Jamaica Anansi Stories

Jamaica Anansi Stories

Martha Warren Beckwith

MINT EDITIONS

Jamaica Anansi Stories was first published in 1924.

This edition published by Mint Editions 2021.

ISBN 9781513290744 | E-ISBN 9781513293592

Published by Mint Editions®

 MINT
EDITIONS

minteditionbooks.com

Publishing Director: Jennifer Newens
Design & Production: Rachel Lopez Metzger
Project Manager: Micaela Clark
Typesetting: Westchester Publishing Services

Contents

Preface

The stories in this collection were taken down from the lips of over sixty negro story-tellers in the remote country districts of Jamaica during two visits to the island, one of six weeks in the summer of 1919, the other of five weeks in the winter of 1921. The music was all recorded during the second visit by Miss Helen Roberts, either directly from the story-teller or from a phonographic record which I had made. In this way the original style of the story-telling, which in some instances mingles story, song and dance, is as nearly as possible preserved, although much is necessarily lost in the slow process of dictation. The lively and dramatic action, the change in voice, even the rapid and elliptical vernacular, can not appear on the printed page. But the stories are set down without polish or adornment, as nearly as possible as they were told to me, and hence represent, so far as they go, a true folk art.

Although some story-tellers claimed to know "more than a hundred" stories, no one narrator gave me more than thirty, and usually not more than four or five at one interview.

To all such story-telling, as to riddling and song, the name of "Anansi story" is applied,—an appellation at least as old as 1816, when Monk Lewis in his journal describes the classes of "Nancy stories" popular in his day among the negroes as the tragical witch story and the farcical "neger-trick." The "neger-trick" harks back to slave times and is rarely heard today; tales of sorcery, too, are heard best from the lips of older narrators. Modern European fairy tales and animal stories (evidently unknown to Lewis) have taken their place. Two influences have dominated story-telling in Jamaica, the first an absorbing interest in the magical effect of song which, at least in the old witch tales, far surpasses that in the action of the story; the second, the conception of the spider Anansi as the trickster hero among a group of animal figures. Anansi is the culture hero of the Gold Coast,—a kind of god—, just as Turtle is of the Slave coast and Hare (our own Brer Rabbit) of the Bantu people "Anansi stories" regularly form the entertainment during wake-nights, and it is difficult not to believe that the vividness with which these animal actors take part in the story springs from the idea that they really represent the dead in the underworld whose spirits have the power, according to the native belief, of taking animal form. The head-man on a Westmoreland cattle-pen even assured me that

Anansi, once a man, was now leader of the dead in this land of shades. However this may be, the development of Jamaican obeah or witchcraft has been along the same two lines of interest. Magic songs are used in communicating with the dead, and the obeah-man who sets a ghost upon an enemy often sends it in the form of some animal; hence there are animals which must be carefully handled lest they be something other than they appear.

Riddling is a favorite pastime of the Jamaica negro. Much is preserved from old African originals in the personification of common objects of yard and road-side, much is borrowed also from old English folk riddling. That this spread has been along the line of a common language is proved by the fact that only a dozen parallels occur in Mason's Spanish collection from Porto Rico, at least ten of which are quoted by Espinosa from New Mexico, while of collections from English-speaking neighbors, fourteen out of fifty-five riddles collected in South Carolina and nine out of twenty-one from Andros Island are found also in Jamaica. Particular patterns are set for Jamaica riddling into which the phrasing falls with a rhythmical swing careless of rhyme,—"My father has in his yard" and "Going up to town." The giving of a riddle is regularly preceded by a formula drawn from old English sources—

> *Riddle me this, riddle me that,*
> *Perhaps you can guess this riddle*
> *And perhaps not!*

generally abbreviated into

> *Riddle me riddle,*
> *Guess me this riddle,*
> *And perhaps not.*

The art is practised as a social amusement, groups forming in which each person in the circle must propound riddles until his supply is exhausted or his riddle unguessed.

My own work as a collector in this engrossing field of Jamaican folk-lore owes much to those collectors who have preceded me and who have enjoyed a longer and more intimate acquaintance than has been possible for me with the people and their idiom;—to Monk Lewis, a true folk-lorist, whose "Journal" of 1816 is of the greatest interest today, to Mr. Walter Jekyll and his excellent volume of songs and stories in the Folk-lore Publications of 1907, and to the writers of nursery tales, Mrs. Milne-Home, Pamela Smith, and Mrs. W. E. Wilson (Wona). I take this opportunity also to acknowledge most gratefully the many courtesies for which I am indebted during my visits to the island. I particularly wish to thank Professor Frank Cundall for his advice and cooperation, and for the use of the invaluable West India library connected with the Jamaica Institute in Kingston where I was able to consult books not easily to be found in library collections. To the Hon. and Mrs. Coke-Kerr, to Mrs. Harry Farquharson and to the Rev. and Mrs. Ashton I am gratefully indebted for many courtesies in the task of finding reliable native informants. To these informants themselves,—to Simeon Falconer, William Forbes, George Parkes, and a score of others I owe thanks for their ready response to my interest. In America also I wish to thank Mrs. Elsie Clews Parsons for suggestions as to method and for the use of her valuable bibliography and Mrs. Louise Dennis Hand for help with Spanish collections, and to express my grateful obligations to Professor Franz Boas for his patient editing and valuable bibliographical suggestions.

Martha Warren Beckwith
The Folk-lore Foundation
Vassar College
April, 1924

ANIMAL STORIES

1. Tying Tiger

a. The Fish-basket

George Parkes, Mandeville

ONE GREAT HUNGRY TIME. ANANSI couldn't get anyt'ing to eat, so he take up his hand-basket an' a big pot an' went down to the sea-side to catch fish. When he reach there, he make up a large fire and put the pot on the fire, an' say, "Come, big fish!" He catch some big fish put them aside. He said, "Big fish go, make little fish come!" He then catch the little fish. He say, "Little fish go, make big fish come!" an' say, "Big fish go, make little fish come!" He then catch the pot full an' his hand-basket. He bile the pot full and sit down and eat it off; he then started home back with the pot on his head and the basket. Reaching a little way, he hide the pot away in the bush an take the basket along with him now.

While going along, he meet up Tiger. Now Tiger is a very rough man an' Anansi 'fraid of him. Tiger said to him, "What you have in that basket, sah?"—speak to him very rough. Anansi speak in a very feeble voice, say, "Nothing, sah! nothing, sah!" So both of them pass each other, an' when they went on a little way, Tiger hide in the bush watching Anansi. Anansi then sit down underneath a tree, open his basket, take out the fishes one one, and say, "Pretty little yallah-tail this!" an' put it aside; he take out a snapper an' say, "Pretty little snapper this!" an' put it one side; he take out a jack-fish an' say, "Pretty little jack-fish!" an' put it one side. Tiger then run up an' say, "Think you havn't not'ing in that basket, sah!" Anansi say, "I jus' going down to the sea have a bathe, sah, an' I catch them few 'itte fishes." Tiger say, "Give it to me here, sah!"—talk in a very rough manner. An' Tiger take it an' eat them all an' spit up the bones. Anansi then take up the bones an' eat them, an' while eating he grumble an' say, "But look me bwoy labor do!" Tiger say, "What you say?" Anansi say, "Fly humbug me face, sah!" (brushing his face).

So both of them start to go home now with the empty basket, but this time Anansi was studying for Tiger. When he reach part of the way, Anansi see a fruit-tree. Anansi say, "What a pretty fruit-tree!" (looking up in the tree). Tiger say, "Climb it, sah!" (in a rough manner). So when Anansi go up an' pull some of the fruit, at that time Tiger was standing underneath the tree. Anansi look down on Tiger head an' said, "Look lice in a Brar Tiger head!" Tiger said, "Come down an' ketch it, sah!" Anansi come down an' said to Tiger he kyan't ketch it without he lean on the tree. Tiger said, "Lean on the tree, sah!" The hair on Tiger head is very long. So while Anansi ketchin' the lice, Tiger fell asleep. Anansi now take the hair an' lash it round the tree tie up Tiger on the tree. After he done that he wake up Tiger an' say that he kyan't ketch any more. Tiger in a rough manner say, "Come an' ketch it, sah!" Anansi say, "I won't!" So Anansi run off, Tiger spring after him, an' fin' out that his hair is tied on the tree. So Tiger say, "Come an' loose me, sah!" Anansi say. "I won't!" an' Anansi sing now,

> *"See how Anansi tie Tiger,*
> *See how Anansi tie Tiger,*
> *Tie him like a hog, Tiger,*
> *See how Anansi tie Tiger,*
> *Tie him like a hog, Tiger!"*

An' Anansi leave him go home, an' a hunter-man come an' see Tiger tie on the tree, make kill him.

b. The Storm

Vivian Bailey, Mandeville

BRER TIGER GOT A MANGO-TREE in his place. Brer Nansi go an' ask if he could sell him a ha' penny wort' of mango. Brer Tiger say no. Brer Nansi well want de mango. Brer Nansi say, "Law pass dat eb'ry man have tree mus' tie on it 'cause going to get a heavy storm." Brer Tiger say, well, mus' tie him to de mango-tree. After Brer Nansi tie Tiger, climb up in de mango-tree, an' eb'ry mango he eat tak it an' lick Brer Tiger on de head. After he eat done, he shake off all de ripe mango an' pick dem up go away leave Brer Tiger tie up on de mango-tree.

Brer Tiger see Brer But pass an' ask Brer But to loose him. Brer But say dat he kyan't stop. Brer Tiger see Brer Ant passing, ask Brer

Ant to loose him; Brer Ant say he kyan't depon[1] haste. Brer Tiger see Brer Duck-ants passing an' ask him fe loose him. An' don' know if him will loose him, for don' know if him will put up wid him slowness, for Duck-ants is a very slow man. After him loose him, Brer Tiger tell him many t'anks an' tell him mus' never let him hear any of Duck-ants's frien's pass him an' don' call up "How-dy-do."

Brer Nansi in a cotton tree were listening when dey talking. De nex' evening, Brer Nansi go to Brer Tiger yard an' knock at de door. An' say, "Who is deah?" an' say, "Mr. Duck-ants's brudder." An' dey tak him in an' mak much of him, get up tea because it was Mr. Duck-ants's brudder, an' after dat go to bed. In de morning provide tea for Mr. Duck-ants 'fore he wake, an' when he wake an' was washin' his face he got to tak off his hat. An' Brer Nansi is a man wid a bald head, an' dey got to fin' out it was Brer Nansi an' dey run him out of de house.

2. Tiger as Substitute

a. *The King's Two Daughters*

William Forbes, Dry River

DEH WAS ANANSI. HE GO out an' court two young lady was de king daughter an' mak dem a fool, an' dem ketch him an' tie him, an' de two sister go an' look a bundle a wood fe go an' mak a fire under a copper[2] fe bu'n him wid hot water. An' after when dem gone, he see Tiger was coming. Anansi said, "Lawd! Brar Tiger, I get into trouble heah!" An' said, "Fe wha'?" An' say, "King daughter wan' lib wid dem, come tie me." Tiger say, "You fool, mak y' loose an' tie *me!*"

Anansi tie Tiger dere now an' Anansi go to a grass-root an' dodge. An' when de misses go t'row down de wood at de fireside, de littlest one say, "Sister! sister! look de little uncle wha' we tie heah, him tu'n a big uncle now!" Sister say, "I soon 'big uncle' him!" an' dem mak up de fire bu'n up de water, tak two ladle an' dem dashey upon Tiger. An' him jump, an' jump, pop de rope, tumble dump on de grass-root whe' Anansi was. Anansi laugh "Tissin, tissin, tissin!"

---

1. *depon* here signifies "because of."
2. A kettle.

An' Tiger jump 'pon Anansi, say, "We mus' go look wood gwine to bu'n *your* back!" Tiger see some good wood on a cotton-tree well dry, an' Tiger say, "I don' care wha' you do!" An' when Anansi go up on cotton-tree, him chop one of de limb pum! an' 'top, an' chop again pum! an' holla, "None!" Tiger say, "Cut de wood, man!" An' holla again, "None!" Tiger said, "Cut de wood, I tell you, come down mak I bu'n you." Anansi say, "You stan' upon de bottom say 'cut de wood, but you know Hunter-man look fe you las' yeah track? Wha' you t'ink upon dis yeah track worse!" an' Tiger run. Anansi say, "He run, Massa Hunterman, gone up on hill-side, gone dodge!" He move from dere gone on ribber-side. Anansi holla, "Him gone, Massa Hunterman, a ribber!" Tiger wheel back. An' Anansi holla to him say go to a sink-hole, an' Anansi get rid of him an' come off.

Jack man dora!

b. *The Gub-gub Peas*

George Parkes, Mandeville

A MAN PLANT A BIG field of gub-gub peas.[3] He got a watchman put there. This watchman can't read. The peas grow lovely an' bear lovely; everybody pass by, in love with the peas. Anansi himself pass an' want to have some. He beg the watchman, but the watchman refuse to give him. He went an' pick up an' old envelope, present it to the watchman an' say the master say to give the watchman. The watchman say, "The master know that I cannot read an' he sen' this thing come an' give me?" Anansi say, "I will read it for you." He said, "Hear what it say! The master say, 'You mus' tie Mr. Anansi at the fattest part of the gub-gub peas an' when the belly full, let him go.'" The watchman did so; when Anansi belly full, Anansi call to the watchman, an' the watchman let him go.

After Anansi gone, the master of the peas come an' ask the watchman what was the matter with the peas. The watchman tol' him. Master say he see no man, no man came to him an' he send no letter, an' if a man come to him like that, he mus' tie him in the peas but no let him away till he come. The nex' day, Anansi come back with the same letter an' say, "Master say, give you this." Anansi read the same letter, an'

---

3. Tall bush peas, one of the commonest and most prized of Jamaica crop.

watchman tie Anansi in the peas. An' when Anansi belly full, him call to the watchman to let him go, but watchman refuse. Anansi call out a second time, "Come, let me go!" The watchman say, "No, you don' go!" Anansi say, "If you don' let me go, I spit on the groun' an' you rotten!"[4] Watchman get frighten an' untie him.

Few minutes after that the master came; an' tol' him if he come back the nex' time, no matter *what* he say, hol' him. The nex' day, Anansi came back with the same letter an' read the same story to the man. The man tie him in the peas, an', after him belly full, he call to the man to let him go; but the man refuse,—all that he say he refuse until the master arrive.

The master take Anansi an' carry him to his yard an' tie him up to a tree, take a big iron an' put it in the fire to hot. Now while the iron was heating, Anansi was crying. Lion was passing then, see Anansi tie up underneath the tree, ask him what cause him to be tied there. Anansi said to Lion from since him born he never hol' knife an' fork, an' de people wan' him now to hol' knife an' fork. Lion said to Anansi, "You too wort'less man! me can hol' it I will loose you and then you tie *me* there." So Lion loose Anansi an' Anansi tied Lion to the tree. So Anansi went away, now, far into the bush an' climb upon a tree to see what taking place. When the master came out, instead of seeing Anansi he see Lion. He took out the hot iron out of the fire an' shove it in in Lion ear. An Lion make a plunge an' pop the rope an' away gallop in the bush an' stan' up underneath the same tree where Anansi was. Anansi got frighten an' begin to tremble an' shake the tree. Lion then hol' up his head an' see Anansi. He called for Anansi to come down. Anansi shout to the people, "See de man who you lookin' fe! see de man underneat' de tree!" An' Lion gallop away an' live in the bush until now, an' Anansi get free.

3. Tiger as Riding-horse

William Forbes, Dry River

TIGER WAS WALKING TO A yard an' see two young misses, an' he was courting one of de young misses. An' as Anansi hear, Anansi go up to yard where de young misses is; an' dey ax him said, "Mr. Anansi, you

---

4. Anansi here claims the power of a sorcerer.

see Mr. Tiger?" An' said, "O yes! I see Mr. Tiger, but I tell you, missus, Tiger is me fader ol' ridin'-horse." An' when Tiger come to misses, dem tell him. An' said him gwine Anansi, mak him come an' prove witness befo' him face how he is fader ol' ridin'-horse!

An' when him come call Anansi, say, "Want you to come prove dis t'ing you say 'fore de misses," Anansi say, "I nebber say so! but I kyan' walk at all." Tiger said, "If I hab to carry you 'pon me back, I will carry you go!" Anansi said, "Well, I wi' go." Anansi go tak out him saddle. Tiger say, "What you gwine do wid saddle?" Anansi say, "To put me foot down in de stirrup so when I gwine fall down, I weak, I can catch up." An' tak him bridle. Tiger say, "What you gwine do wid it?" Say, "Gwine put it in you mout', when I gwine to fa' down I can catch up." Tiger say, "I don' care what you do, mus' put it on!" An' him go back an' tak horse-whip. An say, "Wha' you gwine do wid de horsewhip?" An' say, "Fe when de fly come, fan de fly." An' put on two pair of 'pur. An' say, "Wha' you gwine do wid 'pur?" An' say, "If I don' put on de 'pur, me foot wi' cramp." An' come close to yard an' close in wid de 'pur an' horse-whip, an' mak him gallop into de yard. An' say, "Carry him in to stable, sah! I mak you to know what Anansi say true to de fac', is me fader ol' ridin'-horse."

Tiger tak to wood, Anansi sing a'ter him, "Po' Tiger dead an' gone!"[5]

1

Si - lay - na, Si - lay - na, Si - lay - na bom, Eb - ry - bod - y (?) Si -
lay - na, Si - lay - na, Si - lay - na bom, (?) Si - lay - na, Si - lay - na.
Po' Ti-ger dead and gone, Si-lay-na, Si - lay - na, Si - lay - na,
Eb - ry - bod - y go look fo' dem wife, Si - lay - na, Si - lay - na,
Eb-ry-bod-y go look fo'dem wife, Si-lay - na, Si-lay - na, Si-layna bom.

5. Record was poor and could only be taken in part.

4. Tiger's Sheep-skin Suit

George Parkes, Mandeville

ANANSI WAS A HEAD-MAN FOR a man by the name of Mr. Mighty, who employed Anansi for the purpose of minding some sheep. The sheep numbered about two thousand. And from the first day Anansi took over the sheep, the man began to miss one. An' he steal them until he leave only one. Well, Mr. Mighty would like to find out how the sheep go. He say to Anansi he would give his best daughter and two hundred pound to find out how the sheep go.

Anansi say the best way to find it out is to make a ball. Anansi have a friend name of Tiger, call him 'Brar Tiger'. He went to Tiger an' tell him Mr. Mighty promise to give his daughter an' two hundred pound to whomsoever tell how the sheep go. Anansi now is a fiddler, an' he say that he will play the fiddle an' Tiger play the tambourine, but before he go to the ball he will give Tiger a sheepskin coat, sheepskin trousers, a sheepskin cap, a sheepskin boot; an' when him, Tiger, hear him play,

"Mister Mighty loss him sheep,
It stan' lik' a Tiger t'iefee,"

him, Tiger, mustn't think him the same one; it's one clear out the country. And he is to play his tambourine, say,

"Fe tre-ew, bredder, fe tre-ew,
It 'tan lik' a it mak me clo'es."

Now then, Anansi go back to Mr. Mighty an' tol' him that there is a man coming to the ball wearing a suit of sheep-skin clo'es,—dat is the man who steal the sheep.

Mr. Mighty give out invitation to all the high folks, all the ladies and gentlemen all aroun', to attend the ball at that same date. The night of the ball, Anansi went with his fiddle an' Tiger with his tambourine in the suit of sheep-skin clo'es. At the time fix, Anansi tune up his fiddle, "he-rum, te-rum, she-rum." Tiger now trim the tambourine, "ring-ping, ring-ping, ring-pong, pe-ring-ping, double-ping, *tong!*" Anansi says, "Gentlemen an' ladies, ketch yo' pardner!" Anansi play,

> *"Mr. Mighty loss him sheep,*
> *Mr. Mighty loss him sheep,*
> *Mr. Mighty loss him sheep,*
> *It stan' lik' a Tiger t'iefee."*

Tiger say,

> *"Fe tre-ew, bredder, fe tre-ew,*
> *Fe tre-ew, bredder, fe tre-ew,*
> *Fe tre-ew, bredder, fe tre-ew,*
> *It 'tan' lik' a it mak me clo'es."*

Anansi go to Mr. Mighty an' say, "Me an' dat man workin' an' I didn't know he was such a t'ief! he steal de sheep till he tak skin an' all mak him clo'es!" An' as they were going back to their places Anansi say, "Hell after you t'-night, only t'ing you don't know!" Tiger say, "What you say, Bra?"—"Me say, you not playing strong enough, you mus' play up stronger!"

Anansi say again, "Gentlemen an' ladies, ketch 'em a pardner!" an' sing,

> *"Mr. Mighty loss him sheep,*
> *It 'tan' lik' a Tiger t'iefee."*

Tiger say,

> *"Fe tre-ew, bredder, fe tre-ew.*
> *It 'tan' lik' a it mak me clo'es".*

Mr. Mighty got right up an' said to Tiger, "Yes, that is the man what steal all my sheep!" Tiger say, "No!!" Anansi say, "Yes, that is the man what steal all the sheep, an' I an' that man eatin' an' I didn't know that man was such a t'ief!" An' Tiger was arrested an' got ten years in prison, an' Anansi get the two hundred pounds an' the best daughter to marry to.

5. Tiger Catching the Sheep-thief

a. The Escape

Joseph Macfarlane, Moneague, St. Ann

ONE DAY WAS AN OLD lady name Mis' Madder, had twenty sheep. Mr. Anansi went an' gi' her a hen an', couple week after, Mr. Anansi went back fe de hen. An' said, "Didn't you gi' me de hen, Mr. Anansi?" An' said, "Oh, no! Missus, me hen wud have hegg, hegg, on hegg, chicken on chicken!" An' said, "De only t'ing I can do' Mr. Anansi, go in de sheep-pen an' tak a sheep!" It went on till de nineteen was gone, leave one. Tiger says, "Mis' Madder, I'll kill de sheep tak a half an' ketch Mr. Anansi." Tiger kill i', put 'e skin over himself. When Mr. Anansi come, Tiger bawl like a sheep "Ba-a-a-a!" Miss Madder say, "All right, Mr. Anansi, I don' wan' to hear any more talkin'; tak' de las' sheep an' go." Anansi say, "T'ank you, Miss Madder, won' come back an' worry you fe no more fowl!"

When he went off, under way said, "Yah! dis sheep hebby, sah!" Went home, de wife an' chil'ren sit roun' him wid bowl an' knife. Mr. Anansi tak de knife cut de t'roat an' say, "Lawd! me wife, dis fellow fat till no hav any blood!" Cut de belly come down, Tiger jump out hold him. Mr. Anansi say, "He! he! Brar Tiger, wha' you do?" Tiger say, "Miss Madder ha' twenty sheep an' if me no tie you, him wi' say you an' me eat dem." Anansi say, "If dem tak dem *big* banana trash tie me, I wi' be glad, but if dey could a tak dat 'itte bit o' banana t'read tie me, I should be *so* sorry!" An' dey tie him wid de small banana trash an' t'row into de sea, an' he jus' open his leg an' run under water. An' from dat time you see Anansi running under water.

b. The Substitute

Samuel Christie, St. Ann's Bay

ANANSI IS A SMART ONE, very smart, likes to do unfair business. So one day was walking t'ru a lady property an' kill a little bird; so him pass de lady yard an' say, "Missus, me beg you mak little bird stan' till me come back?" Lady said, "Put it down, Anansi." Lef' de bird an' he never come back till he know de bird spile. De lady t'row de bird. He come back, say, "Missus, me jus' call fe de litt'e bird me lef' t'odder day." Say, "Anansi, de bird spoil an' me t'row it away!"—"No, missus, you kyan' t'row 'way me bird! Jus' call an' me want i'!" Lady say, "Well, Anansi, before you ill-treat me, go in de sheep-pen an' tak a sheep."

Anansi was quite glad fe dat, get a sheep fe de bird! An' go down fin' a sheep-pen wid plenty of sheep. Anansi go an' tak dat one, an' after dat, ev'ry night he tak one. Lady fin' all de sheep was los', so tell de head man mus' keep watch of de sheep-pen. So de head-man was Tiger. Tiger tak out dat sheep was in de sheep-pen an' dress himself wid sheep-skin. Anansi have suspicion an' get a frien' to go wid him dat night, ask de frien' to catch de sheep. So as him frien' t'row on de rope on Tiger head, Anansi fin' it was Tiger an' him ask excuse, go to a good distance where can mak escape, holla, "Dat somet'ing you ketch deh no sheep,—Brar Tiger!"

Tiger tie de frien' carry him up to de yard tell de mistress dis is de man been destroying de sheep all de time!

c. In the House-top

Thomas White, Maroon Town, Cock-pit country

Mr. Goolin pay Anansi a hundred poun' to mak him wife talk,[6] an' Anansi was live upon Mr. Goolin ev'ry day an' go to Mr. Goolin yard ev'ry day fe money. Mr. Goolin get tired of Anansi an' couldn't get rid of Anansi out of him yard. Tiger hear, an' go to Mr. Goolin tell him dat him will stop Anansi from comin' in yard. An' so Tiger did; Tiger turn a big barrow an' go lie down in de common. Anansi come now an' say, "Mawnin', Mr. Goolin." Mr. Goolin say, "Mawnin', Mr. Anansi." Anansi says, "I might well tell you de trut'! De amount of what money you pay me fe yo' wife, it is not enough!" Mr. Goolin says, "Well, I have no more money to pay you again." Anansi says, "O Mr. Goolin! you couldn't tell me a word as dat!" Mr. Goolin says to Anansi, "Mr. Anansi, all I can do fe you, go in de common see a big barrow lie down dere. You can go catch it."

Anansi tek him rope an' go in de common an' him tie de big barrow an' him put it jus' right across him shoulder. An' he was goin' along till

6. See story 96.

him ketch part of de way, him says to himself, "Ha! if I didn't cunnie, I wouldn't get dis big barrow t'-day." So look an' see a long beard come down on him face. Dat was Tiger! Tiger go fe shake him an' he say, "O Brar Tiger, no shake! no shake! no shake!"

Anansi[7] run fe him house an', when he get near, him holler to him wife say, "Shet de back do', open de front do', Brar Tiger come!" Wife say, "Wha' you say? say wash out de pot?"—"No! shet de back do, open de front do'!"—"Wha' you say? put on de pot, come?" Him say, "No-o-o! s-h-e-t de b-a-c-k d-o-o-o-o! o-p-e-n de f-r-o-n-t d-o-o-o-o!"

Wife put up all dem chil'ren quite a-top, and, as Anansi put down Tiger, Anansi fly up a-top, too.

An' Tiger was layin' down in de hall middle, an' all de chil'ren an' de wife, dem all upon house-top. Anansi have six chil'ren. De chil' one of dem, says he hungry. As de chil' say he hungry, Anansi shove down dat chil' t' Brar Tiger. Tiger swallow him. Anodder cry out hungry again; Anansi shove him down, Tiger swallow him. Anodder one cry hungry again; Anansi shove him down gi' Tiger, Tiger swallow him. Deh's t'ree gone. Him was deh again till anodder one cry hungry; Anansi shove him down to Tiger, Tiger swallow him. For a good time again de odder one cry out hungry; Anansi shove him down gi' Tiger, Tiger swallow him. Good time again, de las' chil' lef', him cry hungry. Anansi shove him down gi' Tiger, Tiger swallow him. Lef' him an' him wife, two single, now. Anansi fell in sleep. De wife tak needle an' t'read an' sew Anansi trouser-foot upon her frock-tail. When Anansi wake out of sleep, him wife cry hungry now. Anansi shove down him wife to give Tiger. De woman frock-tail sew up on Anansi trouser-foot an' ketch him up back. An' de lady was deh for a good time until him cry hungry again an' Anansi shove him down gi' Tiger an' Tiger swallow Mrs. Anansi.

Anansi was deh on de house-top until he feel hungry now. An' says to Tiger, "Brar Tiger, you know what you do? I's a man dat's so fat, if I drop on de bare eart' I's goin' to mash up; so if you want me to eat, you want to cut a whole heap a dry trash." An' Tiger went an' cut a whole heap a dry trash an' carried de dry trash come an' he t'rown de dry trash.

Anansi said to Tiger, "Brar Tiger, ketch, ketch, ketch, comin' down!" An' Anansi let himself off of de house-top an' drop in de trash, an' Tiger was upon hard sarchin' an' couldn't fin' Anansi until t'-day!

Jack man dora, choose none!

---

7. The misunderstood warning is inserted from another narrator.

6. Tiger's Breakfast

Richard Morgan, Santa Cruz Mountains

ONE DAY, HANANSI GO TIGER house an' eat breakfas' every day, an' tell Tiger, say, "Brar Tiger, tomorrow you mus' come a my house; but when you hear me makin' noise you mus' come, for dat time breakfas' is on, but when you hear me stay still you mustn't come at all." So when Tiger go, Hanansi eat done. And say, "Brar Tiger, you foot short!" Tiger say, "No, me no hear you mak noise!" Hanansi say, "No, *so* me said, for when man makin' noise he kyan' eat." An' say, "Well, nex' day come back." When Tiger come, Hanansi tak shame, gi' him little breakfas' but say, "Brar Tiger, when we go fe eat, when I say 'Nyammy nyammy nyammy' you mus' say, 'Nyam a wha' eat'."[8] So Hanansi stay deh eat everyt'ing, Tiger never get one.

Tiger study fe him. Nex' day he go to Tiger yard. When Tiger gi' him breakfast an' gi' him enough meat he said to Tiger, "Brar Tiger, a whe' you get meat every day so?" Tiger said, "You know how me come by dis meat? When I see a cow lie down, I go up an' run me han' inside of de cow an' hol' de man tripe, so I never out of meat." So Hanansi went his way an' do de same. De cow frighten on de hill-side an' turn head right down to low-land. Hanansi say, "Do, Brar Cow, don't shut up me han'!" Cow fasten de han' de better an' gallop right down de hill an' drag Hanansi over de stone. Dat's de reason let you see Hanansi belly white.

7. Eggs and Scorpions

William Forbes, Dry River, Cock-pit country

BLINKIE[9] AN' ANANSI WAS GWINE in a wood. Dem gwine in a wood fe go look egg, bird egg. An' Anansi tell Blinkie when little bird say, "Who wan' little egg?" Blinkie fe say him want little egg, an' when de big bird say, "Who wan' big egg?" Anansi say, "Me wan' big egg!" An' in de night when he get all de big egg, Blinkie get vex' an' lef' Anansi in de bush an' him fly away wid de light.

---

8. This means, "Eat, cat, eat";—"Don't want anything to eat."
9. Fire-flies are common in Jamaica.

An' Anansi come a Tiger house in a night. Tiger had a sheep in yard. Anansi say, "Brar Tiger, if you gi' me dinner fe eat t'-night, I gi' you all de egg." An' Tiger say yes, an' Tiger go to de sheep an' say, "Lay out, lay out, sheep!" He lay out roas' fowl, roas' duck, an' all sort a t'ings. Anansi get at it.

When he eat, say want to sleep Tiger house. Tiger set 'corpion roun' de egg. When Anansi put han' in to tak de egg, 'corpion bite him. An' holla, "Aye-e-e!" Tiger say, "Brar Anansi, wha' ha' you?" An' say, "Me t'ree litt'e pickney an' me wife mak me a cry!" Den, when Tiger gone t' bed, he t'ief away de sheep.

8. Tiger's Bone-hole

William Forbes, Dry River, Cock-pit country

TIGER HAD A BIG POT o' meat, an' him boil an' lef' it gone a groun'. An' he have a bone-hole; when he ate de meat, t'row it into de hole. An' Anansi tak him wife an' t'ree pickney an' he say dey five gwine to de house an' get into de pot eat de meat. An' after dey hear Tiger was coming, him an' him wife an' de t'ree pickney, five of dem, go in de hole. An' Tiger come an' say, "Not a creetur nyam dis meat but Brar Nansi!" An' Tiger begin now eat meat, an' de first bone him t'row into de hole, him knock one of de pickney. An' as he go fe holla, Anansi says, "Shut yo' mout', sir, don' cry!" An' he eat again, t'row out anodder bone, knock anodder pickney. As him go fe cry, say "Shut yo' mout', sir!" As he eat anodder bone again, he knock de las' pickney, mak t'ree. Tell him say him mustn't cry. Ate anodder bone an' t'row it in de hole, knock de mudder. As him go fe cry, say, "Shut yo' mout!" An' de las' bone he eat, knock Anansi in a head. Anansi say, "Mak we all holla now in a de hole!" So dey all holla "Yee! yee-e-e!" in a de hole, an' as dey holla, Tiger get frighten' an' run lef' de house, an Anansi an' wife an pickney come out tak all de meat go away, run him out of his house 'count of dat bone-hole!

Jack man dora!

9. The Christening

Charles Wright, Maroon Town, Cock-pit country

ANANSI AN' TIGER BOT' OF them fin' one keg of butter. Anansi says to Tiger, "Let us hide it in the bushes." Some days after, Anansi says to Tiger, "I receive a letter for a christening." When he return, Tiger ask him the name of the chile. He says the name is "Top take off." Another week came again. He say receive another letter for another christening. After he come back, Tiger ask him what's the name of the chile again. He says, "Catch in de middle." An' the las' week he went back for another christening. Tiger ask him when he come back what's the name of the chile. He says, "Lick clean."

Now he says, "Tiger, let us go look for this keg of butter." He carried Tiger all over the place walkin' until he get tired, an' when he nearly catch to the place where they hid the butter he said, "Tiger, we are tired, let us go for a sleep!" An' after Tiger was sleeping, he went to the keg, he took a bit of stick an' he scrape as much as he can get from the keg, an' he wipe a little on Tiger mouth an' he wipe a little at the tail. Then he climb a tall tree now and he make a wonderful alarm that Tiger eat butter until he melt butter!

10. Eating Tiger's Guts

a. The Tell-tale

Simeon Falconer, Santa Cruz Mountains

BRER TIGER AND BRER ANANSI went to river-side. Brer Anansi said, "Brer Tiger, tak out your inside an' wash it out." Brer Tiger did so. "Now, Brer Tiger, dip your head in water wash it good." The moment Brer Tiger put his head in water, Anansi took up the inside and run away with it give to his wife Tacoomah to boil.

Next morning he heard that Tiger was dead. He called all the children to know how they were going to cry. Each one come say, "Tita Tiger dead!" The last child he called said, "Same somet'ing pupa bring come here las' night give Ma Tacoomah to boil, Tita Tiger gut."—"Oh, no!" said Anansi, "Pic'ninny, *you* can't go." So they lock up that child. So man hear him crying ask him what's the matter. "I wan' to go to Tita Tiger's funeral!" Let him out to go. When Anansi see him coming, he run away and tak house-top and since then he never come down.

MARTHA WARREN BECKWITH

b. The Monkeys' Song

Henry Spence, Bog, Westmoreland

ANANSI AND TIGER BADE. So Anansi tell Tiger, "Meanwhile bading, tak out tripe!" Tiger tak out tripe. Anansi firs' come out an' eat Tiger tripe, an' say if Tiger wan' to know how him tripe go he mus' go down to Monkey town. So Anansi go down, go tell Monkey when dey see Tiger coming mus' sing,

"Dis time, we eat Tiger gut down!"

So after, as Tiger hear dem all a-singing, kill off all de Monkey. An' catch one of de Monkey an' he say Anansi come down larn him de song yesterday!

11. Throwing away Knives

a. Tiger and Anansi

Benjamin Collins, Mandeville

ONCE UPON A TIME BRER Tiger an' Brer Anansi was gwine on. Brer Anansi tell Brer Tiger says, "Brer Tiger, I'm gwine to t'row away my knife an' when you see I t'row away mine, you mus' t'row away yours, too." Brer Anansi tak somet'ing an' t'row it away, an' Brer Tiger tak his knife an' t'row it away. An' when dem reach de fiel' to eat pine,[10] deh comes Brer Nansi had *his* knife, he was eating pine, an' Brer Tiger didn't get none. Brer Nansi say to Brer Tiger, "Brer Tiger, no man a knife nyam pine; no man no have knife no nyam pine!"[11]

b. Sheep and Anansi

William Forbes, Dry River, Cock-pit country

MR. ANANSI AN' MR. SHEEP GOING OUT walking over de country. Carry two spoon; Sheep carry one, Anansi carry one. Anansi tell Sheep,

---

10. Pineapple.
11. Anyone whe has a knife can eat pineapple; anyone who has none cannot eat pineapple.

"Mr. Sheep, lef' you spoon here, don' carry it." Den go to de second house an' get some breakfas' again. After him get de breakfas' him say, "Mr. Sheep, where you spoon?" An' said, "Don't you tell me to lef' it at de firs' house?"—"You mus' go back for it now!" Mr. Sheep gone for it, him eat off all de breakfas'.

An' said, "Come, Mr. Sheep, but you mus' lef' you spoon."—"Me won't carry it at all." Den go up to de nex't yard an' get dinner now. Night is coming. An' said, "Mr. Sheep, where is you' 'poon?" An' said, "I lef' it at de las' yard you eat." Well, den, Sheep have to go back fe his spoon again; tell Sheep come back again an' Anansi eat off de dinner. Sheep couldn't get not'ing to eat.

12. Grace Before Meat

a. Monkey and Anansi

Samuel Christie, St. Anne's Bay

ANANSI AND MONKEY WERE TRAVELLING; they were two good friends together. Anansi ask Monkey, "Brer Monkey, how much cunnie you have?" Said, "Brer, me have plenty plenty!" Anansi said, "Brer, me only have one one-half; I keep the one fe meself an' give me friend the half."

Trabble on, trabble on, until they see Tiger in one deep hole. Anansi say, "Brer Monkey, you have plenty cunnie an' long tail; sen' down tail into the hole an' help Brer Tiger!" While him sen' down him tail, Anansi climb one tree. Tiger come out of the hole now, lay hold on Monkey, say, "I nyam you t'-day!" Anansi on the tree laughing. Monkey into a fix now, don't know how to get away. So Anansi call out to Tiger, "Brer Tiger, you ketch Monkey now you gwine eat him?" Tiger say, "Yes, I gwine eat him." Anansi say, "Do like me, now. Open you two hand an' clap wid joy, say, 'I get Monkey!'" That time he open his two hand, Monkey get free. Tiger run after Monkey, Anansi mak his way down from the tree, go home.

b. Goat and Anansi

Henry Spence, Bog, Westmoreland

ANANSI AND TIGER GO OUT hunting one day. Tiger catch one wild goat, Anansi no catch one. Anansi say to him, "Brar Tiger, wha' you say when you catch dis goat?" So Tiger say, "Not'ing!" Anansi say, "Brar Tiger, nex' time when you catch goat so, you mus' put goat under yo' arm an' knockey han' at top say, 'T'ank de Lord!'" An' Tiger did so an' de goat get away gone; de two lose.

13. Day-time Trouble

a. Rabbit and Anansi

Susan Watkins, Claremont, St. Ann

BRAR NANSI AND BRAR RABBIT went for a walk one day. Brar Babbit ask Brar Anansi to show him "daytime trouble". An' while dey go on, Brar Anansi saw Tiger den wid a lot of young Tiger in it. Brar Anansi took out one an' kill it an' give Rabbit a basket wid a piece of de Tiger's meat to carry for de Tiger's fader, an' took Rabbit along wid him to Tiger's house an' tol' Brar Rabbit to han' Tiger de basket. Anansi run, an' Tiger catch at Rabbit to kill him, but he get away. Brar Anansi run up a tree an' say, "Run, Brar Rabbit, run! run fe stone-hole!" Took a razor an' give it to Rabbit. An' Tiger got up a lot of men to get Rabbit out de hole an' Tiger sent for Reindeer to dig him out, as he had a long neck to put down his head an' dig him out; but Anansi tol' Rabbit when Reindeer put down his head in de hole, he mus' tak de razor an' cut it off. A lot of people gadder to see Reindeer tak Rabbit out of de hole, but instead, Reindeer head was taken off an' he drop an' was dead an' de whole crowd run away wid fright. After Rabbit come out, Brar Nansi say to him, "Brar Rabbit, *so* 'daytime trouble' stay. So, as long as you live, never ask anybody to show it to you again!"

b. Rat and Anansi

Moses Hendricks, Mandeville

RAT AND ANANSI WENT OUT one day. They came across Tiger's four children,—Anansi knew exactly where they was. He had a handbasket, Rat had one. So Anansi said, "Brer, two fe me, two fe you!" Anansi tak up one, mak the attempt as if he going to kill it but he didn't do so, put it in his basket alive. Rat t'ot Anansi kill it, an' he tak up his now an' kill it an' put it in his basket. Anansi did the same with the second one,—didn't kill it, put it in his basket. Rat took up the other one an' him *kill* it. So Rat had two dead ones an' Anansi had his alive.

Anansi knew exactly which way Tiger would walk coming home. They met Tiger. Said, "Brer Tiger, I see yo' baby them crying hungry, I tak them up come meet you. I carry two, Brer Rat two." Tiger lay down now to nurse them. Anansi took out one alive. Rat took out one dead, got frightened. Tiger looks cross. Anansi took out the other one alive. Rat took out his dead. Tiger got into a temper an' made a spring at Rat to catch him. Rat was runing. The track was along the side of a wall. Anansi call, "Brer Rat, 'member stone-hole!" Tiger say, "What you say, Brer Nansi?" Anansi say, "Tell you mus' min', him go into dat stone-hole now!" Rat hear now, get into de stone-hole. Tiger wheel roun' to revenge himself on Anansi. Anansi get under de dry trash. That is the reason why rat so fond of stone-hole, an' Anansi, always find him under dry trash an' rubbish.

Jack man dory!

c. *Goat and Anansi*

Ethel Watson, Santa Cruz Mountains

ANANSI AND GOAT WAS WALKING one day. Dey met on Tiger nest. Dey saw seven pic'ny in de nes'. Hanansi said, "Goat, you know what we do? Mak we wring de neck t'row 'way in de bag!" Dey wring de pickney neck t'row it in de bag.

Dey met wid Bredder Tiger. Hanansi said, "Bredder Tiger, we get at' yo' nes' an' we tak yo' pic'ny an wring dem neck t'row 'em in de bag." Tiger say, "You mus' be *kill* me pic'ny!" Anansi say, "No-o-o-o-o!" Tiger say, "T'row 'em out let me see dem!" Hanansi t'row out; dey didn't dead. "Goat, t'row out yours now let me see!" Goat t'row dem out; de Goat's was dead.

Tiger start after Goat. Hanansi say, "Run, Brer Tiger! run, Brer Goat!" Goat slip into a hole. Tiger begin to dig de hole. De stick get broke. Hanansi say, "Bredder Tiger, go look better stick." Bredder Tiger went. Hanansi give de Goat some salt, say, "When Tiger come, blow dis in a eye!" Tiger come back, begin to dig. Hanansi say, "Bredder Tiger, dig an peep down in a hole!" Tiger begin dig an' peep. Goat blow de salt in de Tiger eye. Tiger say, "Brer Hanansi, blow in dis fe me!" Hanansi blow, say, "Bredder Tiger, after eye-water sweet so, what t'ink upon de meat?" Hanansi an' Goat come out an' kill Tiger, den dey put Tiger in de bag wid de pic'ny, an' bot' of dem went home.

14. New Names

Samuel Christie, St. Ann's Bay

THERE WAS FOUR FRIENDS; ONE was Anansi, name of the other was Tiger, name of the other Tacoomah, name of the other Parrot. So they go for a journey, and Anansi bargain with them that the four mus' change their name an' when they come home, each one mus' go to their mudder house an' if their mudder call them the old name they mus' eat their mudder. So the new name,—Anansi name was Che-che-bun-da, Parrot new name was Green-corn-ero, Tiger name was Yellow-prissenda, Tacoomah name was Tacoomah-vengeance,—the four new name. Any mudder call them the ol' name, they mus' eat the mudder.

So they come to Tacoomah house first. Anansi say Tacoomah name "Tacoomah-vengeance". The mudder didn't understand the new name, so she say, "Look me pickney Tacoomah come!" An' kill Tacoomah mudder an' eat him. Second, 'em go to Tiger mudder. Anansi say Tiger name "Yellow-prissenda". So they fall upon Tiger mudder, eat *her*. So that night Anansi cry to excuse the night an' go over to his mudder house an' say, "Mudder, if you call me Anansi', dey will kill you! but de name 'Che-che-bun-da'." The next night they come to Parrot house. Anansi say Parrot name "Green-corn-ero". Eat Parrot mudder the same. At night, again Anansi cry excuse an' go to his mudder, say, "Mudder, las' night wha' me tell you say me name?" The mudder say, "Me pickney, you no name Anansi?" Anansi say, "Ma, coming here tomorrow night an' if you call me so they *kill* you! You mus' call me *'Che-che-bun-da'!*" Ask his mudder again, "Wha' me tell you say yo' pickney name?" She say, "Anansi?" Anansi say, "*No*, mudder! dey *kill* you! Me name Che-che-bun-da, Che-che-bun-da, Che-che-bun-da, *Che-che-bun-da!*" Keep tell the name over an' over that the mudder no forget.

So the night now Anansi turn come and they come along singing,

"Anansi name a Che-che-bun-da,
Cherry-senda, Yellow-prissenda,
Parrot name a Green-corn-ero,
Cherry-senda, Yellow-prissenda,

Tiger name a Yellow-prissenda,
Cherry-senda, Yellow-prissenda,
Tacoomah name Tacoomah-vengeance,
Cherry-senda, Yellow-prissenda."

An' as Anansi mudder see Anansi coming an' the rest, say, "Look me pickney Che-che-bun-da!" Call the new name, so her life save, an' didn't eat Anansi mudder. Anansi make the bargain to feast on the others an' save his mudder!

15. Long-shirt

Moses Hendricks, Mandeville

ANANSI, TACOOMAH AND TIGER MADE a dance; Anansi was the fiddler, Tacoomah the drummer and Tiger the tambourine man. They travel on till they get to a country where all the people were naked—no clothing except the head-man, who wore a long shirt; he had a wooden leg. So they invite up all these people to come to the dance. Mr. Ram-goat was in the lot. So they start playing and the people start dancing, dance until they get so tired everybody fell asleep; and Anansi stole the head-man's shirt—good shirt!—and put his own old one upon him while he was sleeping.

The man got awake, miss his shirt. Now this shirt could talk. The man call out, "Long-shirt, whe' you deh?" Longshirt answer, "Brar Nansi have me on-o!" They start up, now. Anansi got *so* frightened! He met Brar Ram-goat. He said, "Brar Ram-goat, I swap me shirt, gi' you one new one fe you ol' one!" Ram-goat readily make the exchange. The head-man call out, "Long-shirt, whe' you deh?" Long-shirt call out, "Bra' Ram-goat have me on now-o!"

Ram-goat run until he was exhausted, couldn't go any further. He dug a hole an' bury himself into the hole leaving one horn outside and didn't know that horn was projecting outside. The man with the wooden leg couldn't go as fast as the rest. All the rest ran past Ram-goat; the head-man came along, buck the wooden leg upon the horn and he fell down. When he got up, he thought it was a stump, so he got out his knife to cut off that stump to prevent it throwing him down again. He cut an' cut an' cut till he saw blood. He call out to the rest, "Look! come now-o, dirtee have blood!" All the rest come around say, "Dig him out! dig him out! dig him out!" After they dug him out, they took off head-man long shirt, put on his own old one, and they wet him with all the dirty slops—they drench poor Ramgoat.

They thought he was dead and they leave him an' go away. After they was gone, Ram-goat got up. He wring the dirty clothes, he wring with all the slop they throw on him; he never remember to wring his beard. Jack man dora! That's the reason the goat have such an offensive smell until this day, he didn't remember to wring his beard!

16. Shut up in the Pot

Simeon Falconer, Santa Cruz Mountains

There was a very hard time, no food whatsoever could they get, so Anansi him family well fear. So when Bredder Tiger and Bredder Tacoomah go see him, he tell them for last three or four days his wife and children didn't eat bread. Say they will go back home and send him some of 'em food, and the two go back from Nansi yard and just dodge him now and hear his wife call, "Heah! dinner ready!" And Bredder Tiger and Bredder Tacoomah go back to the house knock on the door. The wife open the door and Anansi go right out of the house—'shamed! The wife give them some of the food to eat and it was only fresh beef.

They come back to Bredder Anansi now and Nansi tell them say, "I will get the beef, but whatever I tell you to do, you mus' be sure to do it." An' he put on a big pot of water on fire, an' him, Nansi, get into the pot of water and gwine tell them shut him up in him pot. An' tell them as soon as him knock the pot, open the pot. An' him come out now, tell Bredder Tiger *he* mus' get in the pot,—Tacoomah long side in the pot too. And shut them up, an' he get a heavy weight an' put it on the pot top. An' he went right outside and tell him wife mus' shove up the fire, mak the fire bigger an' bigger. An' when him come back, them was properly cooked. They gwine eat now, he was tuning up his fiddle—

"I got them now! I got them now!
Them think they got me, but I got them now!"

17. House in the Air

a. Tracking Anansi

Simeon Falconer, Santa Cruz Mountains

ANANSI LIVE INTO A TREE with wife and children, then go about and robber the others and they can't find where he live. So Tiger and Bredder Tacoomah dog him and see when he send down the rope and swing up whatever he provide for the family. So Bredder Tiger go to a tin-smith to give him a fine v'ice and went to the tree and him sing,

> *"Mama, mama, sen' down rope,*
> *Sen' down rope, Brer Nansi deh groun' a!"*

Then the mother find out it was not Bredder Nansi from the coarseness of the v'ice. So he go to a gold-smith now, and he come back again and sing again. Now he get a v'ice same as Bredder Nansi.

> *"Mama, mama, sen' down rope,*
> *Sen' down rope, Brer Nansi deh groun' a!"*

Then the mother let the rope down to receive him. Brer Nansi coming from a distance see the mother swinging him up in the tree now and say,

> *"Mama, cut de rope! mama, cut de rope!"*

And she cut the rope and Bredder Tiger fell and broke his neck. Bredder Nansi tak him and have him now for him dinner. They couldn't eat Bredder Nansi at all; him was the smartest one of all.

b. Rabbit and Children going up to Heaven

William Saunders, Mandeville

ONCE DE RABBIT AN' CHIL'REN was going up to Heaven. Dey was singin' dat dey goin' up to Heaven t'-day, an' Brar Anansi want to go along wid dem to have a feed. Having got in de merit dey sing,

> *"Mammy an' Harry,*
> *Pull up de merit, pull up de merit!"*

An' when Anansi quite away on de journey was goin' up to heaven, he was singin',

> *"Pull up de merit, pull up de merit!"*

an' de Rabbits say, "What is dat? Dat is Anansi voice!" De chil'ren say, "Yes, dat is Anansi voice." Rabbits say,

> *"Mammy an' Harry,*
> *Cut down de merit, cut down de merit!"*

Lan' de merit cut down an' from dat day poor Anansi's waist was cut off, leave a little bit!

c. Duppy's House in the Air

Harold Tulloch, Queen Anne's Bay

ONCE BRER DUPPY[12] MAKE HIS house in de air. So he have a sling to sling down himself every morning, an' as soon as he' come down he say to de sling, "Go up, me chin-chin, go up!" So Bredder Nansi come to find out Duppy house, an' he was wondering how to get up in dis house, so he dodge one side in de evening. An' when Bredder Duppy come he said, "Come down, me chin-chin, come down!" an' it came right down. He get in an' said, "Go up, me chin-chin, go up!" an' it go right up. By dis time Anansi was listening. Nex' morning, as soon as Bredder Duppy move off about a mile, Bredder Nansi went right up an' said, "Come down, me chin-chin, come down!" an' it came down. Den Bredder Nansi get in it and said, "Go up, me chin-chin, go up!"

After he went up, he search de house an' eat off all what he found in de house. He want to come down now, but he couldn't remember de name. So he lay off dere until de duppy come catch him in de house.

---

12. A duppy is a ghost, spirit, or any supernatural apparition, but here probably refers to the Devil.

Brer Duppy said to him, "Lawd! Brer Anansi, what you doin' up heah?" He said, "Brer Duppy, was jus' goin' up a-top heah to look fe me family, win' ketch me on de way an' I' stop heah." An' Bredder Duppy tak some boiling water an' t'row on him an' he was dead.

d. Carencro's[13] *House with a Key*

Richard Morgan, Santa Cruz Mountains

KYAN-CROW GOT A HOUSE. De libber de key to de house. When him gwine out den ca' out, "Libber me yum yum!" Ev'ry door shut up. Hanansi stan' aside saw; when him gone, him go up said, "Libber me yum yum!" de door open. An' get inside. As him go in he say, "Libber me yum yum!" de door shet. De fust t'ing him do, him eat de libber so den when Brar Kyan-crow come an' ca' out, "Libber me yum yum!" do' kyan't open. An' say, "Somet'ing de matter a me house t'-day!" When den get little crebbice a de windah gwine in at de house, den didn't see de key at all. Well, Hanansi run out, an' him ketch Hanansi.

Hanansi say, "Brar Kyan-crow, you know you do? You no lob dance? I wi' play fe you!" Kyan-crow say all right. Hanansi say, "But me banjo kyan' play widout hot water." When dey goin' along hall, when de banjo playin' "Ba cimba cimba," Hanansi say, "All right, Brar Kyan-crow, turn back-way come." He tak de packey, he dippy up full of de hot water an' say, "All right, Brar Kyan-crow, dance come now!" As Kyan-crow come, he meet him wid de packey hot water. Kyan-crow tumble down. So from dat day every Kyan-crow got peel-head.

18. Goat on the Hill-side

Julia Gentle, Santa Cruz Mountains

THE TIME HARD. ANANSI SAID to Tacoomah, "How going to manage wid de hard time?" So Tacoomah said, "You know we do? I will get me machete[14] an' I go half shut de door, den I will say, 'Police, I sick!'" Den, when people come, Tacoomah take de machete an' chop dem, put dem in de barrel for de hungry time. Anansi say, "Brar Tacoomah, barrel

13. Crow's name in French stories.
14. A machete is a broad heavy knife used to clear brush, cut cane, etc.

nearly full?"—"No, Brar." He cry out again how Tacoomah poorly; an' de people come an' as dey come, he kill dem put in barrel to serve in hungry time.

Den Goat up on de hill-side say he see everybody goin' in, nobody come out; de house so little, how is it gwine to hold all doze people? So Goat come down now off de hill-side to see how Tacoomah. He peep in. Tacoomah say, "Come in!" an' Goat run right back up hill-side. An' from dat day, Goat stay up on hill-side.

19. Dog and Dog-head

Richard Morgan, Santa Cruz Mountains

HANANSI AN' TACOOMAH DEY GOIN' out huntin' to steal cow. De two of dem have der dog. Dey walk. Hanansi, hungry tak him; he eat de dog body an' tak de dog-head put into his side-bag. Me'while dey gwine in de bush, Tacoomah dog tackle a cow. Hanansi run drive away Tacoomah dog an' tak fe him dog-head fasten on de cow an' call out to Tacoomah, "I tackle one fellah!"

Tacoomah know dat was fe him dog ketch de cow. Tacoomah lef' him went away get one whip an' go to clear place. He fire de whip an' say, "A no me, sah! a pupa, sah!" Hanansi holla, "Brar, wha' dat?" Tacoomah fire de whip again, say, "Don' my dog ketch buckra cow, sah! a pupa dog ketch it!" Hanansi call out to Tacoomah, "Tacoomah, you fool! you ever hear so-so[15] dog-head kyan ketch cow?" So Hanansi run leave de cow; Tacoomah go an' clean it up.

20. Tacoomah's Corn-piece

Adolphus Iron, Claremont, St. Ann

TACOOMAH PLANT A PIECE OF corn. When it commence to dry, den begin to t'ief it. Tacoomah charge Hanansi. Hanansi say, "Brar, no me!" By dis time Hanansi was a fiddler. Hanansi tell Tacoomah say, "Brar, you say me broke you' corn, you mek one dance an' get me fe play." Tacoomah say yes. De night of de dance, Hanansi get one gang tell dem

---

15. *So-so* means "only."

say, "As you hear me begin play, you start a-brekkin'." De tune Hanansi play was dis fe de whole night:

> *"Two two grain, broke dem go 'long,*
> *Eb'rybody broke, broke dem go 'long,*
> *Green an' dry, broke dem go 'long."*

In de morning when de dance finish, Tacoomah go down a him cornpiece. Him holla out, "Lawd! Brar Nansi, come heah! not one lef'." Hanansi turn 'roun' say, "Tink you say a me a t'ief you corn. Las' night you no get me fe play a you dance? den if dem broke out you corn, how you say a me?" Tacoomah tak it to heart an' drop down dead.

21. Anansi and the Tar-baby

a. *The Escape from Tiger*

Richard Morgan, Santa Cruz Mountains

TIGER GOT A GROUN' PLANT some peas an' get Hanansi to watch it. Me'while Hanansi are de watchman, himself stealin' de peas. Tiger tar a 'tump, put on broad hat on de 'tump. Hanansi come an' say, "Who are you in de groun'?" Him don hear no answer. He *hol'* him. His han' fasten. He *hol'* him wid de odder han'. Dat han' fasten. He said, "Aw right! you hol' me two han', I bet you I buck you!" He head fasten. Said, "I bet you, I kick you!" Him two feet fasten. Den he say, "Poor me bwoy! you a watchman an' me a watchman!" So begin to sing,

> *"Mediany dead an' gone."*

Nex' mawnin' Tiger come an' say, "Why Brar Hanansi, a *you* been mashin' me up?"[16] Tiger tak him out. Tiger said wha' fe him do wid him now? Hanansi say, "What you fe do? Mak a fire, *bu'n* me." Tiger go 'way, mak up him fire, ketch Hanansi go fe t'row him in de fire. Hanansi say, "Brer Tiger, you don' know to burn somebody yet? You mus' jump ober de fire t'ree time, den me a count." Tiger jump one, an' jump again, two,

---

16. Colloquial for "getting me into trouble."

an' jump again, t'ree, an' go fe jump again. Hanansi kick down Tiger into de fire, den go back now go finish off de peas.

b. The Substitute

George Parkes, Mandeville

Tacoomah is Anansi friend an' neighbor, live very near in one house but different apartment, so whenever one talk the other can hear. Anansi an' Tacoomah both of them work groun' together at one place. Anansi don't wait upon his food till it is ripe, but dig out an' eat it. Tacoomah wait until it fit to eat it. After Anansi eat off his own, he turn to Tacoomah an' begin to t'ief it. Every morning Tacoomah go, he find his groun' mashed up. He said, "Brar Nansi, tak care a no *you* deh mash up me groun' a night-time!" Anansi said, "No-o, Brar, but if you t'ink dat a me deh t'ief a yo' groun' a night-time, you call me t'-night see if me no 'peak to you."

Tacoomah went to his groun' and get some tar an' tar a 'tump an' lef' it in de center of de groun'. Now night come, Anansi get a gourd, fill it wid water, bore a hole underneat' de gourd jus' as much as de water can drop tip, tip, tip. He cut a banana-leaf an' put it underneat' de gourd so de water could drop on it. After dey bot' went to bed, every now and again Tacoomah called out and Anansi say, "Eh!" Afterward Anansi say, "Me tired fe say 'eh', me wi' say 'tip'." So Anansi put de gourd of water up on a stand wid de banana-leaf underneat', so when Tacoomah say, "Anansi?" de water drop "tip." An' at dis time Anansi gone to de groun'.

He saw de black 'tump which Tacoomah tar an' lef' in de groun'. So Anansi open his right han' an' box de 'tump. His right han' fasten. He said to de 'tump, "If you no let me go I box you wid de lef' han'!" He box him wid de lef', so bot' han' fasten now. He say now, "Den you hol' me two han'? If you not le' me go I *kick* you!" He then kick de 'tump an' the right foot fasten first. He kick it with the lef' foot an' the lef' foot fasten too. He say, "Now you hol' me two han' an' me two foot! I gwine to *buck* you if you don' le' go me han' an' foot!" He den buck de 'tump an' his whole body now fasten on de 'tump. He was deh for some minutes. He see Goat was passing. He said, "Brar Goat, you come heah see if you kyan't more 'an we t'-day." So Goat come. Anansi say, "Brar Goat, you buck him!" Goat buck de 'tump; Anansi head come off an' Goat head fasten. He said, "Brar Goat, you kick him wid you two foot!" An'

Goat kick him an' Anansi two han' come off an' Goat two foot fasten. He said, "Brar Goat, now you push him!" Goat push him, an' Anansi two foot come off an' Anansi free an' Goat fasten. So Anansi go back home an' say to Tacoomah, "Me tired fe say 'tip', now; me wi' say 'eh'."

In de morning, bot' of dem went to groun'. Anansi say, "Brar Tacoomah, look de fellah deh t'ief yo' groun', dat fe' a Goat!" Goat say, "No, Brar Tacoomah, Anansi firs' fasten on de 'tump heah an' he ask me fe buck him off!" Anansi say, "A yaie,[17] sah!" an' say, "Brar Tacoomah, no me an' you sleep fe de whole night an' ev'ry time yo' call me, me 'peak to you?" Tacoomah say yes. He say Tacoomah, "Mak we ki' de fallah Goat!" So dey kill Goat an' carry him home go an' eat him.

c. The Grave

Stanley Jones, Claremont, St. Ann

ONCE MRS. ANANSI HAD A LARGE feed. She planted it with peas. Anansi was so lazy he would never do any work. He was afraid that they would give him none of the peas, so he pretended to be sick. After about nine days, he called his wife an' children an' bid them farewell, tell them that he was about to die, an' he ask them this last request, that they bury him in the mids' of the peas-walk, but firs' they mus' make a hole thru the head of the coffin an' also in the grave so that he could watch the peas for them while he was lying there. An' one thing more, he said, he would like them to put a pot and a little water there at the head of the grave to scare the thieves away. So he died and was buried.

All this time he was only pretending to be dead, an' every night at twelve o'clock he creep out of the grave, pick a bundle of peas, boil it, and after having a good meal, go back in the grave to rest. Mistress Anansi was surprised to see all her peas being stolen. She could catch the thief no-how. One day her eldest son said to her, "Mother, I bet you it's my father stealing those peas!" At that Mrs. Anansi got into a temper, said, "How could you expect your dead father to rob the peas!" Said, "Well, mother, I soon prove it to you." He got some tar an' he painted a stump at the head of the grave an' he put a hat on it.

When Anansi came out to have his feast as usual, he saw this thing standing in the groun'. He said, "Good-evening, sir!" got no reply.

---

17. "A lie, sir!"

Again he said, "Good-evening, sir!" an' still no reply. "If you don' speak to me I'll kick you!" He raise his foot an' kick the stump an' the tar held it there like glue. "Let me go, let me go, sir, or I'll knock you down with my right hand!" That hand stuck fast all the same. "If you don' let me go, I'll hit you with my lef' hand!" That hand stick fas' all the same. An' he raise his lef' foot an' gave the stump a terrible blow. That foot stuck. Anansi was suspended in air an' had to remain there till morning. Anansi was so ashamed that he climb up beneath the rafters an' there he is to this day.

22. Inside the Cow

George Parkes, Mandeville

Anansi an' Tacoomah while they were frien's they had a quarrel, so it was an envy between both of them an' they never speak. One day Anansi sen' one of his chil' over to Tacoomah's yard fe some fire. Tacoomah give him the fire an' some beef-fat. Anansi see the fat in the chil' han', said, "Whe' yo' get dat nasty t'ing from?" So the chil' said, "Brar Tacoomah give it to me."—"Mak a t'row it away, nasty t'ing!" The chil' give it to him. He turn away from the chil' an' do *so* (like him fling it away), an' put it in his mouth; he then out the fire an' send back another chil' fe more fire. She come with the fire an' some more fat that Tacoomah give to her. Anansi said, "You carry back that nasty thing come here again? you give it to me here!" He turn his back an' did same as he did on first occasion. He himself now go to Tacoomah yard, said, "Mawning, Brar Tacoomah." Tacoomah said, "Mawning, Brar Nansi." Anansi said, "A wha' you get all the fat heah from, an' yo' won't tell me mak me go get some too?" Tacoomah say, "I would tell you, but yo' so craving you will go deh an' go mak trouble." Anansi said, "Oh, no, Brar! you t'ink if you tell me wha' such good t'ings is, me wen' deh go mak trouble?" Tacoomah say, "All right. Tomorrow four o'clock, when you hear cow-boy deh drive up cow a ribber-side, you come wake me an' you an' me go."

Anansi scarcely sleep fo' the night, only listening out fo' cow-boy. While on the way Tacoomah said to Anansi, "When you go to de cow, you fe say, 'Open, sesema, open', an' cow will open de belly; an' when you go in you fe say, 'Shet, sesema, shet', an' then you mus' cut de fat out of de belly. But you *mustn't* cut de back-string, fo' if you cut it de cow will dead an you can't get fe come out again. So after you done cut de fat, you mus say, 'Open, sesema, open', an cow will open an' you come out. You say, 'Shet, sesema, shet', an' de cow will shet."

So both of them go down. Anansi go to one cow, an' Tacoomah go to one use the same word, "Open, sesema, open!" Anansi go in, say, "Shet, sesema, shet!" an' the cow shet; an' then he cut a whole basket of fat an, after the basket fill he said, "Open, sesema, open!" an' cow open. He come out, say, "Shet, sesema, shet!" an' cow shet. An' both of them went home.

The nex' morning, Anansi, as he hear the cow-boy, never call to Tacoomah at all. He run down to the river-side an' go to a fat cow an' said, "Open, sesema, open!" The cow open. He go in an' said, "Shet, sesema, shet!" The cow shet. He begun to cut. Whilst cutting he cut the back-string. The cow now drop down dead.

The cow-boy went an' tell the master an' he order them to have it cleaned up. Anansi hide in the *ma*. The master give his darter the belly to go an' wash at the river. She carry it in a bowl, dash it down in the water. Anansi then jump out an' say to the girl, "Look! I in the river having a bathe an' yo' carry that nasty t'ing come an' t'row on me!" The girl begun to fret an' cry. Anansi say, "You got to carry me to your father mak him pay me for it!" She then tak Anansi to the father an' Anansi say will tak a cow in payment.

Anansi said he not going to carry the cow come home so to give any of his family any, so he went into a t'ick wood, kill the cow, mak up a large fire an' put it in to roast. He then started to look for ol' yams in the bush. He saw two eyes in the earth. He said, "Lawd, from me bwoy bo'n is de firs' me know say dirtee can hab yeye!" So now he start to dig out dese yeye,[18] dig up Bredder Dry-head.[19] He go fe put him down back in de eart'. Dry-head say, "No, jus' carry me go where dat big smoke is yonder!" Anansi refuse to carry him. Dry-head said to him, "If yo' don' carry me, de whole of you' body will catch fire!" Anansi start to run. His whole body begin to blaze, have to run back an' tak up Dry-head. On reaching the fire, Dry-head order Anansi to bring the cow to him. Anansi with a sulky heart got to comply with "Dry-head", order. Dry-head start eating the cow an' eat off every bit,—Anansi never taste it!

---

18. *Yeye* is Jamaican for "eyes".
19. "Dry-head is one of the same species, but he is a different man from them." "Dry-head is a man always hide himself in the bush to eat up what Anansi or Tacoomah have," Parkes says.—He figures as a kind of old man of the sea in the Anansi stories.

23. Cunnie-More-Than-Father

George Parkes, Mandeville

ANANSI HAS SEVEN CHILDREN. HE ask them how they would like to name. Six of them like different name, but one boy say he would like to name "Cunnie-mo'-than father." So for every tack[20] Anansi put up, Cunnie-mo'n-father break it down. One time he work a groun' very far away into the bush, an' in going to that bush he pass a very broad flat rock. So one day a man give him a yam-plant; that yam name "yam *foofoo*."[21] The same day plant the yam, it been bear a very big one same day. So nobody in the yard know the name of that yam save him, Anansi, alone. So when he go home, he cook the yam an' call the wife an' chil'ren aroun' to eat, an' say, "Who know name, nyam; who no know name, don' nyam!" So as no one know the name, they didn't get none of it; Anansi alone eat off that yam that night. The nex' day go back to the groun' and the yam bear a larger one. He bring it home an' bile it again, call the wife an' chil'ren an' say, "Who know name, nyam; who no know name, don' nyam!" The nex' day he went back an' the yam bear a larger one than the previous day. He cut it an' carry it home, cook it, call up the wife an chil'ren; he alone eat it.

Cunnie-mo'n-father say, "Look here! I *mus'* fin' out the name of that yam!" He got some okra an' went to the place where the broad rock is an' mash up the okra an' have the place quite slippery, an' hide himself away in the bush near by. Anansi now coming with a larger yam this time. As he reach to the rock, he make a slide, fa' down, an' the yam smash. He said, "Lawd! all me yam foofoo mash up!" Cunnie-mo'-n-father now catch the name, an' he ran home now an' tell mother an' other chil'ren, "Remember! yam foofoo!" Anansi then take up the pieces, put them together and carry home. He cook it an' ca' all of them roun' to eat. He say, "Who know name, nyam; who no know name, no nyam." They began to guess all sort of name; after that, whole of them say, "Yam foofoo! yam foofoo!" Anansi get vex, say, "Huh! eat! nobody fin' it out but Cunnie-mo'n-father!"

Anansi then get to hate Cunnie-mo'n-father, want to make an end of him, but he didn't know what way was to do it. So one night Brar

---

20. *Tack* means a "trick".
21. A yellou yam, the favorite vegetable food of the negro is called "afoo yam".

Tiger came to pay a visit to Anansi at his house. While both of them sittin' an' talkin', at that time Cunnie-mo'n-father was lying down underneath the table fawning sleep.[22] Anansi said to Tiger, "Look heah! ev'ry tack dat I put up, Cunnie-mo'-n-father break it down. I wan' to mak an end of him, but I don' know what way to do it." That time, Cunnie-mo'-n-father listen. Tiger said, "I wi' kill him fo' you." Anansi say, "How you will manage it?" So Tiger said to Anansi, "You mus' put up a tack, an' I wi' ketch him." Anansi said, "Look heah! Tomorrow night jus' at dinner-time you come here hide yo'self in the pepper-tree; behin' that fattest limb, you hide yo'self there, an' I will sen' him to pick some pepper an' as he put his han' on the pepper-tree, you mus' hol' him." So the nex' night at dinner-time Tiger went to hide himself there. Anansi call Cunnie-mo'n-father, say, "Go get pepper from the pepper-tree." Cunnie-mo'n-father start for de pepper-tree. On his way going he call in the kitchen an' take a fire-stick, an' as he went to the pepper-tree, he shove the fire-stick right in Tiger face. Tiger cry out, "W'y-ee!" an' gallop away. Cunnie-mo'n-father return to Anansi an' say he hear something in the pepper-tree cry, so he don' pick any. Anansi eat his dinner that night without pepper.

A few minutes after, Tiger come back in the house an' tol' Anansi what have taken place. Anansi say, "Well, the boy have tack! but we *mus'* ketch him." At that time the boy go under the table lay down an' study for them again. Tiger say, "How mus' we ketch him?" Anansi said, "You come here tomorrow twelve o'clock an' I'll sen' him up on a cocoanut tree an' while he in the tree, you wait underneath; when he come down you ketch him." The nex' morning, Cunnie-mo'n-father get two bags, fill it with red ants go up same cocoanut tree an' hide it, preparing for Tiger. At twelve o'clock Tiger come to Anansi yard. Anansi call for Cunnie-mo'n-father an' said, "Go an' get me some cocoanuts off'n that tree." He went, an' Tiger lay wait under the tree for him. He shout to Tiger he mus' look up an' show him the bes' cocoanut he want, an' while Tiger do that, he open one of the bag an' throw it down in Tiger face. Ant begun to bite him an' he has to run away. Cunnie-mo'n-father slip right down off the cocoanut tree, so he didn't get any cocoanut.

In the evening, Tiger went back to Anansi to tell him how Cunnie-mo'n-father do him again. While the two of them was talking an' setting up another tack, Cunnie-mo'n-father was underneath table listening to

22. *Fawning* means "feigning".

them again. Anansi said, "The boy smart! but I goin' to put you up a tack fo' ketch him! Look heah! Tomorrow at twelve o'clock, you fin' yo'self at me groun' an' you will see a fat root of yam near to a tree. You mus' hide yo'self in the bush an' I will sen' him there to come cut yam, an' as he come there, hol' him." Tiger then went an' fix himself in the yam bush. At twelve o'clock Anansi call Cunnie-mo'n-father an' sen' him to groun' to cut yam an' tell him that very spot whe' he is to dig them. Cunnie-mo'n-father went to the groun' an' shout out "Yam-o-e-e! yam-o-ee! yam-o-ee!" t'ree times. Nobody answer. Cunnie-mo'n-father say, "I t'ink father tell me say that when I come to groun' call fo' yam, yam wi' speak, an' de yam don' speak!" Call again, "Yam-o-ee!" So Tiger answer him, "O-ee-e!" So Cunnie-mo'n-father say, "From me bwoy born, the firs' I hear that yam can talk!" So run home back lef' Tiger.

So Tiger leave the groun' an' come home an' tell Anansi what happen. Anansi said, "Well, 'cunnie mo' than me' fe trew, but we goin' to ketch him!" At that time Cunnie-mo'n-father underneath the table fe listen, an' unfortunately he fell fas' asleep. So Anansi an' Tiger ketch him an' make a coffin an' put him in. Anansi tell Tiger he mus' take him t'row him far away in the sea where he kyan't come back again. Tiger lif' up the coffin, put it on his head an' start on the journey. On reaching to a bush he help down the coffin an', as the sun was so hot, went underneath a tree an' fall asleep. Now there was a little hole in the coffin, an' looking thru that hole, Cunnie-mo'n-father saw an ol' man comin' along drivin' a flock of sheep. He began to cry, sayin' they want him to go to heaven an' he don' ready to go yet. The ol' man said, "Bwoy, you too foolish! Heaven's a good place an' you don' ready to go there yet? You open the coffin put me in!" The ol' man open the coffin, Cunnie-mo'n-father come out, put in the ol' man an' nail up the coffin back with him in it. He then drove the sheep a little way up inside the bush. Tiger now wake out of his sleep, lif' up the coffin an' away he went to the sea with it, an' go as far he could an' t'row the coffin down in the sea drown the ol' man, fe' a heaven he want to go! He then go back to Anansi yard an' tell him that he has finish with the fellow,—no more of him, fe' he has drown' him in the deepest part of the sea.

Later in the evening, while Anansi an' Tiger was sitting down an' talking about the badness of Cunnie-mo'n-father, Anansi look an' see a flock of sheep was coming up to his house an' some one driving it. The driver was Cunnie-mo'n-father. Anansi says to Tiger, "But now look at the bwoy what you drown' today, look at him driving a flock of sheep coming up!" Tiger said, "No! 'cause I t'row him in the farthest part of the sea!" They waited until he drove them up to the yard. Tiger said to him, "Boy, don't it was you I t'row into the sea today?" Cunnie-mo'n-father said, "Yes, the place whe' you t'row me I get these sheep, an' if you did t'row me a little further, I would get double more than this!" Anansi, hearing that, said that he would like to get some himself an' Cunnie-mo'n-father mus' carry him an' t'row him at the part where he can get the sheep. Cunnie-mo'n-father then get a coffin make an' put Anansi in it carry him to the sea-side, hire a boat, an' carry him far far away in the sea an' drown him. An' that was the las' of poor Anansi in *that* story.

24. The Duckano tree

William Forbes, Dry River, Cock-pit country

DEH WAS ANANSI.—TACOOMAH WAS ANANSI son. Den was a hard time. Anansi had a Duckano tree had some Duckano on it. An' he had t'ree pickney; when he go out a night, eat him belly full, come back carry 'em a bag. Now when him wife mak a little dinner fe him, tell him no, he don' want it, gi' it to pickney dem. Tacoomah tell mama cut little hole in Anansi trab'ling bag an' t'row ashes in it. Fast as he go 'long, ashes drop straight to de Duckano tree. Den Tacoomah follow de ashes till him fin' out de Duckano tree. An' when him fetch to de Duckano tree, pick off all, lef' one; an' him tell de Duckano, "As Anansi come fe pick you, drop a dirt!" An' as de Duckano drop a dirt, Anansi say, "Yes, dat de bes' place I want you fe go!" Come down to pick him up, Duckano go back on tree. Anansi say, "Cho! dat de bes' place I pick you t'-day". Go back on tree, couldn't catch it. An' not a creature can pick de Duckano, but Tacoomah!

Den, as Anansi go up de Duckano tree, him see Dog a come. An' said, "Brar Dog, go pick up Duckano fe me!" an' as de Duckano drop, dog come pickee up; den, as Dog pick him up, Dog *nyam* de Duckano. Dog run 'round so, Anansi go after him *so*. Dog go into one deep hole, jus' two eye look out a deh. Little out de two eye, Anansi pass an' see him, draw him out of de hole an' 'queeze out de Duckano. Wha' mak de two sink place in Dog side, Anansi 'queeze out Duckano.

Jack man dora!

25. Food and Cudgel

a. *The Handsome Packey*

Moses Hendricks, Mandeville

ONCE THE TIMES WAS VERY hard. So Anansi had a wife an' six children dependent on him; wherever he goes he gets something, so he gets seven plantains, one apiece. His wife said to him, "Where is yours?" Said 'he mustn't mind him; when they cook it, each one mus' give him piece-piece. At the end he got more than anyone 'cause he got seven pieces.

He went out another day in search of food and he saw a calabash tree with one calabash on it, an' he look at it an' said, "My! there's a han'some packey!" The packey say, "I han'some an' I can do han'some work." He said, "Do it let I see!" Packey put a table before him full of nice eatables; when he eat to his satisfaction, packey shut up everything.

He took the packey home with him an' he shut it up in his loft overhead. Every day he hide from the family an' go up there have his good feed an' whatever little rubbish he bring in, he give it to them. His wife an' children watch him an' fin' what he have. After he was gone out, they play the same game—"What a han'some packey!"—"I han'some an' can do han'some work."—"Do it let we see!"—They carelessly let the packey drop from them an' crack. When Anansi go home, go to his feed, say, "What a han'some packey!" packey don't give him any answer. He find that something was wrong.

Went out another day an' saw another packey (which was the same packey), says, "There's a han'some packey!" Packey said, "I han'some an' can do han'some work." He said, "Do it let I see!" Packey took out a cow-whip an' give him a handsome flogging. He t'ought of having a good joke on the family an' pick it an' hung it up in the loft upon the same place. So the wife an' chil'ren went to this packey again, expecting the same thing; so the wife said, "There's a han'some packey!" Packey said, "I han'some an' I can do han'some work!" The six chil'ren were around the packey. The wife said, "Do it let we see!" and the packey out with the cow-whip an' fall in to lash them right an' left. Some tumble down, some get into the shingle hide themselves all around in the crevice. Jack man dora! That's the reason why you see Anansi live in the crevice!

b. The Knife and Fork

William Forbes, Dry River, Cock-pit country

ANANSI WAS CUTTING A GROUND 'gainst a ribber-side an' he had a hatchet an' de hatchet get 'way from him into de sea. An' him pull off him clo'es go dive fe de hatchet an' in'tead of fin' de hatchet him fin' a knife an' fo'k. An' when him come home, he put knife an' fo'k 'pon table an' say, "Lay out, knife an' fo'k, lay out!" An' it lay out anyt'ing he ax fe. Well, den, him get a party, lots of people into de house to show dem what knife an' fo'k can do. An' after de people come into de house, he put dem knife an' fo'k on de table an' say, "Lay out, me knife an' fo'k, lay out!" An' all de people eat.

An' ants mak nest 'pon de knife an' fo'k now. Well, den, nex' day mo'ning when he tak out knife an' fo'k, say, "Lay out, me knife an' fo'k!" not'ing at all come out. It spoil! Well, him go back to de ribber-side wid anudder hatchet an' was chopping, fling away in de sea. An' after him dive, dive an' fin' a horse-whip in de sea. An' as he go home say, "Lay out, horse-whip, lay out mak a eat!" An' de horse-whip lay out an' flog him, wattle him well till he holla.

An' he only sen' back fe all doze people who eat wid de knife an' fo'k, say he going to mak a great dinner an' all de people mus' come. An' when de people dem come, he put dem into de house an' tak out his chil'ren an' wife, put a kitchen. An' put de horse-whip on de table an' lock up de windeh, say if do' an windeh open can not get dinner. An' he tell de horse-whip mus' lay out mak dem eat. An' de horse-whip flog dem all till dey break down de house.

"Anansi is a man nobody can fool him—only Brar Dead!"

26. The Riddle

Moses Hendricks, Mandeville

TACOOMAH AND ANANSI WERE GREAT friends. Tacoomah got into trouble. He was tried and sentenced to be hung. Anansi said, "Brer Tacoomah, no fret! I'm a good liar; I play you off." Anansi went to the king to beg for Tacoomah. The king said to him, "If you give me a puzzle that I can't answer, I will let him off."

Anansi went home. Tacoomah had a mare that was heavy with colt. He said, "Brer Tacoomah, if you do as I tell you, I can get you off." Tacoomah said, "Brer Nansi, I will do anything to save me life!" Go for the mare—the one heavy with colt—open the mare's stomach and took out the colt, then took a bit of the mare's skin and cut out a bridle. Then Tacoomah got some fresh dirt and filled his hat and put it on, got some silver and put it into one boot and throw some gold into the other boot. Next, Tacoomah mount the colt. Anansi said, "Come now, Brer Tacoomah, go now and see king." He told Tacoomah all that he was to say to the king when he met him; Anansi put him up to all the talk. They said to the king:

> "Under the earth I stood,
> Silver and gold was my tread,
> I rode a thing that never was born,
> An' a bit of the dam I hold in me hand."

The king couldn't guess it; he said, "You must explain to my satisfaction." And he said, "I have me hat full of dirt" (took off his hat and show him), "one boot with silver" (he was standing on silver), "the other boot with gold" (he was standing on gold also). He rode "a colt that was never born" (he cut that out of the mother's belly), and "a bit of the dam" he held in his hand—that was the mare's skin he had as a bridle. The king reprimanded him and said, "Go on, me good man, go about your business!"

Jack man dory! Anansi got him off, Anansi was a smart man!

27. Anansi and Brother Dead

a. Brother Dead's Wife

Grace Doran, Whitehall, Cock-pit country

ONE DAY ANANSI WAS WALKING an' walk till he go into a wood and see a man have a barbecue[23]—plenty of meat. An' him go an' say, "Hi, Brar! how you do?" Man no 'peak. "Brar, you have plenty of meat an'

---

23. A cement platform for drying coffee or piment berries.

you want some one fe 'top wid you?" Man no 'peak. Say, "Brar, gi' me little breakfas' now?" Man no 'peak. Say, "Oh, Brar, you no talk, but me going to tak litt'e fe me breakfas'." Man no 'peak. Nansi go up on barbecue say, "Brar say me mus' tak meat." No 'peak to him yet. Tak de meat an' say, "Brar, gi' me you pot?" Man no 'peak to him. Say, "Brar, mus' put on yo' pot go get meat." Man no 'peak. Put on de pot an' go on de barbecue fetch meat. When he cook done, tak him bag, load up, say, "Brar, me gwine now." Man no 'peak. "Tomorrow I come back see you, an' I see you need servant an' I going to bring one of me daughter." No 'peak.

De nex' day say, "Wife, I go in Dead country an' buck up Brar Dead. Have plenty of meat. Gwine a carry me daughter down to country to work for him an' cook for him." Daughter name Sindy. When he go again, Dead sit down got him comb combing hair, long hair cover him face. Say, "Brar Dead, I promise bring a servant for you, but him hungry so me going to tak me eat." Dead no 'peak. An' tak de jug, put on pot, tak water, an' go up on barbecue tak meat an' him cook, say, "Brar Dead, I gwine, but I coming back tomorrow." An' go back say, "Enough meat dar, an' Brar say come back tomorrow." Nex' day come back. Dead no say one word, got long bow an' arrow in hand. Don't see him daughter. Go up on barbecue an' see him daughter finger have a ring. Say, "I mak you 'peak t'-day!" An' tak Dead hair and tak one long pla't tie *heah,* and tak one long pla't tie *deah,* and tak two pla't behind tie up on tree. An' as him gwine away, pile up dry trash an' light up de head wid fire. Dead shake head when de plat' burn off; and shake again, de odder pla't pop off; an' tak up him bow an' arrow an' run after Anansi.

Run up to house an' say, "Wife an' pickney, go up alof', Brar Dead dah come!" Brar Dead come in sit down *so* in de house wait 'pon dem. Pickney cry out, "Pupa, me hungry!" Say, "Brar Dead, open you han', pickney a come!" Six pickney now, de las one come, say can't do any more. Now Mrs. Anansi cry out, "Brar Dead, open yo' han', me a come!" Anansi drop now, drop in de dirt. From dat time you see Anansi live in de dirt.

b. Goat and Plantain

Rennie Macfarlane, Mandeville

GOAT PLANT HIS PLANTAIN TREE an' when it begun to bear he go an' look at it, an' when he look at it he say it will soon fit. The nex' day he go again an' say, "It is fit; it will soon ripe!" An' the nex' day when he come to cut it, Br'er Nansi cut it an' eat it. Br'er Goat said, "Baa-a-a, where's me plantain?" He go to Anansi house an' Anansi an' his wife an' two children run up in housetop. Br'er Goat wait down below. Anansi daughter said she was tired, wanted to drop on the groun' an' she drop an' Goat cut her up an' put her in his tread-bag, an' he said, "Baa-a-a, here's me plantain!" Anansi son say he wanted to drop an' he drop. An' Br'er Goat cut him up an' put him in his tread-bag, an' he said, "Baa-a-a, here's me plantain!" An' Anansi wife say, "I want to drop!" an' she drop an' Goat cut her up an' put her in the tread-bag, an' said, "Baa-a-a, here's me plantain!"

An' Br'er Anansi said, "As I'm so fat, sprinkle some ashes on the groun' an' when I drop I won't mash." An' Br'er Goat sprinkle it on the groun' an' Anansi drop an' the ashes fly up in Goat face an' blind him. An' Br'er Nansi keep the plantain-tree for himself an' when it bear, he eat it.

28. Brother Dead and the Brindle Puppy

Charles Roe, Maroon Town, Cock-pit country

DEH WAS AN OL' WITCH call Brar Dead, never talk to nobody; if him talk to anybody, him be dead. But him only making some bow all day an' set it to catch all wil' animal, an' when he catch dem, he put dem over fire an' dry dem, but him no eat dem. So Mr. Anansi go deh one day an' say, "Brar Dead, gi' me some of you meat now." But he never 'peak to Mr. Anansi, for him can't talk to nobody. So Anansi goin' in an' tak a whole bagful of de dry meat an start to eat it.

So Brar Dead has a brindle puppy. So Brar Dead pick some green bush an' gi' to de brindle puppy. So Mr. Anansi going to mak him talk dat day now. So when him come out an' tell little dog say when him sing an' people drop dead, puppy mus' t'row de bush on dem, because first day him gwine hear him voice. So him tak one de a arrow now an' start, an' de dog mus' follow him now. So when he stick him lance, blood don' come; Anansi don' walk dere. So go on; so when he stick at odder cross-road, blood come an' he say dere Anansi walk. So when he sing, Anansi got to stop. He sing,

"Anansi ma shway, Anansi ma shway,
A pupa yan kin baw, eh, eh, wa-eh!

A yan kin baw yeh, ke ya ma-dee,
Eh, eh, wa-eh, eh, wa-eh!
Eh, ey-eh wa-ey-eh!"

So he goin' till he ketch Anansi, an' when he see Anansi, tell de little puppy say mus' ketch Anansi. So de puppy ketch him, an' when he ketch him, poke de bow t'ru Anansi two ears an' he buil' up a fire an' burn up Anansi to dust.

29. The Cowitch and Mr. Foolman

Moses Hendricks, Mandeville

A GENTLEMAN HAD A COWITCH[24] property. He wanted to have it cut down, but whoever cut it must not scratch their skin. Anyone who cut it down without scratching, he would give the pick of best cow on his property. Many tried, but failed. Anansi says that he will cut it down. So the gentleman sent his son to watch and see that he cut the tree without scratching his skin at all. Anansi began cutting and the juice of the tree began to eat him. He wanted to scratch. He said to the boy, "Young massa, de cow yo' papa goin' to gi' me, white *here* (scratches one side), black *here* (scratches the other), had a red *here*, had anodder black *here*, blue jus' down at his feet." He went on that way until he cut down the tree.

He got the cow, but he couldn't manage the removal of the cow alone, and he didn't want to get any intelligent person to assist him, he wanted a fool; so he got a man by the name of Foolman. Foolman wasn't such a fool as he thought. They removed the cow to a place to butcher it near to Foolman's yard, but Anansi did not know that. So he said to Foolman, "Brer Foolman, we mus' get fire, roast plenty of meat." Foolman said he didn't know where to go to get fire. Anansi pointed out a little smoke a long distance off. Foolman refused to go. He got vexed and started to go for the fire himself. He was no sooner gone than Foolman called up his family, butchered the cow, and removed all the parts, leaving the tail. He dug a hole in the earth and drove the root of the tail down as tight as he could. When he thought it time for Anansi to come back, he held on to the hair of the cow-tail and called

---

24. A kind of plant with poisonous juice.

out, "Brer Nansi, run! Brer Nansi, run!" Anansi come and he say, "Brer Nansi, de whole cow gone, only tail!" He held on to the tail and both of them thought to pull up the cow. While pulling, the tail broke in two. So Anansi had to give Foolman a piece of the tail that popped off. So with all his cunning, he got but a very small piece.

30. Dry-Head and Anansi

a. Go-long-go.

George Parkes, Mandeville

ONE TIME ANANSI WIFE HAVE a very large pig. She value the pig for ten pounds, say she was going to sell the pig an' buy a piece of land. Anansi wanted the pig to eat an' he wanted to eat him one,[25] so he fawn sick, very very sick; all what the wife could do for him he wouldn't take nothing. He then call his wife an' tell her him gwine to die an' she mus' take care of herself an' the chil'ren.

The wife said to him she has to go nex' day to see the doctor about him, so the nex' day she dress herself an' start for the doctor, leaving Anansi very sick at home. When the wife gone one way, Anansi get up, dress himself an' go short cut the other way. He change himself into a different man. The wife say, "Good-morning, sir." He say, "Good-morning, ma'am." He say, "What is the matter?" The woman said, "My husband is sick unto death!" He said, "Well, I am the doctor. Have you any hog at home?" Say, "Yes." He says, "If you want your husband to live, you better kill the hog and let him alone eat it." The woman turn back with a very heavy heart. Anansi run back by the short cut, reach home, an' be in bed sick. When the wife return home he say to her, "Have you seen the doctor?" She says, "Yes."—"What him say?"—"He say I am to kill the hog an' let you alone eat it; then you will get better." Anansi say, "Cho! Doctor talking nonsense! How he t'ink I eat such a big hog like dat?" The woman said, "To get you better I got to comply with the doctor's order."[26]

Anansi took away the hog an' carry into a wood, him one alone. An' scrape it an' put it into a copper to cook. An' he see a wil' thing called

---

25. By himself, alone.
26. From this point the story follows a Lacovia version.

himba[27] an' he dig it to cook with the meat. He saw Mr. Go-long-go[28] come up. Say, "Brar Anansi, wha' you do here?" Say, "I boil buckra meat, sah." Tell him mus' tak out piece of meat gi' him. Say, "I kyan' tak out fe a buckra meat, sah!" Brar Go-long-go say, "If you don' tak it out I 'top you mout', I 'top you breat'!" An' he take it out an' gi' him to eat. An' say, "Tak out de whole of it!" an' he tak out the whole an' put it before Brar Go-long-go. Eat off the whole of it!

An' he said, "Brar Go-long-go, I no pass some plenty guineapea deh?" An' they went there, an' carry a pint of oil an' put him into the middle of the plant-trash an' t'row the oil right around it, an' him light an' whole take fire. Brar Go-long-go say, "Come take me out!" Anansi say, "Nyam meat no gimme me no!"[29]

b. Dry-head

Ezekiel Williams, Harmony Hall

BRAR NANSI TRABBLE AWAY. HIM was a man very fond of duckano. So while he was going on, hear somet'ing drop "*woof!*" An' say, "Makey stan' deh!" fe him duckano. At de same time deh was Brar Dry-head drop off de tree. Brar Dry-head say, "Ef you tak me up, you tak up trouble; an' ef you put me down, you put down yo' luck!" So Brar Nansi never know *what* to do. Brar Nansi say, "Brar Dry-head, have big fat barrow in a stye; mak we go kill it!" An' so dey do. Well, when de pot boil wid de barrow, Brar Nansi say, "Brar Dry-head, you know what we do? Who can't eat wi'out spoon not to taste it." So Brar Dry-head, he never have no hand, so Brar Nansi eatee off clean!

c. Brother Dead

Emanuel Johnson, Brownstown

ANANSI RUN TILL HE MEET up Bredder Dead. . . Br'er Dead say, "If you pay me, I will save you."—"Br'er, me have not'ing to gi' you, but me have one cock a yard fe me wife, me tek him come gi' you." Br'er Nansi

---

27. Wild yam.

28. "Go-long-go" corresponds with "Dry-head" in other versions. See note to 22.

29. "You ate the meat and gave me none."

run to de yard, get de cock, meet Br'er Dead in de corn-piece an' gi' it to him. Now Br'er Dead goin' to kill him jus' de same. After Br'er Dead tie de cord gone away to odder side of de corn-piece, Anansi t'ief de cock back from Br'er Dead, get a hawk an' put up de hawk. Hawk catch Dead now in de corn-piece. Anansi say,

Fly along, BrudderHawk, fly a-long.   Fly a-long, BrudderHawk, fly a-long.

Car-ry him go 'long,   Car-ry him go 'long,   Car-ry him go 'long, Brud-der

Hawk,   Car-ry him go 'long.

An' Br'er Hawk fly along wid him till drop him into a sea-ball.[30] Jack man dora!

31. The Yam-hills

George Parkes, Mandeville

ONE TIME ANANSI START TO work a groun' at the road-side. After clearing up his field, he dig nine yam-hills. Now no one is allowed to count up to the nine. If he say *nine,* he drop down dead. So Anansi say, "I got to eat somet'ing out of this." So he sat down an' begin to cry. Hog was passing, say to him, "Br'er Anansi, wha's the matter with you?" Anansi said, "My dear Bredder Hog, from mawning I dig these few yam-hills an' trying to count them, but I can't manage to count them yet." Hog said, "Cho! you too wort'less! You mean say you can't say, 'One, two, t'ree, four, five, six, seven, eight, *nine?*'" And as Hog say "nine," Hog drop down dead. Anansi take him up, put him in his bag an' carry him home an' eat him.

The nex' day he came back an' eat up Goat, who share the same fate as Hog, an' every day he went back dig the same hills. At that time Monkey was on a tree watching an' seeing all that take place. He came

---

30. A pit in the ground near the sea-coast, into which the waves wash is called a "sea-ball."

down from off the tree, an' while Anansi dig the same nine hills again an' was sitting down crying, Monkey come up an' said, "Br'er Anansi, wha' the matter with you?" Anansi said, "My dear Bredder Monkey, from mawning I dig these few yam-hills, an' I'm trying to count them but I can't manage!" Monkey said, "I will count them for you, but you mus' sit down 'pon one." Monkey then said, "One, two, t'ree, four, five, six, seven, eight, an' the one Br'er Anansi sit down upon." Anansi said, "*That's* not the way to count them!" Monkey said, "I'll count them *good* for you now!" Monkey began, "One, two, t'ree, four, five, six, seven, eight, an' the one Br'er Nansi sit down upon deh." Now Anansi is a man with a very short heart.[31] He got vex an' say, "You mean to say that you can't say 'One, two, t'ree, four, five, six, seven, eight, *nine?*" An' as the word *nine* come out, Anansi drop down dead. Monkey took him up an' said, "You can fool the others, but you can't fool *me!*"

32. The Law against Back-biting

a. Duck's Dream

George Parkes, Mandeville

ONE TIME ANANSI WERE LIVING in a country an' the country were very hard; so they pass a law that anyone talk one another, that man will drop down dead. So Anansi say he *mus'* eat something out of it, because he's going to fix himself into a place where people *mus'* talk him. So he get a hoe an' a pick-axe an' a machete an' go to a broad flat rock near the side of the road where everyone pass, begun to knock, pong pong pong. Hog was passing. Hog say, "Mawning, Brar Anansi." Anansi say, "Mawning, Brar Hog." Hog say, "Wha you do deh?" Anansi say, "Governor pass law an' say famine coming upon lan' an' ev'rybody mus' work groun', so me deh try see wha' me kyan' do." So Hog went on. As he went a little way he say, "Odder people work groun' a good place; Anansi deh work groun' 'pon rock!" As Hog say so, drop down dead. Anansi turn roun', pick him up put him in his bag, said, "Dat de way *oonoo*[32] talk a man!" So now he carry Hog go home go eat him.

---

31. "A very hasty temper."
32. *Oonoo* is Jamaican for "you."

MARTHA WARREN BECKWITH

The nex' day he went back. Cow was passing. He began to knock, pong pong pong. Cow say, "Mawning, Brar Anansi." Anansi say, "Mawning, Brar Cow." Cow say, "A wha' you deh do deh?" Anansi say, "governor pass a law that a great famine come 'pon land an' everybody mus' work groun'." So cow went on. When he go a little distance he said, "Odder man work groun' have good place; Anansi work 'pon rock stone!" Cow drop down dead. Anansi tak him up put him in his bag, said, "Dat's how *oonoo* talk a man!" He carry home Cow an' eat him.

Horse and Goat come and they share the same fate. Now a day or two after, while Anansi was there knocking, Duck came up. He said, "Mawning, Brar Anansi." Anansi said, "Mawning, Brar Duck." Duck said, "A wha' you do deh?" Anansi say, "Governor pass law say great famine coming 'pon lan' an' ev'rybody mus' work groun', so me deh try see wha' me can do." Anansi said to Duck, "What is all de strange news a fe you side?"[33] Duck say not'ing strange but only thing he dream a dream las' night that he's on the worl' so long an' no married yet; so him a go down a bottom yonder go see if him kyan' get married. So he went on. Anansi then said, "Good people, they get married. Duck an' all say *him* want fe married too!" So Anansi drop down dead. Duck turn roun' an' pick him up, swallow him, an' said, "Dat's de way *oonoo* talk a man!"

b. Guinea-chick

Alexander Archibald, Mandeville

ANANSI MAKE LAW IF ANYONE talk de odder one, he dead. He get up on one cave roadside, go working ground. Cow a pass, go see him. Anansi say, "Des a try a work one groun' heah." So when Cow go long, pass him, Cow say, "Chuh! man fool! man kyan't work groun' 'pon rock-stone!" As Cow say so, Cow tumble down dead. Den Anansi go pick him up, go eat.

Hog came. Hog ax him say, "A wha' yo' a doin' heah?"—"A try a work a groun'." Hog pass him.—"Chuh! man kyan't look upon rock-stone an' say me work groun'!" As Hog say so, him drop dead. Anansi pick him up, go eat.

Guinea-chick say, "I will go deh!" Guinea-chick put on him clo'es same as a go market. So when he come an' see Anansi upon de stone a

---

33. "In your district."

dig, tie him head wid a check handkerchief—dat are Guinea-chick—
an' pass Anansi, no'peak to him. Dat time him go long Anansi say, "Dat
dar fool!" Den Anansi drop dead.

Jack man dory!

c. Dry-head at the Barber's

Charles Thompson, Harmony Hall

ONCE ANANSI AND BUT[34] MADE agreement that they wasn't to talk
one another. Anansi went to a road and But went to one. Part of the
day, Dry-head was passing where Anansi was working and complain to
Anansi that he going out to a ball tonight and he going to a barber-shop
to get his hair barber. And after he gone Anansi say, "Pardon me, me
Lord! whe' Brar Dry-head get hair on his head to go to de barber-shop
to barber?" An' Anansi fell down an' died, an' But went back an' pick
him up an' eat him.

33. Fling-a-mile

George Parkes, Mandeville

ANANSI ONE DAY WENT TO a river to catch fish, an' while fishin' down
the stream, he came across a hole. He put his han' down in the hole an'
something hol' the han'. He said, "A who hol' me?" The something said,
"No *me!*"—"Me who?" The thing said, "No me Fling-a-mile!" Anansi
said, "Fling me a mile mak I see." The t'ing wheel Anansi, wheel him,
an' fling him one mile from the spot. When Anansi drop, he nearly
knock out his senses.

He said, "I mus' eat somet'ing out of dat hole!" He went an' get six
iron fork an' six wooden one an' stick up at the place where he drop.
Nex' day he was going back down fe fishing. He meet up Hog. He said,
"Bredder Hog, mak we go down a river go ketch fish now?" Hog said
yes. When they reach the river, both of them started. Anansi, he walk
on the side where the hole are not, Hog, he walk on the side where the
hole are. Anansi look over to Hog way and said, "What a pretty hole in
front of Bredder Hog deh! You mus' get somet'ing out of de hole deh. I

---

34. Butterfly.

don' min' if it befo' me!" So Anansi tell Hog to put his han' in the hole see if him feel anyt'ing. Hog put in him han'. Hog said, "Somet'ing hol' me han'!" Anansi said, "Ax a who hol' you!" Hog said, "A who hol' me?" The t'ing say, "A *me!*" Anansi say, "Ax him, say 'A me who?'" Hog say, "A me who?" The t'ing say, "No me Fling-a-mile!" Anansi said to Hog, "Tell him fling you a mile mak you see." Hog say, "Fling me a mile mak I see!" The t'ing wheel Hog, wheel him, wheel him, drop him right on the fork Anansi fix up. Hog drop dead. Anansi tak up Hog put him in a bag and said, "I well wan' fe eat you long time!" At that time Monkey was on the tree watching Anansi.

The nex' day Anansi start back to the river, meet up Bredder Goat. He say, "Bredder Goat, mak we go down a river, go ketch fish?" Goat say yes. Anansi tol' Goat to walk on the hand where the hole is an' he walk on the opposite side. While going along Anansi said, "What a pretty hole in front of Br'er Goat deh! You *mus'* fin' somet'ing in a hole like dat. I wish it were me de hole we' deh befo'!" Anansi said to Goat, "Put yo' han' in deh see if you can fin' anyt'ing." Goat put the han' in the hole. Somet'ing hol' him. He said, "Somet'ing hol' me!" Anansi said, "Ax a who hol' you!" Goat said, "A who hol' me?" The t'ing said, "No *me!*" Anansi said, "Ax 'A me who?'" Goat say, "A me who?" The t'ing say, "No me Fling-a-mile." Anansi said, "Tell him fling you a mile mak you see!" Goat say, "Fling me a mile mak I see!" He wheel Goat, whee' whee' wheel, an' drop him right on the fork one mile. Goat drop dead. Anansi took up Goat an' put him in his bag, said, "I well wan' you fe eat a long time!" At that time Monkey was still watching him.

The nex' day he start to go out again; he met up Br'er Dog. Anansi said to Dog, "Mak we go down a river go ketch fish!" Dog say yes. On reaching to the river, Anansi tell Dog to walk on the side where the hole is an' he walk on the opposite side. On reaching to the hole Anansi said, "What a pretty hole in front of Br'er Dog! You *mus'* fin' somet'ing in *dat* hole. I wish it we' deh befo' me!" Anansi say to Dog, "Put yo' han' in deh if you feel anyt'ing." Dog put the han' in the hole. Something hol' him. He said to Anansi, "Somet'ing hol' me!" Anansi said, "Ax 'A who hol' me?'" Dog said, "A who hol' me?" The somet'ing say, "No *me!*" Anansi say, "Ax him 'me who?'" Dog say, "Me who?" The somet'ing say, "No me Fling-a-mile!" Anansi say, "Tell him fling you a mile mak you see!" Dog said, "Fling me a mile mak me see!" The t'ing fling Dog whee'-a, whee'-a, whee', an' dash him one mile on the stake. Dog drop on the stake dead. Anansi tak up Dog, put him in his bag an' said, "A well wan' you fe eat long time!"

Now Monkey couldn't bear it no longer, come off the tree. The nex' day while Anansi was going down, Monkey put himself in the way where Anansi was to meet him. Anansi said, "Br'er Monkey, mak we go down a river go ketch fish." Monkey say, "Yes, a well wan' company fe go down too!" On reaching to the river, Monkey walk on the side where the hole is an' Anansi on the opposite side. On reaching to the hole Anansi said, "What a pretty hole in front of Br'er Monkey! You *mus'* fin' somet'ing in a hole like a dat. I wish a we' me i' deh befo'!" Anansi said to Monkey, "Put yo' han' in deh, see if you fin' anyt'ing." Monkey say, "No, Br'er, me go put me han' in deh, somet'ing go *hol'* me!" Anansi said, "No, man, me no t'ink not'ing wi' hol' you!" Monkey said, "You come put yo' han' in deah." Anansi said, "No, as you de closee, you put fe *you* han' in deah." Monkey said, "No! somet'ing wi' hol' me!"—"No! not'ing no in deah fe hol' you!" So Anansi go near to the hole now and tell Monkey *mus'* put down him han', an' Monkey refuse. Anansi now make attempt to put his han',—like *that*—in the hole, an' Monkey push it down, an' the somet'ing hol' Anansi han' now. Monkey said to Anansi, "Tak out de han'!" Anansi say, "Me han' kyan' come out; somet'ing hol' it!" Monkey says, "Ask a who hol' you." Anansi speak in a very feeble v'ice, say, "A who hol' me?" The t'ing say, "No *me!*" Monkey say to Anansi, "Ax 'A me who.'" Anansi said in a feeble tone of v'ice all 'e time, "A me who?" The t'ing say, "A me Fling-a-mile." Monkey say, "Tell him fe fling you a mile mak you see." Anansi now said in a feeble tone of v'ice, "Fling me a mile mak I see!" So tak Anansi an' wheel him, whee', whee'! An' while it was wheeling him he said to Monkey, "Br'er Monkey, run one mile from heah, whe' you see some iron an' wooden fork,—jus' haul dem out fe me!" Monkey tak off him hat an' run half way an' stop where he could see when Anansi drop. Anansi drop on de fork an' belly burst 'tiff dead! An' Monkey take him an' put him in his bag, take him go eat him.

34. But-but and Anansi

Richard Morgan, Santa Cruz Mountains

BUT-BUT AN' HANANSI DEM GWINE up to town. When dem ketch a pass Hanansi said, "Brar But-but, let we eat fe you pone!" an' dey eat half of But-but pone. As' dem gwine along, But-but feel hungry. He said, "Brar Hanansi, me hungry now." Hanansi say, "Brar But-but, you too foolish! we no half get to town yet" But-but walk till him faint away. Hanansi travel ketch roun' one turn, he 'top an' eat off of his pone deh.

Hanansi gwine a town an' get one big cutacoo.[35] Him buy everyt'ing in de whole town gill-gill. But-but lay wait for him part of de way. When he see Hanansi a come, But-but fly go before. He turn one red pocket-han'kerchief. Hanansi come down an' talk in a head. He took up de han'kerchief an' say, "Yah! der's a good red pocket-han'kerchief, but Brar But-but so cunnie, maybe he turn 'e!" an' fling it down. An' go on a little furder, But-but fly go on before again an' turn one cup, one nice silver cup. Hanansi come down. He took up de cup, say, "Der's yer luck him boy buck up t'day, but Brar But-but so cunnie maybe he here turn 'e!" an' t'row 'e down. When Hanansi get to de horse-pond whe' Hanansi wife was washing clo'es, But-but went before turn one old drawers. When Hanansi go takey up an' look 'pon it, say, "Careless, eh! look at me ol' drawers! Des ol' drawers heah kyan mak baby not skin!"[36] an' tak de ol' drawers t'row in de cutacoo. But-but begin an' eat out everyt'ing 'pon de head.

Hanansi got t'ree sons. When him goin' a house, put down him basket. As he open de basket, But-but fly out an' go upon de firs' pic'ny head. Hanansi say, "'tand 'teady, me baby, mak I kill him!" An' tak a morter-stick an' lick upon head an' kill de pic'ny. An' go up upon de nex' head again. An' say, "'tand 'teady, me baby; dat no deady, on'y sleeping!" an' he lick de odder one dead. Dat was two gone. An' go up on de las' one now. An say, "'tand 'teady, me baby, put yo' neck good mak I lick him!" an de t'ird one dead. An' he fly upon de wife head now. An' he said, "'tand 'teady, me wife, you is de 'tronger head now!" an' lick de wife dead. An' But fly upon *him* head now. An' him go up on de ridge-pole of de house an' tu'n down him head a bottom fe kill But-but 'pon him head. As' him fall down an' ketch half-way, But-but fly off, an' Hanansi broke him neck. So But-but destroy de whole family.

---

35. A Jamaican food-basket, woven deep and square in shape.
36. A soiled garment should never be left about lest it be used by the sorcerer to bewitch the owner. Burning such a garment produces a skin disease exactly like a burn, according to the common belief.

35. Tumble-bug and Anansi

Moses Hendricks, Mandeville

ANANSI AND TUMBLE-BUG TOOK A job once. After they got their pay Anansi said to Tumble-bug, "We mus' buy something so as to have a good feed." They bought a bunch of plantain and a keg of butter.

They commence to eat. Anansi dip, Tumble-bug dip. Anansi said, "No, my Tumble-bug, when I go 'pluck-um', you mus' go 'tip'!" However, Tumble-bug dip all the same. Anansi got vex an' box him. Tumble-bug fawn dead. Anansi get frightened, said, "Hi! Tumble-bug, the least bit of fun I make with you, you dead?" Tumble-bug never shake. Anansi run, leave the butter an' the plantain an' everything, take to the woods for it. Tumble-bug wake up an' eat up the plantain an' the butter. After that he fly away after Anansi now.

When he got in the woods near where Anansi was, he hid himself against a tree give a sound like a man cutting. Anansi sing out, "Who are you?" Tumble-bug said, "Gentleman servant cutting bread-nut fo' gentleman horse." Say, "Hear any news?"—"Yes."—"What you hear?"—"Anansi kill Tumble-bug,—life for life!" Anansi start running an' Tumble-bug after him. He run out to a place call "Dead man country", get among the dry trash, and that's where he live ever since.

36. Horse and Anansi

Alexander Archibald, Mandeville

ANANSI CALL HORSE A GO bush cut plantain. When dey cut done, dey carry out in de open, dey begin to play stick, lick stick. Den Anansi said, "Brar Horse, we hungry now, we don' have no fire fe roast plantain." So say to Horse, "Go see fire quite yonder? Go deh, go tak fire come, mak we roast plantain!" Horse fling up him tail on back, gallop, gone. Meanwhile him gone, Anansi 'trike him tinder-box an' buil' a fire roast every plantain; eat all de plantain, leave only four. Horse gallop away an' kyan' ketch de fire an' turn back. Anansi say, "Brar Horse, when you gone, one man pass heah gi' me fire an' me roast de plantain; as me roas'ee done, one man come beat me an' tak away de plantain on'y lef' dem four heah gi' me!" So Brar Horse say, "Never min'! you tak two, me tak two." So Horse takee.

Dat time Brar Goat go bush kneel down watch Brar Anansi, watch what take place; so de nex' day, Goat say *him* will go wid Anansi. Dem two go, dem two cut plantain, an' dem come out 'pon de open an' dem play. So Anansi said, "Brar Goat, we hungry now an' we ha' no fire. See fire quite yonder? gallop go get fire an' come." Goat gallop, go roun' clump of bush, go kneel down on knee go watch him. Him 'trike him tinder-box mak a fire, peel ev'ry plantain put a fire. When de plantain roast, he 'crape ev'ry bit. As him 'crapee, Goat get up a come. Goat cut 'tick an' him jump one side so him put circle roun' de fire-side, an' say to Anansi, "Put you han' in now, sah!" an' jump de odder side an' put circle again. So den Anansi begin to beg, an' Goat tak away eberyt'ing didn't gib him one!

Jack man dory!

37. Anansi in Monkey Country

a. Bunya

Elizabeth Hilton, Harmony Hall, Cock-pit Country

ANANSI GO TO MONKEY COUNTRY. Put on a big pot of water an' tell the Monkey when him get in the pot of water, when him say "Bunya", they mus' take him out of the pot of water. When they take him out, they mus' go in. So when he go in the pot of water, as soon as he feel the water hot he say, "Bunya." They take him out. An' put all of them one time into the pot of water. An' when them said, "Bunya!" Anansi said, "No bunya yet!" An' said, "Bunya!" Anansi said, "No bunya yet!" Anansi wouldn't take them out until them boil. Anansi take them out an' eat them.

One little one lef' at the top of the pot that the water didn't scald. That one run go to the next Monkey country an' tell them the story about Anansi an' the "bunya." When Anansi eat, he start to the other country, an' him go there an' tell the Monkey mus' put him into the pot of water an' when he say, "Bunya," mus' take him out. So when Anansi feel the water hot, he say, "Bunya!" Monkey say, "No bunya yet!" Anansi say, "Bunya!" Monkey say, "No bunya yet!" Monkey keep Anansi in that pot till him kill him.

b. *Christen Christen*

Adolphus Iron, Claremont, St. Ann

ONE TIME HARD TIME KETCH Brar Nansi. Him couldn't get not'ing to eat. Him trabble away to Monkey country fe go preach. When him ketch deh, him say, "Well, frien's, I come here to chris'en, but I chris'en wid a large oben." De Monkey, dem glad fe hear. Dem jump an' buil' up de oben. Anansi say, "You mus' pack it wid wood an' light it wid fire. When it well hot, me will go in first, an' when you hear me say, 'Chris'en,' you mus' open de door." De Monkey, dem agree.

De oben buil', de oben light, Anansi go in. Anansi holler, "Chris'en!" Dem open de door. Anansi jump out, dem begin jump in. When de las' monkey jump in, Anansi shet de door. Monkey begin holler, "Chris'en! chris'en!" Anansi say, "No chris'en yet!" When Anansi t'ink dem a well roas', him open de door. One scorch-side one jump out an' run fe de odder Monkey country an' tell all wha' done.

Anansi stan' deh till him eat off de whole ob de roas' one dem. Him trabble again till him ketch de odder Monkey country. All was prepare to meet him. De scorch-sided one meet him first. Anansi say, "Brar, I fink I know you!" De Monkey said, "No, sah, a de firs' me an' you buck up!" Anansi say, "Well, I come here to chris'en, but I chris'en wid an oben." De Monkey, dem buil' up de oben quicker yet. Anansi say, "I will go in firs'; when you hear I say, 'Chris'n!' you open de do'." All de Monkey say yes. When Anansi feel de fire, him holler, "Chris'n, chris'n, chris'n!" De Monkey say, "No chris'n yet!" An' dey let Anansi stay all roas' till he burst!

38. Curing the Sick

a. *The Fishes*

Rennie Macfarlane, Mandeville

THREE LITTLE FISH PICKNEY MOTHER was sick an' Anansi said, "If you want, I get you' mother better for you!" an the three little fish said, "Yes!" An' said, "You give me a frying-pan an' some sweet ile, an' you lock up in that room an' when she better, I let you know." An' he fry the fish an' eat it an' tell the fish pickney that they can come out the room now. An' they ask, "Where is our mother? Did you get her better?" an' he said, "No, I eat her!" an' the fish run after him an' he run away.

An' a mule ask the fish, "Do you want me to catch him for you?" an' they said, "Yes!" And the mule said, "Give me those peas that you have now an' I catch him for you." An' the mule go out to Anansi gate an' lie down there an' when Anansi come out, Anansi run up into his belly an' the mule gallop away again. An' Anansi cry out in the mule's belly, "If he go to sea-side, stop him; but if he go anywhere else, let him go!" An' he gallop to the sea-shore an' give Anansi to the fish.

An' he say, "You know what you do, fish? Put me under the trash an' burn me!" An' when the fish put him under de trash, Anansi run under a stone, hide, an' the fish t'ot he was burn.

b. *The Six Children*

George Parkes, Mandeville

An old woman had six children, three sons and three daughters. They grew up to be big men and women. They were living near the roadside. The old woman was sick with sore eyes, so the children came out by the wayside and began to cry. Hog was passing by, said to them, "What's the matter with you, now?"—"Well, Mr. Hog, our mother became blind and we cannot cure it!"—"I can't do no good, I can't cure it!" So Hog went away. Little after that there was Goat come up. Children were still crying. Goat said, "What's the matter with you, now?" Children said, "Well, Mr. Goat, our mother took in with blindness and we cannot cure it!" Goat say, "I cannot cure it!" and he went on his way. A little after that Cow came up. "What's the matter with you, now?"—"Well, Mr. Cow, our mother took in with blindness an' we cannot cure it!" Cow say, "I can't do no good!" an' he went on his way. Afterward they heard Jack-ass galloping come along say, "Hee-haw, hee-haw! What's the matter with you? what's the matter with you?" The children say, "Well, Mr. Jack-ass, our mother took in with blindness an' we cannot cure it!" Jack-ass say, "I can't do no good! I can't do no good! I can't do no good!"

Little after that, Anansi come up, hear the children crying, said, "An' w'at de mattah wid you, now?"—"Well, Mr. Anansi, our mother took in with blindness an' we cannot cure it!" Anansi said, "I can cure it!" He said, "You know wha' you all do? Put a barrel of water in the kitchen, get two barrels of white yam put in the kitchen, a pound of butter, a pound of lard, 'nuf meat, an' put dem in de kitchen, an' I'll come back anodder day an' cure it!" So the day appointed he came back an' said, "Carry you mother now an' put in the kitchen," an' said, "I am going to shut the door an' when you heah somet'ing say 'fee-e-e-e', you all mus' say, 'T'ank God, mama have a cure!'"

So Anansi kill the ol' lady, cook off all the yams an' flour an' everyt'ing, fry up the ol' lady with the butter an' the lard. He go "fee-e-e-e" an' the children, hearing that, said, "T'ank God, mama have a cure! t'ank God, mama have a cure!" Anansi now eat off the ol' lady an' all the t'ings, take all the bones an' pack it put at the fire-side, an' come out an' fasten the door, say that they mus' not open the door until nine days time. That time, take himself away. On the seventh day, the chil'ren couldn't bear it no longer, went an' burst the door open fin' all their mother bones at the fire-side.

They come out, start crying again. Hog pass by, said, "What's the matter with you now?"—"Well, Mr. Hog, Mr. Anansi come heah an' kill our mother an' we cannot catch him!" Hog said, "I can't help you!" and went his way. A little after, Goat came up, said, "What' the matter now?"—"Well, Mr. Goat, Mr. Anansi came heah an' kill our mother eat her off an' we cannot catch him!"—"I can do no good, I can't catch him!" Goat went on his way. Cow came up. "What's the matter with *you* now? what's the matter with you?"—"Well, Mr. Cow, Mr. Anansi come heah an' kill our mother an' eat her off an' we cannot catch him!" Cow said, "I can't do no good! I can't do no good!" an' he went on his way. A little after, Jackass come, say, "Hee-haw! what's the matter with you? what's the matter with you? what's the matter with you?"—"Well, Mr. Jack-ass, Mr. Anansi come heah an' kill our mother an' eat her off an' we can't catch him!" Jack-ass said, "I will catch de fellah! I will catch de fellah! I will catch de fellah!"

Jackass went to Anansi gate an' lay down fawn dead with his belly swell up. Anansi come down an' said, "Lawd! dat's a lot me bwoy meet up t'-day!" An' said, "Me wife, bring de big pot an' de big bowl an' de big yabba[37] an' de big knife!" So when it come, Anansi cut Jack-ass

---

37. A shallow flaring bowl.

under the belly, put his han' t'ru the cut. He full the big pot with the fat, and the big bowl, an' shove his han' now to fill yabba, clear to his shoulder. Jack-ass hol' him. He said, "Br'er Jack-ass, me no t'ink you dead!"[38] an' said, "A little fun me mak wid you, no mean i'!" Jack-ass say, "Fun or no fun, come we go!" an' Jack-ass get up, gallop straight to the children yard. An' they make up a big fire an' put Anansi in an' bu'n him an' bu'n him till him belly burst!

39. Anansi, White-belly and Fish

Mrs. Ramtalli, Maggotty

ANANSI IS ACCUSTOMED TO LIE in the sun every morning watching the birds going to feed. One day he said to White-belly, "Brar White-belly, whe' you go to feed eb'ry day? tek me wid you." So White-belly promised on condition that he would behave himself. He fitted him out with a pair of wings to fly, and they went to the feeding-trees. These overhung a river. Every tree White-belly went on, Anansi said, "A fe me tree dat!" and White-belly went away to another. Anansi eat so much that he fell fast asleep. White-belly got annoyed. When Anansi was sleeping, he went and took off the false wings. Anansi turned in his sleep and fell into the river.

The Fish picked him up and took him to their home. He said, "Cousin Fish, no eat me!"—"If we are 'cousin' we wi' see!" Fish boiled some hot rice-pop. Anansi said, "It no hot enough! putee in the sun mekee hot more!" When he thought is was quite cooled off, put it to his head, never stopped drinking until it was finished. Then Fish say, "Yes, me cousin fe trew!"

It was getting night and Fish told him to remain over until next day. Fish had a barrel of eggs in the kitchen. Anansi wanted to eat them off, asked Fish to make his bed in the kitchen for the night. He poached all the eggs in the ashes, left one, and they went "pop!" The pickney say, "A wha' stranger man a do deh?" The Fish mother said, "Have manners, pickney! Let you cousin prosper." Morning dawn, the mother sent the children to bring the eggs to her to count them. Anansi said, "Mek the child'ren keep quiet; me wi' work!" and he took the one egg, took it to

---

38. "I thought you were dead."

the mother Fish. Each time she marked it he would wipe it off, take back the same egg, until he had taken the whole barrel full.

After that, he said he wanted to go. Fish said to two of the children, "Me son, get the canoe an' tek you cousin over the river." It was looking very breezy and rainy. When they got half way across, Fish bawled out at the top of her voice, "Bring stranger man back he-e-ah! fe he eat off all me eggs; only one is heah!" The children say, "Wha' ma say?" Anansi said, "You ma say you mus' row quickly, squall ahead!" The children rowed across. Anansi took them up, put them in his bag and took them home, eat them. And from that day, fishes are eaten!

40. Goat's Escape

a. The Rain

Richard Pottinger, Claremont, St. Ann

ANANSI AND GOAT HAVE A little quarrel. Anansi said to Goat, "Brar Goat, I gwine ketch you!" Goat say, "You never live, me frien', to ketch me!" Goat 'fraid fe rain. So one moist night Goat was coming from his field had to pass Anansi's house, drizzle drizzle rain fall; Brar Goat have to run up Anansi's house.—"Come in, me frien'!" Goat go in. Anansi step in a room tak out him fiddle:—

> *"Me t'ank Brar Rain*
> *Fe run wil' meat from bush*
> *Come a house."*

Goat didn't like it, keep to de door-way. Anansi not notice him, only playing de same song. Goat jump down de bottom door Anansi cut after him. Goat can't cross river, run to de river-side turn a white little stone. Dog see, de odder side of de river, when Goat turned a little stone. Anansi run up de river now.—"Brar Dog, see Brar Goat pass?"—"Yes, Brar! see one little stone a riverside deh? takee up t'rowee, I show you whe' him deh." Anansi tak up de stone, t'row it de odder side, give Brar Dog. Goat drop on him four feet. Anansi say, "Luck in me han' an' it get 'way!"

b. The Dance (1)

Elizabeth Hilton, Harmony Hall, Cock-pit country

Assono[39] an' Anansi make a dance and invite Goat and Dog to the dance. Anansi make bargain with Assono that when Goat an' Dog come in, he mus' sit down at one door an' Anansi at the other. Assono sing, (repeat three times)—

> *"I sit down a me house deh fe dey come!"*

So Anansi sing,

> *"Whe' me been tell you!"*

Dog sing,

> *"The somebody kyan't run, you no hearie?"*

Goat sing,

> *"I kyan't run, but I cunnie do!"*

Anansi say to him, "Brar Goat, you no play de fiddle good! mak me tak de fiddle stan' 'pon de do'mat play better." That time he gone to shut the door, Dog and Goat run thru' the other door before Assono catch them. Assono an' Anansi run after them an' get to a big river. Dog can swim an' Goat kyan't swim, so Dog swim over the river an' lef' Goat. Goat turn a big rock an' lie by the roadside. Dog say to Anansi, "Brar Anansi, tak a rock-stone, lick me down an' I wi' stay mak you come pick me up!" Anansi tak a big rock *so* an' fling over the river. Goat get up an' holla "Baa-a-a-a!" Assono so vex with Anansi that he eat him up same place.

---

39. Assono is a large animal, unidentified. See story 75.

b. The Dance (2)

Alfred Williams, Maroon Town

HANANSI GIVE A DANCE, INVITE any amount of company, an', de night, everbody come. He invite Brar Goat, an' when him come, Brar Goat stay outside on de landing, an' Brar Hanansi inside say him gwine to play, an' he play,

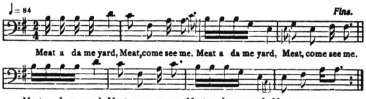

Meat a da me yard, Meat, come see me. Meat a da me yard, Meat, come see me.

Meat a da me yard, Meat, come see me. Meat a da me yard, Meat, come see me.

Brar Goat den dance. When he dance he holla,

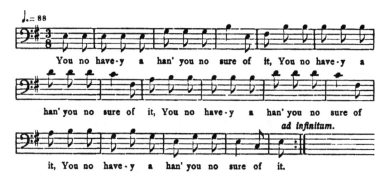

You no have-y a han' you no sure of it, You no have-y a

han' you no sure of it, You no have-y a han' you no sure of

it, You no have-y a han' you no sure of it.

ad infinitum.

41. Turtle's Escape

Henry Spence, Bog, Westmoreland

TURTLE FOOL ANANSI ONE DAY. Anansi go out one day an' him catch one turtle,—quite glad of de turtle! So when he go home, Turtle know Anansi gwine eat him an' said to Anansi, "Brar Anansi, you know me fat? When you put me on, as de water boil up you tak me off, 'cause fat will mash." So when de water get warm, him blow him nose mak de water boil up. Anansi get frightened, said de turtle wi' mash! So he lay him down at de pan-side let de fat cool so him no mash. Turtle run away in de pond. Anansi lose him dinner.

42. Fire and Anansi

Henry Spence, Bog, Westmoreland

ANANSI AN' FIRE WERE GOOD frien'. So Anansi come an' see Fire an' dey had dinner. So he invite Fire fe come see him now. So Fire tell him he kyan't walk. So Fire tell him from him house him mus' lay path dry bush, an' him walk on top of dry bush. Anansi married to Ground Dove. Ground Dove tell him no, he mustn't invite Fire; him wi' bu'n him house an' bu'n out himself. Anansi wouldn't hear what him wife say, an' he laid de trash on. An' Fire bu'n from him house, an' when he come near Anansi house he mak a big jump, bu'n Anansi, bu'n him house, bu'n eb'ryt'ing but him wife. Fire fool Anansi!

43. Quit-quit and Anansi

a. Tailors and Fiddlers

David Roach, Lacovia

ANANSI AND LIZARD GO TO a ball. Anansi is a fiddler, Lizard is a tailor. Quit-quit was the fiddler. Anansi was playing, "tum, tum, tum" and all the girls were going round Brar Quit-quit. So Anansi play, "Me nyam-nyam taya!" an' it please the people. All love taya; all the girls crowded round Brar Anansi. Brar Quit-quit says, "Taya no somet'ing!" Then Anansi comes in with his music—"Me nyam de somet'ing! If taya no somet'ing, whe' are de somet'ing?"

Brar Anansi said mus' mak a suit of clo'es for him that kyan't match. Brar Quit-quit tell him mus' mak a suit out of maggot-fly. An' after the ball they went to dinner an' when the maggot-fly smell the meat, they run off leave him naked.

b. Fiddlers

Henry Spence, Bog, Westmoreland

ANANSI AND TIGER BOT' OF dem are fiddler an' go play fe de king ball. So Tiger could play more dan Anansi. So de king say de man could play de best would get married to de king daughter. Dem had dinner after de ball, so after dem play, play, play, Anansi find Tiger playing more dan him, so de lady more cleave to Tiger. So Anansi whisper to Tiger, say Tiger mus' play,

Nyam nyam no not'ing!

As he commence play, de lady say de meaning "Belly-feed no not'ing, but *mus'* somet'ing!" So Anansi set *him* fiddle, play,

Bittle no somet'ing, what is somet'ing?

De lady cleave to Anansi an' drive away Tiger.

44. Spider Marries Monkey's Daughter

May Ford, Newmarket

BREDDER MONKEY HAD A DAUGHTER whom Bredder Spider wanted to marry. Monkey didn't want Bredder Spider to marry his daughter as he thought Bredder Spider was too fast and beneath him; he only kept Bredder Spider company as he thought him useful to him. So he jump to Bredder Green-lizard and said, "Bredder Green-lizard, what you think of such cheek? Fancy! Bredder Spider want to marry me daughter! I don't want to hurt his feelings as he is useful to us, so help me to get out of it." So Bredder Green-Lizard say, "I tell you a way, man. Call her 'Miss Nennan-kennan-wid-a-turn-down-gown' and whoever guess her name marry her, for Bredder Spider never can guess that!" So Bredder Lizard went direc' an' tell Bredder Spider, "When dey call you all up to ax Bredder Monkey daughter name, you fe say, 'Miss Nennen-kennan-wid-a-turn-down-gown'." So Bredder Monkey send out word to all the gentlemen who want to marry his daughter to come and guess her name. Not one could tell her name till when he catch to Bredder

Spider, Bredder Spider say, "Miss Nennen-kennen-wid-a-turn-down-gown." So Bredder Spider got Bredder Monkey daughter an' marry her.

So when Bredder Spider wife had a baby, she left Bredder Spider put the pickney to bed while she go to pond. When Bredder Spider think wife gone, him start to sing,

> *"Hush, me pickney, hush me baby,*
> *A me cunnie mak me get yo' mama!"*

Spider wife turn back an' say, "A what a dat you sing?" Spider say, "Me only sing,

> *'Hush, me pickney! hush, me baby!*
> *It's a good t'ing marry yo' mama?'"*

Bredder Monkey been a come see him an' hear what Bredder Spider singing. Bredder Monkey say, "Wa' *so* you get me daughter!" an' grab away the baby an' kill Spider. And as him kill Spider the pickney drop out his hand dead.

So never kill a Spider, as whatever you have in hand will be sure to break.

45. The Chain of Victims

Richard Morgan, Santa Cruz Mountains

HANANSI SAW BRAR HOG AN' said, "Brar Hog, lend me a dollar, tomorrow, twelve o'clock, come fe it." An' saw Brar Dog an' said, "Brar Dog, len' me a dollar, tomorrow, twelve o'clock, come fe it." An' saw Brar Monkey an' say, "Brar Monkey, len' me a dollar, tomorrow, twelve o'clock, come fe it." An' saw Brar Tiger an' said, "Brar Tiger, len' me a dollar, tomorrow, twelve o'clock, come fe it." An saw Brar Lion an' say, "Len' me a dollar, tomorrow, twelve o'clock, come fe it."

Nex' day hear some one knock at de door. Hanansi said, "Who come deah?"—"Me, Brar Hog." An' he say, "Come in." He an' Hog stay dere talkin' an' hear anodder knockin'. An' say, "Who come deah?"—"Me, Brar Dog." He say, "Brar Hog, you run go in dat room, fe Dog too bad; if him catch you him are goin' to kill you!" Dog come in. Him stay dere talkin' until hear anodder knock an' said, "Who come deah?"—"Me,

Brar Monkey." An' say,' "Come in"; an' say, "Brar Dog, you run go in dat room dere an' When you go you see Brar Hog un'er de bed, kill him." Him an' Monkey talk till Tiger come knock at de door, an' Hanansi say, "Who knock deah?"—"Me, Brar Tiger." An' say, "Brar Monkey, run go in dat room hide or Tiger ketch you!" When Brar Tiger come in, him an' Hanansi deh talkin' till he hear annodder knock. An' say, "Who come deah?"—"Brar Lion." An' say, "Brar Tiger, you run go in dat room deh; you see Brar Monkey, kill him!" So as Lion come in he tell Brar Lion, "Look heah! have plenty o' meat. Brar Tiger gone in dere; you gwine go kill him!" Lion went in an' kill Tiger. Me'while de Lion kill Tiger, Hanansi go out de kitchen door dig one deep hole an' ca' say, "Brar Lion, run come heah! We go put on little hot water fe clean up doze fellah!" As Lion jump out of de house, feel so glad, gallop on to de kitchen, he got down in de hole an' bre'k his neck. So Hanansi said, "You brute! look how much money I borrow from you, an' I have all yo' bone to crack t'-night!"

46. Why Tumble-bug Rolls in the Dung

William Forbes, Dry River, Cock-pit country

DEH WAS MR. ANANSI AND TUMBLE-BUG. Deh was a young lady, was de king daughter. Her fader said who come wid a jar of money will get dat young lady to marry. Tumble-bug get a jar of money. Anansi get a jar an' couldn't get no money to put in it, get some cow dung an' some horse dung fill up de jar. And after dem was going up to de young lady, dem ketch to a shop. And de two jar favor one anodder. An' Anansi said, "Brar Tumble-bug, let we go in de shop go get a drink." An' Anansi said, "Mus' buy a bread come," an' as he come out, him tak up Tumble-bug jar and lef' fe him jar. An' Tumble-bug tak up Anansi jar. And when dem go up to de young lady in de king yard, Anansi said, "Massa, mus' bring a clean sheet go t'row out money out of jar!" An' he t'row out. Money—wa-a-a-a! An' as Tumble-bug t'row, him t'row out horse-dung an' cow-dung.

Anansi said, "Tak it up, tak it up, tak it up, you nasty fellow, carry out de missis yard!" Dat is why you see Tumble-bug roll in filth today today.[40]

---

40. The repelition is distributive and means "until today."

47. Why John-crow has a Bald Head

a. The Baptism

Margaret Brown, St. Anne's Bay

ANANSI ALWAYS HAS A GRUDGE wid John-crow; he say whenever he make his nest, de Crow fly on it an' catch it up an' he never can make his nest, so he have a hatred for Crow. He say he was going to married and he was going to invite no one but Crow. An' he have a big dinner an' no one was at de table but Crow. So after de eat an' drink done, he said he was going to have a baptism but he don't baptize wid not'ing but boiling water. So after de water's boiling, he took it off an' order Crow to sit round de copper an' so he dip ev'ry one head into de water, an' dat why Crow have bald-head today.

b. The Dance

Henry Spence, Bog, Westmoreland

ANANSI AND JOHN CROW HAD a ball one night, so dey fin' dinner de night fe all de dancer. John Crow a great 'tepper, can 'tep better'n Anansi. So as Anansi fin' John Crow can dance neater dan him, he get bex. So after de dinner de pop was hot, so he said to John Crow him mus' dance up to de pop. So jus' to get rid of John Crow de night, he got a ladle an' dash on John Crow wid de hot pop right up on de head, an' all John Crow head 'trip off. All de John Crow in dis worl' never have ne feder upon i' head *heah;* Anansi bu'n 'em off wid hot pop.

48. Why Dog is always Looking

Moses Hendricks, Mandeville

ANANSI AND DOG WERE FRIENDS. They wanted to go into cultivation, so both of them went out in search of good lands to rent. They came across a nice bit of land. Anansi fell in love with the spot; Dog fell in love with the spot too. Anansi said to Dog he remembered when he was a little boy his father planted yams on that very spot of land,—"An' the yams did bear." Dog said, "How they bear big?" Anansi said, "Brar

Dog, they bear *big*, they bear big like me leg!" (Anansi's leg is jus' like a thread!) Brar Dog say, "Before I work an' plant yam, an' the yam not bigger than you leg, I sooner walk round an' look!" That's the reason why, when you're eating, a dog 'sure to be looking at you.

49. Why Rocks at the River are covered with Moss

Sarah Vessel, Bog, Westmoreland

ANANSI WAS GWINE OUT ONE day an' he stop a ribber-side a-eatin'. A rock-stone beg him, an' wouldn't gi' him none. After eat done, wan' to get up; rock-stone hol' him an' he couldn't get up. An' began to bawl. A man was coming pas' same time an' ask him, "Bredder Anansi, who been a cry heah?" Anansi said, "Don' know!" An' de man go inside de bush, go hide. Anansi holla, an' he come out an' he catch him by his two han' an' draw him right up. Half a him 'kin lef' on de stone. Moss a grow upon rock-stone a ribber-side, Anansi skin a grow deah.

50. Why Ground-dove Complains

Simeon Falconer, Santa Cruz Mountains

TIGER PLANTING CORN, AND BIRDS and everyt'ing destroying de corn, so him get Dove to help him fe watch who is destroying de corn. So after dey sit up de whole night fo' to watch de corn, next day Tiger him go sleep. Bredder Dove go back in de day now and destroy de corn. So de nex' day, Tiger went in de day and dodge in de ground. Bredder Dove have a gang, an' Tiger were slap him on de ears and he sing out, "Me ears! me ears! me ears!" An' from dat day to dis de dove singing, "Me ears!"

51. Why Hog is always Grunting

Norman Hilton, Harmony Hall

BRAR HOG AND BRAR DOG live close by river-side, so Brar Dog said to Brar Hog, "Come! we get a bathe!" Brar Hog said yes, so Brar Hog took off his mout' and Brar Dog an' Brar Hog jump in the water. Brar Dog said to Brar Hog, "Come! let us see who can dive longer than the other." So two of them dive underneath the water. Brar Dog come up, jump out of the water, take Brar Hog mout' and went away with it. When Brar Hog come out of the water, searching for his mout' and couldn't fin' it, an' said, "Humph! Brar Dog tak a me mout'!" That's why Brar Hog always grunting.

52. Why Toad Croaks

Richard Morgan, Santa Cruz Mountains

ONE MAN GOT A DARTER. He said, "Got one cotton tree; de man cut dat cotton tree, he marry to me darter." Every man go cut, soon dey cut de chip fasten back; so dem couldn't get de girl to marry. Toad said him go fall him. Toad full in pocket a hashes an' every chop him chop him fling de hashes upon de tree when de chip fly, and 'ey kyan't fasten. So Toad do an' do till he fell de cotton tree.

De master hab a long barbecue an' tell him say, "Now you mus' go down dere and 'trip yo'self an' I wi' pour on de water to let you skin." All dis time one big pot hot water on de fire boil up, so dem turn over de pot o' hot water an' say, "Brar Toad, water come! tak you rubbin' clot'." An' Toad jump in wild pine; up to dis day, ev'ry night you hear him cry out, "Kwoka soaka!"

53. Why Woodpecker Bores Wood

Samuel Wright, Maroon Town, Cock-pit country

THERE WAS A BIRD NAME of Woodpecker promise his mother to bury him into a stone, an' go all about an' tell all his frien' dat him gwine to bury him mother into a stone. An' de mother was poorly unto death an' he went to go an' bore a stone, an' he turn back an' said, "Mother, I try the stone but I can't bore it. I'll bury you into a wood." An' he bore de wood. An' after de death of his mother, he buried him into a wood. That is the reason the wood-pecker bore the wood.

54. Why Crab is afraid after Dark

Richard Morgan, Santa Cruz Mountains

CRAB GO TO GOD TO gi' him head. God tell him he mus' go back, "Tomorrow come, I will give you head." After Crab gwine home, he rej'ice into him, he singin',

> *"T'ank God, tomorrow God a'mighty gi' me head!*
> *T'ank God, tomorrow God a'mighty gi' me head!"*

He dance until he muddy de water. Nex' day he went to God a'mighty fe get head. God tell him say, "Stop! after you don' get head yet you go an' muddy water; den if you get head you will do worse. So you mus' carry your head upon your shoulder all de days of you life." So when Crab returning home, when him ketch Orange Bay[41] an' stan' der call Daniel name, said him wouldn't trust a shadder after dark, for him don't know when dey pick him up t'row him into his basket.

55. Why Mice are no Bigger

Richard Morgan, Santa Cruz Mountains

DEH IS A MAN DE name of Robin Mice-rat gwine to his uncle house. Him an' de uncle stay dere in dark de whole time. When him gwine away, he tell de uncle good-by an' tak a stick an' he lick 'e uncle. At dis time he went to our Saviour an' said he want to turn big man, so de Savior tell him say if he wan' to turn big man he mus' go an' kill his oldest uncle. So, as he never died, he went back de nex' night. So him an' his uncle talking an' his uncle said to him, "Dat fellow Robin come here las' night; when him gwine away, tak a stick an' lick me in de head. But, me pickney, if a *heah* (pointing to the temple) him ketch me, de fellow would a got me." So as de uncle show him de place, as him get up, meet his uncle at de said place, kill him 'tiff dead.

Nex' day he went to his Savior fe let him turn big man. De Savior said to him, "You little bit of man go kill you' oldest uncle, den if me let

---

41. A local place-name.

you turn bigger you will do worse!" So from dat day das de reason let you see mice don't bigger to dis day.

56. Rat's Wedding

Thomas Williams, Harmony Hall, Cock-pit country

RAT GOT MARRIED, AN' DERE was rice and peas provide for de helping of food fe de dinner. It was so richly cook an' so much dat it get burn. So Rat remember dat de rice burn in de pot, an' Rat like 'crapin', an' while he was goin' home wid his wife in de way, when he get part way he said to her, "I forget somet'ing very valuable in de wedding house, have to go back fe it!" She said yes, an' put out de buggy on de water-table[42] an' run back to de wedding house, never went in where everybody in de house merrying himself, went to de kitchen. So de pot wid de bu'n rice was lean up by de side of de wall. So de force he go to de pot wid trouble de pot,[43] an' de pot, 'stead of rolling away, tu'n over cover him underneat'. An' when he fin' dat he couldn't come out, he said, "Chut! what about dat? I wouldn't give a biscuit fe a man who kyan't lose his night rest!" and he begin to 'crape bu'nt part *kur-ur-rup krup krup krup.*

His wife calling now, "Mr. Rat! Mr. Rat!"—"Me head fasten in pot o!" Tu'n back *'crape 'crape.* So de cook hear de noise and went but in de kitchen, find it was Rat underneat' de pot an' call out fe help. An' come out lift up de pot an' kill him. Dat's why so many widows in de world, because dere husband died and left 'em.

57. Cockroach Stories

a. Cock's Breakfast

Richard Morgan, Santa Cruz Mountains

ONE DAY COCKROACH SAID TO Cock, "Brar Cock, get little break-fas' so I will come an' have breakfas' wid you." Cock said yes. Cockroach come, Cockroach eat. When he done 'e said, "Brar Cock, when you

---

42. A wooden foot-path is laid above the level of high water at the side of a road likely to be flooded in high water. This is called a "water table".
43. The pot's equilibrium was disturbed by the impact.

know time my breakfas' ready, come." Cock said, "How mus' I know?" Cockroach said, "I wi' gi' you a sign. When you hear I mak noise, don' come; but when you hear I stay still in de yard, you mus' come." When Cock go, he didn't fin' Cockroach. Cock return back to his yard. Secon' day, Cockroach come an' say, "O Brar Cock! from I lef' you heah, pain all over my skin so I go an' lie down, I couldn't look a t'ing; but t'-day you can come." Cock do de same, go to de yard, didn't fin' him, return back. When he ketch half way, he hear in Cockroach house,

> "Ring a ting ting,
> Me know nigger fe nigger!"

Cock tak time, tip on him toe. An' go long to one gourd, he hear Cockroach in a de gourd. An' Cock tak him bill, lick him at de gourd. Cockroach run out. Cock pick him up an' swaller him. So from dat day, not a cockroach walk a fowl yard any more.[44]

b. Feigning Sick (1)

Eliza Wright, Maroon Town, Cock-pit country

COCKROACH AN' FOWL, DE TWO of dem keep house, an' de two of dem mak up to plant de groun'. An' ev'ry day Fowl ready fe go plant de groun', Cockroach fawn sick in bed. An' Fowl get up an' do everyt'ing in de house an' get Cockroach breakfas' an' bile it an' put it up, an' he go plant de groun'. An' when he catch part of de way, Cockroach come out of bed an' boil him break-fas', an' he didn't eat what Fowl left fe him, he fawn sick. An' he took up him fiddle an' sit down an' play now,

> "Brar Fowl, I mak you plan' a groun'!
> Cro-co-ty.
> Brar Fowl, I mak you plan' a groun'!
> Cro-co-ty!"

So one day when Fowl go out, he go half way an' put down de plant an' dodge him. Cockroach tak him fiddle an' play again,

---

44. This is a reference to the common saying, *Cockroach never so drunk, no walk a fowl yard.*

> *"Brar Fowl, I mak you plan' a groun'!*
> *Cro-co-ty.*
> *Brar Fowl, I mak you plan' a groun'!*
> *Cro-co-ty."*

An' Fowl run in an' pick him up an' swaller him, an' from dat day, Cockroach, if he ever so drunk, won't walk a fowl yard.

b. Feigning Sick (2)

George Barrett, Maroon Town, Cock-pit country

ONE DAY ANANSI AN' COCKROACH make a bargain to give a day in groun' weed grass. Anansi was to go wid Cockroach to weed grass. De day fe him to go he sick, have fever. When Cockroach come, Anansi say he got fever. When Cockroach gone, he began to sing,

> *"Groun' too far!*
> *Rikity.*
> *Groun' too far!*
> *Rikity."*

Cockroach turn back, say, "You want to mak me a fool!" Anansi say, "Oh, no, no! fever!"

c. The Drum

Mrs. Matilda Hall, Harmony Hall

ONCE THERE IS DOG, MONKEY, Tiger, Puss and Cockroach. So Christmas coming and hear them playing all about music and them has none. An' said, "We have to make up to make a drum now, then how will we manage?" So they says, "The only way, we have to cut a little little of our skin to make a drum." The Roach said, "I have none", so them drive him out of the company and he got into a banana tree to live; then he turned round to them and said, "I first will play that drum!"—"How will you get it to play?" them ask him, an' said, "I first will play it!"

Well, them fit up the drum now with the skin, hang it up to get cure. So Christmas eve fall now. Then going to the market to buy up all them things, catch about three quarter of a mile they heard the drum playing, said, "Biddy bwoy! who playing our drum?" So it is Roach took down the drum, put it between his feet and began to play;

> *"Kelly money better kelly better,*
> *Kelly money better kelly better,*
> *Tira coota na tira ding ding,*
> *Tira coota na tira ding ding!"*

is the Roach singing. The Puss come see him and kill him, and Puss eat Roach until this day.

58. Hunter, Guinea-hen and Fish

Thomas Williams, Harmony Hall, Cock-pit country

Hunter always hunting an' he meet up a spendid piece of land, rich land, and he t'ink to cultivate it an' he begin same day cut bush. Piece of land is Guinea-hen feeding-ground. Guinea-hen come out at night,—Guinea-hen don' walk in de day. "Massa is good, know dis is my feedin' ground an' begin to clean it so I can get my pullin' clear! Let me help myself." Make a little chopping himself too.

Ol' man coming in de morning. "Hi! t'ankful! I commence work yesterday, do somet'ing good an' massa help me!" Start to do a little himself 'side what he do first day. T'ird day come, he burn what he cut, an' Guinea-hen burn dere too. Ol' man come in morning say, "Hi! t'ankful! massa burn de balance!" Begun to clean up. Guinea-hen come de night, give t'anks an' clean up de balance of what de ol' man lef'.

Nex' day, ol' man t'ankful, begun to plant peas an' corn. Guinea-hen come in night, say, "Massa is good! I don' need to plant any", begin to eat dat which de ol' man plant. Ol' man come in de morning see de damage, say, "Hi! what insec' do dis?" Plant some more.

Go on so until de peas begin to ripe—about eight weeks. Ol' man say, "Goin' to gadder it in tomorrow." Guinea-hen hear what ol' men say, went to de sea an' call de fish wid his trombone an' tell de fish what he want: "I plant a bit of corn and peas, an' gettin' ripe an' ol' man coming tomorrow an' I wan' to go tonight gadder it in before he come tomorrow." Fish accept an' say, "Well, yes, I'll go, but, Friend Guinea-hen, I kyan' walk an' I kyan' fly, my wing is not strong enough. So, as you have foot an' wing, you give me one of dem, I'll go." Guinea-hen says, "Yes, I'll lend you my wing but I kyan' tak me legs off to give you. See de straight road? You can fly an' drop, an' I'll run on quick on my feet." So Fish fly an' drop, an' Guinea-hen run on till came to de groun'. "Here is my own field; gadder an' eat as much as you like."

When day commence to light, de time man is to come, Guineahen commence to eat an' look out. Fish say, "What you lookin' so fo', Friend Guinea-hen?" Guinea-hen see ol' man coming, say, "It's a butterfly I see jumpin' about. Lend me yo' wings, I go ketch it fe you." An' he sail away quietly out of groun'. Ol' man come, see damage an' begin to grumble an' pick what he can till he get whe' de Fish is, say, "Lawd! see him whe' he mak him bed!" an' when he hawl up a big root an' see Fish a-flutt'ring an' a-trembling, he say, "O Fish! is it you do dis damage all dis time?" Fish says, "No, not I! Don' kill me an' I sing you some song." Ol' man like music, put him in a tub o' water to sing an dance.

Fish says, "Tak me to de neares' sea-side you has!" Ol' man tak up de tub, put it on his head goin' to de sea-side. Fish begin,

> "She man yerry me bra, hay!
> She man yerry me bra!
> Guinea, guinea, quot amba tory."

Ol' man dance, Fish sing, until big wave coming an' Fish aim for it an' go long wid it. Ol' man stay dancing, don' know dat Fish is gone. Look in tub, Fish gone. Run home fe hook an' line an' t'row it into de sea to catch Fish. An' dat is why we always have to catch fish at sea.

59. Rabbit Stories

a. The Tar Baby

Rennie Macfarlane, Mandeville

WHEN BRER FOX TRIED TO catch Brer Rabbit, he could not catch him. He stick up a tar-pole in his common, an' when Brer Rabbit come an' see it', say, "Come out of Brer Fox place or I kick you!" An' the tar-pole wouldn't come out. An' kick him an' his foot fasten. "Let go foot, else I kick you with the other one!" An' he won't let it go, an' kick it with the other one an' the other foot fasten. An' he box him an' his han' fasten. An' say, "Let go me, else I box you!" an' he box him with the other han' an' his han' fasten. An' he said, "Let it go, else I buck you!" An' he buck him an' head fasten. An' said, "Let me go, else I bite you!" an' when he bite him, mouth fasten an' he couldn't move or talk.

An' Brer Fox said, "Think I couldn't catch you!" An' Brer Fox said, "Out of burn you an' drown you an' hang you an' dash you over de bramble, which one you rather?" He said, "Do anything you like but don' dash me over dat bramble!" An' Brer Fox take him an' dash him over the bramble, an' he said, "Oh, what a fool!"

b. Saying Grace

Rennie Macfarlane, Mandeville

BRER FOX CATCH BRER RABBIT again. So he gwine kill him, an' Brer Rabbit said, "Do, Brer Fox, as you gwine kill me, have prayers." An' he said, "Clasp you hands an' say what I say: 'O God, bless an' blind us!'" but Brer Fox thought he say "Bless an' help us," an' he say it. An' Rabbit run away an' they never see him.

c. Pretending Dead

Rennie Macfarlane, Mandeville

WHEN BRER FOX WANT TO get Brer Rabbit again, he an' Bear make up to catch him. Brer Bear go to Brer Rabbit yard an' tell him that Brer Fox dead an' he mus' help him bury him, for he an' Brer Fox friends. When he go to Brer Fox yard, he see Brer Fox lying down. Brer Rabbit put on his bonpon[45] hat an' coatie an' spectacle an' sit up in a rocking-chair an' say, "I never see it so! What a style! what a funniness! I think that when folks fall down die, they always cock up their foot in the air an' make 'pooh!'" An' Brer Fox cock up his foot in the air an' say, "Pooh!" an' Brer Rabbit go away an' say, "A man like you never dead yet!"

---

45. A round tin cooking pot is called a "bonpon". So is a high round hat.

60. The Animal Race

a. Horse and Turtle

Alfred Williams, Maroon Town, Cock-pit country

HORSE BET TURTLE SAY A get to Kingston before him. Turtle bet him say him will get to Kingston before him, Brar Horse. An' Turtle tak up one of him pickney an' drop dem ev'ry mile-post, an' drop de last one in at Kingston at de wharf-house, tell 'im 'em going for a sack of salt. An' de night when dem start, as Brar Horse catch to de firs' mile-post an' sing out in a harsh note,

Turtle answer quite yonder, an' sweet,

Horse say, "Well! Brar Turtle gone!" Gallop, draw rein an' 'pur As he get to de nex' mile-post, hear,

"I-ya-a ya-o sa, nom-be, ya-o ya."

Gallop an' gallop till he get to de nex' mile-post. Turtle sing,

> *"I-ya-a ya-o sa, nom-be, ya-o ya."*

Trabbel on, ride on, ride on, ride on, catch to de nex' mile-post, sing out,

> *"I-ya-a ya-o sa, nom-be, ya-o ya."*

Turtle answer de same song quite at de mile-post,—

> *"I-ya-a ya-o sa, nom-be, ya-o ya."*

As Horse catch to dat mile-post go in to Kingston, drop down dead!

b. Pigeon and Parrot

Julia Gentle, Santa Cruz Mountains

PIGEON AN' PARROT WAS CO'RTIN' one girl an' she say whichever one firs' come in de house de mornin' she would marry dat one. Parrot could not fly very fas'. He went an' mek bargain wid anodder Parrot. He went before an' leave de odder one to follow Pigeon behin'. He went near to de girl house an' sit down in a tree. Pigeon call, saying,

> *"Come on, me pretty Poll, come on, me pretty Poll,*
> *Stay on de tree so long,*
> *For de sun an' de moon gwine down,*
> *Stay on de tree so long."*

Parrot answer Pigeon behind,

> *"Go on, me pretty Pigeon, go on, me pretty Pigeon,*
> *Stay on de tree so long,*
> *Go on, me pretty Pigeon, go on, me pretty Pigeon,*
> *Stay on de tree so long."*

Pigeon sail again. He stop, call again,

> *"Come on, me pretty Poll, come on, me pretty Poll,*
> *Stay on de tree so long,*
> *Come on, me pretty Poll, come on, me pretty Poll,*
> *Stay on de tree so long."*

Parrot answer,

> *"Go on, me pretty Pigeon, go on, me pretty Pigeon,*
> *Stay on de tree so long,*
> *Go on, me pretty Pigeon, go on, me pretty Pigeon,*
> *Stay on de tree so long."*

Pigeon sail. When Pigeon nearly catch to de house, call again in de same tune. Parrot answer before now. Pigeon say, "Stop! a lil' while Parrot was behin'; how Parrot get before?" When Pigeon went to de house, Parrot was in de house. Pigeon has to stay outside an' Parrot married to de girl.

61. The Fasting Trial (fragment)

Julia Gentle, Santa Cruz Mountains

JUMPIN' DICK SAY HE WOULD bear longer hunger than White Belly. So White Belly up a tree where a grape a drop, an' Jumpin' Dick pick up on de ground.

White Belly say,

> *"Coo coo, me lovin'! coo coo, me lovin'!*
> *Everybody goin' to look for dem dandy."*

Jumpin' Dick dance an' sing,

> *"Every Monday morning,*
> *Zum zick a zum zum!*
> *Every Monday morning,*
> *Zum zick a zum zum!"*

62. Man is Stronger

Simeon Falconer, Santa Cruz Mountains

THE LION AND THE TIGER were very good friends. Tiger says, "No one beat us in strength!" Lion said, "No, my friend, somebody that's stronger than we. Tiger said no, no, he cannot believe that. Lion said there was a little something called "Man" that was stronger. So Tiger says he will have to find that something called "Man."

And he go hunting the Man and he buck up Mr. Ram-goat and he ask him if him name "Man". Goat says yes. And he asked him if the two things he had up here (horns) called "gun". And he asked him if that long scar he have on belly, called "ram-rod." And he asked him if that bag he had, called "shot-bag." And Goat said yes. And Tiger walk up and lick him flat on the ground. Goat holla "Wi-i! wi-i-i!" And Tiger went back to Lion and say he find something called "Man" and single lick he lick him, fa' dead. Lion say, "No, me friend! dat no 'Man', for Man have two feet an' dat you tell me have four legs." Tiger say *will* have to go back again find Man, for he bound to have that something called "Man".

And he went out again seeking after "Man", and a Hunter was out. And he saw the Hunter and he said, "Now this yeah *mus'* Man!" And so him gwine up to de man, de Hunter aiming for him with the gun, and ask if him name "Man". And the Hunter drive at him with the gun. And he run back to Lion and could only say, "I find 'Man' an' him single answer him answer me, blood fly all t'ru me body!" and him dead. Lion says, "I tell you; you no believe me; but you believe me now!"

63. The Pea that made a Fortunej

Etheline Samuels, Claremont, St. Ann

ONE DAY AN OLD LADY was traveling on the road and she picked up a green pea and she planted it. And after it grew, her goat ate it off. She cried upon the goat and told it that she wanted the peas. The goat said that he didn't have anything to give her, but she could take one of his horns. She took the horn and went to the river-side to wash it. The river took it away from her. She cried upon the river, and the river said it didn't have anything to give her but a fish. She went further. She met a man who was very hungry. She gave the man the fish. After the man ate it, she cried upon the man. The man gave her a moreen. She went a little further and saw a cow-boy. She gave him the moreen. After he had worn it out, she cried upon him for it. He said he didn't have anything to give her but his whip. She went a little further and saw a man driving cows. She gave the whip to the man. After the man had lashed it out, she cried upon him, so he gave her a cow; and from the cow she made her riches.

64. Settling the Father's Debt

Simeon Falconer, Santa Cruz Mountains

A MAN OWE ANOTHER ONE five pounds, and the other called in and asked the son who was at home, "Where is your father?"—"Me father gone to break a new fence to mend a rotten one."—"Where is your mother?"—"Me mother gone to the market to sell sweet to buy sweet."—"Where is your older brother?"—"Gone to sea to catch what in catching will kill and what him don' catch will carry home alive."— "Where is your sister?"—"Me sister in the house weeping over what she was rejoicing about last year."—"What are you doing?"—"Taking hot bricks out of oven."—"Now, me good boy, you give me some hard puzzle. If you tell me the meaning I'll give you five pounds."—"When I tell you me father gone to break a new fence to mend an old one, mean to say me father owe you five pound and gone to borrow five pound to pay you. When I tell you me mother gone to the market to sell sweet to buy sweet, gone to sell honey to buy sugar. When I said me brother gone to the sea to catch what in catching he kill and what him don' catch him bring home alive, I mean to say he goes to bed and he will catch the lice from his head and kill them; what he don' catch he mus' carry back in the head. When I said me sister was in the house weeping over what she was rejoicing over last year, she was rejoicing last year in getting her baby; she is weeping over it now because it is dying. When I tell you I'm taking hot bricks out of oven, I am pulling chiggers out of me feet."—"Now all your puzzles are put through, you are worthy of the five pounds."—"Please settle me father's debt, then." So he make a receipt and give his father five pounds.

65. Mr. Lenaman's Corn-field

George Parkes, Mandeville

THERE WAS A MAN NAMED Mr. Lenaman. He went to a place to rent a piece of ground. He didn't know that it was a burial ground. It was about twenty acres of land. When he went, he chopped with his machete "pom!" He heard a voice say, "Who chop bush deh?" He answered, "Me, Mr. Lenaman." The v'ice said,

> *"Big an' little, get up an' help Mr. Lenaman chop bush!*
> *No mo' bush mustn't lef' today."*

So all de ghosts, big an' small, get up chop off de bush clean.

Mr. Lenaman was very glad. He went home and told his wife of the luck he had met. When the bush dry up, he went back to burn it an' starting to burn it he hear de v'ice say, "Who burn bush deh?" He said, "Me, Mr. Lenaman." The v'ice said,

> *"Big an' little, get up an' help Lenaman bu'n bush!*
> *No mo' bush mustn't lef' today."*

An' all de ghost get up an' help Mr. Lenaman bu'n off de bush clean.

The nex' day, himself an' wife went to plant corn. As they make the firs' chop say "pom!," hear de v'ice say, "Who plant corn deh?" He say, "Me, Mr. Lenaman." De v'ice say,

> *"Big an' little, get up help Lenaman plant corn!*
> *No mo' corn mustn't lef' today."*

An' all de ghost get up an' help him plant de corn, plant off de whole twenty acres.

When de corn grow up, he went back to mol' it. As he started, the v'ice says, "Who mol' corn deh?" He said, "Me, Mr. Lenaman." The v'ice said,

> *"Big an' little, get up help Lenaman mol' corn!*
> *No mo' corn mustn't lef' today."*

An' all de ghost get up an' help dem mol' off de corn dat day.

Now de corn grow up an' bear an' dry. Mr. Lenaman send his wife an' boy one day to go an' see how dey stay, an' tol' 'em not to break any because if dey break one, de ghosts will break it all off an' den Mr. Lenaman won't get none. He is going to get a lot of people to go there with him one day to help him break them, so that he can get a plenty. Now the wife an' boy went to the groun', but when they go, they forget what Mr. Lenaman tol' them. In coming away, they broke one each. They hear the v'ice say, "Who broke corn deh?" They said, "Mr. Lenaman wife an' boy." The v'ice say,

> *"Big an' little get up an' help Lenaman wife an' boy break com!*
> *No mo' corn mus' be lef' today."*

An' dey break off every bit!

The wife an' boy went home an' tol' it to Mr. Lenaman. The three of them went back to the groun'. Mr. Lenaman got vex an' started to beat the wife an' boy. The v'ice said, "Who beat wife an' boy deh?" He said, "Me, Mr. Lenaman." V'ice said,

> *"Big an' little, get up go an' help Mr. Lenaman beat wife an' bwoy!*
> *No mo' wife an' bwoy mustn't lef' today."*

So dem beat de wife an' boy so dat dem kill dem.

So Mr. Lenaman stan' up now didn't know what to do, start to scratch his head. The v'ice said, "Who 'cratch head deh?" He said, "Me, Mr. Lenaman." The v'ice said,

"Big an' little, get up an' help Lenaman 'cratch head!
No mo' head mustn't lef' today."

An' de whole of dem start to 'cratch his head, 'cratch it until he dead.

66. Simon Tootoos

Thomas White, Maroon Town, Cock-pit country

DER WAS ONCE A WOMAN dat have a child. Him name was Simon Tootoos. De mudder him was a church woman, an' him used to send de boy to church; and after, de mudder come an' die. An' when de mudder die, he take de world upon his head. And Simon Tootoos mek colbon[1] and set it on Sunday day, and he go to wood on Sunday to go and search his colbon. And when he go to catch him bird, he catch a snake in de colbon. When he go to raise up de colbon an' fin' it was a snake, him leave it. An de snake answer to him,

Come take me up, Come take me up, Si - mon Too - toos,
len-non boy. Come take me up, oh, len-non boy, Too na too.

It was his dead mudder cause de snake to sing like dat. And when he go to leave—

"Come back you' colbon, come back you colbon.
Simon Tootoos, lennon boy,
Come back you' colbon, O lennon boy!
Too na too!"

make him come an' tek him up carry him come back to yard. And him put him down—

---

1. A trap.

> *"Come 'tretch me out, come 'tretch me out,*
> *Simon Tootoos, lennon boy,*
> *Come 'tretch me out, O lennon boy!*
> *Too na too!"*

And stretch him out and cut him neck.—

> *"Come wash your pot, come wash your pot,*
> *Simon Tootoos, lennon boy,*
> *Come wash your pot, O lennon boy!*
> *Too na too!"*

And wash de pot. And cut him up an' put in de pot, an' he set it on de fire, mak up him fire under him, and him start boiling. After it start boiling, it boil until it tell him to season in skelion[2]. When it boil, it tells, him to come down pot off de fire. So

> *"Come wash you' plate, come wash you' plate,*
> *Simon Tootoos, lennon boy,*
> *Come wash you' plate, O lennon boy!*
> *Too na too!"*

He wash de plate.

> *"Come clean you' knife, come clean you' knife,*
> *Simon Tootoos, lennon boy,*
> *Come clean you' knife, O lennon boy!*
> *Too na too!"*

He clean him knife.

> *"Come lay you' table, come lay you' table,*
> *Simon Tootoos, lennon boy!*
> *Come lay you' table, O lennon boy!*
> *Too na too!"*

---

2. A cooking-pot.

He lay him table. An' say,

> *"Come pick me out, come pick me out,*
> *Timon Tootoos, lennon boy,*
> *Come pick me out, O lennon boy!*
> *Too na too!"*

And pick him out.

> *"Come lay me on table, come lay me on table,*
> *Simon Tootoos, lennon boy,*
> *Come lay me on table, O lennon boy!*
> *Too na too!"*

Put him on table.

> *"Come draw you' chair, come draw you' chair,*
> *Simon Tootoos, lennon boy,*
> *Come draw you' chair, O lennon boy!*
> *Too na too!"*

He draw him chair.

> *"Come eat me now, come eat me now,*
> *Simon Tootoos, lennon boy!*
> *Come eat me now, O lennon boy!*
> *Too na too!"*

He eat him dead mother now.

> *"Come call you' grave-digger, come call you' grave-digger,*
> *Simon Tootoos, lennon boy,*
> *Come call you' grave-digger, O lennon boy!*
> *Too na too!*

> *"Come call you carpenter, come call you' carpenter,*
> *Simon Tootoos, lennon boy,*
> *Come call you' carpenter, O lennon boy!*
> *Too na too!"*

As him eating done—

"Come say you' prayer, come say you' prayer,
Simon Tootoos, lennon boy,
Come say you' prayer, O lennon boy!
Too na too!

"Come go to you' bed, come go to you' bed,
Simon Tootoos, lennon boy,
Come go to you' bed, O lennon boy!
Too na too!"

After him go to him bed, him mudder come out of him belly; an' dat was de las' of Simon Tootoos.

67. The Tree-wife

Thomas White, Maroon Town

IT WAS A MAN DIDN'T have no wife an' he was a hunter-man; he hunt in de bush all day. An' one day he go in de bush, go an' shoot, an' when he coming home, him saw a pretty tree name of Jessamy, an' he say, "O me biddy boy, das a pretty tree!" An' he says, "If dis tree could tu'n a wife to me, I would like to be marry to him!" An' so he said, it done de very same as what him said; de tree do tu'n a wife for him. De woman was naked, an' he lef' him at de said time an' went home back, an' he get some clot'ing for de woman, an' got him dress up nicely an' carry him home at house.

An' deh he an' de woman was fo' a long time until one day he were gwine out a bush fe gwine shoot, an' leave him wife a house. Him go an' sleep an' never come home till de nex' day. An' after he gone to de wood, it's anudder man go dere an' inveigle him wife an' tek' him away from him house an' go to dis man house. An' when de poor man come home from bush de nex' day, he couldn't fin' him wife. An' what de wife did, after de wife come out dis man's house go to de nex' house, she was frighten how him husban' gwine fin' him. An' de nex' man house about a two mile off him husban' house, an' as she leaving for him house, she spit all de way until she ketch to dis odder man's house.

An' de man was into a rage dat him couldn't fin' him wife an' didn't know what was to ever do. An' him sing,[3]

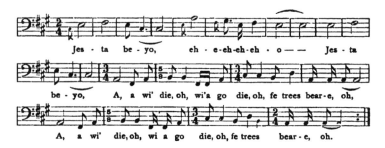

Jes - ta be - yo, eh - e-eh-eh-eh - o — — Jes - ta be - yo, A, a wi' die, oh, wi'a go die, oh, fe trees bear-e, oh, A, a wi' die, oh, wi a go die, oh, fe trees bear - e, oh.

When de man sing, de spit dat de woman spit answer him,—

> *"Jesta be-yo, eh, eh, eh, o!*
> *Jesta be-yo, a wi' die-o,*
> *Wi' a go die-o, fe trees bear-e o!"*

To every place where de woman spit, de man go dere an' stan' an' call—

> *"Jesta be-yo, eh, eh, eh, o,"*

at each stopping-place of half a mile until two miles are passed. An' jus' as de woman hear de voice of de man, stan' at door-mout' an' see dat de man coming. An' de man go tak him wife an' catch him right back to home yard.

Jack man dory, choose none!

68. Sammy the Comferee

Thomas White, Maroon Town

IT WAS A WOMAN HAD one son, an' it was a boy dat very unruly by him mudder an' fader. He had not'ing to do but fire bow an' arrow all day. An' one day he tek up him bow an' arrow an' fire de arrow an' de arrow drop in a Massa Jesus yard. An' he went in de yard to go an' pick up de arrow, an' Massa Jesus wife was in de yard an' Massa Jesus was gone

---

3. The song sung is the Koromanti Death Song, always used by the Maroons at a burial.

out—wasn't at home. An' all dem clo'es was out of doors sunning. An' de wife detain de boy in de yard fo' de whole day until rain come de day an' wet up all Massa Jesus clo'es a-do'. Dis boy was Sammy de Comferee, an' jus' t'ru Sammy de Comferee mek de clo'es a wet up a-do'. An' when Massa Jesus come in, him was wet an' him want some dry clo'es to put on an' him couldn't get no dry clo'es to put on. An' him tu'n to him wife an' ask him what him was doin' de whole day at de house an' mek him clo'es wet up a-do'. Him answer to Massa Jesus dat as he, Sammy de Comferee, was in de house, das why came de clo'es to wet a-do'. Massa Jesus say to him as he was along in de house de whole day if is de reason to mek him clo'es a wet up a-do', an' de woman reply to Massa Jesus dat if him been pretty as Sammy de Comferee, him would a do more. An' Massa Jesus answer to him wife dat him know dat is him made Sammy de Comferee, an' if Sammy de Comferee is prettier den him, him would see about it.

An' Massa Jesus put up iron rod, an' de iron rod hot as a fire, hot until it red. An' him sen' for Sammy de Comferee. An' when Sammy de Comferee come, Massa Jesus says to him what he was doin' in him yard de whole day. An' he says dat him fire him bow an' arrow an' de arrow drop into de yard, an' after, he went in de yard to pick up de arrow an' de wife detain him in de yard an' him couldn't get away from de woman until rain tek him in de yard. And Massa Jesus said dat de wife tell him dat Sammy de Comferee is prettier 'an him dat made him. An' he order Sammy to climb de iron rod. An' he commence to melt away an' he sing,

Ah, me Sam-my de Con-fa-ri-a - e-ro, Gi-ra
no, ah, in din ro. Ah, e do me da de a, Gi-ro no.
Ah, me Sam-my de Con-fa-ri-a - e-ro, Gi-ro no, ah, in din
ro. Ah, e do me ma me-a, Gi-ro no. Ah, me Sam-my de
Con-fa-ri-a - e-ro, Gi-ro no, ah, in din ro.

He melt off to him leg. An' sing again—

> *"A me Sammy de Con-fa-ri-a!"*

He melt off to his middle. He sing again—

> *"A me Sammy de Con-fa-ri-a!"*

an' him melt off one of him hand. He sing again—

> *"A me Sammy de Con-fa-ri-a!"*

an' him melt off to him neck. An' him sing again,

> *"A me Sammy de Con-fa-ri-a!*
> *Gi-ra no a in din ro!"*

an' him melt off to not'ing. An' when you look at de iron rod, de whole heap of fat heap up about de iron rod. An' all de pretty men dat come into de worl' get some of Sammy de Comferee's fat, but all de ugly ones don't get none of it.

Jack man dory, me story done!

69. Grandy-Do-an'-Do

a. Moses Hendricks, Mandeville

THERE WAS AN OLD WOMAN, a witch, but she was very wealthy. She lived quite to herself. Plenty of stock—horses, cows, sheep, mules, each kind kept by itself in a separate pasture. The old lady's name was Grandy Beard-o, but nobody knew that name. She wanted a person to sup with her. She came across a little girl one day. The took that girl home. After she prepared her meal, she called the girl and asked her if she knew her name. The girl said, "No, ma'am." She said to the girl, "Unless you tell me my name, I will not give you anything to eat."

She started out the girl to go and fetch some water. The girl had to go through all the pastures to get where the water was—mules to themselves, cows to themselves, horses to themselves, sheep to themselves. She went along crying, being hungry. So she got into cow-pasture—that was first pasture. The cow said to her, "What's the matter with you, me baby?"

The girl said, "The old lady will not give me anything to eat exept me can tell her her name!" Cow was afraid to tell her.

From there she went into mule pasture, crying all the same. Mule said, "What's the matter, me baby?"

The girl said, "The old lady will not give me anything to eat, except me can tell her her name!" Mule wouldn't tell her.

She got into horse pasture, crying all the way. Horse said, "What's the matter, me baby?"

"Old lady in there won't give me anything to eat except me can tell her her name!" Horse wouldn't tell her.

From there she went into bull pasture, still crying. Bull said, "What's the matter, me baby?"

"Old lady won't give me anything to eat except me can tell her her name!"

Bull says, "Cho! when you go home, tell her her name Grandy Beard-o." Bull was a mighty man; he didn't care!

The girl was so glad, hastened home so as to get something to eat. Old lady said, "You can tell me my name make me give you something to eat?"

The girl said, "Your name Grandy Beard-o, ma'am."

Old lady got so indignant! She gave the girl a good feed and after that she started to find who told the girl. Went into cow pasture.

> *"You cow, you cow. you cow,*
> *Why you tell the girl*
> *Me name Grandy Beard-o?"*

Cow said,

> *"A ring ding ding, mamma, ring ding ding;*
> *A ring ding ding, mamma, ring ding ding;*
> *No me tell."*

She jump into horse pasture now.—

> *"You also horse tell the girl*
> *Me name Grandy Beard-o?"*

Horse said,

> "A ring ding ding, mamma, ring ding ding;
> A ring ding ding, mamma, ring ding ding;
> No me tell him."

She got into bull pasture now.—

> "You bull, you bull, you bull,
> Why you tell the girl
> Me name Grandy Beard-o?"

Bull said,

> "A ring ding ding, mamma, ring ding ding;
> A ring ding, ding, mamma, ring ding ding;
> Damme, me tell 'm!"

The old lady gripped the bull and tossed him in the air. The bull dropped; nothing happened. The bull tossed her in the air now, and she dropped; one leg broken. She tossed the bull again; the bull came down unhurt. The bull tossed her up again; she came down, another leg was broken.

She tossed the bull; nothing happened. The bull tossed her; she came down, one arm broken. She tossed the bull again; the bull came down unhurt. The bull tossed her again; she came down, the other arm was broken.

She tossed the bull again; the bull came down unhurt. The last toss the bull made, her neck broke. That was the end of her. The girl became mistress of all she possessed, and that is why the land goes from hand to hand in legacy up to today.

Jack man dory!

b. Julia Gentle, Malvern, Santa Cruz Mountains

A VERY BAD WOMAN HAVE only one daughter an' say, "Go to the river for water an' when you come back, if you cannot tell my name I will destroy you." When him goin' fe water see Crab. An' Crab axin' where him go. An' say, "Grandy sen' me go a river fe water an' say when me come back, if me cannot tell him name, her will kill me." The Crab tell him say, "When you go, tell her dat her name Grandy Do-an-do."

So when she come back, she forget the name. An' she say mus' kill him, so dash away the water an' send him back. Then when she go back, the Crab say, "Sing it all the way!" Then when the girl go back she sing,

> *"You name Grandy-do-an-do.*
> *You name Grandy-do-an-do."*

Then the woman mad when she hear it an' she travel. An' she meet Cow, an' say,

> *"You Cow, a you tell de girl a name Grandy Do-an-do?"*

Cow say,

> *"No, no me tell him so you name Grandy Do-an-do!"*

She travel an' she meet Sheep, an' say,

> *"You Sheep, a you tell de girl a name Grandy Do-an-do?"*

Sheep say,

> *"No, no me tell him so you name Grandy Do-an-do!"*

Meet Horse, say,

> *"You Horse, a you tell de girl me name Grandy Do-an-do?"*

Horse say,

> *"No, no me tell him so you name Grandy Do-an-do!"*

Meet Duck, say,

> *"You Duck, a you tell de girl a name Grandy Do-an-do?"*

Duck say,

> *"No, no me tell him so you name Grandy Do-an-do!"*

Meet Crab, say,

> *"You Crab, a you tell de girl a name Grandy Do-an-do?"*

Crab say,

> *"Yes, a me tell him a you name Grandy Do-an-do!"*

An' tak de machete an' chop after de Crab, an' Crab sink in de hole an' stay in de hole till now.

70. Jack and Harry

William Forbes, Dry River, Cock-pit country

JACK AN' HARRY, DE TWO was gwine out for a walk. An' de mo'ning was cool, an' catch to an ol' man dah in watch-house. Harry said, "Ol' Massa, beg you a little coffee if you have any." An' he said, "Yes, me pickney!" an' him give Jack a cup o' coffee an' Harry a cup o' coffee. An' de ol' man didn't drink fe him coffee yet. Jack say, "Harry, I gwine drink fe de ol' man coffee." Harry said, "No, Jack, don' do it!" An' Jack tek 'way fe de ol' man coffee an' drink it. An' de ol' man tek him 'tick after dem, dem run.

An' when dem run, see a hen wid some chicken. Harry said, "Do, me good hen, cover me wid you wing!" An' cover dem wid her wing de same as her own chicken. An' de ol' man was coming after dem didn't see dem, tu'n back. An' Jack say, "I gwine to pop de hen wing." An' Harry say no, an' Jack say *mus'* pop it. An' de hen begin to flutter after dem an' Jack an' Harry run an' de hen was after dem.

An' see a poor lady 'tan' up in de way. An' Harry said, "Do, lady, tek you coat an' cover we up!" An' after she cover dem up, Jack had a stick an' say, "I gwine to choke de ol' lady." An' Harry say, "Don' do it!" An' as he choke de ol' lady, ol' lady shake dem out an' run after dem.

An' when dey run, dey see a kyan-crow[4] in de way an' Harry said, "Do, me good kyan-crow, tek we up on you wing, carry we away from dis ol' lady!" An' de kyan-crow tek up Jack an' Harry an' fly up wid dem right up in de sky, an' de ol' lady couldn't catch after dem. An' Jack say, "I gwine to pop de kyan-crow wing mek him drop." Harry said, "No, Jack, don' do it!" An' as 'em drop, 'em knock 'emself out of senses.

An' when dey come to demselves, see a land turtle was coming. An' Harry call to de land turtle, an' as he shove out his head. Jack cut off de head.

71. Pea-fowl as Messenger

a. John Studee

Matilda Hall, Maroon Town

THE HUSBAND AND WIFE MARRIED people, and the husband a great gambler, never at home with the wife; until the wife going to have a baby, and the ninth month come now. So they send for the mid-wife; so when the mid-wife come, there is no husband in. She said she want some one to go call the husband, name of him is John Studee. So she call for all the thing they have in the yard. She call for a fowl, a cock, and say, "What will you say to call the husband?" The cock crew,

> *"Ko ku ru ku-u-u!"*
> *"You won't do."*

She calls for the dog and says, "What will you say?" Dog says,

> *"Hoo-oh!"*
> *"No, won't do."*

Said to Puss what he will say. Puss says,

> *"Me-oo!"*
> *"Won't do."*

---

4. Carencron.

Then 'he call for the pea-fowl now; 'he provide a quart of corn for the pea-fowl, ask what he will say. Pea-fowl sing,

"You John Studee, you John Studee,
Fe me master, John Studee,
There's a pretty gal from Silo,
There's a handsome gal from Silo,
Want the care of a new John bwoy,
't almost deh."

"Yes, you'll do!"

Then when the pea-fowl fly miles off, he didn't see the master, John Studee. He fly, he fly away now, take up the quart of corn and fly away. Then he pitch upon the house-top, sing,

"You John Studee, you John Studee,
Fe me master, John Studee!
There's a pretty gal from Silo,
There's a handsome gal from Silo
Want the care of a new John bwoy,
't almost deh!"

The people say, "John Studee, was here, but jus' gone away,—that great gambler!" He fly about a mile off again, go to another great house, go upon the house-top. He sing loud of voice now,

"You John Studee, you John Studee,
Fe me master, John Studee!
There's a pretty gal from Silo,
There's a handsome gal from Silo
Want the care of a new John bwoy,
't almost deh!"

John Studee come now, say, "Who call my name?" See the bird up on the house-top, say, "Well, he want me!" Then he took up the fowl an' get the buggy in haste; and take off his gold chain off his neck an' put it on the pea-fowl. Pea-fowl have the golden feather round his neck on account of that gold chain. So when the feather came home, he got a boy chil' an' call his name John Studee after him.

b. Contavio

Oliver D. Witter, Santa Cruz Mountains

Miss Nancy married Contavio. One day, Contavio went to market, but before he left home he locked up Miss Nancy till he came back. He did not come back that day, and as Miss Nancy was hungry and saw a sheep passing she said, "Do, my dear sheep, call Contavio for me and I will throw a lump of gold on your head." Bra Sheep goes, "Bep, baah baah baah." She said, "No, my dear Bra Sheep, that will not do." Soon after she saw a billy goat and said the same thing to him. Bra Billy said, "Bep, bep, ba, ba, ba, bep-ba-ba-bep, bah, bah." She said, "No, my dear Bra Billy, that will not do." She then saw Bra Peacock coming up an' she said, "Bra Peacock, if you call Contavio, my husband, for me, I will give you a lump of gold," and Bra Peacock flew right away until he saw Contavio, and he picked him in his head and picked off all the feathers, and spurred him the whole way home until all Bra Peacock's spurs dropped off. When he got Contavio home, Miss Nancy flung the lump of gold on Bra Peacock's head and that's why the feathers on a peacock's head look like gold. That's also the reason why it has no spurs, and a crow has no feathers on its head.

72. The Barking Puppy

Alfred Williams, Maroon Town, Cock-pit country

Deh is old lady live at home wid one little puppy, an' ev'ry night a gentleman come to pay her a visit, but dis little puppy snap an' bark, have fo' to tu'n back. An' de ol' lady catch de puppy an' mak up a big fire an' bu'n de puppy. Nex' night again de gen'leman come back. Ol' lady sing,

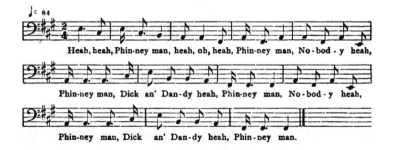

$\quad$ = 84

Heah, heah, Phin-ney man, heah, oh, heah, Phin-ney man, No-bod-y heah,

Phin-ney man, Dick an' Dan-dy heah, Phin-ney man, No-bod-y heah,

Phin-ney man, Dick an' Dan-dy heah, Phin-ney man.

De ashes bark as de puppy. De ol' lady get up, tak up de ashes dash 'em in de river, say, "Dis gen'leman goin' to pay me visit an' kyan' because de ashes bark!"

Nex' night, de gen'leman come back again, holla out, "Hulloo!" Ol' lady sing,

> *"Heah, heah, Phinney man,*
> *Nobody heah, Phinney man,*
> *Dick an' Dandy heah!"*

De puppy ashes bark in de river an' de gen'leman wouldn't come. De ol' lady tak de river water dash in de sea to hinder Dick an' Dandy from barking. Nex' night de gen'leman come back fo' de las time; counsel a sing now. Old lady raise up an' sing,

> *"Heah, heah, Phinney man,*
> *Nobody heah, Phinney man,*
> *Dick an' Dandy heah!"*

Meanwhile de gentleman dance. He come in now, draw a chair, say, "So long I couldn't come on account of Dick an' Dandy!" an' say, "I coming to marry you." Old lady say yes, but don' know but dog shadow come; sometime shadow come back. Ol' lady sing,

> *"Heah, heah, Phinney man,*
> *Nobody heah, Phinney man,*
> *Dick an' Dandy heah!"*

An' de gentleman catch de ol' lady an' tear him up to inch pieces.

73. The Singing Bird

a. Fine Waiting Boy

Alfred Williams, Maroon Town

A GENTLEMAN HAVE HIM SERVANT, and one day he said to de servant, "Collin, go an' look about de horse harness my buggy." An' Collin go an' harness him master horse an' put in de buggy. Well, him master drive on an' him drive on till him get to a well; an' de master said, "I want some water." An' Collin said, "Massa, der's a well is down before. An' he an' Collin come out de buggy against de well-side, an' meanwhile de massa sit against de well-side, Collin pitch him master in de well. An' Collin tu'n back an' go on half way wid de buggy, an' when he get home de missus ask him, "Where is de master?" an' Collin said, "He goin' pay a visit an' comin' tomorrow; de buggy goin' meet him." Collin go de day wid de buggy. When he went back, de missus said, "Where is de master?" He said, "Go to pay a visit, won't be back till tomorrow." When Collin gone, de nex' servant in de yard say, "Missus, hear what little bird singing?" Missus come to de doorway an' listen, an' hear de little bird whistling,[5]

When de missus hear de little bird singing so, couldn't understand, called a sensible person understand de bird. An' go search de well, fin' de master body, an' go tak Collin hang him.

b. The Golden Cage

William Harris, Maggotty

A KING HAD A DAUGHTER. He had two servants who did not like the daughter. One day the two servants were going to the well for water and the daughter said she wanted to go with them. And they catch the little girl and cast her in the well. Three days after, the little girl went home to her father an' the father catch the two servants and throw *them* in the well. And he get his child and thus end the story.

---

5. Sung by Mrs. Williams.

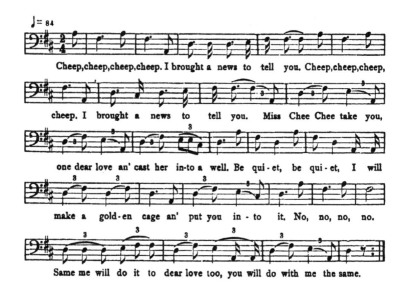

Cheep, cheep, cheep, cheep. I brought a news to tell you. Cheep, cheep, cheep, cheep. I brought a news to tell you. Miss Chee Chee take you, one dear love an' cast her in-to a well. Be qui-et, be qui-et, I will make a gold-en cage an' put you in-to it. No, no, no, no. Same me will do it to dear love too, you will do with me the same.

74. Two Sisters

Margaret Morris, Maroon Town, Cock-pit country

Two SISTER DEY TO HOUSE. One sister fe servant to a Busha[6] in one pen[7], an' tell de Busha marry odder sister. De sister name Miss Grace my fair lady, de older sister Lady Wheel. An' Miss Wheel servant to him sister. Busha gone to him work, never come back till midnight. Busha come, never hear not'ing stir. Till one day him gone out, Miss Wheel call Miss Grace to let dem go pick peas. So dem went away an' tek a basket pick de peas, an' have a baby in de hand, Miss Grace my fair lady baby. An' when dem pickin' de peas aroun' sea-ball, Miss Wheel mek Miss Grace tek off dress an' Miss Wheel shove Miss Grace my fair lady in de hole. She pick up de peas an' come home, tek water wash her breast, tek de baby fe her own self; when night come, suckle de baby. So when de Busha come home midnight, she give him de dinner, eat an' drink dat time, no notice him wife at all. T'ree day after dat he keep on coming but never notice. Till a day when he come, he ax fo' de servant. Say, "No, my dear, I sen' her out to de common, soon

6. An overseer on an estate.
7. An estate devoted to cattle-raising.

MARTHA WARREN BECKWITH

come." De husban' fall in sleep an' never hear if de servant come in. Till one day when de husban' coming back, one of de neighbor call to him, "Busha, you don' hear what harm done in your house?" He say no. Dem tell him he mustn't even drink cold water into de house de night an' him hear what alarm done. So de Busha go, an' what de lady gi' him he never tek, never drink cold water even. Him force him an' he never touch it. An' de Busha lay down midnight an' seem to doze asleep, but he no 'sleep.

Have a little dog an' call de dog "Doggie." Dog see when dead woman come. She call to de dog,

> *"Han' me my baby, my little doggie."*
> *"O yes, Miss Grace, my fair lady."*

Gi' him de baby.

> *"Gi' me some water, my little doggie."*
> *"O yes, Miss Grace, my fair lady."*

> *"Han' me my bowl, my little doggie."*
> *"O yes, Miss Grace, my fair lady."*

> *"Gi' me some water, my little doggie."*
> *"O yes, Miss Grace, my fair lady."*

> *"Gi' me my comb, my little doggie."*
> *"O yes, Miss Grace, my fair lady."*

> *"Gi' me my baby, my little doggie."*
> *"O yes, Miss Grace, my fair lady."*

De gentleman hear ev'ry word. De lady say, "Oh, not'ing, my dear!" Don' want de Busha fe hear not'ing. An' de las' night come, de neighbor put him up to put a pail of milk an' a pail of hot water at de doorway an' to cover it wid a sheet. De dead woman come an' call out de same:

> *"Gi' me my clo'es, my little doggie."*
> *"O yes, Miss Grace, my fair lady."*

"Take my baby, my little doggie."
"O yes, Miss Grace, my fair lady."

Tek de baby an' put it to bed. An' step in de hot water, pitch into de milk cover wid de white sheet. Take him out of de cover an' wrap her up, an' she look up eyes fix up. De gentleman say, "What do you, me dear?" An' say, "My sister shove me down in de ball. Him call to me fe go an' pick peas an' shove me in deh." When de gentleman fin' out wife dead, take Miss Wheel, build a lime-kiln an' ship into a barrel an' pitch down de hill-side roll it in de fire.

Jack man dory!
Dat's de end of de story.

75. Asoonah

Philipp Brown, Mandeville

ASOONAH IS A BIG SKIN t'ing. When it come in you' yard it will sink de whole place. One day, de lady have t'ree chil'ren an' leave dem out an' him go to work. An' den dis Asoonah comin' in eb'ry day, an' de chil'ren know what time it comin' an' deh 'tart a singing—

"Hol' up fe me 'coolmaster tail,
Limbo, Limbo, Limbo,
Hol' up fe me 'coolmaster tail,
Limbo, Limbo, Limbo."

An' come again, he ax de small one, "Whar yo' mudder?" An' say, "Gone a washin'-day." An' ax, "Whar de pretty little one?" Tell him, "Inside de room." Ax, "Whar de house whar's de guinea corn?" an' holla out, "Whar's de mortar?" Tell him, "Inside de kitchen." So one day now when de mudder come, de chil'ren say, "Eb'ry day a big t'ing come in yeah an' kyan't tell what is what." De mudder said to de husban', "Well, you better 'top an' see a wha' come yeah a daytime." Got de gun an' go off in de loft in de kitchen-top an' sit. When him see Asoonah come, he was so big he get frightened an' dodge behin' de door soon as Asoonah mount de hill. . . As he reach de gully, he fire de gun and Asoonah fall down in gully an' break him neck.

An' de king hear about dis Asoonah, but he couldn't tell what it is. De king say anybody can come in dere and tell what is dis, he give t'ree hundred pound. De little boy hear about it an' he was so tear-up about it. An' de ol' lady keeping a jooty at de king gate said, "What way Asoonah 'kin a go bring in yeah t'-day?" When de king ax eb'rybody an' couldn't tell what is it, he went an' call up de little boy. De boy went to tek it up an' de king ax him if he know what is it. An' him hol' it up like *dis* an' say, "Eh! no Asoonah 'kin?" Eb'rybody got frightened and come right out, an' de king offer de boy t'ree hundred pound and give a plenty ob clo'es an' got de boy work again.

76. The Greedy Child

a. Crossing the River

George Barrett, Maroon Town, Cock-pit country

DE CHIL'REN WAS GWINE TO school an' ev'ry day de ol' man tek de chil'ren dem ober de ribber. De ol' man ax dem fe some of 'em breakfas'. All de chil'ren gi' him some but one don' gi him some. Till he 'point a day come, de ol' man say he wan' somet'ing from him, an' he wouldn't gi' it. When he coming back, de ribber come down. Tek ober de rest of de chil'ren an' wouldn't tek ober dat. Little boy sing,

> *"Mudder Galamo,*
> *I gwine dead t'-day!"*

De ol' man says, "Stop singin'." Eb'ry time sing, de water come up a little higher. Jus' to heah, dat time his mudder comin'. Ol' man say, "I mus' hev two pounds." She say all right, an tek him ober. An' dat time, eb'ry day he offer de ol' man breakfas'.

b. The Plantain

Philipp Brown, Mandeville

EB'RY NIGHT DE DEBBIL GO out. An' as him go out, come in an' say, "Wife, I scent fresh blood!" De wife said to him, "No, me husband, no fresh blood in heah!" Was de wife's sisters come an' look fe him. So eb'ry night when de debbil coming in, de wife know when him coming in an' put up de sister into a barrel.

Daylight a mo'ning, de Debbil gone back ober de ribber gone sit down. So gi' de sister a plantain an' tell her when she reach de hill, him will see her husband sit down right ober de hill, an' de Debbil will say, "Go s'y (go your way), madame?" An' mus' say, "No one go s'y, no two go s'y, no t'ree go s'y, but, 'im go s'y fe him mamma," an' de Debbil let him pass. Got a little small sister. Dis sister greedy. An' de Debbil come in de night say, "Me wife, eb'ry night I come, I smell fresh blood!" An' de wife said, "No, me husband!" An' when de daylight, de Debbil go away ober to de hill an' de sister send away de little girl an' gi' him a plantain. An' when de little girl go on de hill, him see de Debbil. De Debbil say, "Go s'y?" De little girl say (him so greedy now), "No, go s'y fe mamma, no one go s'y, no two go' s'y, no t'ree go s'y, no go s'y fe mamma." De Debbil ketch him ober de hill an carry him right ober to de ribber an' kill him. An' from dat day, de Debbil hair off him head at de sea-side; an' from dat de sea got moss.

77. Alimoty and Aliminty

Julia Gentle, Santa Cruz Mountains

ONE DAY A LADY HAVE two daughter, but her sister have one. Sister daughter name Alimoty. An' everybody love Alimoty, but nobody love him daughter. An' him go to de Lion an' say to de Lion he *mus'* kill Alimoty for him. Den de Lion say him mus' put on red frock on Alimoty an' blue frock on to him daughter when him going to bed. An' after him going to bed, de girl say, "Cousin Alimoty, yo' red frock don' fit you; let us swap!" An' deh swap. An' de Lion kill de lady daughter, lef' one. Den de lady tell de Lion *mus'* kill Alimoty whom everybody love an' don' love him daughter. Den he said, "Tonight you mus' *sew* on de red frock on Alimoty an' de blue frock on to you daughter, an' I come an' kill him tonight." And when deh go to bed, deh swap again, an' de Lion kill de lady daughter,—have none now! Den de Lion said, "Tomorrow sen' Alimoty to me yard; I *will* kill him." Den Alimoty was going t'ru de yard an' de dead mudder give him a bottle of milk, drop it an' run off. Alimoty sing,—

> *"Poor me, Alimoty,*
> *Poor Alimoty,*
> *A me Dickie sahnie o-o,*
> *See me go long a wid two."*

An' Aliminty was a hunter and hear de singin' an' say, "Dat is Alimoty v'ice!" An' he came to de Lion yard an' kill de Lion.

78. The Fish Lover

a. Timbo Limbo

Thomas White, Maroon Town

A MAN HAD ONE DAUGHTER an' de daughter was name' Lydia. An' him wife die an' him married to anudder woman. An' she have some chil'ren fe de man, an' she like fe him chil'ren more 'n de daughter-in-law. Mostly it's de daughter-in-law she impose upon to do de work. An' she sen' Lydia fe water, give him a big jug fe go to de ribber; an' de jug is mor'n Lydia weight, dat she alone can't help up de jug, an' de mudder-in-law won't sen' none fe him pickney fe go an' help up Lydia. When Lydia get to de ribber-side, Lydia was crying dat de jug is too hebby an' him kyan't get no one to help him up. An' a Jack-fish was in de ribber hear de lament, an' went up an' said to de young woman if him wi' be a wife fe him he wi' help him up when him come to de ribber-side. An' Lydia consent to de Jack-fish to be a wife to him, an' Lydia fill him jar wid water an' de Jack-fish help him up an' 'he went to de yard.

De mudder-in-law ask him who 'he had a ribber-side to help him up wid de jar, an' Lydia says dat 'he has no one. De mudder-in-law says, "Yes, you mus' have some one!" She says, "No, mudder-in-law, I had no one to help me but me alone; it's me alone helping up myself." An' one mo'ning Lydia tek up de jug an' went to de ribber-side. An' what de mudder-in-law did, him sen' one of him chil'ren to follow Lydia an' to watch him at de ribber-side to see who help him up wid de jar. An' when Lydia go, him had to sing to call de Jack-fish; when de Jack-fish hear de voice of Lydia, him will come up to help her. De fish name is Timbo Limbo an' de song is dis,

♩ = 88

Tim - bo, Lim - bo, Tim - bo, Lim - bo, Tim - bo, Lim - bo,

Same gal, Ly-di - a, Tim - bo, Lim - bo, Tim - bo Lim - bo,

Tim-bo Lim-bo, Tim-bo Lim-bo. Same gal, Lydi - a. Tim-bo Lim-bo.

A slight variation which sometimes appeared in the third measure, but without regularity was:

Tim - bo Lim - bo.

An' de little child do see de Jack-fish dat were helping up Lydia, an' went back home an' tell him mamma, "Mamma, me sister Lydia do have a man-fish at de ribber-side fe help him up." At night when de man come from work, him wife said to him dat Lydia have a big Jack-fish fo help him up at ribber-side. So de man tell him wife, "When daylight a mo'ning, you mus' get Lydia ready an' sen' him on to Montego Bay an' buy black pepper an' skelion." In de mo'ning, mudder-in-law call de girl fe sen' him on to de Bay. Lydia start crying, for Lydia mistrus' dat is somet'ing dey gwine do in de day. When him gone, de fader load him gun an' him call de little girl fe dem go to de ribber-side. De little girl gwine sing, sing t'ree time, change him voice,—

> *"Timbo Limbo,*
> *Same gal Lydia,*
> *Timbo Limbo o-o-o!"*

An' de water go roun' *so,* an' de Jack-fish come out. An' de fader shoot him eh-h-h-h, an' de Jack-fish tu'n right over; an' de fader tek off him clo'es an' jump in de water an' swim an' tek out de Jack-fish an' carry to de yard.

An' as him begun to scale de fish, one of de scale fly all de way some two miles an' go an' meet Lydia an' drop at Lydia breast. An' when Lydia tek off de scale of de fish an' notice de fish-scale, him fin' it was Timbo limbo scale. An' she start crying an' run on to de yard, an' didn't mek no delay, only tek up him jar an' went to de ribber an' him 'tart him song,—

> *"Timbo Limbo,*
> *Same gal Lydia,*
> *Timbo Limbo o!"*

De Jack-fish didn't come up. An' 'tart a-singin' again,

> *"Timbo Limbo,*
> *Same gal Lydia,*
> *Timbo Limbo o-o!"*

De water stay steady. An' tek up de song again,

> *"Timbo Limbo,*
> *Same gal Lydia,*
> *Timbo Limbo o-o-o!"*

An' de water tu'n blood. An' when him fin' dat Timbo Limbo wasn't in de water, Lydia tek up himself an' drown himself right in de water.

Jack man dory, choose none!

b. Fish fish fish

Florence Thomlinson, Lacovia

IT WAS MOTHER AND TWO daughters. One of the daughters go to river-side worship a little fish. She commence to sing and the fish will come up to her,

Fish, fish, fish, fish, pen-ge leng, Come on the ri-ver, come pen-ge leng.

So the little fish come to her and she play play play, let go the fish and the fish go back in the river.

An' when she go back home, her mother quarrel, say she wait back so long. Next day, wouldn't send her back to river, send the other daughter. So when the other daughter went, she sung the same song she hear her sister sing,—

> *"Fish fish fish fish, pengeleng,*
> *Come on the river, pengeleng."*

She catch the fisch, bring it home, they cook the fish for dinner and save some for the other daughter. When she came, she didn't eat it for she knew it was the said fish. She begin to sing,

> *"Fish fish fish fish, pengeleng!"*

The other sister said, "T'ank God, me no eat de fish!" The mother said, "T'ank God, me no eat de fish!" She go on singing until all the fish come up and turn a big fish, and she take it put it back in the river.

c. Dear Old Juna

Richard Pottinger, Claremont, St. Ann

A MAN AND A WOMAN had but one daughter was their pet. The girl was engaged to a fish, to another young man too. She generally at ten o'clock cook breakfas' for the both. That man at home eat, then she took a waiter wid the fish breakfas' to the river. When she go to the river, she had to sing a song that the fish might come out,—

> *"Dear old Juna, dear old Juna,*
> *Oona a da vina sa,*
> *Oona oona oona oona,*
> *You' mudder run you fader forsake you,*
> *You don' know you deh!"*

Fish coming now, sing

> *"Kai, kai, Juna, me know you!"*

The fish come out to have his breakfas'.

Go on for several days, every day she sing the same; the fish give her the same reply. The young man thought of it now. One morning, he went a little earlier wid his gun, sing the same tune. The fish come out, sing the same tune as it generally do. The young man shot it, carry the fish home, dressed it, everybody eat now, gal an' ev'rybody. At the end of the eating, she found out it was the said fish. She dropped dead at the instant.

79. Juggin Straw Blue

David Roach, Lacovia

THERE WAS A WOMAN HAVE a daughter and a neice, and the neice was courting by one Juggin Straw Blue. She love the daughter more than she love the neice and always want the neice to do more work than what the daughter do. Well, the lady send the neice to a river one day with a big tub to bring water in it. The girl went to the river and get the tub fill and she couldn't help it up. An Old Witch man was by the river-side, and he help her up and tol' her not to tell nobody who help her up with the water. But when she went home, the aunt pumped her to know who help her up and she told her. Therefore the aunt know that the Old Witch man will come for her in the night, and she lock her up into an iron chest. Part of the night, the Old Witch man comes in search of the girl. So the girl was crying into the iron chest and the tears went through the keyhole and he wiped it and licked it and says, "After the fat is so sweet, what says the flesh!" And he burst the door open and take her out.

And the Old Witch man travel with the girl and he have a knock knee and the sound of his knee was like a music,—

Na koo-ma no year-ie de knee bang cri' bang cri' bang.

And the Old Witch man says to her, "Your head and your lights is for my dog, and your liver is for my supper!" So the girl started a song,—

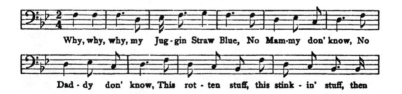

Why, why, why, my Jug-gin Straw Blue, No Mam-my don' know, No Dad-dy don' know, This rot-ten stuff, this stink-in' stuff, then

car - ry me down to gul - ly   True Blue, you'll see me no more.

So as this girl was courting by Juggin Straw Blue, his mother was an Old Witch too. And the courtyer's mother waked him up and gave him eight eggs; for the Old Witch man has seven heads and seven eggs, and each egg is for one of the Old Witch head. Well, the boy went after the Old Witch man and overtake him and mash one of the egg, and day light. And he cut off one of the head. An' the Old Witch man mash one of *his* egg and night came back. An' the boy mash the next one of his, and day light again; an' the Old Witch man mash one of his egg and night come back again. And so they went on that way until the boy mash seven egg and cut off the Old Witch seven heads and take away his girl. And he went home with his girl and marry.

80. The Witch and the Grain of Peas

Thomas White, Maroon Town

IT WAS A MAN WERE married to a woman first and he had one child wid de first woman he were married to. An' de first woman dat he married to dead an' he go married to anodder one; an' de girl has to call her "mudder-in-law." An' de mudder-in-law doesn't like de daughter-in-law. An' one day de mudder-in-law go to him field gone work. In de morning she wash some peas an' put on de peas on fire an' went away to ground. An' de daughter-in-law doesn't live at dis house, live in house by herself. An' de daughter-in-law come deh, ketch de daughter, louse and comb him hair. At de same time de mudder-in-law is Old Witch, know dat de daughter-in-law come to house. So as she was gwine away de eb'ning, de daughter said, "Look yeah, sister, mamma put on some peas on de fire; why don' you tek one grain of de peas?" An' she open de pot an' tek out one grain of de peas. An' when de Old Witch woman know dat de daughter-in-law tek out one grain of de peas, shet put up de hoe an' went from ground an' come back to house an' tek down de pot an' tu'n out all de peas in bowl, an' she couple eb'ry grain of de peas until she fin' one don' have a match. And said to child, "Look yeah! you' sister come today?"—"No, never come today!"—"Yes, don' control me, for I see at de grain dat you' sister come an' tek out one grain from de pot." An' gwine to swear him at de river to drown her because she tek de peas. An' she say, "If you don' eat my peas today you won' drownded, but if you eat my peas you will drownded." So de girl took up de song,—

Oh, me dear-est ma-ma, me mu-ma, oh, Poor me one, oh, Peace, oh, a ring down. Ah, me dear-est ma-ma, ring down peace, oh, a ring down, Ah, ye ring down.

And at de said time, de young girl had a sweetheart outside name of William. An' William mamma heard de song 'pon de ribber-side and send away to carpenter-shop an' tell William heard his girl singing quite mournful on ribber-side. An' him go up on lime-tree an' pick four lime an' gwine a fowl-nest an' tek four fowl-egg an' gwine a turkey-nest an' tek four turkey-egg an' tek four marble, an' call de girl an' put her before him. An' William an' de girl mudder-in-law come to a battle at de ribber-side an' William kill de woman. An' he put de girl before him an' carry her home an' marry her.

81. Bosen Corner

Martha Roe, Maroon Town, Cock-pit country

A WOMAN HAVE TWO DAUGHTER; one was her own chil' an' one was her daughter-in-law. So she didn't use her daughter-in-law good. So de place whe' dem go fe water a bad place, Ol' Witch country. De place name Bosen Corner. One day she sen' de daughter-in-law fe water. So when she go long, she see so-so[8] head in de road; she put her hand on belly mek kind howdy. Go on again, see two foot go one in anudder *so* (crossed) in de road. An' say, "Howdy, papa." So-so foot say, "Gal, whe' you gwine?" She said, "Mamma sen' me a Bosen Corner fe water." He say, "Go on, gal; good befo' an' bad behin'." She go on

8. "Only."

till she ketch to a little hut, see one ol' lady sit down deh. She say, "Howdy, nana." De ol' lady say, "Whe' you gwine?" Say, "Ma sen' me a Bosen Corner fe water, ma'am." De ol' lady say, "Come in here; late night goin' tek you." De Ol' Witch go pick up one piece of bone out dungle-heap an' choppy up putty in pot, an' four grain of rice. Boil de pot full of meat an' rice an' get de gal dinner. De gal eat, an' eat done call her say, "Me gal, come here 'cratch me back." When she run her han' 'cratch her back *so*, back pick all de gal han' so it bleed. Ol' Witch ask her, "What de matter you' han'?" Say, "Not'ing, ma'am." Even when it cut up all bleed, never say not'ing. When she go sit down, ol' lady go out of door come in one ol' cat. De ol' cat come in de gal lap, an' she hug it up an' coax de cat an' was so kin' to de cat. An' de gal sleep an' get up to go away in de mo'ning. De ol' lady tell her say mus' go roun' de house see some fowl-egg. She tell de gal say, de egg whe' she hear say "Tek me! tek me!" dem are big egg; she musn't tek dem; small egg say, "No tek me!" she mus' tek four. First cross-road ketch, she mus' mash one. Firs' cross-road she mash one de egg, an' see into a big pretty common. Second cross-road she mash udder one; de common pack up wid cow an' goat an' sheep an' ev'ryt'ing dat a gentleman possess in property. De t'ird cross-road she mash anudder one; she saw a pretty young gentleman come out into a buggy. De fourt' cross-road she mash de las' egg an' fin' de gentleman is a prince an' he marry her.

De daughter-in-law come, her an' her husban', drive into de yard see mudder-in-law. She expec' de Ol' Witch kill de gal didn't know she was living. So she sen' fe her own daughter, sen' a Bosen Corner fe water, say de udder one go get fe her riches, so she mus' get riches too. De gal tek a gourd an' going now fe water too. Go long an' see so-so head an' say, "Ay-e-e! from me bo'n I nebber see so-so head yet!" So-so head say, "Go long, gal! better day befo'." An' go long an' meet upon so-so foot, an' say, "Eh! me mamma sen' me fe water I buck up agains' all kind of bugaboo, meet all kin' of insect!" An' say, "Go long, gal! better day befo'." An' go de ol' lady house now. De ol' lady go tek de ol' bone go putty on de fire again, an' say, "Nana, you gwine tell me so-so bone bile t'-day fe me dinner?" An' when she see de four grain of rice she say, "Nebber see fo' grain of rice go in a pot yet!" Till it boil de pot full de same wid rice an' meat. De ol' lady share fe her dinner give her, an' she go tu'n a puss an' come back in. When de puss beg fe little rice, de gal pick her up fling her out de door. Ol' lady call her fe come, 'cratch him back too, an' put him han' to 'cratch him back, draw it back say, "Nebber see such a t'ing to 'cratch de back an' cut han'!" Nex' mo'ning, de ol' lady tell her mus' look in back of de house tek egg. De big egg say, "Tek me! tek me!" mus'n't tek dem; de little egg say, "No tek me! no tek me!" mus' tek four. She don' tek de small one, tek four of de big egg. De firs' cross-road she break one an' see a whole heap of snake. At de secon' cross-road she break anudder an' see a whole lot of insect. At de las' cross-road she massoo one, an' see a big Ol' Witch man tear her up kill her 'tiff dead in de road.

82. The Three Dogs

a. Boy and Witch Woman

Thomas White, Maroon Town

OLDEN TIME IT WAS A young man an' him brudder. Dem two of 'em was bred up on a property penning cow. Eb'ry morning dat dey wan' to pen, carry dem breakfas' an' carry dem fire. An' one morning dat dem going, 'em carry food but dey didn' carry no fire. An' dem pen cow until twelve o'clock in de day an' de smaller one feel hungry. He say, "Brar, me hungry! how we gwine to get fire?" An' dey look 'pon a hill-side,— jus 'as out deh, an' see a smoke an' de smaller one go look fe fire. An' he go right up de hill an' see a big open house; lady in open kitchen. An' she was Old Witch. An' he frighten an' come back. So now de bigger brudder go, name of William. An' as he go up, stop behin' one big dry 'tump, stan' up deh an' look what de Ol' Witch do. An' dis Ol' Witch got on a pot on fire, an' tek off de pot an' him dish out all vessels right t'ru, de boy don' see no pickney in kitchen, only de Ol' Witch. An' Ol' Witch knock on side, pon pon pon, an' all pickney come out, twenty big man and small children, women and boy pickney. An' dey all sit down deh an' eat. When dey done, who fe smoke de pipe dem smoke. An' Ol' Witch get up an' knock, pon pon, an' all de chil'ren go up in him back.

An' den de boy call to him now, say, "Mawnin', Nana!" She frightened and ask if he been deh long time an' he say, "No, jus' come up to beg fe fire." An' she says, "Tek fire, but don' tek me fire-stick; an' de boy tu'n back an' break a piece o' rotten wood an' hol' it 'gainst de steam of de fire an' ketch de rotten wood. An' Ol' Witch say to him, "Boy, you jus' a good as me!" Boy said, "No, Nana, I'm not so good!" An' de boy go down in cow-pen an' when in de height of penning up de cow, tell de smaller brudder not to mek up fire, pen de cow an' go home quick quick. An' dis bigger brudder was a witch himself an' know all about what come after him, an' when he go home, go inside de house, fawn sick.

An in a quick time de Ol' Witch was upon dem. An' she go in de yard, say, anyone as would knock de packey off 'im head she would tek for a husband. De smaller brudder fling an' couldn't knock off de packey. De Ol' Witch woman call to William mamma if she don' have a bigger son. "Yes, but he have fever in bed, kyan't come out." An' de Ol' Witch never cease till William have to come out. As he come out, he pick up a little trash an' knock off de packey. Ol' Witch say, "Yes, you is my husban'!"

An' him sleep at William house de night; nex' mo'ning dem gwine to go 'way. In de night, when William an' de wife gone to bed, part of de night when William was in dead sleep, de Ol' Witch tek one razor to cut William t'roat. An' William have t'ree dog, one name Blum-blum, one name Sinde, one name Dido. An' when de Ol' Witch tek de razor, Blum-blum grumble an' de razor mout' tu'n over. William wake. He drop asleep again, Ol' Witch raise up,—

Sharp-en me ra-zor, Sharp-en me ra-zor, shar come schwee, sho am schwee!

Sinde grumble an' razor mout' tu'n over. An' drop asleep again, an' when de Ol' Witch raise up again, Dido grumble an' de razor mout' tu'n over.

Daylight a mo'ning, get up William mamma, boil coffee, give dem chocolate. William an' wife gwine away now, an' he tell him mudder chain dem t'ree dog dey got, Blum-blum, Sinde, Dido; an' him get a big white basin an' he set de basin jus' at de hall middle, an' him tell de mudder dat as soon as see de basin boil up in blood, him mus' let go de t'ree dogs. An' he tell good-by, gwine now in witch country. Travel an' travel till dem come to clean common. An' he fling a marble so far, de place wha' de marble stop is one apple-tree grow, had one apple quite in de branch top. An' 'he said, "My dear William, I ask you kindly if you will climb dis tree an' pick dis apple fo' me." When William go up in de apple-tree, Ol' Witch says to William, "Hah! I tell you I got you t'-day!

for de place wha' you see me knock out pickney out o' me skin, you wi' have to tell me t'-day." William says, "Yes, I know about dat long time, for it will be 'iron cut iron' today!" For oftentimes him an' fader go to wood an' him saw fader fall a green tree an' leave a dry one. As Ol' Witch got William on apple-tree, Ol' Witch knock out ten axe an' ten axemen, gwine fall de tree. Den William start song,—

Blum-blum, Sin-de, Di-do di - i - i - i - i - i. Blum-blum, Sin-de, Di-do.

Den de Ol' Witch sing,—

Chin, fal-lah, fal-lah, Chin, fal-lah, fal-lah, Chin, fal-lah, fal-lah, Chin.

When de tree goin' to fall, William said, "Bear me up, me good tree! Many time me fader fell green tree, leave dry one." De witch knock out twenty axe-men, t'irty axe-men.

> *"Blum-blum, Sinde, Dido,*
> *Um um eh o,*
> *Blum-blum, Sinde, Dido!"*

Den de Ol' Witch sing,

> *"Chin fallah fallah, chin fallah fallah."*

When de tree goin' to fall, William said, "Bear me up, me good tree; many time me fader fell green tree, leave dry one." De Witch knock out twenty axe-men, t'irty axe-men.

> *"Blum-blum, Sinde, Dido-o-o!"*

Den de Ol' Witch sing,

> *"Chin fallah fallah, chin fallah fallah."*

While William in de tree, white basin boil up wid blood. An' William got a deaf-ears mamma. An' de nex' neighbor come in an' chattin' wid William mudder de whole day; an' in height of basin boil over an' run a stream slap on de frock of de ol' lady chattin' in de kitchen. When de ol' lady see de blood hot, she cut de chain of Blum-blum an' Sinde. Dido cut de chain himself, an' de t'ree dog gallop 'way. When William up tree see de t'ree dog coming, he only shake his hand an' de t'ree dog drop. An' de t'ree dog wait till de Ol' Witch get forty axe-man round de tree. In de height of cutting de tree, de t'ree dog destroy ev'ry one of dem an' kill de Ol' Witch herself.

An' William come down off de tree an' tek his machete an' scatter Ol' Witch over de whole earth, an' everywhere you go you can see dat bad *cowitch* is not'ing else den de pieces of de Ol' Witch.

Jack man dory, choose now!

b. Lucy and Janet

Martha Roe, Harmony Hall, Cock-pit country

ONCE A WOMAN HAVE TWO daughter. Lucy an' Janet were de two girl name. She sen' dem far to school. Der is Ol' Witch live along de road. An' she had t'ree dog, one name Dick, one name Dandy, an' one name Bellamo. August, Lucy was going home, going spend time wid her mamma, an' de mudder has to sen' dose t'ree dog to go carry her home. An' all her breakfas' fe her an' t'ree dog she put all togedder. Lucy were kind. When Lucy catch to her breakfas', she an' de t'ree dog eat togedder; she never consider dem as dog, she take dem as frien'. So when she catch half-way, de t'ree dog stop back an' one big Ol' Witch man come out to destroy Lucy. Dat time, de dog leave her quite back; now she gwine call dem:

> "Yah! Bellamo, Dick an' Dandy,
> Yah! Bellamo, yo!"

De t'ree dog run in an' dem tear up de Ol' Witch an' kill him. So ev'ry time Lucy come, dose t'ree dog guide her to her mamma go an' spen' August, an' de t'ree of dem carry her back to her school-missus place.

Well, Christmas, Janet a go. De dog come to carry home Janet. When dey come, she say, "I wonder what you all doin' so long!" an' begin to quarrel. When she ketch fe to eat breakfas', she eat her breakfas' first den she divide what left give de t'ree dog. So as she started on, de dog dem start back de same as usual. When de Ol' Witch man come out, going call de dog now. And say, (harshly)

"Yah! Bellamo, Dick an' Dandy,
Yah! Bellamo, yah!"

Dog wouldn't come. An' de Ol' Witch kill dat girl t'ru her bad manner. So you fin' plenty of young people don' have manners.

"Money won't take you 'round de island like civility."[9]

83. Andrew and his Sisters

Thomas White, Maroon Town

A WOMAN HAVE T'REE DAUGHTER an' one son, an' de son was a yawzy 'kin.[10] De t'ree sister, one name Madame Sally, one name Madame Queen Anne, one name Madame Fanny, an' de brudder name Andrew. De t'ree sister don' count much by de brudder. An' one day dem goin' out to see frien', an' bake pone an', in de mo'ning, tell der mudder good-by an' tell der fader good-by; dey never speak to de yawzy boy Andrew. Travel de whole day till late tek dem. An' dey look out on a common, dey saw a big white house an' dey call up an' ax fe a lodging fe de night, an' de woman in de house tell dem yes. An' it was an Ol' Witch house dem goin' to sleep. De Ol' Witch woman cook dinner give dem, an' bed-time get a nice bed to sleep in. An' de Ol' Witch woman drug dem, an' dey fallen in sleep.

At de said time, de yawzy 'kin brudder Andrew was half Ol' Witch an' he know what his sister was goin' to meet in de night. An' he follow dem whole day, until night, when de girl gone to bed, de Ol' Witch brudder fin' himself under de Ol' Witch house. An' dis Ol' Witch woman had t'ree copper hung up into her house. An' part of de night when de girl were in sleep, Ol' Witch went to kill one of de girl. As him catch de girl t'roat for go cut i', yawzy boy Andrew cry out,—

9. The proverb is added from an old mammy of over a hundred years.
10. Framboesia, popularly called "yaws" is a contagious though curable skin disease common among young negroes of the West Indies. It begins with a blister and spreads over the whole body. See Lewis, *West Indies*, p. 208.

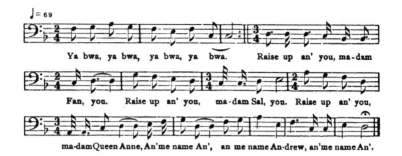

Ya bwa, ya bwa, ya bwa, ya bwa. Raise up an' you, ma-dam
Fan, you. Raise up an' you, ma-dam Sal, you. Raise up an' you,
ma-dam Queen Anne, An'me name An', an me name An-drew, an'me name An'.

As him sing out, razor-mout' tu'n over. Ol' Witch woman said, "But, bwoy, whe' you come from come here?" Andrew say, "Hi, Nana! me follow me sister dem come deh. But I have yawzy an' when de yawzy bite me, me mudder kill a cow an' tek de blood an' wash me." De Ol' Witch kill a cow an' tek de blood an' wash de boy, an' de boy fall in sleep back. So she go an catch Madame Queen Anne to cut him t'roat, an' de boy Andrew bawl out again,

> "Ya, bwoy, ya, bwoy, a me name o
> A me name Andrew,
> Rise up, Madame Fanny,
> Rise up, Madame Queen Anne,
> Rise up, Madame Sally,
> A me name o,
> A me name Andrew, a me name o."

Ol' Witch razor mout' tu'n over. Ol' Witch gi' out, "Bwoy, whe' you come from, torment me so?" Boy said, "Hi, Nana! when me to home, when me yawzy bite me, if it is de bigges' barrow me mamma got, 'm kill him an' tek de blood wash me." An' Ol' Witch kill a barrow an' wash him, an' de boy gone to bed, gone sleep. Day coming fast, Ol' Witch mad to eat de girl. When she t'ink dat Andrew asleep, him not sleeping. Well, de ol' lady wait for a good time an' him went in de room an' him catch Madame Fanny t'roat to cut him. An' him hear,—

> "Ya, bwoy, ya, bwoy,
> A me name Andrew, a me name o
> Rise up, Madame Fanny,

Rise up, Madame Queen Anne,
Rise up, Madame Sally,
A me name o
A me name Andrew, a me name o."

Boy jump out an' say, "Hi, Nana! de yawzy bite me dat I kyan' sleep. Nana, when I to home me mamma tek de bigges' sheep, tek de blood wash me." Dat time, Ol' Witch copper deh 'pon fire was boiling hard, an' Andrew ketch de Ol' Witch an' knock him down in de copper an' kill him dead. An' Andrew detain de t'ree sister 'pon Ol' Witch property, an' him claim de property as his own, an' sen' away for his mudder an' his fader, an' tek all de Ol' Witch riches an' live upon it, mek himself a man.

Jack man dory, choose none!

84. The Hunter

a. The Bull turned Courter

George Barret, Maroon Town, Cock-pit country

DEH IS AN OL' MAN live into a big large city an' ev'ry day he go out an' shoot some cow. Ev'ry time he go out an' see dem come to de pond drink water, he shoot one. An' when de rest mek a'ter him to come an' kill him, he say "Chee!" an' he tu'n a stone; an' dey come an' couldn't see him an' dey have to leave him. An' he tek up dat one, cut it up an' carry to his house. When dat done, he come again, an' dey come drink water until de las' one come out, an' he shoot him. An' ev'ry day continually de one t'ing.

So he leave one bull, an' go a'ter de bull many days an' couldn't overtake him. An' dat ol' man get dead an' leave his wife an' one daughter, big woman now. Den de bull change himself into a man. He go to de tailor an' mek him a suit of clo'es an' a pair o' boot to put on, an' was comin' soon in de mo'nin' about ten o'clock. An' de daughter say, "Well, since I live here, deh is not a man come here yet an' dat is me husban'!" An' on de day he come, say, don' eat beef, anyt'ing else gi' it to him he wi' eat. Den 'he begin to tell him say, "When me fader go to de pond-side an' shoot a cow, he say 'Chee!' an' tu'n a stone." De mudder in a dif'rent room say, "De firs' time you get a husban' you tell him all yo' belly-word? Save somet'ing!"

Nex' day dem gwine away. Den de young woman walk wid him t'ru de common till him ketch de place whe' him hide him skin; den he say, "You sit down an' wait a while." Den, she sit down *dis* way, an' hear a stick broke, an' when she tu'n round *so,* see de bull was comin' on upon him. Den him buck him, an' say "Chee!" an' tu'n dry trash. He 'crape up all de trash an' mash dem up to lint. Dat time de girl say "Chee!" an' she tu'n a tree. He buck de tree, 'crape off all de bark. Girl say "Chee!" an' tu'n a needle fasten at de tail; when him going away swinging tail, him drop 'pon a leaf. When see him gone to a distance, him say "Chee!" an' tu'n de same somebody again. An' run to him house, holla "Mamma, open do'!" De ma say, "Wha' I tell you? Save somet'ing! De firs' day you get a husban', you tell all yo' belly-word."

b. *The Cow turned Woman*

Elizabeth Hilton, Harmony Hall, Cock-pit country

ONE TIME A WOMAN HAVE one single child,—a boy. An' choose out a hunter. Mother fret an' cry a good deal an' say not a good trade, he might get dead in the bush. Sometime, go 'way for two or three months an' don' return, and where he shooting, only wild cow is there. The cow is so cross he has to turn stick an' stone to live amongst the cow.

One day when he go shooting, he see a beautiful young lady—one of the cow turn a beautiful young lady. An' he married her an' carried her home. When he go a-bed a' night his wife say, "How you live among those wil' cow an' they never kill you, an' no other hunter ever could return home?" Said, "Me love, when the cow come to buck me, I turn a piece of stick, an' they buck me all the same, I turn a rock,—I turn all different things." An' the mother call to him an' say, "Hi, me son! you jus' married to a 'trange woman, you tell him all you secrets? Tell some, lef' some!" Only one thing that he didn't tell,—that when he turn something, he fasten at the cow tail an' the cow couldn't buck him. An' the girl turn a cow, go back in cow country; an' the nex' time he go back in bush, all the cow buck him no matter what he turn an' the only way he escape, he fasten at the cow tail.

85. Man-Snake as Bridegroom

a. The Rescue (1)

Richard Morgan, Santa Cruz Mountains

DER IS A WOMAN TO court. Every man come to court her, she said she don' want him, till one day she saw a coal-black man, pretty man. 'he said, "O mudder, dis is my courtier!" She tek de man. Breakfas' an' dinner de man don' eat, only suck couple raw egg. So her got a brudder name of Collin. She didn't count de brudder. De brudder tell her, said, "Sister, dat man you gwine to marry to, it is a snake." She said, "Boy, you eber hear snake kyan tu'n a man?" Collin said, "All right! De day you are married, me wi' be in de bush shootin' me bird."

So de weddin' day when de marry ober, de man took his wife, all his weddin' garment, he borrow everyt'ing; so him gwine home, everywhere him go all doze t'ing him borrow, him shed dem off one by one till de las' house he tek off de las' piece an',—de Bogie! He walk wid his wife into de wood an' to a cave. He put down his wife to sit down. He tu'n a yellow snake an' sit down in his wife lap an' have his head p'int to her nose to suck her blood to kill her. An de woman sing,

> *"Collin now, Collin now,*
> *Fe me li'l brudder callin' come o!"*

De Snake said,

> *"Um hum, hum he,*
> *A han'some man you want,*
> *A han'some man wi' kill you."*

De woman sing again,

> *"Collin now, Collin now,*
> *Fe me li'l brudder callin' come o!"*

De Snake say,

> *"Um hum, hum he,*
> *Deh han'some man,*
> *Deh han'some man wi' kill you."*

Collin said, "Wonder who singin' me name in dis middle wood?" an' he walk fas' wid his gun. When he come to de cave, de snake-head jus' gwine to touch de woman nose. An' Collin shoot him wid de gun an' tek out his sister. So she never count her brudder till her brudder save her life.

a. The Rescue (2)

Matilda Hall, Harmony Hall, Cock-pit country

A WOMAN GOT ONE DAUGHTER that mother and father had, a very loving daughter to them. So draw up to womanhood, a young man come for her; she don't like. Another young man come; she don't like. An' a nice young man come one day to the yard, an' when that one come she was well pleased with him, say, "That is my beloved! me like him well!" An' that time was a Yellow Snake jes' come fe her now.

So them well pleased of it, father an' mother, an' them marry, Snake an' daughter. An' when the wedding-day come, everything was well finish until getting home now at the husband house in a wil' wood. An' when he got half way, begun to drop the clo'es now that he wear, drop him trousers, drop him shirt, an' jacket, an' going into one hole an' long out his head. An' he lay hol' of the leg of his wife an' he swallow to the hip an' he couldn't go further. Yellow Snake begin to sing,

> *"Worra worra, me wi' swallow yo',*
> *Worra worra, me wi' swallow yo'.*
> *Swallow yo' till yo' mamma kyan' fin' yo'!"*

So the girl sang now,

> *"I'm calling fe me hunter-man brother,*
> *Harry, Tom an' John!*
> *I'm calling fe me hunter-man brother,*
> *Harry, Tom an' John!*

Yellow Snake a wi' swallow me,
So me mamma kyan' fin' me!"

The brothers were hunter-men, heard her crying and run to see what is was. And they killed the Snake and took away the sister and said, "Well, you will have it! Pick an' choose isn't good. You wasn't pick an' choose, you wouldn't marry to Yellow Snake that was going to kill you now."

b. Snake Swallows the Bride

William Forbes, Dry River, Cock-pit country

A LADY HAD ONE DAUGHTER. All de young men come co'tin', she didn't like none. Till Snake tu'n a man, come in wid epaulette, everyt'ing, well dress up, an' he ax fe de girl fe marry. Say, "You is de man I want!" An' give up 'hem daughter to dat man de said night. Very well, middle of de night de girl was singing in de bed,

"Me me me me!"

Snake go,

Snake go

"Um um do kom go yerry."

Well, him singing de whole night till him swallow her. When de mamma get tea, papa get up an' drink, say, "Where dese young people? past time!" Mamma say, "Dem is young people, let 'em lie down!" An' when de fader shove de door gwine see, de Snake swallowed de daughter.

Jack man dory fe dat!

86. The Girls who married the Devil

a. The Devil-husband

William Forbes, Dry River, Cock-pit country

THERE WAS TWO SISTER AN they had a yawzy brudder who de two sister didn't care about. They was faderless and mudderless. An' see a man come to court de two sister to carry dem away; an' de man tek dem into de boat to carry home, an' de little yawzy boy tu'n a cockroach an' get into de boat. An' when deh get home, de house-maid tell de two girl, "Wha' you follow dis man come heah now? He is Devil!" An' de Devil tell de house-maid dat she mus' feed dem well, an' de little boy come out of de boat.

Well, deh had a big cock a de yard, an' de house-maid said, "I gwine to sen' you home into de boat." An' t'row out a bag o' corn gi' de cock, say, "When him fe eat it done, de boat will catch home". So de cock commence to eat de corn—

> *"Hock kaluck kum ka tum swallow!*
> *Hock kaluck kum ka tum swallow!"*

knock him wing bap bap bap bap! After he knock him wing, he crow—

> *"Ko ko re ko!*
> *Massa han'some wife gone!"*

Devil didn't hear him, crow again—

> *"Ko ko re ko!*
> *Massa han'some wife gone!"*

Devil hear now; as he hear, he come—

> *"Zin-ge-lay, wid dem run come,*
> *Zin-ge-lay, wid dem jump come,*
> *Zin-ge-lay, wid dem walk fas'!"*

So de boat name "John Studee." As he run into de yard, stamp him foot an' said, "John Studee!" An' stamp again, "John Studee-ee-e!" So de boat tu'n right back wid de two girl an' de little boy. An' as dey mos' come, de little boy tu'n cockroach again; go in garden. Devil didn't see him.

Nex' day mo'nin', Devil go back in fiel' put up de two girl again. De maid t'row out a bag o' corn an' a bag o' rice. Same t'ing happen. Las' day when him gone, de maid t'row out a bag o' corn, a bag o' rice an' a bag o' barley. An' after him t'row, de cock commence to eat—

> *"Hock kaluck kum ka tum swallow!*
> *Hock kaluck kum ka tum swallow!"*

After dem bag o' corn, tu'n upon rice now—

> *"Hock kaluck kum ka tum swallow!*
> *Hock kaluck kum ka tum swallow!"*

An' de rice he eat now, tu'n upon de barley—

> *"Hock kaluck kum ka tum swallow!*
> *Hock kaluck kum ka tum swallow!"*

Eat off de t'ree bag, time de girl catch home; leave de boat at de shore-side. De cock clap him wing—

> *"Plop plop plop plop*
> *Massa han'some wife gone!"*

As Devil hear, him come—

> *"Zin-ge-lay, wid dem run come,*
> *Zin-ge-lay, wid dem jump come,*
> *Zin-ge-lay, wid dem walk fas'!"*

As he come, 'tamp him foot an' say, "John Studee-e!" De boat t'un right back come home. If it wasn't fo' dat little yawzy boy, de Devil will kill 'em.

b. The Snake-husband

Emilina Dodd, Lacovia

A WOMAN HAVE A DAUGHTER, oftentimes engaged and wouldn't marry, said that the gentlemen weren't to her sort; until one day she see a well-dressed gentleman, came and proposed to her. But she has a brother was an Old Witch, told her that man was a snake. She said the man was too well-dressed to be a snake, but the brother was going home with them under the carriage as a lizard. The first place, as he was going on, somebody ask, "Mr. Snake, I beg you give me my collar," and the next, "Mr. Snake, I beg you give me my jacket," and so on until he show himself plain as a snake.

When they get home, he lock her up wanting to kill her, but couldn't kill her without the thing called "bump." Go out in the yard looking for it. After them gone, the mother-in-law said, "Me daughter, dis man you marry going to kill you because he is a bad man and he marry a wife already and kill her and he gwine to kill you too. I would let you go, but him have one cock, him so chat!" So she threw a barrel of wheat an' a barrel of corn. When the cock was picking it up he say, "I don' care a damn, I will nyam an' talk!" sing,—

> *"Ko ko re kom on do!*
> *Girl gone, him no gone,*
> *Ko ko re ko kom on do!"*

Then they throw a double quantity. The cock pick it up an' sing'

> *"Ko ko re ko kom on do!*
> *Girl gone, him no gone,*
> *Ko ko re ko kom on do!"*

Then Snake come from the wood while the brother was taking her on the water. Snake overtake her, take her home again and lock her in, go back in the wood again in search of "bump." And mother-in-law throw a double quantity of wheat and corn. Cock say again, "I don't care a damn, I will nyam an' talk!" The cock eatey all and sing,—

> *"Ko ko re kom on do!*
> *Girl gone, him no gone,*
> *Ko ko re ko kom on do!"*

So when Snake come out from the wood, he couldn't get her again because she was near on land. So he went back home an' tek a stick an' lick the mother-in-law on the head, kill her.

(The following songs are taken from other versions of the Snake-husband story.)

I will lick you so fine, I will lick you so sweet, yo' fad-der an' mud-der will nev-er fin' de hair ob yo' bone.

Poor me Lyd-ie gal, oh, poor me Lyd-ie gal, oh, han'-some man sin-ake un-done me.

Car-lie, oh, me Car-lie, oh. If a no been Car-lie come heah,

1. Variant.

yal-low snake could' a' swal-low me whole.

Mu-ma, mu-ma, snake a swal-low me. You lie, you lie, me dis I put ma han''pon you, you cum come tell yo' lie on me, you

2. Variant.

cum come tell yo' lie on me.   cum come tell yo' lie on me.

87. Bull as Bridegroom

a. Nancy

Richard Morgan, Santa Cruz Mountains

DEH IS ONE WOMAN GET a daughter. One day in de yard 'he saw a man, big stout man. He put co'tin'ship to her. De woman said yes. When de man come to de yard breakfas' time, he didn't eat; always went away where some clean grass is. 'he got a brudder watchin' him all 'e time. When he go, de man begin to sing,

> *"See me, Nancy, a wind,*
> *T'ink a me, Nancy, me come."*

De man tu'n bull an' eat his belly full o' grass. When he eat done, he sing again,

> *"See me, Nancy, a wind,*
> *T'ink a me, Nancy, me gone."*

Den he tu'n de shape a de man back.

When day of de wedding, de boy said, "Sister, you know wha' dat man coming here is? Dat man a bull." His sister said, "O bwoy, go 'way! Where you ever hear cow can tu'n a living soul?" Dey come home from church, sit roun' de table, everybody giving toast. Dey call upon de woman brudder to give toast. De brudder said, "I won' give toas', but I wi' sing." De man said, "No, give toas' better 'an de sing!" De guest said dat dey would like to hear de sing as much as toast; so de little boy commence to sing,

> *"See me, Nancy, a wind,*
> *T'ink a me, Nancy, me come."*

De man begin to bawl out an' knock his head, call out fe toast. De boy begun to sing again,

> *"See me, Nancy, a wind,*
> *T'ink a me, Nancy, me come."*

MARTHA WARREN BECKWITH

De ha'r of de cow grow, an' de four foot, an' de big bull begun to jump an' buck down all de people in de house, an' he gallop an' dey never see him no more again.[11]

b. The Play-song

George Parkes, Mandeville

DEH WAS AN OL' WOMAN who had a daughter an' a son. De son was an Ol' Witch, an' de girl was well kep' up by de ol' woman. Deh were several gentlemen who make application fo' de girl to marry, but de mudder refuse dem. At las' de debbil dress himself nicely an' went, an' he was accepted by de ol' lady, an' begun to co't de girl.

De boy, being an ol' witch, know dat it was de debbil. He tol' de mudder not to allow his sister to marry to de man, for de man is de debbil. De mudder said, "Go 'way, sah! what you know? You can call a gentleman like dat de debbil?" So when de debbil walking, his knee sing a song like ringing a bell. It go like dis:

> "Dirt i' room a yerry, double bing, double bing,
> Dirt i' room a yerry, double bing, double bing,
> Dirt i' room a yerry, double bing, double bing,
> Belling belling beng, bell i' leng beng."

De boy overhear de debbil knee singing. But, now, anybody else sing de song, de debbil clo'es will drop off, a horn grow on head, an' tail grow out on him too. So one night while he was in de house talking, de little boy was underneat' de table singing de song quietly:

> "Dirt i' room a yerry, double bing, double bing."

---

11. Thomas White's version of this song is as follows:

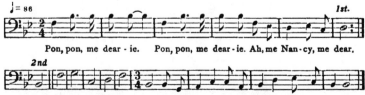

♩ = 86

Pon, pon, me dear-ie. Pon, pon, me dear-ie. Ah, me Nan-cy, me dear.

dear. Oh, oh, you, oh, oh,   you, da me Nan-cy, da me Nan-cy, What a fine gal!

When de debbil hear dat he say, "Look heah, mistress, stop dat bwoy from singing dat song! I don' like it." De ol' woman say, "Massah, me kyan' stop him singing, because it mus' of been his little play-song[12] what he have singing." So de debbil say, "Well, I don' like to hear it!"

De boy now sing de song much louder, an' de debbil knee begin to sing it very loud—

"Dirt i' room a yerry, double bing, double bing!"

an' de clo'es drop off an' de tail an' horns grow out. So de boy say to de mudder, "Didn't I tell you dat man was a debbil, an' you would not believe it!"

c. Gracie and Miles

Florence Thomlinson, Lacovia

THERE WAS ONCE A GIRL by the name of Gracie and a man Miles. They were engaged. And Miles always came to see Gracie most every evening, and he would always sing for her. Song was about Gracie; says that Gracie is a fine girl, but he is going to kill her.

---

12. Jamaica children compose a "secret song" which they amuse themselves with at play or sing when they are walking alone.

She didn't know he would kill her fe true.

She has a little brother stop in the yard with her. (Miles) worked in the field every day; they would send his breakfast by the little boy to him. When (the boy) nearly got to him, he wasn't a man; he was a bull. When he see the boy coming, he turn a man. The boy tell his sister, "You know that man is not a man, he's a bull!" and she said, "Oh, cho! nonsense! How you could expect that?" The little boy said, "If you think it is not true, you go with me, stop back." Next day she went after the boy and stay far back and see it was a bull eating grass, not a man. He sing,

> *"Me a Miles a moo, me Gracie is a fine girl,*
> *Me Gracie me wi' kill her."*

She know it is a bull now. When he come, the sister say tomorrow evening must have a ball now. So he says he will come. So she get up a lot of men with ropes and have music and all in the house. So the little boy begin to sing the song now:

> *"Me a Miles a moo, me Gracie is a fine girl,*
> *Me Gracie me wi' kill her."*

Miles said, "Oh, where that little boy come from? Turn him out!" Hoof begin to grow, horn begin to grow, tail begin to grow and he get a big bull, and they toss him and rope him and pole him, turn him out.

88. The Two Bulls

Alexander Foster, Maroon Town, Cock-pit country

ONE TIME THERE IS A bull range the common,—call the pen "Garshen pen." That bull wouldn't 'low no bull-calf to born an' to raise in that pen barring out him one; but every heiferborn, him nurse them, go about lick them, nourish them, make them grow fine! Until one time cow was heavy, climb up into a high mountain an' have a calf, an' when the calf born he is a bull calf. Now that ol' bull we call him "Ol' Moody," an' the young bull name "Tep'y-tep'y today."

The mother stay until the calf grow a tremendous bull, carry down that bull come to de river to drink water. Every time the father come to drink water, him go away, so then when the son come, the son try to put foot in the father track, an' the bull mamma say to him, "No, me son, de track no fit fo' you fader yet," make her carry him back a couple of days more. Now at twelve o'clock in the day, mother carry down the bull again, try foot for him father again. Now he feel to himself that he come a man, an' he stan' up same place an' say to him mother, "Mus' see me father today."—"Massy, me son, yo' pa so cruel, have a dread to carry son go!" He stan' up holla, "Ma, I gwine go! I gwine try to see me father!" an' he raise a sing now,—

> *"Santy Moody o, Tep'y-tep'y deh!*
> *Santy Moody o, Tep'y-tep-y deh!"*

De ol' bull gwine answer him now,—

> *"Hum–um–m, wha' you say?*
> *Me jus' a go a brudder Dickey an' Sandy,*
> *Moody say me mustn't go."*

Coming up the common to meet him father, (like) when a pretty man coming up, you see all de young girl for dat gentleman; an' he sing coming,

> *"Santy Moody o, Tep'y-tep'y deh!"*

De ol' bull answer him,

> *"Hum–um–m, wha' you say?*
> *Me jus' a go a brudder Dickey an' Santy,*
> *Moody say me mustn't go."*

Meet to fight now, an' de ol' toss up him son into the air an' he drop on four feet. An' the son lif' him up in de air now; when de fader coming down, one foot break. An' he 'tamp on de t'ree foot an' lif' him son higher again. An' him son lif' him up again in de air, an' when he comming again, break one of de other foot. An' all de cow now running to the river for water wouldn't bother with the ol' bull at all, everybody for the young one. An' lif' up de young bull again deh 'pon him two foot, lif up in de air, an' de young bull drop on him four foot back. An' de young bull lif' him up again; when he drop, he break de udder foot Lif' up de son again, but he couldn't go too far wid him; an' his son lif' him up in de air again break de udder foot. An' he lay down on him belly fe fight an' lif' up him son, but him couldn't go too far wid him foot. An' him son lif' him up de las', now, lif' him up in de air; an' when him come down, break him neck. An' from dat day, all young bull grow in pen; not'ing to destroy dem.

89. Ballinder Bull

Richard Morgan, Santa Cruz Mountains

DER IS A BULL DE name of Ballinder Bull, but dem right name King Bymandorum. It is a wicked bull. De king said whoever kill Ballinder Bull, he will get his two daughter to marry to. All de men in de worl' try, an' couldn't kill him. One day, an' ol' lady stood by an' a woman was breedin' go to de horsepon' to tek water. De bull buck out de baby out of her an' went away. De ol' lady tek de baby an' rear him. When him come a good-sized boy, he send him to school. Every twelve o'clock when dey play marble, he lucky to win. De res' a chil' tell him said, "A *da* you mek so!" Four o'clock when him coming home, him say, "Ma, why de reason when I win doz odder chil' sai, "A *da* you mek so?" Him ma tell him tomorrow twelve o'clock get one switch play wid de least one an' after you win him tell you "A *da* you mek so!" gi' him two good lick an' you will come to know why dey use de word. So twelve o'clock he play an' win, an' tell him "A *da* you mek so!" He gi' him de two lick, an' after he give him de lick he said, "Hit let Ballinder Bull buck you out of you mudder belly." When de boy return home he said, "O mudder, you is not me right mudder!" De ol' lady said no, begun to tell him all dese t'ings were happen. De boy said, "Anywhere Ballinder Bull, a gwine kill him!"

Dis bull got gol'en tongue an' gol'en teet'. When de boy gwine along, him meet some noblemen and said, "My little boy, where am you goin'?" An' said, "I gwine a fight Ballinder Bull." De men said, "Boy, we after Ballinder Bull fe dis many year an' kyan't ketch him; what you t'ink upon you?" De boy said, "Never min', I gwine fight him!" De boy went where him feedin'. Bull never see him, go drink water. De boy go to de cotton-tree an' say, "Bear down, me good cotton-tree, bear down!" De cotton-tree bear down. Said, "Bear up, me good cotton-tree, bear up!" When de bull was coming, he hear de singin',

> *"Anywhere Ballinder Bull,*
> *De' will kill him today!"*

Ballinder Bull say, "What little boy up in de air jeering me as dis?" When he come, he fire bow an' arrow; de boy catch it. Him fire anodder one, an' he fire out de seven; de boy caught every one. De boy look on him an' sen' one of de bow an' arrow, peg down one of de han'. An' tek de odder one an' sen it t'ru de odder han'. He sen' anodder an' peg down one of de foot. He sen' anodder an' peg down de odder foot. He sen' anodder, he peg down one of de ears. He sen' anodder an' peg down de odder ear. De las' one, he sen it t'ru de head. An' he say, "Bear down, me good cotton-tree, bear down!" When de cotton-tree bear down, he catch de ears an' pinch it an' fin' dat de bull was dead. An' he came off an' say, "Bear up, me good cotton-tree, bear up!" an' de cotton-tree bear up. An' tek a knife an' tek out de teet', tek out de tongue an' travel.

De same day, he never went to de king yard. Hanansi goin' to ground an' saw de bull an' said, "Buck, Ballinder Bull! buck, Ballinder Bull!" De bull don' shake. Hanansi said, "You damned son of a bitch, you won' get me fe kill today!" an' tek up de stone an' stone him an' fin' out dat de bull dead. De gladness in Hanansi! He went up chop off de bull head, bear it on to de king. When he go he said, "I kill Ballinder Bull, Sir!" De king say, "Oh, yes! you shall be my son-in-law tomorrow morning." Now der is a bell, every gate has a bell. So Hanansi gettin' ready to go to church, dey hear de bell ringin' at de gate an' dey sing,

> *"A who a knock a Nana gate, bing beng beng?*
> *A who a knock a Nana gate, bing beng beng?"*[13]

---

13. In a Brownstown version of the same story, the song is as follows:—

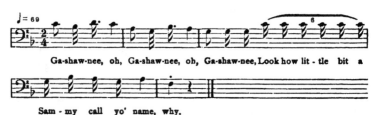

Ga-shaw-nee, oh, Ga-shaw-nee, oh, Ga-shaw-nee, Look how lit-tle bit a

Sam-my call yo' name, why.

When de boy come, de king say "What you want?" An' say, "I kill Ballinder Bull, Sir." Hanansi come out. (King says) "You's a little liar! Little boy like you couldn't fight Ballinder Bull!" An' Hanansi run in, said, "Der is de head!" De boy put his han' in his pocket said, "Der de tongue an' de teet'!"

Dey ketch Hanansi an' 'tretch him out on a ladder, an' beat him. After dat, dey sen' him to look wood fe de weddin'. Dey sen' Dog to watch him. Hanansi carried de wood, carry about ten bundle. Ev'ry trip, Dog go wid him. When him come back, 'im say, "Brar Dog, you love meat? I hear one hog over yonder; run go see if we kyan' get little!" By time Dog return back, Hanansi gwine under wood 'kin an' hide, an' all de hunt Dog hunt, kyan't fin' him till dis day.

90. Bird Arinto

Mrs. Ramtalli, Maggotty

THERE WAS A BIRD ARINTO; it used to feed on human flesh. In the district there was a little boy by the name of David Lawrence who was lame in both feet. When the boy heard the bird fly, he asked his sister to take him; but she refused, saying if she remained Arinto would eat her too. The boy, having no other resource, dug a hole in the ground where he lived for some time. When the bird came and perched on the house-top, he said, "Smell flesh; somebody about here!" Then David Lawrence sang,

You Ar-in-toe, You Ar-in-toe, Shake, shake, come down to Da-vid Law-rence.

Then the bird pitched off the house to the spot where he heard the singing. As it was an underground passage, the boy would move along and the bird would follow him up and down. As he went to the foot (of the passage), the bird would go there; as he went above, the bird would go there,—all day like that. At night the bird would go to rest,—couldn't eat he was so tired. But the boy cooked at night and had his rest.

It went on for some weeks until the bird got tired an' weary and one night fell off the roost. David Lawrence came out, cut out the tongue, and took it to the king, who had promised whoever killed Arinto would get his daughter's hand in marriage. Anansi, passing the nex' day, saw the dead bird, cut off the head and hurried with it to the king. A wedding feast was made to have Anansi married to (the king's) daughter. Just as that was going on, a ragged boy called at the gate, but Anansi told the king to have nothing to do with him. But he appealed so loudly that the king after all went out, and the boy said to him, "Anansi is a usurper, because, king, have you ever seen a head without a tongue?" Anansi, on hearing that, ran under the table and from there into the house-top. David Lawrence was taken in, dressed, married to the king's daughter, and lived happily.

Jack man dora!

91. Tiger Softens his Voice

George Parkes, Mandeville

ONCE UPON A TIME A woman had one daughter, an' that daughter was the prettiest girl in an' around that country. Every man want the girl to marry, but the mother refuse them as they come. Tiger, too, wanted the girl, an' demands the girl, an' the mother says no. Tiger said if he don't get the girl he will kill her. So they remove from that part of the country and go to another part, into a thick wild wood where no one live. And she made a house with a hundred doors and a hundred windows and a large staircase; and the house is an upstairs, an' there both of them live.

Tiger hear of it, always loafing aroun' the house to see if he can catch the girl, but the girl never come out. During the day, the mother went to her work, leaving the girl at home. When going out, the mother fasten all the doors an' windows; coming home in the evening, at a certain spot where she can see the house an' notice that all the windows an' doors are close as she leave it, then now she have a song to sing, go like this,—

"Tom Jones, Tom Jones, Tom Jones!"

(that's the name of the girl). Girl now—

"Deh lo, madame!"

Woman said to her now,

> *"Fare you well, fare you well, fare you well,*
> *Fare you well, me dear; fare you well, me love!*
> *A no Tiger, deh la, ho, deh la, ho?*
> *Me jus' come, ho!"*

Then the door open, *so*—

> *"Checky checky knock umbar,*
> *Checky checky knock umbar,*
> *Checky checky knock umbar."*

The door don't open without that song now, and when it open, the mamma go into the house.

At that time, Tiger in the bush listening to the song. So one day while she was away, hear time for her to come home, Tiger approach the spot where she always sing. He now in a very coarse voice sings the song,—

> *"Tom Jones, Tom Jones, Tom Jones!"*

The girl look from the window, said, "Tiger, a who no know sa' a you!" So now Tiger go 'way an' hide till mamma come. When she come, he listen good. Next day, Tiger go to a blacksmith an' ask de blacksmith what he t'ink can give him, Tiger, a clear v'ice. De blacksmit' say he must hot a long iron an' when it hot, mus' take it push down his t'roat. An' de blacksmit' give him a bit of meat to eat after he burn the throat an' that will give him a clear v'ice. So Tiger go away eat de meat first an' den burn de t'roat after. Nex' day he went to the spot where the woman always sing from. An' that make his v'ice more coarser. He sing now—

> *"Tom Jones, Tom Jones, Tom Jones!"*

The girl look thru the window an' say, "Cho! a who no know sa' a you!" So Tiger got vex' now, an' he went home, burn the throat first and afterward eat the meat, and that give him a clearer v'ice than the woman. The nex' day, when most time for the woman to come home from her work, Tiger went to the spot where he can see the house. He begin to sing,

"Tom Jones, Tom Jones, Tom Jones!"

The girl answer (tho't it was her mother now)—

"Deh la, madame!"

Then Tiger say,

"Fare you well, fare you well, fare you well,
Fare you well, me dear; fare you well, me love!
A no Tiger deh lo o-o-o
Me jus' come, h-o-o-o!"

The door commence to open now,—

"Checky checky checky knock umbar,
Checky checky checky knock umbar,
Checky checky checky knock umbar!"

And as the door open, Tiger step up an' caught the girl an' swallow her.

And when the mother coming home, reach to the spot and saw the doors and windows open, she throw down what she carry and run to the house. And she saw Tiger lay down. And the mother then went away an' get some strong men come an' tie Tiger, kill him, an' open de belly an' take out de daughter. At that time, little life left in her an' they get back the life in her. The woman then leave the house an' go off away far into another country, and that is why you always fin' lot of old houses unoccupied that no one live in.

92. Hidden Names

a. Anansi and Mosquito

George Parkes, Mandeville

An ol' lady have a daughter which no one know the name, an she never call the name at all make no one hear it So she offered a hundred pound to anyone who could tell the girl name. Anansi say he *mus'* get that money. Now he went an' mak a bargain with Mosquito that Mosquito mus' go in the girl room, as he's a small man an' can go thru crevices, an' he, Anansi will go underneath the mother room. In the night while the girl was sleeping, Mosquito went an' sing at her ear; an' the girl then knock her han' up on Mosquito an' say, "Go 'way!" At that time the mother stop into her room an' hear. After a little time, Mosquito went back to the girl ear an' sing again. The girl knock after him an' say, *"Go 'way!"* again. Anansi underneath the mother's room give a clear listening. A little time after, Mosquito went back to the girl an' sing at her ear. She then knock after him again an' say, *"Go 'way!"* The mother then called to the girl, said, "Zegrady, Zegrady, what's the matter?" The daughter said, "It is something worrying me in my sleep, mum." Anansi never wait now for Mosquito, run right to his house, take up his fiddle an' begin to play,—

> *"Zegrady, Zegrady, Zegra, Zegrady,*
> *Come shake up Anansi hand,*
> *My dear!"*

The next morning he start for the house and play. So the girl hear her name and say, "Mother, I heard someone call my name!" So the old woman invite Anansi to come in an' Anansi get the money, never give Mosquito none. So from that day is why Mosquito flying at poeple ear making noise, because Anansi rob him out of the money.

b. Anansi plays Baby (1)

Eliza Barrett, Harmony Hall, Cock-pit country

THERE WAS T'REE SISTER LIVING to a house. Nobody was to know their names. An' Anansi want to hear them an' he couldn't get them. An' he have a young man an' turn the young man into a baby (an' turn himself the baby mother), an' he carry the baby go an' ask them if they min' the baby for her; tell 'em say, when part of the day the baby crying they mus' bathe the baby for her. An' one of the sister name Santa Cruka. Santa Cruka take the baby an' 'trip him an' put him into a bowl, an' Santa Cruka said, "Run come a sister Aminty! ever see such a little baby have such a big man place?" An' Aminta say, "Run come, Sister Amata! ever see such a little baby have such a big man place?" So when de baby mother come now an' carry the baby under a tree, the baby tell the mother, "That one name Santa Cruka, an' the other one name Aminta, an' the other one name Amata." An' he put down the baby an' he turn a big tall man before him. An' he go up to de t'ree lady an' said, "Missus, is not you name Mistress Santa Cruka? An' she go into her room an' drop down dead. An' go back to Aminta an' say, "Sister, is not you right name Sister Aminta?" An' she drop down die. An' go back to Sister Amata an' say, "Is not you right name Sister Amata?" An' (she) drop down dead. An' (Anansi) take all the richness of the three sisters an' never care to go home.

b. Anansi plays baby (2)

Henry Spence, Bog, Westmoreland

ANANSI GO TO A GROUN'. Nobody know dose two sister name, not from dem born. So he come bet dat him will fin' out dem two sister name. When he come home, he said to his wife him going to fawn himself a baby an' de wife mus tek job grass-weeding at de groun' fe dem two women, when him gwine, mus' put him quite unter de shady tree as a baby. An' de wife did so. So when de two woman go under de tree, mek much of de baby, nice baby! So as dem woman play wid de baby, de baby laugh, mout' full of teeth. Two sisters frighten to see young baby have so much teeth. So one of de sister say, "Sister Agumma, run see Anansi baby mout' full of teet'!" Sister Agumma run come an' see. Anansi catch dat name. Sister Agumma come say, "O sister Agumme, a-a-ah! Anansi baby mout' full of teet' fe true!" Anansi catchy bot' name an' win de money.

b. Anansi plays baby (3)

Richard Morgan, Santa Cruz Mountains

DER IS A MAN LIVIN' at a town for eight years, nobody know his name. Hanansi say, "Ma tek off me trousers, put on me long shirt, kyar' me go a man yard, let him nurse me till you come home from ground." De baby stay good all de while. When he see h' mudder comin' home, de baby creep, cryin', go to his mudder. De man went to tek him back, said, "What kind of baby dis count fe, he see he mudder he start to cry?" Meanwhile he go to tek de baby an' saw de shirt jump up in de back. Him 'toop down, him peep, him knock him han'. "Mercy, me Lord! what kind of a baby got such long hair on him so, poor me, Tom Goody!" Den de baby gwine to his mudder cryin' "Tommy Goody!" So from dat day, de whole town fin' out de man dat he name Tommy Goody.

93. Anansi and Mr. Able

Thomas White, Maroon Town

ABLE HAVE TWO DAUGHTER AN' dey was pretty young women. Anansi hear about dese two women, did want dem for wife, didn't know what way he was to get dem. Able is a man couldn't bear to hear no one call him name; for jus' as he hear him name call, him get disturb all to kill himself. So Anansi get two ripe plantain an' give de young women de two ripe plantain, an' dey tek de two ripe plantain from Anansi an' dey eat de two ripe plantain. Das de only way Anansi can get dese two young women.

An' Able nebber know 'bout it until one day Mr. Able deh at him house an' him hear de voice of a singin',—

"Brar Able o, me ruin[14] *o*
Me plant gone!"

Brar Able say, "Well, from since I born I never know man speak my name in such way!" So he couldn't stay in de house, an' come out an' went to plant sucker-root. Anansi go out,—

---

14. Pronounced "roon".

> *"Brar Able o, me ruin o,*
> *Me plant gone."*

Mr. Able went out from de sucker-root an' he climb breadfruit tree. Anansi go just under de breadfruit tree, sing,

> *"Brar Able o, me ruin o,*
> *Me plant gone."*

Mr. Able went up in a cotton-tree. Anansi went up to de cotton-tree root, give out—

> *"Brar Able o, me ruin o,*
> *Me plant gone."*

An' Mr. Able tek up himself off de cotton-tree an' break him neck an' Mr. Anansi tek charge Mr. Able house an' two daughters.

Jack man dory, choose one!

94. The King's Three Daughters

Vincent Morrison, Mandeville

ONCE A KING HAD THREE daughters and the king die and some young fellows go up to the fence, but as they come they run them. The fellows meet Brar Nansi one day and they said to Anansi, "I bet you never go to that house!" Mr. Anansi said, "I bet you I go up there!"

Anansi went an' got some horse-mane and get a cotton-tree spar an' dig out a fiddle. An' he come out de road de evening, an' he start to play de fiddle say,

> *"Tom body tom ting,*
> *Tweety tweety tweety tweety tweety twee*
> *Linga linga loo*
> *Nobody never go deh yet,*
> *Linga linga ling*
> *Anansi go deh t'-night*
> *A go linga linga ling."*

The ladies call out and ask who is it playing that sweet music. Anansi say, "It's me, missus!" And the ladies ask who. He says, "Me, Mr. Anansi, missus." The ladies carry him up to the house and he play for two hours and come away. So the fellows who did bet him, he win them.

Jack man dora!

95. The Dumb Child

George Parkes, Mandeville

THERE WAS ONCE A LITTLE child born into a country, born with golden tongue an' golden teet', an' from de day she born, nobody see de teet' excep' de mother an' de father; she never talk for no one to hear her nor to see neither the teeth nor the tongue. Now the king of the country hear of it, an' he offer a gran' reward for anyone who would get to make the chil' talk, because he, the king, never seen a golden tongue an' teet' yet. So lot of men went to the house an' try all sort of mechanic; the chil' wouldn't talk.

So Anansi heard off it, went to the king an' tol' the king that he would make the chil' talk; an' the king say if Anansi make the chil' talk before him, he will make the reward much larger, but if he don't make the chil' talk before him, he, the king, will kill Anansi. So Anansi went away, got his fiddle, cord it up, an' went to the place of the little chil'; an' he played on his fiddle to make the chil' hear,—

> *"Poly don ya sin do,*
> *Poly don ya sin do,*
> *Poly don ya sin do,*
> *Merry day t'-day ya,*
> *Merry day t'-day ya,*
> *Sin do, sin do-o!"*

The chil' look upon Anansi an' smile; Anansi shake his head. He play the tune again—

> *"Poly don ya sin do,*
> *Poly don ya sin do."*

The chil' laugh; Anansi get to see de teet'. Now Anansi play stronger again de same t'ing,—

> *"Poly don ya sin do,*
> *Poly don ya sin do."*

The chil' begin hum it now,—

> *"Poly don ya sin do,*
> *Poly don ya sin do."*

Anansi play again harder now,

> *"Poly don ya sin do,*
> *Poly don ya sin do,*
> *Poly don ya sin do,*
> *Merry day t'-ay ya,*
> *Merry day t'-day ya,*
> *Sin do, sin do-o!"*

The chil' make,

> *"Poly don ya sin do,*
> *Merry day t'-day ya."*

Anansi shake de head an' laugh an' he play much stronger now,

> *"Poly don ya sin do,*
> *Poly don ya sin do."*

The chil' now sing louder,

> *"Poly don ya sin do!*
> *Poly don ya sin do!"*

As the chil' sing that time, Anansi pick up the chil', run right away to the king palace, call for the king, put the chil' in the chair, tol' the king he make the chil' sing, see tongue an' teet'. The king wouldn't believe him. Anansi play him fiddle before the king, play the same tune,—

> *"Poly don ya sin do,*
> *Poly don ya sin do,*

Poly don ya sin do,
Merry day t'-day ya,
Merry day t'-day ya,
Merry day t'-day ya,
Sin do, sin do-o!"

Chil' begin now,

"Poly don ya sin do,
Merry day t'-day ya!"

And the king was very glad, an' Anansi was nicely rewarded and the king took the child in his own home, an' dere she live wid de king forever.

96. The Dumb Wife

Thomas White, Maroon Town

DEH WAS A MAN NAME of Goolin. He had a wife. He married him wife fe so many years dat de wife turned dummy,—she couldn't speak to nobody. An' Mr. Goolin reward out a certain amount of money, if anyone could make him wife talk, he would pay dem dat amount of money. Anansi hear about it an' go to take up de job from Mr. Goolin. Anansi says if he had a mountain groun', an' Mr. Goolin says yes. An' Mr. Anansi an' Mr. Goolin go up to de mountain groun' an' Mr. Anansi tell Mr. Goolin he mus' get a coffin made an' send get up some men to carry de coffin. An' Mr. Anansi sen' tell de wife dat Mr. Goolin dead; an' when de message reach Mrs. Goolin dat her husband dead, Mrs. Goolin commence to cry; an' when she look an' see de amount of men goin' up to de mountain fe gwine carry down Mr. Goolin, de wife was crying but she couldn't talk. An' Anansi come down wid Mr. Goolin, an' dey hev' to come down a high hill, an' de house was upon a flat before de hill. Well, Mrs. Goolin da in de house, she hear de great noise was coming down de hill an' come jus' at de house door, she come an' stan' up an' look out an' see de majority of men comin'. Anansi gi' out,

"Goolin gone, t'de-e-e,
Goolin gone, Goolin gone,
Goolin gone home t'de-e-e!"

An' when de wife hear dat mournful singin' de wife sing now very faintly,

> *"Goolin gone, t'de-e-e,*
> *Goolin gone, Goolin gone,*
> *Goolin gone home t'de-e-e!"*

An' when Goolin hear he say, "Sing up, man!" Anansi sing,

> *"Goolin gone t'de-e-e,*
> *Goolin gone, Goolin gone,*
> *Goolin gone home t'de-e-e!"*

An' wife sing now,

> *"Goolin gone, t'de-e-e,*
> *Goolin gone, Goolin gone,*
> *Goolin gone home t'dee-e-e!"*

So Mr. Anansi tek out Mr. Goolin out of de coffin as a live man, an' Mr. Goolin an' him wife was talking up to t'-day.

97. Leap, Timber, Leap

a. Old Conch

Emanuel Johnson, Brownstown, St. Anne

THERE WAS A KING HAVE a lumber to bring into the palace, an' that lumber was one mile in length and there was not one man could carry it except one old man name of Old Conch. The king sen' for him; him tek five days to do one mile. Anansi hear, an' he can walk a little faster than him, an' went to the king an' say he will go an' the king say if he can carry it quicker than Old Conch, he can go. Anansi mek a cotta an' travel for the lumber, an' when Old Conch ketch up the five days, fin' Anansi beside the lumber trying to lift it up and couldn't lift it. Old Conch were beside the timber an' comence a song,—

Fol-low, timber, follow, fol-low 'long road, timber follow. Leap, timber, leap,
Leap, tim-ber, leap, leap, tim-ber, leap. Fol-low, 'long road, timber fol-low,
fol-low, 'long road, tim-ber, fol-low. Leap, tim-ber, leap, leap tim-ber, leap.

Timber pick up himself an' mek a leap in two mile.

Anansi went on before an' stood beside the timber trying to help it on again. Now when Old Conch went up and see Anansi by the timber again, Old Conch go beside the timber an' say,

> *"Follow long road, timber, follow!*
> *Follow long road, timber, follow!*
> *Follow long road, timber, follow!*
> *Leap, timber, leap! leap, timber, leap!*
> *Leap, me timber, leap! leap, timber, leap!"*

Timber pick up himself mek one jump two more mile; that's four miles timber gone now. Now go on, an' fin' Anansi beside it again, an' start him song say,

> *"Follow long road, timber, follow!*
> *Follow long road, timber, follow!*
> *Follow long road, timber, follow!*
> *Leap, timber, leap! leap, timber, leap!*
> *Leap, me timber, leap! leap, timber, leap!"*

The timber pick up himself two more miles an' drop in the king yard now.

Then Old Conch go on, an' Anansi run ahead an' say, "King, I brought de timber!" King were very glad to see the timber come an' say, "You done well, Anansi!" an' say, "I wan' de timber in dat corner." Anansi go beside the timber an' couldn't fix it in; were trying an' frying an' couldn't fix it in. Now Old Conch come, says, "King, I brought de timber." King says, "No! Anansi brought it; but, however, I wan' de timber to go in dat corner, an' I'll prove out of de two of you which bring it!" Anansi first go to the timber, an' couldn't manage it. Now Old Conch start an' say,

> *"Follow long road, timber, follow!*
> *Follow long road, timber, follow!*
> *Follow long road, timber, follow!*
> *Leap, timber, leap! leap, timber, leap!*
> *Leap, me timber, leap! leap, timber, leap!"*

The timber pick up himself an' fall in the corner. Now the king tek after Anansi was to kill him, couldn't catch him, run under a stone an' by the time they get up the stone, slip beneath the door crevice!

Jack man dora!

b. Grass-quit (fragment)

Howard Robinson, Retirement, Cock-pit country

GRASS-QUIT WENT TO THE BOTTOM place an' he haul a little grass-straw an' tak a knife an' slit the timber-head like *this* an' he fix the grass-straw into it, an' he say,[15]

15. The song appears twice in the story, the first time only four measures; it was explained that the second time the song must stop as given because that is how the Anansi Story ends.

An' the timber follow him right into man yard, an' as it catch into the yard, the daughter marry Grass-quitt same time. An' he sen' for a police an' tak up Anansi same time. When Anansi come out of prison, he make Grass-quit ride grass-straw until today.

98. The Boy fools Anansi

Richard Morgan, Santa Cruz Mountains

ONE BOY WENT TO HANANSI yard, an' Hanansi an' he mudder made up to kill de boy. Me'while, de boy hear what dem say. Hanansi went away fe one of his country-men help him to kill de boy. As Hanansi gone, de boy kill Hanansi mamma, tek off de coat an' de sucker, put it on an' cook up de ol' lady. When Hanansi come, de ol' lady gi' dem deh dinner. An' he say, "Ma, wha yo' got stren't te kill a big big boy?" De boy said, "Yes, me pickney."—"Ma, a wan' water." De ol' lady gi' him de water. An' said, "Lawd, dis fellah fat!" De boy tek time an' tek off de coat an' de sucker, t'row it down an' run, went away. Hanansi tumbled down,—"Lawd! a me mamma been nyam!" An' run after de boy but couldn't catch him. So it's only de boy ever fool Hanansi!

99. The Water Crayfish

Moses Hendricks, Mandeville

THERE WAS A WEALTHY WOMAN, but she had no children. She was always wishful of adopting a child. So she went down to the river to bathe one morning as usual and she saw a pretty baby. She was so glad she took it home and she made a pet of it. She employed a girl called Tamanty to care for the child, and Anansi to be the watchman to watch and see if the girl cared for the child.

So it happened one day she had to go out, so she left them to take care of the child. Anansi wanted all along to get rid of this girl Tamanty. Tamanty was sweeping the house and the little child was playing with the broom. Anansi winked to the girl and said, "Lick him wi' the broomstick! lick him wi' the broomstick !" The girl took the broomstick and hit the child. The child started running for the river. Anansi and Tamanty started after her, calling out, "Come back, Miss Nancy, come back!" The child said,

"No na no, Tamanty! no na no, Anansi!
Me a river craw-fish, me no have a mu-ma,
Poor me, river craw-fish! river a me mu-ma."

The child ran right into the river and became a cray-fish.

Modern European Stories

100. Ali Baba and Kissem

Alexander Townsend, Flamstead, St. Andrew

ALI BABA WAS THE BROTHER of Kissem, but Ali Baba was a poor man and Kissem was a rich man. Ali Baba had two donkeys and an ox,—all his living. Ali Baba was cutting wood one day, he heard a company of horse coming afar. Took his donkeys and hid them in the bush, hid himself in a tree. Forty men were coming on; the head man came right to the cave where he was. Name of the cave was "Sesame." This cave was shut, would open by the word "Open, Sesame." And they brought forty bags of gold an' put in. Shut without word. Ali Baba saw them from the tree-top. When gone, Ali Baba came down to the cave, said, "Open, Sesame, open!" Ali Baba took all the money he could, loaded it on the donkey.

Must measure the money, but didn't have any measure. Brother said, "What Ali Baba got to measure?" Took stuck the measure. Ali Baba measure, measure, measure, measure thousands of dollars. One piece stuck on the bottom. Brother aska; Ali Baba tells all about it, teaches brother, "Open, Sesame, open." Next day, Kissem took wagon, oxen, servants, went to the place, said, "Open, Sesame, open!". When he went inside, cave shut. When he went on, saw all the money, he forgot the word, said, "Open, kem! Open, wem! Open, rim! Open, sim!" Forgot that word entirely, can't get out. The men came back; "Open, Sesame, open!" Find Kissem. "How came you here?" No answer. Cut Kissem up in five pieces, hung them up in the cave.

Kissem's wife went to Ali Baba, said, "Kissem no come here yet!" Ali Baba went next day to the place. "Open, Sesame, open!" Finds the five pieces, takes them down, gets a cobbler to sew the five pieces up into a body. Robber comes back, finds body gone. Who took away that body, signifies some one knows the place; must find out who that is. Goes about town, finds a cobbler who said he joined five pieces into a body. Cobbler shows the house. He gets jars, puts a robber in each jar; one jar has oil. Takes the jars to Ali Baba, says will he buy oil. Ali Baba says yes.

He makes sport for the great governor. Ali Baba had a maid by the name of Margiana, and she was very wittified,—discovered the whole thing, but she didn't say anything. She danced so well, danced up to the governor to give her something. He put his hand in his pocket to get her something; Margiana get one dagger, killed the governor dead. Margiana got the oil red-hot, poured into all the jars that got men. Ali Baba said, "Well, Margiana, you saved my life and you shall have my son and as much money as you want, and as much money as will put you in heaven!"

101. Bull-of all-the-Land

William Forbes, Dry River, Cock-pit country

DER WAS A BULL NAME King Henry and, in de day, Bull-of-all-de-Land. Well, in de day him put on bull clo'es an' de night him turn man. An' one night de wife him lib wid mek up fire and bu'n de bull clo'es, an' after she bu'n de bull clo'es, de man lef' de wife. Have t'ree pickney; an' she tell him to give him clo'es and she take her finger, prick, an' drop t'ree drops of blood on de shirt-front. An' him go away lef' 'em fe t'ree years.

An' after him lef' 'em, she mash t'ee pairs of shoes to fin' him. An' she walk till she catch a river-side see a washer-woman. An' he said who would wash but de t'ree drops of blood, him will marry to her. Den de woman dat was washing de shirt-front say, "Me lady, if you wash out de t'ree drops of blood, I will show you King Henry." Well den, only cut a lime an' 'queeze it pon de t'ree drops a blood an' wash off! An' de washer-woman run leave de woman at river-side an' run up to King Henry, say, "I wash de blood!" An' after she go up, him kep' her in de yard, send off fe a minister, say in t'ree days fe marry de woman a wash out de blood.

In de night, dem put de strange lady into a close room against King Henry, but de woman didn't know de king is dere. And dis woman dat say him wash out de blood, gib him laudanum in tea an' he drop asleep. Den when de minister come, him hear it de two night de woman was singing; and he talk to King Henry say what woman singing to him at night. And say, "What woman?" And say what he drink in his tea. Nobody in de district know his name Bull-of-all-de-Land, only dis woman; all other know him King Henry. Well de next night sing again:

Phonograph record 35, transcribed by Helen Roberts.

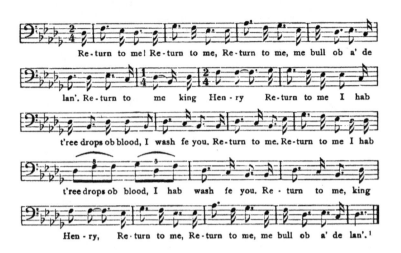

Re-turn to me! Re-turn to me, Re-turn to me, me bull ob a' de lan'. Re-turn to me king Hen-ry Re-turn to me I hab t'ree drops ob blood, I wash fe you. Re-turn to me. Re-turn to me I hab t'ree drops ob blood, I hab wash fe you. Re-turn to me, king Hen-ry, Re-turn to me, Re-turn to me, me bull ob a' de lan'.[1]

As King Henry hearing de singing, jump right up. An' de nex' day marry de woman, mek her a lady. Fe nobody else know he is Bull-of-all-de-Land.

102. The Boiling Pot

Maud Baker, Dry River, Cock-pit country

ONCE CINDERELLA AND HER GODMOTHER lived together, and godmother told her there was a certain room in the house that she wasn't to enter at all. One day while godmother was out, Cinderella said she must see what was in that room. After going there, she was extra frightened to meet up a large pot boiling with blood and no fire underneath. When godmother came back, she found out that Cinderella had gone into the room. Calling her to her, she told her that she must tell her the truth now; when she went into the seventh chamber, what did she see? Cinderella replied, "Dear Godmother, I saw nothing and nothing shall I talk until my dying day!" She asked her the same question again, and Cinderella repeated the same answer. Then she was so annoyed that she took Cinderella into a deep wood

---

1. The record is uncertain in places.

about ten miles away and asked again, "Cinderella, when you went into the seventh chamber, what did you see?" The girl again repeated, "Dear Godmother, I saw nothing and nothing shall I talk until my dying day!" The godmother threatened to cut out her tongue if she wouldn't tell her the truth, but she kept saying the same as before, so then the godmother was so annoyed she cut out her tongue and left her there weeping extra.

Well, after a day passed, there was a king travelling through the woods and he saw this lovely little girl. And she was stripped naked and still weeping. The king asked her what she was doing there and she couldn't tell at all, only cry. And the king took his silk handkerchief, wrapped her up and took her home with him. Some time after, the girl had a boy child for the king. The godmother heard of it all right, and when the ninth night came, godmother came in and stole away the baby and put a cat in the bed. When the king got up and saw the cat, and asked what she had done with the baby, she couldn't tell, only weep all the time. Some time after, she had a girl baby. When the nine nights went round again, the goddie went to the bed, took the baby and put a big block of rotten wood in the bed. And the king was again amazed, asked her what she had done with his baby and she couldn't tell, only cry. Well, the king threatened to imprison her for his two babies, but seeing her so fretful and pitiful, he gave her a chance. Some time after, she had a boy baby again. After the nine days came round again, they put up soldiers to keep guard in the room and all outside and round about the yard, and at the gate soldiers with guns and bayonets. And godmother came in and took away the baby and plastered up the mother's mouth and everywhere in the bed with blood. So when the morning awoke now, the king believed that the girl had been eating all his babies, and he advertised around the country that she was to be hung on such a day.

Well, after the day came around, all the high men gathered at the place to see her hung. After the sentence was passed and she was about to receive her death, some one called to them they must stop because some nobleman was coming. And they spied afar off one of the most beautifulest carriages glittering in the sun. So they waited until the carriage came, and it was that old godmother with the three children grown to a big size. And she came in and put the two boys on the king's leg and the girl in the middle, and put in the girl's tongue, and she was able to talk for herself now. Also, the godmother got a good sum of money from the king for the good care she had taken of the three children; and instead of sorrow, they had a merry day. And the king went home and married the girl and they lived very happily after that.

103. The Twelve One-eyed Men

Henry Pottinger, Claremont, St. Anne

I'LL GIVE YOU A PLAIN story that you may be able to write it down and the words may not puzzle you to spell,—all plain words.

There was a lady and her maid lived in a palace upon a very high mountain. There was nobody allowed to go up the mountain except a fisherman alone. The maid had a baby who was her first son. A couple of days after, her mistress had a baby who was her first son. Next morning the fisherman came up and saw the two babies. The fisherman owned the two children as his sons. The fisherman broke a limb from a rose and stuck it in the ground as a plant. Immediately it grew a tree with a beautiful shade. Under the tree he placed a golden table, for his two sons to play their billiard under. Day by day they went under the tree and played their billiard there.

The first son's name was Adam; the second son, his name was Bob. One morning early Adam said to Bob, "I am going today to see what the world is like." He called for his mare and a cane-stick and a hound, and he mounted his mare and he started away. He rode that day long, till night came down. He saw beautiful light on the top of a hill. He went up to the house. A lady met him at the door. The lady asked him where he is going. "I am travelling to see what the world is like." The lady said to him, "You best to remain here with me, for ten young men have passed this same way and never returned again." The first one came, and she gave him one hundred keys to open ninety-nine doors, but never open the hundred. The first door that he opened he saw beautiful things, until he opened ninety-nine and every one he saw better things. He was forbid not to open the hundred, but he would like to see what (was) inside the hundred and he opened the hundred and he saw (a) beautiful green pasture with a coal-black horse standing there full-rigged with saddle and bridle, and there he mounted on. And the horse made one rear and he dropped into a palace and there he saw ten young men sitting upon ten chairs. There were two chairs left, nobody thereon. He sat upon one. The eleven men that were sitting on the eleven chairs now, all had one eye.

Bob, his brother, who (was left) at home, next morning broke a branch from the tree and threw it on the ground, and it withered at once. "Mischief befalls me brother!" He called for his mare, he took his cane-stick, he called for his hound, he mounted his mare. He said to his mother, "My brother is dead; wherever he is, I must find him today."

He rode for that day till it was night. He saw the light on the hill. He went up the hill. The same lady met him at the door. She asked him where he was going. "I am going to look for my brother Adam." The lady said to him, "Eleven came here before and have gone the same way and never returned again; there is one chair left and you will sit thereon!" She gave him one hundred keys to open ninety-nine doors, and forbid him not to open the hundred. The first door he opened he saw beautiful things, and he opened ninety-nine doors. The one key was left. "It is just as well for me to open the hundred!" And he saw the same black horse, the handsomest animal in the world, with saddle and bridle thereon. He mounted the horse, and he reared and dropped in the same palace where his brother was. There was a chair provided there for him, and (he) found that he had only one eye the same as the other eleven had. If he had heard what the lady had said, he wouldn't have gone to look for his brother who was lost.

The lady and the maid lamented for their son,
But not so bad as the poor fisherman.

104. Bird and Hunter

Elizabeth Hilton, Harmony Hall, Cock-pit country

"THE KING HAVE TWO SON. The first one went out to hunt. He see a pretty little bird!" An ol' man said to him, "Say, massa, you better not follow dat bird!" He see the bird a pretty golden bird and he still follow the bird. Then him go to a place where he didn't see anybody at all but an old hut, an' he gwine in an' see a big fire. Come off an' hitch up him horse an' warming by the fire an' was hungry an' see a sow an' t'ree pig, an' he shoot them an' was roasting them by the fire an' see an' ol' woman come up. 'He say, "Beg you little fire, massa." An' say, "Come an' take it." An' say, "Hol' yo' dog fe I 'fraid of it." An' the ol' woman pop one of her hair an' give it to the gentleman to tie the dog. She pop another an' give it to him to tie the horse. Said, "I beg you a piece of the meat now, massa." An' give him the four tripe. She said, "That is not enough!" She jump on the gentleman and begin to beat him. The gentleman said, "Dog, dog, help me!" Dog said, "I would help you, but I am 'ready chained!" He said "Horse, horse, help me!" Horse said, "Master, I would help you but I am ready chained!" An' him killed him.

The next day, the other brother didn't see him come home and went to look for him. He travel and when he get to the ol' woman house, he see the same little bird was singing. He said, "What a beauty! I'd like to catch that bird!" The ol' man said to him, "Massa, don' go off wid dat bird! About t'ree days ago a noble gentleman pass here an' never return, an' dat's where all de kings' an' nobles' sons los' der way." The gentleman said, "I'll just fin' out how my brother go." And went to the same place an' see the same ol' hut, an went in an' see a big fire. An' he went in an' was warming a' fire an' see a sow an' t'ree pig an' kill the sow an' the three pig. An' see the ol' woman come out; "Massa, beg a little fire." An' say, "Come an' take it!" An' say, "Chain yo' horse an' yo' dog," an' pop off two more hair an' give it to him; an' the gentleman t'row the hair into the fire an' hear them pop. The ol' woman go into the bush and pop two green withes an' tie the horse an' the dog an' begin to fight the gentleman. The gentleman call to the dog, "Dog, dog, help me!" an' the dog pop the withe an' begin to bite the ol' woman. He say, "Horse, horse, help me!" The horse began to trample her. When she fin' out that they were going to kill her she say, "Massa, don' kill me, I will show you something! Raise up all those black stone that you have seen here and you will find all the kings' son and all the nice lady an' beautiful princess that I have enchanted and turned into stone. An' you will find your brother, horse an' dog." An' the gentleman kill her an' raise up all the stone and fin' his brother and all the ladies and gentleman.

105. Jack and the Devil Errant

Elizabeth Hilton, Harmony Hall, Cock-pit country

JACK WAS A GREAT GAMBLER,—NO one could ever beat him a game; and he went and gambled with the Devil Errant. Jack won the first, second and third games; the Devil Errant won the fourth and the fifth games. The Devil Errant said to Jack, "I require nothing of you but to find me in three months." No man knew where the Devil Errant lived, and if Jack doesn't find him in three months, the Devil Errant will take his head. And the Devil Errant knew where Jack lived.

Jack was fretting and didn't know what to do. He asked every one of his friends and they said they didn't know the Devil Errant and didn't know where he lived. He went to the keeper of the world and asked him where the Devil Errant lived. He said, "How could you play cards with a man like that! However, I am keeper of all the beasts. In the morning I will ring the bell and all will come and I will ask them if they know the Devil Errant." In the morning he rang the bell and all the beasts came. Everyone said he didn't know the Devil Errant. So he said, "I don't know what to do, Jack; but I have a brother who lives three hundred miles from here, and I will roll a barrel and you must go after the barrel; where the barrel stops, that will be where my brother lives."

In the morning, he rolled the barrel and Jack followed the barrel, and it stopped in the brother's yard and Jack stopped too. And he asked the brother if he knew the Devil Errant and he said no, didn't know a man like that. And he said, "Well, I am the keeper of all the fish in the sea. In the morning I will ring the bell and all the fish can come und I will ask them if they know the Devil Errant." In the morning, he rang the bell and all the fish came and they said they didn't know a man like the Devil Errant.

Jack was fretting, for it only needed three days and the three month would be gone. The brother said, "Well, I don't know what to do, but I have another brother who lives two hundred miles from here. Tomorrow I will roll the barrel and where that barrel stops that will be the place. In the morning, he rolled the barrel and Jack followed after the barrel, and when he got to the other brother the brother said, "Well, I don't know such a man by the name of the Devil Errant, but I am the keeper of all the birds in the year, and in the morning I will ring the bell and they will come and I will ask them if they know the Devil Errant." In the morning, he rang the bell and all the birds came exept one named the Quack, and everyone said he didn't know the Devil Errant. Little after, the Quack came up. The keeper asked him why he didn't come all this time and he said, "I was just at the Devil Errant's yard picking up a few grains of corn." The keeper said to Jack, "This is the only one who can take you to the Devil Errant's yard."

Jack had to kill a cow now and cut it up in pieces and put it on the bird's back along with himself, and every time the bird said "Quack," give him a piece of meat. The Quack was a greedy bird; said "Quack" and gave him a piece, "Quack" and gave him a piece, "Quack" and gave him a piece, "Quack" and gave him a piece, till he gave him the whole cow, didn't have any more to give him. The bird said "Quack" and he gave him his hat, "Quack" and he gave him his boots, "Quack" and didn't have anything more to give him, and the bird dropped him at the river-side.

As Jack was there crying he saw an old man come. The man said, "Jack, what you doing here?" Jack said, "I was gambling with the Devil Errant and he won me the fourth and fifth times and he said I was to find him in three months, and the three months are up today." The man said, "Well, I advise you to stay here for a few minutes and you will see the Devil Errant's two daughters come to bathe. You must not trouble those two, but when you see the third one come, when she goes to bathe take her clothes and hide them, and when she comes out to look for the clothing say to her, 'Your father played me a trick and I will play you one too!'"

Jack did so. When the girl looked for her clothes, Jack said, "Your father played me a trick and I will play you one too." And the girl fell in love with Jack and told him all her father's secrets and said, "Now, Jack, when you go to my father's gate, if he tells you to come in you mustn't go in at the gate; for there will be a sword ready to cut off your head. Let him come and open the gate for you." So when Jack went to the Devil Errant's yard, the Devil Errant said, "You are very clever indeed, Jack! Open the gate and come in." Jack said, "No, you come and open it." The Devil came and opened the gate.

The Devil said, "As you are so clever to find me in three months. I will give you another task to do." He dropped his gold ring into an empty well and said, "Go and pick it up." When Jack went, the well was full of water. Poor Jack was hungry and crying. He saw the girl coming with his breakfast and a bag with a machete in it. And she said, "Why are you crying, Jack?" He said, "Because your father has given me a task I can't do." She said, "What is it?" He said, "He dropped his ring into the well when it was empty, and when I went to pick it up, it was full of water." She said, "Well, what you must do is to take this machete now and cut me up in pieces and I will be a ladder, and when you are coming back, you must take up every piece and put it into this bag and I will become the same woman. Jack said he couldn't do it at all, but she forced him to and so he did it. He chopped her up and put her down and she became a ladder, and every time in coming up he took up a piece until he had taken up the whole, only one little piece he forgot, till at last she became the same woman, only she had lost one of her finger-joints; but she said, "Never mind for that, Jack!"

Jack took the ring to the Devil Errant and he said, "Since you are so clever, I will give you another task; take this house, now, and shingle it with dove feather." Jack was crying and he saw the girl coming with a barrel of corn. She said, "Now, Jack, dash this corn about the house and every bird will come to feed; and pick the feathers and shingle it with dove feathers." And so Jack did.

And the Devil said, "You are so clever I will give you another task to do, and when you have done that I will set you free." And he gave him a bit and said, "Go and catch my horse in the pasture." When Jack went to the pasture he saw it was a mountain of sea. Jack was crying and he saw the girl coming with a gun and a stone. She said, "Don't cry, Jack! take the bridle and stone, fire the gun and dash into the sea. The horse will come and put his head into the bit, as my grandfather was buried here."

When Jack carried the horse to the Devil Errant, the Devil Errant said, "You are very clever indeed. I will give you one of my daughters to marry." He had the three girls dress alike and gave a grand dance and said when they were dancing he must pick out the one that he loved the best. The girl told him that she would wear a different branch and told him what branch she would wear, so he picked out the youngest daughter. The Devil Errant said he couldn't give him that one at all because she was too young, but Jack said she was the only one he loved, and the Devil Errant couldn't break his promise and had to give her to him, and they got the parson to come and marry them.

That night the wife said, "Well, Jack, father is going to kill you tonight." When they went to bed, the wife made two wooden babies that would cry and put them in the bed; and they went into the pasture and got the best riding horses her father had and started for home. The devil got a pot of boiling water and threw it trough the chimmey into the room on the bed. When he heard the babies cry, he went to cut their throats and he found the two wooden babies. So he went after them. The horse's name was "Supple Jack." The girl said to Jack, "Look, look behind you and see what you see!" Jack said, "Your father is at the horse's tail!" She said, "Take this grain of corn and throw it and it will turn a wood of trees that he can't pass." The Devil went back for his axe, and felled the wood. She said, "Look, look behind you, Jack, and see what you see!" He said, "Your father is at the horses tail!" She said, "Take this sweat and drop it behind you and it will mount to a great river he can't cross." The devil went back for his ladle and ladled the water till he drowned; he couldn't go any further!

The girl said to Jack, "As you have been away so long, don't take me with you; leave me at the lodgings and come back tomorrow for me. But you must not kiss anyone; if you kiss anyone, you will forget me and never remember me any more." So Jack went home. His mother and sisters and everybody came to kiss him, but he refused to kiss them. He lay on the sofa sleeping and a pet dog came and kissed him, and Jack never remembered his wife any more for four years. Then they made a great entertainment. Jack was just about to marry the next day to another woman, and he and his bride went to the entertainment. The first wife sat down at the window sad. They asked her to go with them to the entertainment. She said no, she was not going, but they forced her to go with them. As everybody was enjoying himself, they asked her to entertain them. She knocked her left side; a rooster came out. She knocked her right side; a hen came out. She knocked her stomach; a grain of corn came out. The rooster took it away from the hen. The hen said, "Get away, you ungrateful rooster! You came into my father's yard, he gave you a task to do and you couldn't do it. He dropped his gold ring into the well and you couldn't take it out, had to mince me in pieces, and now I have lost one of my little finger joints!" She knocked again and another grain of corn came out. The rooster took it away from the hen. The hen said, "Stop, you ungrateful rooster! You came to my father's yard, he gave you a task to shingle a house with dove feathers and you couldn't do it; I had to do it for you!"

Jack said, "I remember something!"

She knocked on her stomach again and another grain of corn came out. The rooster ate it up. She said, "Get away, you ungrateful rooster you! You came to my father's yard. He gave you his bridle to go and catch his horse and you couldn't catch it and I had to show you how to do it!"

Jack said, "I just remember my fault!" Jack fell down at her feet and begged her to forgive him. He said to the company that a man had lost a key and was about to buy a new one when he found the old one just as good, and everybody told him there was now no occasion to buy the new one. Jack said, "Well, this is my wife that I forgot for four years, and I have found her!" He put her in his buggy and drove home and left the other one in the same place. And they both lived happy forever.

106. The Magic Hat and the Staff of Life

Maud Baker, Dry River, Cock-pit country

ONCE JACK'S WIFE GAVE HIM a cow to sell, and she told him the cow cost twenty pounds. Three men bet they could get the cow cheap. They hid at different places along the wayside, and one came out and asked Jack if he was selling that goat. Jack said, "No, me man, it's a cow, not a goat! because me wife told me it's a cow and I can't sell it for a goat." The man told Jack his wife was making a fool of him and he would give him a dollar for the goat, but Jack refused. After he had gone for a couple of miles, a second man came out and repeated to him all that the first had said. And Jack refused to sell the cow and went on. After a couple of miles again, the third man came out and said he must sell him the goat. Jack got angry himself now, and the man offered him three dollars and he took it and returned to his wife with it and told her all that had happened to him with this goat she gave him for a cow. The wife was angry and told him she would have nothing more to do with him until she got her twenty pounds for the cow.

Jack took the three dollars and started off in a deep study. He went to a shop and called for a bottle of whiskey, which cost a dollar. After paying for it, Jack asked the man to let it remain until he returned back, and the clerk consented. He went to a second shop and bought a bottle of whiskey for a dollar and asked the clerk to put it up also till he returned. He went to a third shop, bought a bottle of whiskey also and asked the clerk to let it remain. After going about three miles, he met up with the three men who robbed him out of his wife's cow and says to them would they mind going to the shop and taking a drink with him; and they said yes. At the shop, Jack called for a bottle of whiskey, the four of them served it in glasses and drunk it all. Jack took off his hat and clapped it on the counter and said, "It's well paid for!" and the clerk said, "All right, Jack, we know that." After they go outside, the three men want to know how Jack didn't pay for the whiskey and yet the clerk believe that he paid for it. Jack said as long as he clapped his hat on the counter, they must say that he paid for it. They bet Jack that he couldn't go to the next shop and do the same, and Jack said that he could; and he went into the second shop and called for a bottle of whiskey again, the four of them drunk it off, and, taking off his hat, he clapped it on the counter again saying that it was well paid for. The clerk said, "Yes, Jack, it is all right." They go to the last shop now, call for the third bottle and do the same thing again. They wonder how he can do that and ask to buy the hat. Jack said no. He asked them one hundred pounds for the hat, and the three of them made it up and Jack gave them the hat and got the hundred pounds and carried them to his wife. She was well pleased now.

The three men started with the hat to see if they could get something by it also. After buying some things, one of the men tried the hat and it wasn't successful. The other two were rowing with him, saying that wasn't the way Jack did with the hat. The second one now took it and went in, but the clerk was angry and was about to call the police; they had to pay for what they called for there. Then there was a big row, the other two saying that wasn't the way Jack had done with the hat. Now the third one tried it and was not successful. They threatened now to catch Jack and to kill him.

Jack knew what would happen and he told his wife he was going to put up a trick. He went to the bed and lay down, and when the wife saw the three men coming she started crying. They asked her what was the matter, and she said her husband was dead and nobody to help her bury him. They said, "A devil act that! should have been dead before now!" and asked to see him. Jack was lying in bed as if dead, and a stick beside him. One of the men said, "Yes, me man, we were looking for you to kill you; we are glad that you are dead already!" and he took up the stick beside him and gave him a wonderful stroke. Jack started up with fright and said to them, "This is the stick of life! it raised me from the dead!" and the wife was so glad to have her husband back again! Well, the three fools asked Jack now to sell them the stick. Jack refused, but they begged and Jack consented. They gave Jack one hundred fifty pounds for the stick because it was the "stick of life."

The men started 'round the village advertising that they could raise the dead. The king's daughter was dead. They went to the king's home and told him that they could raise the dead, and he was glad and carried them inside where the daughter was lying dead. They began beating her with a stick and crying, "Princess, arise from the dead!" but nothing happened. The king was angry, ordered the furnace well heated and had them thrown into it. That was the end of the three men, and Jack was well rid of them.

107. Uncle Green and Jack

Thomas Williams, Harmony Hall, Cock-pit country

Uncle Green is a rich old man and he never married. Jack is a young man and is poor and preparing to get married, but cash is hard to get; so he t'ink to get somet'ing from Uncle Green. So he appoint his wedding for a day an' invite Uncle Green. So when de day came, he make bargain wid his cook an' everybody, make up good fire in de kitchen an cook good all what dey have. An' make way outside in open yard where all de guests can sit, an' dere he provide vessels an' stones, each pot have his own place. Pick up de pot hot off de fire, put on de stone. No fire under dat; everyt'ing shut down quite close; no heat escape. So all de guests came from church, coming to dinner. So, nearly to dinner-time, somebody say, "Hi! how is it nearly dinner-time an' not'ing doing? All de pot is on de stone an' no fire under it!" All de chief men know all dat will happen, so dey say, "Never min', frien's, keep quiet, we soon have dinner!" Guests say, "All right, dis is strange wedding!" When dinner-time, Jack, de bride, come out an' say, "Frien's, we soon have dinner. I have a shell an' a whip which know dere duty, an' wi' do it as I speak to dem." So when de hour come, he rise up an' took de shell an' de whip an' came out in de yard among de cooking vessels dat was on de stone, an' blow de shell, to-hoo, to-hoo, to-o, an' fire de whip at de same time an' say, "Boil, pots, boil!" He did dat twice, an' said, "Butler an' cooks, everyt'ing to your posts!" Each one came an' take charge of what dey have to occupy. Jack stand up dere an' say, "Come, now, cook, dish up an' hand to de butler!" So all de guests looking wid amazement and wonder, looking how t'ings going to be. As dey lift up de cover, de steam begin to fly out of every pot and evert'ing well cooked!

Uncle Green propose to get married too an' propose to buy de shell an' de whip. "How much you take for de shell an' whip, Mr. Jack?" Jack say, "Oh, Uncle Green, me hatful of money." His hat was a big hat. Uncle Green send t'ree time to de bank to draw his hat full of gold and silver, notes, an' everyt'ing whatever he could find to fill up his hat.

No instruction given to him how doze t'ings were cooked before and never ask how t'ing was done; say, "Only blow de shell an' crack whip an' everyt'ing wi' cook." So wedding day came, an' he invite, an' prepare to marry today. He kill an' cut up an' put up everyt'ing in de pot wid cold water, put on de cold stone outside in de yard. When de hour for dinner come, say, "Frien's, keep quiet; we soon have dinner." De same t'ing as Jack said before he said, only not'ing of fire. So as de cook take up de cover, everyt'ing is raw same way as it was put in. Say, "Good heavens! dat fellow Jack deceive me. Wonder where I will fin' him!" an' some one say he is at home.

Jack know what will happen. He make himself plain in de way for anyone to see. Constable an' cart come, take up Jack, t'row him into a bag an' carry him to Uncle Green. Uncle Green say, "I want your life! Take him on to de sea an' drown him." So while dey driving on going over a bridge nearly got to de sea, Jack said to de cart-man, "You driving me on an' you forget you' valuable golden horse-whip! Put me on de water-table at de road-side lef' me dere, go for you' whip." While he dere, Jack commence to cry in de bag, "Don' wan' king! Carry me go tu'n king an' I don' wan' king!" A poor old man was passing by at de same time, hear de cry, stop, listen. He was a shepherd driving sheep to de pasture. He say, "'top! what a foolish bwoy! Bwoy, if you don' wan' to go an' tu'n king, come out an' mek me go!" Old man jump in de cart an' loose de bag, an' Jack come out de bag. Old man quick go down in de bag an' Jack tie him an' tek charge of de flock of sheep an' drive dem on. Cart-man come an' take his seat an' drive on wid de ol' man; so drive to de sea, take up de bag an' dump de ol' man. He was drown. So came home to Uncle Green. Say, "Did you drown him?"—"Yes."—"A rascal dat!"

Some day after, Uncle Green was going on de road in de district an' hear big flock of sheep before him coming. Said, "Dat voice is not Jack voice?" When he get up to sheep, sheep pass, Jack arrive, dey meet up. He say, "Stop, Jack!" Jack say, "Yes, sir?"—"You alive?"—"Yes, sir! an' if you t'row me furder I would get gold an' diamond; where you t'row me, it only sheep an' goat I get dere!"—"All right, bwoy! I forgive everyt'ing in a hurry, you go an' show me where de gold an' diamon' is!" An' so it was done. Jack drive de cart himself. When he get to a shallow place he say, "It is here de sheep an' goats are."—"I don' want e! Go on, go where de gold an' diamond is!" Drive on furder to de bank, take up de bag, t'row him in de deep water and drown him. An' dat was de end of de craving man, Uncle Green, an' Jack take all his riches.

108. Big Begum and Little Begum

Emily Alexander, Mandeville

There was two sons named Big Begum and Little Begum. Big Begum was very rich ane Little Begum was very poor. One day, Little Begum found a bag of money and sent to Big Begum to borrow his quart pan to measure the money. Big Begum was very envious, didn't like to see Little Begum prosper. So he wondered what Little Begum was doing with the quart pan. He got some grease and greased the bottom of the pan to find out Little Begum measured the money and, not looking in the pan to see that a coin had fastened in the bottom, sent it back to Big Begum. Big Begum saw the money in the pan and was surprised to know where Little Begum got this money from, so he threatened Little Begum if he did not tell him he would kill him.

So Little Begum told him that he had killed three of his horses, carried the meat to the market and hung it up in the market crying out, "Fresh meat for sale, bit a pound!" Big Begum now went home, killed three of his horses and carried the meat to the market and gave the same alarm; but no one came to buy it. So he was so sorry!

He went back home, called Little Begum, put him in a bag and tied him on a tree to stay till he came back. While Little Begum was there, he saw a man passing with a herd of sheep and he cried out. The man went up and asked what was the matter. He said that Big Begum wanted him to go to him and he did not want to go. So the man with the herd of sheep said he wanted to go, and Little Begum told him to take him out the bag if he wished to get there. The man took him out and went into the bag; Little Begum tied it as tight as he could, and the man told him to take charge of the herd of sheep. So he went away with the herd of sheep, leaving the man there.

Big Begum came up now with his cutlass and chopped the bag so fine that he could hardly believe it was a man, and buried it. So when he buried it, he went round the corner whistling and singing beautiful songs, feeling quite happy that he had killed Little Begum. But as he turned the corner, he saw Little Begum with the herd of sheep. He was so surprised! He said, "Is that you, Little Begum? I thought I had chopped you up a while ago and buried you!" Little Begum said, "If you had chopped me up a little finer and buried me a little deeper, I would get a herd of cows instead of a herd of sheep!" So Big Begum told Little

Begum to chop him up as fine and bury him as deep, so he might get the cows. So Little Begum chopped him up very fine and buried him. That was the End of Big Begum!

109. The Fool and the Wise Brother

Emily Alexander, Mandeville

ONCE A LADY HAD TWO sons; one was very foolish and the other was very wise. The wise one was hired to look after some sheep while the foolish one was to stay at home and mind the mother. One day the mother became very ill and the wise brother had to leave his work and come home, so he sent the foolish brother to go mind the sheep. So the foolish boy took a stick and broke the legs of the sheep and brought them home in the yard.

The wise brother had on a bath on the fire for the mother. It was piping hot. So the wise brother went to the owner of the sheep to tell what had happened to the sheep and to ask for pardon, so he told the foolish brother to take off the pot off the fire and give the mother a sponging while he was away. The foolish brother took off the piping bath and put his mother in a tub and poured the hot bath on her, and she died.

When the wise brother came home and found that his mother was dead, he was so disappointed because the owner of the sheep said as soon as their mother died he would take away their lands to pay for his sheep. So the sheep-owner took away the land and left them with only an iron gate. So both of them lifted the iron gate on their backs and began to travel. As they reached a tree they sat down to rest. While they were there, they saw a band of robbers coming; so both of them with the iron gate mounted the tree. The robbers came and sat under the tree and began to eat. But they had no custard and no vinegar and they wanted some. So the foolish brother in the tree said, "Brother, I want to werine!" So he said, "You may do so," and so he did. The robbers underneath saw it coming down. Thinking it was vinegar, they took a pan and caught some and said, "Thank the Lord! the Lord has sent vinegar for us." Again the foolish brother said, "I want to dédé!" So he did, and the robbers caught some, thinking it was custard, and said, "Thank the Lord! the Lord has sent down custard for us." So both of them in the tree now became tired of holding the iron gate, so they dropped it. The robbers were so frightened that they ran away leaving everything, and the two brothers came down out of the tree and took up all the money that was left and a knife.

The robbers sent one of the men to see what it was, and the two brothers took the knife and cut off his tongue and sent him back. When the robbers saw him coming, they ran to meet him and asked him what was the matter. He could only say to them, "Bla, bla, bla!" They were so frightened that they started running, he running after them calling out "Bla! bla! bla!" They ran until they were out of breath and fell down and could go no further.

110. The Children and the Witch

Emily Alexander, Mandeville

THERE WAS A POOR MAN and his wife and two children. He had nothing to give them but a slice of bread and cold water for the day. So one day he got up, took the children into the bush and pretended to be chopping the tree; then, as the children were playing, slipped away. When the wife asked for the children, he told her he had left them in the bush and she fretted and worried all day. Life became easier for them day by day, and the man became sorry that he had left them in the wood.

The children, when they missed their father, started to travel through the wood to see if they could find their way home. A little black bird said to them, "Follow me and I will show you your way home!" but this little black bird was an Old Witch. It carried them to a house made out of nothing but cakes, sweets and all manner of nice things, and then the bird vanished away from them. But they were so glad to get the cakes and sweets that they began eating at once. Immediately as they touched the first cake, the door of the house opened and a very ugly-looking blind old woman came out to them and asked them what they were doing there; so they told her how they had been lost in the bush. She took them into the house, put one in a cage and had one to do all the work of the house. Every evening she went to feed the one in the cage, and asked him to stick out his hand to see if he was getting fat; so the one left in the house gave him a bone to stretch out instead, because the Old Witch was blind and could only feel. The one in the cage was getting very fat and rosy. One day she went to the cage and asked him to stretch out his hand and the child stretched out the bone; so she became very impatient, said she couldn't wait any longer and would kill him that very day for dinner, and asked the one in the house to heat up the oven. Then the Witch told the one in the house to see if the oven was hot enough; the Witch was going to shut the door on her and let her stay in there and bake. But the girl was smart and said she did not know how to get into it, she must show her the way. As the Witch went into the oven, she pushed her in and shut the door, and the Witch stood in there squealing till she was burned to death. Then the girl ran and took the boy out of the cage, took some of the cakes and nice things off the house, and ran to their own home. The parents were so glad to see them that they kept a ball for them that night, and they told the story how they had killed the Witch.

111. The Boy and the Mermaid

Emily Alexander, Mandeville

ONCE A LITTLE BOY WENT to the river to bathe. He was washed away to sea and his parents heard nothing about him, but he was told before going that if he went he would be drowned.

But he was a smart little boy. A mermaid came and took him and carried him to the bottom of the sea and asked him certain questions: If he ate fish? he said "No." If he ate beef? he said "No." If he ate mutton? he said "No." If he ate pork? he said "No." If he had said "Yes," the mermaid would have killed him, because its body was made of fish, beef, mutton and pork. So, as he didn't eat any of those things, the mermaid carried him to the shore, threw him out, and a sheep took him up. The master of the sheep asked him certain questions,—where he was from and what was his name. He told him and they carried him to his home. They were so glad to see him they went and invited friends to come and help them enjoy themselves and make merry.

112. Difficult Tasks

Julia Gentle, Santa Cruz Mountains

A BOY LIVE WITH A very rich gentleman, and he have no children and he believe that when he die, the boy get all the fortune; so he want to kill the boy. And he throw out a barrel of rice and say boy must pick up every grain before he come back. And dead mother come and pick up every grain.

And when he come and see the boy pick up all the rice, say, "You mean to get all me fortune!" He tell the boy must go to the headman town and carry away the duppy-man one bell. An the dead mother go with the boy and the mother tell the boy what time the duppy lie down he must mash them hard. And he go take the bell out the middle of the town where the duppy is, and must run to four cross-roads before he come home with the bell. Then all the duppy scatter; one go one crossroad and one another, and the boy run home to massa with the bell.

Then after he carry the bell come home, the man say, "I don' know what to do! I believe you going to get me fortune!" And him tak one sword, the sharpest sword, and give the boy the dull sword and say, "We now play sword!" And the boy take the dull sword and kill the man and get all the fortune.

113. The Grateful Beasts

James Smith, Claremont, St. Anne

A POOR MAN WAS ONCE traveling and saw a dog and a lion and a crow and ants fighting over dead prey. The poor man had nothing but a knife. He said, "Let me try and see if I can help you all." He cut one quarter gave to the lion, cut one quarter gave to the dog, cut one quarter gave to the crow, gave the last quarter to the ants. The lion said, "My good man, I have nothing to pay for you kindness, but any trouble you get into just call upon the lion and you shall be ten times stronger than the lion." The dog said, "Any trouble you get into just say, 'The grey the dog,' and you shall be ten times quicker than the dog." The crow said, "Say, 'The grey the crow,' and you shall fly ten times higher than the crow." The ants said, "Say, 'The grey the ants,' and you shall be ten times smaller than the ants."

Some time after that, a great seven-headed giant who had one daughter, made a rule that any man coming to his house he would surely put to death. That poor man heard about the saying of the seven-headed giant and said he would marry the daughter. They laughed at him, but he found himself at the giant's yard. There he found the daughter, but the giant was not at home. He told her that he would marry her, and she said that the giant would kill him. He said that he would give the giant a fight. He went back the second day, went back the third day. The father caught him there, said to his daughter in the house, "Aye! I smell fresh blood!"—"No, papa, nothing of the kind!" The giant went into the room she was hiding the man in. The man said, "The grey the ants," and he was ten times smaller than ants; found his way through the crevices, ran down the stair-case, found himself out on the green, and he came back into his man's shape. The giant came out and caught hold of him. He called upon the lion and he was ten times stronger than a lion. He flashed off three of the giant's heads.

All the giant's treasure was hidden in a round hill and the key was two marbles on an iron rod. The two marbles and the rod dropped from the giant's pocket. "The grey the dog," and he was ten times quicker than a dog and caught the marbles and the rod. The giant caught after him and he said, "The grey the crow," and flew ten times higher than a crow, and flew down and hit off the other four heads. The giant was lying down dead. With the advice of the girl he walked straight up to the hill, joined the iron rod on the top of the hill, set the two marbles at the other side at the foot of the hill, and both marbles rolled to the iron rod. So the man went in and got all that hidden treasure and he married the daughter and got all the possessions.

So you can never be too strong to be brought low.

114. Jack and the Bean-stalk

Clarence Tathum, Mandeville

JACK'S FATHER DIED AN' LEAVE he an' his mother. And all them money finish an' they didn't have more than one cow leave. An' the mother gave him to go to the market an' sell it. When he catch part of the way, he swap it for a cap of bean.

When he get home, the mother get annoyed and t'row away the bean, so he get dread if the mother beat him. He went away an' sat by the roadside, an' he saw an old lady coming. 'He beg him something. he show him a house on a high hill, an' him tol' him de man live up dere is de man rob all him fader riches an' he mus' go to him an' he get somet'ing. An' so he went home back.

An' so in de morning, he see one of de bean-tree grow a large tree outside de window, an' 'tretch forth over de giant house; an' he went up till he reach to de giant house. An' when he go, de giant was not at home an' he ax de giant wife to put him up an' give him something to eat. De wife tell him she will give him something to eat, but she can't put him up, for anywhere him put him de giant will find him when him come home. He said to de giant wife him must tek a chance. De wife put him into a barrel. When de giant come home, de giant smelled him. He ax him wife where him get fresh blood. So she told him she have a little somet'ing to make a pudding for him tomorrow. Said 'he mus' bring it. Said no, better to have fresh pudding tomorrow than to have it tonight. After de giant finish his dinner, started to count his money. He fall asleep on de table, an' Jack went down take be bag of money an' went away to his house. He climb on de bean-tree right outside his window an' went home back an' gave his mother the money.

115. Jack and the Devil

Richard Pottinger, Claremont, St. Anne

DEVIL HAD HIS COMPANY IN his house, had a woman also locked up while Jack, his servant, was heating the oven. Somebody was expected from home. Jack was very fond of that girl, promised her that if anybody will come from home, he will keep heating the oven. The two of them arrange that she will keep singing—

> *"Wah wah oo, wah wah oo, wah wah oo,*
> *Nobody coming from Prince of Wales?"*

Jack now (answers),

> *"No, no, madame; no, no, madame; no, no, madame;*
> *Nobody coming from Prince of Wales."*

The master came to the window; "Jack, is the oven hot?"—"No, Master, not yet hot." Jack put in two bundles of wood more. About an hour after, the girl began the same song. Jack gave the same reply. Master came again; "Jack, is the oven hot?"—"No, Master, not yet hot."
The girl's father came. The girl started singing—

> *"Wah wah oo, wah wah oo, wah wah oo,*
> *Nobody coming from Prince of Wales?"*

Jack says,

"Yes, yes, madame! yes, yes, madame! yes, yes, madame!
Somebody coming from Prince of Wales!"

The master came to the window; "Jack, is the oven hot?"—"Yes, Master, red-hot!" Coming down the staircase the father drew a revolver and shot him. Jack has to put him in the oven, and Jack, the girl, and all the company make a feast of him. The father took Jack and the girl back to his house and married them both for life.

116. Jack's Riddle

Clarence Tathum, Mandeville

A LITTLE BOY ONCE HEARD of a king's daughter who would answer any riddle, and so he told his mother that he was going to ask the king's daughter a riddle. Whatever riddle the king's daughter asks him, if he can't answer, the king's daughter will kill him; or else, he will get the king's daughter. And the mother made some dumpling and gave to him, made six, poisoned one. And he eat four and gave two to the donkey he was riding, and one of those two was the one that was poisoned. So "Poor Lo" died. So seven John-crow came to eat Poor Lo; so while the seven John-crow were eating Poor Lo, they were dying one after another by the poison of Poor Lo. And he saw an orange-tree with one ripe orange on it, and he went and picked it and eat it, and he picked up one under the tree and eat it. And Jack went to the king's daughter, and she asked him the riddle; and after he answered it, he asked her this one:

"Two kill one and one kill seven; the top of the tree was sweet, but the bottom was sweeter yet."

117. Jack as Fortune-teller

T. Brown, Claremont, St. Anne

DER WAS A DAY JACK says he was a fortune-teller. De king call him dat his wife los' her marriage ring and he want him to tell him where it go. Jack didn't know not'ing all de same, but jus' working his head.

De king got t'ree servant in his house. De t'ree of dem steal de ring.
De king give Jack four days to tell him. One mo'ning, one carry Jack
breakfas'. Jack says, "Praise de Lord, I got one!" Same day, one carry
his dinner; same day, one carry his supper. Jack says, "Praise de Lord,
I got de t'ree!" (Jack meant he get t'ree meals, but de servant think
Jack mean them.) One of the servant go in the house, say, "Let us
tell Jack we get de ring, for he know it." De t'ree of dem come to
Jack one night and told Jack dat 'ey steal de ring. Jack said, "Oh, yes,
I did know a long time dat it you t'ief it!" Jack says, "If I tell de king
about de ring, king will behead de th'ree of you." Jack says, "Make a
little ball and put de ring in it and put it down a big turkey's mout'."
De morning, nine o'clock, de king called Jack to tell him where
his wife's ring goes; if Jack can not tell him, he will kill Jack. Jack
says, "If you want to know how you' wife ring go, kill dat big turkey
an' look in his craw." Dey kill de turkey, an' saw de ring; and from
dat day, de king believe what Jack do and give Jack his daughter to
marry. And I pass roun' de house last week and I saw dem an' dey
give me a good piece of beef-bone. Dear how Jack got his richness
by working his head!

118. Robin as Fortune-teller

Henry Spence, Bog, Westmoreland

Robin fawn himself to be fortune-teller. So he bet a lot of money
dat whatever dey have fe dinner tonight, him will tell it. So Robin name
Fox,—call him "Mr. Fox Robin,"—an' dey didn't know his name. So
it was a fox underneat' de dish fe de dinner. So when him come in,
frighten', t'ink him goin' to lose, him sit down, say, "Aye, poor Fox is
caught today!" When dey hear him say dis, everybody give a shout.
Him win; for it was a fox underneat' de dish.

Once de good man again go out to shoot. So him coming home,
hear about Fox too,—same Fox. So him catch a robin redbreast an' kill
it an' roast it an' put it under de dish de very same as dey do de fox. So
at dinner when he come to a certain time, say, "I want to know what
underneat' de dish now, Mr. Fox?" So said, "Well, poor Robin is well
caught today!"

119. Jack and the Grateful Dead

Richard Morgan, Santa Cruz Mountains

A BOY AN' A GIRL made match to marry, an' doze people who dey call de fairy t'ief away de girl from Jack. But dey give one anodder different name; dis girl name "Catch 'em" an' dis boy name "If-you-can".

An' Jack was travelling. When he get part of de way, he see whole heap of people beatin' a dead man. He say, "O my! what de reason dey do dis?" Dey said, "De man owe me a lot of money!" Jack pay all de money an' bury de man. He went a little furder an' see anodder an' he do de same. He went a little way off again, he see anodder, he do de same.

So he get broke now. He hear dat de fairy want a servant. De fairy said, "Yes, I want a servant!" an' gi' him every key open all de door excep' one room. Jack said, "All right, sir!" De fairy is a people dey go out every day. Jack open every door, an' after him open de las' door he fin' de girl in dat room. An' 'he say, "Jack, what you open dis door for? De fairy bin goin' kill you, for dey dey got me here an' fatten to kill." Jack said, "I am jus' as smart as dem!" an' tek down de girl an' comb her hair, ketch her louse, gi' her somet'ing to eat an' hang her up same way. When de fairy come an' say, "Jack, you goin' into dis room?" Jack said, "No, sir." De fairy tek de key, he walk in de door an' fin' de girl same way as he leave her.

Every day Jack do de same t'ing, till de las' day he took down de girl an' dey walk. He goin' in a vessel. De girl was so pretty, one of de men dat in de vessel grudge Jack an' fling Jack overboard. Anodder little boy, gi' de name of Jack, he t'row one piece of board, said, "Poor man! paddle on dis." An' de girl is de king daughter who was going to marry to Jack de nex' day. An' Jack paddle till him get one part of de sea upon some stone an' sit down hol'ing his head. Dat was night. Pelican fly an' pick him in his head, gi' him a piece of bread, tek him up an' sail wid him drop him into anodder place. Anodder pelican tek him an' sail wid him drop him into anodder place again. De las' pelican gi' him somet'ing to eat, fly wid him right into town. So dat was de t'ree dead men he buried; dat t'ree dead save his life.

Nex' morning in de whole town nobody to be found in de street. An' when Jack couldn't get a house to rent, all de house was rented, one woman said 'he don' get nowhere only a loft to de roadside. Jack said, "Dat's de place I want!" an' was dere until de couple going to church. Den, after she come at de said place, Jack look out an' saw her, an' Jack said, "Catch him!" De girl said, "If-you-can!" an' she call to de coachman to turn back home to de yard. An' after she went home, she sent a constable t'rough de whole town, an' everyone he bring she said no. De las' one de ol' lady said, "Only one man lef' here an' he drunk, for he drink a great bottle of rum!" but Jack do dat in gladness as he saw de girl. An' de girl said, "Bring him come!" An' after him come, he catch him an' kiss him an' goin' in de house bathe an' shine himself an' tell all what distress happen to him.

Dey catch de man what do dis t'ing, hang him by de p'int of his tongue.

120. The Boy and his Master

Richard Morgan, Santa Cruz Mountains

DER IS OLD WITCH. ONE boy larnin' old witch, too. De man want a book-clerk. De boy go to him and said, "You want a book-clerk, sir?" An' say, "Yes, but you cannot read?" Boy say no, an' say, "All right, you shall be my clerk." He never trouble de boy on de book for a long time. When he going tek up de book, 'e say, "Oh-h-h-h! you expect to be my master!" an' de man say, "Go home!"

Him mudder an' fader was poor. He said, "Ma, I gwine to turn a fat pig tomorrow; kyar' me go sell, don' lef' de rope on me." He ma get two pound. Nex' day he say, "Ma, I gwine to turn a pretty mare; kyar' me sell me, don' lef' de rope." When de fader get part of de way, he meet a man. De man say, "Ho-o-o, what a pretty mare! How much you want?"— "One hundred." De ol' man go to tek off de rope. De man said, "What a damn fool is you! I buy de mare an' you want de rope!" De Old Witch tek de mare. At de same time de Old Witch know dat de mare is de boy an' de boy know dat is de Old Witch. So he hitch him in de market an' gwine in de shop to tek a drink. Some school-children gwine past. De mare said, "Do, you kyan' slip off dis rope off me head?" De chil'ren said, "'top! you ever hear a horse talk?" De mare said, "Never mind! you slip it off." As dey slip off de rope, de mare gallop away. De chil'ren call out, "You' mare get away!"

De Old Witch come out. He turn a stallion, an' two race fo' it. An' de mare up again a pigeon-hawk an' she fly. De Old Witch turn a big fowl-hawk an' dey sail in de air. De mare turn a dove an' sail till she 'py a house wid glass windeh. De dove sail right t'ru de windeh, drop into a woman lap; de dove turn a ring, get on de woman finger. De fowl-hawk fly exactly to de door. When de hawk fly away, de ring come off de finger an' turn de boy an' tell de woman a man will come here in de mo'ning; he will have her marry fo' dis ring, but don' receive it. Nex' day de boy turn de ring, get on de finger. De man dribe up an' said, "You have a ring here?" De woman said yes. He said, "I give you one husband," an' de woman said yes and slipped off de ring to give to de man. De ring drop on de floor an' turn a corn-grain. De man come out of de buggy, turn a rooster to pick up de corn-grain. De corn-grain jump up, turn a puss an' wipe off de cock head. So dat de boy get up and tek de buggy an' go to de Old Witch yard and tek all what he get.

So de boy learn one mark more dan de Old Witch.

121. The Language of Beasts

Richard Morgan, Santa Cruz Mountains

ONE BOY WAS ALONG WID a man. He was a shepherd boy; every Wednesday he go in de wilderness go look after his master sheep. He saw one snake. De snake said, "Do, I beg you carry me go to me fader; but when you go, if me fader give you money, don' you tek it, but ax him to give you de knowledge of every animal." So de boy tek de snake to his fader. When he go, de snake ax him if he want money. He said, "No, I wan' to understan' de knowledge of every animal." De snake tol' him to lie down, an' he spit in his mouth an' tol' him whatever animal dat he hear talk he mus' not tell it to nobody, fo' de day he venture to talk it he shall surely die.

De odder Wednesday he went de same place, he saw some pigeon on one tree. De pigeon was cooing, an' de pigeon tell him he mus' come an' dig under de tree an' he will fin' a lot of money. De boy went an' dig, an' he fin' de money. He tek it home to his master. His master deliver all dat money to him, he tek it, settle himself an' married a wife.

One evening him an' his wife went for a ride. He was before, de lady was behin'. De horse turn round and whicker to de mare which de lady was riding. De mare answer him an' said, "I kyan' go wid you; for you, it is two of you, but me, it is four of us. I have to carry meself an' me colt, de missis an' de missis baby in her, so I cannot walk fas' as you." De man turn roun' an' laugh. De lady said, "Why de reason let de two animal whicker an' you look pon me an' laugh? Der is somet'ing in dis matter!" She nag her husband to tell her de meaning why mek him laugh. De husband said to her, "De day dat I tell you, I will surely die. Sen' for a carpenter mek me box an' den I wi' tell you!" De carpenter come mek de box, an' he went an' lie down in it.

He got one rooster in his yard. De rooster come near de box an' begin to crow. De missis said, "Oh, go away! makin' such a noise over yo' master head!" De master said, "Let de bird stay!" De rooster said to his master, "Master, you fool to gi' up yo' life fo' de count of woman! Look how much wife I have in de worl', an' de least nonsense all of dem come round me, I begin to peck 'em an' walk away from dem. So, Master, you come out of de box an' tek yo' supple-jack an' go in de house give yo' wife two good lick, an' den you fin' if she would 'noy you again." De man do so. He got up, he went in de house, he tek de supple-jack an' hit her t'ree lick over de shoulder; an' from dat day de woman never ax him a word again.

122. The Three Pieces of Advice

Richard Morgan, Santa Cruz Mountains

DER IS A MAN; HE married; he got t'ree chil'ren, he became poor. He said to his wife, "I goin' to look somet'ing to do." She said, "Yes, me dear husban'." He went an' walk one hundred mile. When he got to a pen de master said, "You little too late; I jus' got a butcher dis mo'ning." He walk anodder one hundred mile an' when he go he succeed a butcher. He was doin' his work one year, never drew no money—one hundred pound a year. When de year was up, de missis said to him, "Out of you money an' t'ree advice, which one you rather?" He said, "I rather de t'ree advice." She give him one revolver an' give him a loaf of bread an' give him some money to serve him on de way; was not to touch de bread till him get home. De t'ree advice—"Not to forsake de bridge which you cross; not to interfere in politics; you mustn't in haste in temper." An' him tek his journey.

When he was going, he went to tek anodder road; he remember de first advice, mustn't forsake de bridge which he cross. He go on a little furder. He saw some people beatin' one dead man; he went to call to dem, but he remember de second advice. He pass. When he go on till he saw his home, he saw his wife an' his chil'ren an' a man walkin' side on side. He took de revolver to shoot de man, he remember de t'ird advice; de missis said, "You mus' not haste in temper," an' he put it by. When he went on a little furder, it was his wife bredder hear dat de husband was not at home, so come to look for his sister.

When dey goin' in de house he began to tell how many mile he went, an' he say to his wife, "De missis gave me t'ree advice, out of me money which of dem I rather; I said I rather de t'ree advice, and she give me dis loaf of bread; not to cut it till I reach home, but she give me my pocket-money." De wife said, "What about de t'ree advice an' lef' yo' money!" De husband said, "I can't help it." De chil'ren cry out, "Papa, cut de bread! papa, cut de bread!" Tek de knife, an' after him cut de bread, de one hundred pound scatter out upon de table.

So de t'ree advice, if he turn a different road he never will see home. De second advice, doze people was beating de dead man, if him was to call to 'em, dem people would destroy him. An' de t'ird advice, he would shoot his own bredder-in-law.

123. Three Brothers and the Life-tree

Richard Morgan, Santa Cruz Mountains

A WOMAN GOT T'REE SON. One day he said, "Mamma, I gwine out to seek fe' a little work." She said, "Yes, me chile, but care me little last son!" De mudder bake two pone an' after dey travel, de little bredder said, "Bredder, I hungry!" He said, "De only way you will get dis pone, let I pluck out one of yo' eye." De little boy said, "Pluck it out now," an' he did so. After dey walk a far way again, de little bredder cry out, "Bredder, I hungry!" He said, "De only way you will taste de odder piece, let I pluck out de odder eye." De little boy said, "What mus' I do after I hungry?" An' him pluck out de odder eye an' gi' him de balance of pone lef'. An' de two bredder walk, lef' dat poor one.

When night come, he went feeling. He feel a tree. He went up into de tree. After midnight, he hear people talkin' come on an' stop right under de tree. So i' was two duppy. One king from de day de king was born, he blin'. De duppy said, "If people know dat dis tree was a life tree, dey would tek it an' cure de king eye."

Me'while de poor blin' boy hearing dem. De boy feel an' tek de leaf an' rub his two eye. De two eye were open. De boy came down. Nex' day morning tek two of de leaves an' went to de king yard. After he went de soldier said, "My man, what you want?" He said, "I want to see de king." Dey let him in. When he gwine to de king he said, "O king!" He said, "What do you want?" De boy said, "I hear dat yo' eye blind; I come to open it" He said, "O my boy, you cannot open my eye again!" De boy said, "I will open it; but when I rub it you mus' not mek alarm." De boy took de leaf out of his pocket and rubbed de king eye. De king eye were open, an' de king let de boy married to his daughter.

An de same week dem two bredder which injure his little bredder eye hear dat de same young king which married lately have plenty of work. So de two bredder went in an' ax fe work. De king said, "O me men, if you come a little sooner! my son-in-law jus' go down to de village." Dey went down after him. When de men go down, 'ey saw him own bredder an' do not know him at all. Dey said, "Good-morning, king!" Dey said, "Yo' fader-in-law send we down here to get some work." De king said, "Oh, yes!" He said, "Seem like you feel hungry." Dey said, "Oh, yes, king!" He let de people den pick some breadfruit an' dey roast it. Me'while dey eating dey was talkin'. De king said, "But, my men, where is de odder bredder that traveled togedder?" He said, "He knock up in de way, so we have to leave him; so we don' know whether if he alive or not." De king said, "Dis is yo' lost brother which you pluck out de eye for that two piece of pone!" An' dey was 'stonish.

So de bredder said all how him get de eye open, an' dey never stop to work again; dey travel on to de said life tree, an' when dey get dere, dey go up in de tree. Part of de night dey hear two somebody talkin'; soon as dey ketch to de tree dey stop dere to res'. One of de duppy said, "But you know, dis odder night when we was talkin' here, some one mus' hear me when I was talkin' 'bout dis life tree, for I hear dat de king eye open." An' after he said dat, one said, "I scent fresh blood!" an' he run right up in de tree an' ketch de two men an' break dem neck.

An' come to a time de king an' his wife go pay de mudder a visit. An' 'e mudder askin' for de rest. He tell his ma all what de bredder hev done to him, an' if don't two duppy, 'he never would see him no more.

124. The Skilful Brothers

Richard Morgan, Santa Cruz Mountains

ONE WOMAN GOT T'REE SON. One of de son name Look-up-in-de-sky, de odder one name Fling-me-stick, de t'ird one name Brer Buck.

One day, Look-up-in-de-sky saw a eagle flyin' away wid de mudder. He said, "Fling-me-stick, de eagle tek away me mudder!" Fling-me-stick lick out of de eagle mout'. Brer Buck stoop down an' ketch de mudder. An' de mudder lef' t'irty pound fe t'ree of dem. Out of doze t'ree son, which of dem deserve de money?

Some said, "Look-up-in-de-sky deserve it!" Odder said, "Fling-me-stick!" De nex' one said, "Brer Buck!" But if Look-up-in-de-sky didn't see de mudder, de eagle would fly away wid her. If Fling-me-stick didn't fling an' lick out de mudder out of de eagle mout', she would be gone. If Brer Buck didn't stoop down an' ketch de mudder, she would mash up. So, out of de t'ree of dem, de t'ree deserve de ten pound apiece.

125. The Three Sillies

Charles Roe, Maroon Town, Cock-pit country

THERE WAS A YOUNG MAN one day was courting a young lady. So when he got to the house, it was one of the young ladies and father and mother in the yard. So the mother said to the daughter, "You mus' go look for some orange for the gentleman breakfas'." So when the young lady gone, the mother wait till she catches the young lady come with the orange. So when she (the mother) come, she say, "Hi! what you doing so long you can't come with the orange?" So the young lady say to her, "Mamma, me considering when me have the first pic'niney, what fe gi' 'im name." So the mother say, "Yes, missis." So they sit down and was considering the name. So the father wait until he can't see them come. Him start, an' when he go to orange tree him say, "Hi! what you so long you can't come yet?" The mother say, "Me husband, me an' me daughter considering what to give the first pickney name." So the father sit down and say, "Yes, missis, we consult now."

So the man there waiting say, "Let me see what these three people gone look for orange in the house, can't come yet!" So when he come he say, "What you a doing so long? You no come pick this orange fe me, I hungry killing me at the yard." Said young lady, "My dear, we considering the first pickney we have, what mus' we give him name." The young man said, "I goin' away. So if I meet t'ree fool as unoo (you), I will come back an' marry you."

So he start, an' when he get to the firs' cross-road, he see one man he wet him finger an' pick it up an' grab it out of the road. So he say,

"What you doing?" The man say, "I pick up the gravel out of the road, see if I could pick out all of the gravel out of the road." The man say, "I saw one fool!"

Him pass him an' go on, till he see another one cut two stick an' hol' up his trousers an' run jump see if he can jump into his trousers. So he say, "Oh! you fool, hol' your trousers an' put you' two foot in. This make two fool I have buck up since I leave the other three fool!"

So pass this one an' go on to the sea-side an' see another one get a pan an' fetch out water, see if he could dry the sea. So him say, "Well done, O you fool! This make three fool since I lef' the other three fool behin'. How mus' you dry the sea? You may fetch water until you are dead you never may dry the sea."

So then he turn back. So when he got back he say, "Well, my dear, I buck up three fool fooler than you three; so I come back to marry you."

126. A Misunderstanding

Florence Tomlinson, Lacovia

THERE WAS A GENTLEMAN ENGAGED to a young lady and he was out riding one evening. And the young gentleman made the lady believe he was rich, go along to a logwood property and told her "all was his". And go on an' go on an' come to another property covered with stock—cow and sheep—and told her it was his. That was two property now. And went to the next property where were horses and mules, and said (wiping his face), "All these are mine, me dear." The lady believed he was rich, and they got married and went home and lived together until all the house things were going, all the crockery was going, want a fresh supply. And she said to him, "Me dear, everything is going now, want a fresh supply. Let me have some money."

"No, me dear, I havn't got any."

"Then why don't you sell some of the things off some of the property?"

"Oh, I have no property, me dear!"

"Yes! don't you remember when we used to go out riding you showed me three properties? One had logwood, one had cows and sheep, and the next had horses. Why don't you sell some of those things?"

"Oh, ho! ho! ho! ho! me dear, I wipe with me pocket handkerchief and I mean me whiskers!"

127. Big-head, Big-belly, and Little-foot

a. Arthur Brown, St. Ann's Bay

ONCE THERE WAS A MAN have three sons, one name Big-head, one name Big-belly, one name Little-foot. Dey went for a walk one evening. Big-head saw a berry-tree. He went up on it an' pick one of de berry an' taste it. Big-belly ask him if it sweet. He bow his head; his head drop off. Big-belly laugh at him till his belly burst Little-foot start running home to tell the news, his foot broke. That was the end of the three.

b. James Smith, Claremont, St. Ann

THREE LITTLE BROTHER WENT OUT to catch meat. So them hunt till the day was in and caught nothing. Return home hungry and jokify, coming out of the forest saw a tar-apple tree have on two fruit on it. Big-Belly couldn't climb. Maugre-Foot couldn't climb. Maugre-Neck climb the tree, pull the first fruit, eat off that one. Pull the second fruit, bite it and tempting the others, his little head broke off fell on the ground. Big-belly laugh till him belly pop. Maugre-Foot set out run fo' carry home the news, till him little foot broke off a pass.

Jack man dory, this story done!

128. The Goat in the Lion's Den

Henry Spence, Bog, Westmoreland

GOAT WID TWO KIDS WERE trabbling one day long trabbling, an' trabble till almost evening, an' rain commence to fa' now. So 'eh see a great rock, an' mudder an' two kids went under de rock to shelter, didn't know dat was de lion house. So de lion see de t'ree goat coming, he grunt like a great rolling. De mudder of de goat frighten. 'He said to de lion, "Good-evening, minister!" an' de lion tell him "Evening." An' he said to de lion him looking fe a minister to baptize dese two kids, an' say, want to give dese two kid a name. De lion said to him, "Dis one name is 'Dinner' an' dis one name is 'Breakfas' tomorrow' an' you, de mudder, name is 'Dinner tomorrow'!"

So after him get dese t'ree name, de goat was well frighten how to come out back; an' de two kid hear de name dem got, so de heart commence to leap bup, bup, bup! De lion ax de mudder what's de matter wid de two kid. De mudder said, "As de room is so hot, dey seem terrify." An' de mudder said as dey is in heah, kyan' go, if he would jus' allow de two kid to go outside get a little air. De lion agree, until when dinner-time come on 'em mus' go in back. An' de mudder whisper to de two kid mus' mek de way as sharp as ever dey can mek it befo' dusk. So when de lion see it coming on evening an' no see de two kid come back, commence to roll again, she commence wonder how dem stay out too long, so ax de lion if de lion allow him to go bring dem back in befo' de time too late. De lion agree. An' when de mudder go out, neber see one back—eb'rybody gone!

Meaning of dat, a woman have more knowledge dan a man.

129. The Donkey, the Cat and the Lion's Head

Joseph Macfarlane, Moneague, St. Ann

ONE DAY A DONKEY AN' a cat was out trab'ling an' when dey went half way, dey saw some lion head, an' de cat pick i' up, put i' in de donkey hamper. An' when dey went round de corner, dey saw two lions working on de road, an' dey lef' de hamper roun' de corner wid de lion head. De lions said, "We are jus' having breakfas'!" De Donkey an de Cat said, "We have plenty!" Donkey said, "Brer Puss, you go tek up de lions' heads fe see which one we eat today." Puss went, took up de head an' said, "Dis one?" Donkey said, "De odder one." An' said, "Dis one?" Donkey said, "De odder one," till dey count about twenty (when it was only one). De lions whisper to each odder, say, "Dey kill so many lion one day, what you t'ink of we couple?" An' dey eat an' went home.

130. Clever Molly May

Emily Alexander, Mandeville

ONCE ANANSI WENT OUT TO invite a friend to dinner. Little Molly May was his servant, so he left her to roast a turkey for dinner. Anansi filled the wine-jug, laid the table, put on his frock coat and his top hat, took his walking-stick and went out for his friend. Molly May roasted the turkey. Seeing that it looked so nice and charming, she thought that she would take a piece; so she did, and it tasted so nice she took another piece. That tasted so nice she took a next piece and a sip of the wine, and she sipped and tasted till at last she had eaten up the whole turkey and drunk the whole of the wine.

She saw the master coming; so she ran in swift haste, took up the bones, fixed them nicely in the dish, covered the dish, and carried it and laid it on the table. When the master came, he sent the visitor into the house and said to Molly May, "Hullo, deh! everyt'ing all right?" She said, "Yes, sah! all is right." So the master took up the carving-knife and went outside to sharpen it. Molly ran inside and told the visitor that the master was sharpening the knife to cut off one of his hands; the visitor in swift haste left the house. Then Molly went outside and told the master that the visitor had eaten all the turkey and drunk the wine. The master ran through one door and, seeing all the bones on the table, went through the other. The visitor was running for his life and Anansi went running after him, calling "Leave one! leave one!" He meant leave one (side of) the turkey, but the visitor thought he meant one of his hands, so he ran for his life.

131. Dancing to Anansi's Fiddle

Sarah Vassel, Bog, Westmoreland

ASSONO A RUN A GANG. Assono sen' one of de men for water. When he go a take water, him couldn't take it; Anansi play fiddle into de water-hole—

"Zing a little ting!"

T'row down de gourd an' begin to dance. Assono a come to look fe de man. When he come, (Anansi stop playing). He call to him say, "Massa, no quarrel!" Him come give de massa de gourd a go fill it. Anansi begin playing. De Massa t'row down de gourd, begin dance. Assono dance till him drop. Anansi cut off him head an' tek de head make a water-cup.

132. Anansi claims the dinner

Edward Daley, Mandeville

ANANSI AN' CERTAIN NUMBER OF men was going to a certain place. Certain men give dey own names; Anansi start to give his name now, said, "Mine is 'Dem-men-came-here-las'-night'." When deh get where deh go to, deh bring out dinner. Deh say it is for 'de-men-came-here-las'-night'. Anansi claim de dinner, an' nobody else get any.

133. Anansi seeks his Fortune

Stanley Jones, Claremont, St. Ann

ANANSI WAS VERY POOR AND he went out to seek his fortune, but he had no intention of working. He clad himself in a white gown. And he met a woman. She said to him, "Who are you, sah? an' whe' you from?"—"I am jus' from heaven." The woman said, "Did you see my husban' dere?" He said, "Well, my dear woman, heaven is a large place; you will have to tell me his name, for perhaps I never met him." She said his name was James Thomas. Anansi said, "Oh, he is a good friend of mine! I know him well. He is a big boss up there and he's carrying a gang. But one trouble, he has no Sunday clo'es." The woman ran away and got what money she could together and gave it to Anansi to take to her husband.

But he wasn't satisfied with that amount; he wanted some more. He went on a little further and saw a man giving a woman some money and telling her to put it up for 'rainy day'. After the man had left, Anansi went up to the woman and told her he was "Mr. Rainy Day." She said, "Well, it's you, sah? My husband been putting up money for you for ten years now. He has quite a bag of it, and I'm so afraid of robbers I'm glad you come!" So Anansi took the money and returned home and lived contentedly for the rest of his days.

134. The Pannier-jar

Vessel Edwards, Retirement, Cock-pit country

THERE WAS A MAN AT slave time had a wife, and the wife kept two other men. The husband of that wife was working out. One night, one came first and then the house-master came home. And they had a big jar called a pannier-jar, and the wife took the man and put him into the pannier-jar. Afterward the other man came in, and when he saw the house-master was frightened and he told the house-master he had come to borrow the pannier-jar. The house-master told him he could take it, and the woman helped him up with the pannier-jar. And when he got part of the way, he said, "Poor me bwoy! if it wasn't for this pannier-jar, I would be dead tonight!" The other man in the pannier-jar said, "Brar, same meself!" And he got frightened and heaved down the pannier-jar, mashed it up and killed the man in there.

135. Anansi kills his Grandmother

William Cooper, Mandeville

ANANSI AN' TIGER WERE TRAVELLING. Anansi kill him old grandmother, him put him into a little hand-cart was shoving him t'ru de town. After him catch to a shop jes' like out here, de shopkeeper was a very hasty-temper man; an' went in de shop an' call fe some whiskey an' give it to one of de shopkeeper carry it to his grandmother. An' said he mus' go up to de han'-cart an' call twice. An' de ol' lady did not hear. So Anansi said to de shop-keeper him mus' holla out to de ol' lady; him sleeping. So de ol' lady didn't hear, he fire de glass in de ol' lady face, an' de ol' lady fell right over. Then the shop-keeper get so frighten he cry out to Anansi, say Anansi mustn't mek no alarm in de town; he will give him a bushel of money to mek him keep quiet.

So dem was going along an' borrow a quart can from Tiger an' was measuring dis money. Tiger said, "Where you get all dat money?" Anansi say, "I kill my ol' grandmother." Tiger, him went home an' kill his grandmother an' put her up in a little hand-cart an' was goin' along t'ru de town hollerin' out to all de people, "Who want a dead body to buy?" So Anansi said to Tiger he shouldn't do anyt'ing like dat; too foolish!

136. White Belly and Anansi

Richard Morgan, Santa Cruz Mountains

WHITE BELLY PLANT SOME PEAS. Hanansi come a White Belly yard and say, "Brer White Belly, dem peas not fat an' you know what you do? if you want 'em to be fat, mek up little fire at de root." Tomorrow morning when White Belly were come, every peas dead!

White Belly is a carpenter. He mek a box. He mek bargain wid de mudder; he say, "Ma, I gwine put you in dis 'ere box, put some money in de box; den I will holla out "Me mudder died!" White Belly put de han' 'pon de head, say, "Me mamma dead o-o-o!" Hanansi run come. White Belly say, "Ma, what you have to give me? Let good an' bad see!" De box turn up an' t'row out all de money. Hanansi go back home an' say, "Ma, I wan' a little water to wash me foot." Mother carried the water come. He dip him feet in dere, say, "Good Lord, ol' lady, you give cramp me!" Tek de mortar stick, lick 'im in de head. An' cobb'e one box an' put his mudder in an' call out, "Me mudder dead!" White belly come. Hanansi said, "Ma, what you have to give me? Give me back good an' bad see!" De box raise up an' 'tamp him down flat. So Hanansi kill him ma, an' White Belly mudder save.

137. Monkey hunts Anansi

Richard Morgan, Santa Cruz Mountains

HANANSI BORROW MONKEY MONEY, so him tell Monkey fe come Wednesday. When Monkey come, Hanansi knock in 'tomach, say, "Broad enough you can knock, oh!" Monkey ketch him, beat him. Nex' day when Monkey come he say, "Mudder Hanansi, whe' you son?" Him say, "Brer Monkey, fe you murder him yesterday, don' know if you him dead!" Monkey call one roos' cock an' cut de craw an' tek out Hanansi an' beat him.

When him gone, Hanansi say, "Ma, you goin' mek Brer Monkey kill me? You know wha' you do, Ma? Put on yo' pot, dig de fire ashes, put me in deh, mek up de fire, put on de pot. I will see if dat fellah, Monkey, wi' fin' me when him come!" Nobody knew Monkey was a Obeah man. When Monkey come he say, "Mo'nin', Mudder Hanansi; wha you son?" Mudder Hanansi said, "Massa, dis two day you beat him, an' don' know wha' he do?" Monkey gwine a kitchen, tek off de pot an' dig out de fire-ashes an' tek out Hanansi an' beat him,

Anodder Obeah woman tell Mudder Hanansi said, "You gwine to let Monkey kill yo' son? Yo' can twis' rope?" De ol' woman said, "No me trade?"[2] She said, "Twis' one rope. When you look out o' one en', you see horse you t'ink o' ants." Put Hanansi upon it When Monkey come, Hanansi deh 'pon de rope. When Monkey go up 'pon de rope, holla

---

2. It is my trade.

till Hanansi cut de rope. Me'while de rope cut, Monkey tumble down broke hi' neck. So Hanansi come down, clean up Monkey.

138. Anansi and the Pig coming from Market

Moses Hendricks, Mandeville

ANANSI TOOK THE JOB TO sweep the market. After he swept the market and got the pay, he bought a pig called "wee pig". On his way home he had to cross a stream. He couldn't get the pig across. He wouldn't carry it himself and he wouldn't pay anyone to assist him,— wanted free help. So he saw a dog coming along. He said, "Br'er Dog, I beg you bite this pig, make this pig jump over the river, make Anansi get home."

Dog said no, couldn't do it.

He saw a stick coming along, said, "Do, Br'er Stick, I beg you lick this dog, make this dog bite this pig, make this pig jump over this river, make Anansi get home."

Stick said no, couldn't do it.

He see Fire, say, "Do, me good Fire, burn this stick, make this stick lick this dog, make this dog bite this pig, make this pig jump over this river, make Anansi get home."

Fire says no.

He sees Water. "Do, me good Water, I beg you out this fire, make this fire burn this stick, make this stick lick this dog, make this dog bite this pig, make this pig jump over the river, make Anansi get home."

Water said no.

He saw a cow coming. "Do, Br'er Cow, drink this Water, make this water out this fire, make this fire burn this stick, make this stick lick this dog, make this dog bite this pig, make this pig jump over this river, make Anansi get to go home."

Cow said no.

He saw a butcher coming. "Do, me good butcher, I beg you butcher this cow, make this cow drink this water, make this water out this fire, make this fire burn this stick, make this stick lick this dog, make this dog bite this pig, make this pig jump over this river, make Anansi get home!"

Butcher said no, wouldn't do it.

He sees Rope coming along. "Do, Br'er Rope, I beg you hang this butcher, make this butcher kill this cow, make this cow drink this water, make this water out this fire, make this fire burn this stick, make this stick lick this dog, make this dog bite this pig, make this pig jump over the river, make Anansi get home!"

Rope said no.

Saw Grease coming along. "Do, me good Grease, grease this rope, make this rope hang this butcher, make this butcher kill this cow, make this cow drink this water, make this water out this fire, make this fire burn this stick, make this stick lick this dog, make this dog bite this pig, make this pig jump over the river, make Anansi get home!"

Grease said no.

He saw a Rat. Said, "Do, me good Rat, gnaw this grease, make this grease grease this rope, make this rope hang this butcher, make this butcher kill this cow, make this cow drink this water, make this water out this fire, make this fire burn this stick, make this stick lick this dog, make this dog bite this pig, make this pig jump over this river, make Anansi get home!"

Rat says no.

Saw Puss coming along. "Do, Br'er Puss, I beg you kill this rat, make this rat gnaw this grease, make this grease grease this rope, make this rope hang this butcher, make this butcher kill this cow, make this cow drink this water, make this water out this fire, make this fire burn this stick, make this stick lick this dog, make this dog bite this pig, make this pig jump over this river, make Anansi get home!"

Puss says, "Yes, I will kill your rat!"

Rat says, "Before you kill me, I will gnaw the grease!"

Grease says, "Before you gnaw me, I will grease the rope!"

Rope says, "Before you grease me, I will hang the butcher!"

Butcher says, "Before you hang me, I will kill the cow!"

Cow says, "Before you kill me, I will drink the water!"

Water says, "Before you drink me, I will out the fire!"

Fire says, "Before you out me, I will burn the stick!"

Stick says, "Before you burn me, I will lick the dog!"

Dog says, "Before you lick me, I will bite the pig!"

Pig says, "Before you bite me, I will jump over the river!"

So away went the pig over the river; and him and Anansi went home safe and without expense.

Dance and Song

139. The Fifer

Richard Roe, Maroon Town, Cock-pit country

THERE'S A BOY ONCE, MOTHER got only the one boy an' 'he love him so much that 'he give him a flute. So one day they go to far groun' an' coming back the boy leave the flute at the groun'. When he catch half-way, he remember it an' he tell him papa. Papa say to go back for it, but he mus' be careful not to blow it coming back because he got a lot of wil' beasts to pass. So as he come home he begin to blow,[1]

Min-nie, Min-nie, wa-yo da Lim-ba, Min-nie, Min nie wa-yo da Lim-ba.

Min-nie, Min-nie wa-yo da Lim-ba, Min-nie, Min-nie wa-yo da Lim-ba.

Wild beast rush out, say, "Who's dat blowing de pipe, sah?"—"Oh, no, not me blowing!" An' go 'way, blow again. Wil' beast rush out. "Ha! you?"—"No, grandpapa, not me blowing!"—"Den who blowing?"—"He gone on befo', massa; not me blowing!"—"Blow, let me see."—"Flee flitty flee, flee flitty flee."

Wil' beast go away. He commence the right tune now,

> "Minnie Minnie, wa-yo da lim-ba,
> Minnie Minnie, wa-yo da lim-ba,
> Minnie Minnie, wa-yo da lim-ba."

(Wild beast rush out, catch him, compel him to play.)

"Ah, I catch you now, sah! Play de tune now, sah! blow, sah!" Then he began to blow the right tune, both dance. Different wil' beats—Tiger,

---

1. The song was sung by Alfred Williams.

Asoonah, all the wil' beasts come out an' dance. An' the father get frightened, come shoot all the wild beasts, all drop save him boy. An' flog the boy.

140. In Come Murray

William Forbes, Dry River, Cock-pit country

It was said when you go you see a man going to play dat Nansi story. Get anodder wid a pint a water, den him gwine to turn a drunkard, begin to totter, say, "Tiger, tiger, lie down"—

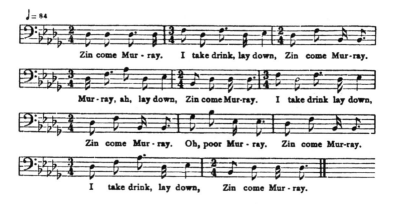

Zin come Mur - ray. I take drink, lay down, Zin come Mur-ray.

Mur - ray, ah, lay down, Zin come Mur-ray. I take drink lay down,

Zin come Mur - ray. Oh, poor Mur - ray. Zin come Mur-ray.

I take drink, lay down, Zin come Mur - ray.

141. Tacoomah makes a Dance

William Forbes, Dry River, Cock-pit country

Tacoomah make a dance, get Anansi for de fiddler, an' Grassquit was coming as a fiddler too. Robin Redbreast was to play de music, Monkey was to blow de bugle. Well, after de night de dance commence. Anansi gwine to play,

"Queena bunna, ring-ki-ting,
You sen' fe great Grass-quit,
You don' sen' fe me!
Anansi draw bow so sweet, ring-ki-ting,
Anansi draw bow so sweet, ring-ki-ting."

Tacoomah say,

> *"You ya, you ya, so ya, me ya,*
> *Wid a fort tumba like a tenky bunna,*
> *Wid a jump, wid a jump, like a tenky bunna."*[2]

Robin Redbreast say,

> *"Jock, Jock, when you coming home?"*

Jock said,

> *"Tomorrow evening."*
> *"What in your right?"*
> *"Boot an' spur."*
> *"What in your left?"*
> *"Bow an' arrow."*[3]

Jock[4] said,

> *"Robin redbreast*
> *Was pretty well dressed,*
> *And he was into his nest,*
> *And a puppy went into his nest*
> *And broke his neck t'ru distress."*

Well, den, Turtle an' Duck goin' in de river fe go an' swim, an' dem is to run to a hill-side in de river. An' Cock is de judge. Den Cock went to sing fe dem—

> *"Co co re co."*

Duck an' Turtle swim—

> *"Shekey, shekey, shee-e-e."*

---

2. The tune is that of the Devil in the Cock and Corn story, number 85.
3. The dialogue is taken from a popular game.
4. I asked, "Who is Jock?"—"Jock man dora."

142. Anansi makes a Dance

William Forbes, Dry River, Cock-pit country

AGAIN, ANANSI MAKE A DANCE. Him playing de fiddle,

Goat dere a dance, say,

"Me kyan' run, but me cunnie do!"

Dog begin to sing,

> *"Na way you lie, Samedy,*
> *Pussy no dead at all!"*

Den Puss an' Rat begin to dance an' say,

> *"Massa Puss an' Massa Rat a jump shandelay,"*[6]

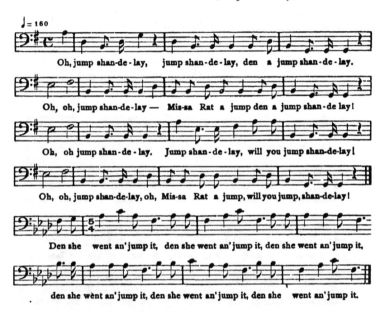

Oh, jump shan-de-lay, jump shan-de-lay, den a jump shan-de-lay.

Oh, oh, jump shan-de-lay — Mis-sa Rat a jump den a jump shan-de lay!

Oh, oh jump shan-de-lay. Jump shan-de-lay, will you jump shan-de-lay!

Oh, oh, jump shan-de-lay, oh, Mis-sa Rat a jump, will you jump, shan-de-lay!

Den she went an' jump it, den she went an' jump it, den she went an' jump it,

den she wènt an' jump it, den she went an' jump it, den she went an' jump it.

Well, Anansi boy was blowing de fife,

> *"Ti-H-harry-ham, handsome ben-in-ben!"*

Den de bull was coming along, hear dem, say,

---

6. Part of the first of the song is missing; phonograph needle was put down too late.

Oh who dey ca' me Tim-mo Lim-mo? Tim-mo Lim-mo, oh?

Zin ku-ma Ya ya ya, oh, Zin ku-ma.

Tim-mo Lim-mo, oh, Tim-mo Lim-mo oh, Zin ku-ma.

Ya, ya, ya, oh, Zin ku-ma. Ah, who dey ca' me Tim-mo Lim-mo?

Ah, who dey ca' me Tim-mo Lim-mo, oh, Zin ku-ma. Ya, ya, ya oh,

Zin ku-ma Tim-mo Lim-mo, oh, Zin ku-ma. Ah who dey ca' me

Tim-mo Lim-mo? Ah, who dey ca' me, Tim-mo Lim-mo,

Tim-mo Lim-mo, oh, Zin ku-ma. Ya, ya, ya, oh, Zin ku-ma.

143. Red Yam

Mary Jane Roden, Brownstown, St. Ann

ANANSI AND TACOOMAH HAVE TWO little boy. So Anansi go to him ground, he have a yam name of "red yam". So when he carry home de yam, if de two little boy don' tell him de name of de yam, don' give 'em no dinner. So one night de little boy say, (dance to the fiddle and drum),

"Poor me bwoy, papa no gi' me no dinner!
If I don' know de yam name, papa no gi' me no dinner!
Poor me bwoy, me go fe dead fe hungry, da la!"

Another day papa go to ground. So the little boy follow him go right outside a bush, go set for him. When him coming back he fall down, say, "Now me little red yam mash up!" So when him come home an' said to the little boy, "Come, me pickney, pupa come an' if you tell me de name of dis yam tonight, I goin' to give you a good supper," the little boy say,

> *"T'ank God, me know him name,*
> *T'ank God, me know him name,*
> *T'ank God, me know him name!"*

> *"Come, now, tell me!"*

> *"Ai! red yam, t'ank God a red yam!"*

(dance and play the fiddle and drum).

When the papa boil the dinner, give him a big dinner fe him call the name. When he eat the big dinner the papa gi' him the night, boy sing,

laugh, ma bwa, laugh, ma bwa, yo' bel - ly full wid de red yam.

Sing, ma bwa, sing, ma bwa, sing, ma bwa, yo' bel-ly full wid de red yam.[7]

144. Guzzah Man

Mary Jane Roden, Brownstown, St. Ann

ONE DAY TACOOMAH, MONKEY AND Baboon were driving a truck with rum to the wharf fe master. When they were going, Anansi said to Tacoomah they have a dance an' they invite Monkey an' Baboon to the dance. An' while they was dancing, Anansi an' Tacoomah go t'ief t'ree puncheon of rum from Monkey an' Baboon, come back to the dance, see Monkey an' Baboon was dancing. Anansi say,

Guz - za man, Guz - za man, Brudder Nan - si drink rum. Oh, Guz - za man,

Guz-za man, Guz-za man. So A-nan-si tie Ti-ger, tie him 'til he jump, Ti-ger.

Guz - za man, Guz - za man, Guz - za man. Tom drunk, but Tom no fool,

7. The narrator continued with the following which, she insisted, belongs with the song:

Tom drunk, but Tom no fool, Tom drunk, but Tom no fool, Tra-la-la-la-la - la.

This last measure may be repeated at will, or the whole three about Tom. The oftener it is sung, the sweeter the song, in Mother Roden's opinion and in that of many others.

This singer was most uncertain; in intonation, repetitions, etc. she varied exceedingly and agreed that any way the song was repeated to her by the transcriber was correct, no matter how it was sung. The transcriber, therefore, will not vouch for these three tunes. The old woman is a cripple and can neither read nor write. H. R.

Tom drunk, but Tom no fool, la - la - la - la - la - la - la.

145. Fowl and Pretty Poll[8]

Mary Jane Roden, Brownstown, St. Ann

FOWL INVITE PRETTY POLL TO chapel, den Pretty Poll said to Fowl, "Kyan't go to chapel for me soso fedder." Poll said to Kyan-crow, "Make go to chapel." Kyan-crow said to Pretty Poll him kyan't to go chapel for him peel-head young man.

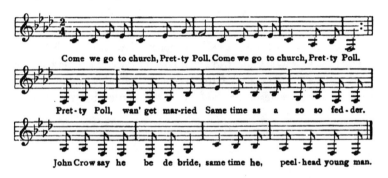

Come we go to church, Pret-ty Poll. Come we go to church, Pret-ty Poll.

Pret-ty Poll, wan' get mar-ried Same time as a so so fed-der.

John Crow say he be de bride, same time he, peel-head young man.

146. The Cumbolo

Sarah Findley, Santa Cruz Mountains

AN OL' MAN AN' A wife was travelling going on walk when they hear a nice music was playing an' the ol' man say to his wife, "O Quasiba,[9] hear

---

8. Jamaica negroes speak of the groom at a wedding as "the bride."
9. Two school-mistresses in Bethlehem, Santa Cruz Mountains, gave the following list of "born-day names" which belong to negro children in Jamaica according to the day of the week upon which they are born. See Jekyll, int. x (l.c.).

An old woman who was telling me of some obeah practises assured me that the obiman (sorcerer) did not use a man's common name when he wanted to bewitch him. but his "born-day" name.

	Boys	Girls
Sunday	Quashy	Quashiba
Monday	Quaco	Juba

dat sweet music singing over yonder. I like to know where dat music come from."—"Ol' man, you tak time walk an' we soon hear where dat music from. . . But Bruddie, dat ol' Cumbolo dat was singing las' night!"—"Den you mus' come let we dance de Cumbolo, Susan, we all a Cumbolo!" (sing and dance)—

Su-san, da'we all a Cum-bo-lo.   Sus-an, da'we all aCum-bo-lo.[10]

147. John-crow and Fowl at Court

Susan Watkins, Claremont, St. Ann

JOHN-CROW AND FOWL WENT TO court. Now as Fowl's baby was prettier than Crow's, Crow had taken Fowl's baby and left her baby for Fowl to take. So Fowl took Crow to court. The judge said whichever could sing the sweetest song should have the prettiest baby. Crow sang,

"Periwe, periwa!"

Fowl sang,

> *"Sun up an' sun down,*
> *I sing the song to cheer me heart.*
> *'Tis my charming baby dear,*
> *Bam, cluck, cluck!"*

So Fowl got back her pretty baby and Crow got her ugly one.

Tuesday	Cubena	Cuba
Wednesday	Cudjo	Bennie
Thursday	Quaw	Abba
Friday	Cuffy	Pheba
Saturday	Quamin	Benneba.

10. The music was recorded by a colored boy who was organist in the church at Bethlehem. The dance (also called "calimbe") is performed at wakes, two men holding a couple of sticks parallel while a third dances upon them to the strains of the song.

148. Wooden Ping-ping and Cock

Matilda Hall, Harmony Hall, Cock-pit country

WOODEN PING-PING (THERE'S A WORM in the dirt name so) and Cock. So then Wooden Ping-ping hid in the earth and the Cock hunted for him, couldn't find him. Wooden Ping-ping said (fine falsetto voice, rising inflection),

> *"Clay den, clay den, see me, ah?*
> *Clay den, clay den, see me, ah?"*

Cock answered,

> *"Na pullee theng theng,*
> *Na pullee theng theng!"*

They kept on singing, this in the earth, that outside; but Cock couldn't find him.

149. Animal Talk

James Anderson Hilton, Maroon Town, Cock-pit country

FOWL TELL DE OTHER FOWL say, "Tell o*d*der, one, o*d*der one, o*d*der one!" till it scatter over de whole worl'.

Cock say, "If it *tre-ew,* yes!"

Horse stamp him foot on de eart', "What in my stomach, mak it stay in deah!"

Jack-ass say, "De worl' don' level!" (for if de worl' level, don' hav to wear crupper on his tail.)

Cow say (slowly and drawlingly), "Mas-sa wor-r-r-k ne-v-e-r don-n-ne!"

Mule say (quickly and with energy), "It *will* done! it *will* done! it *will* done! Massa work *will* done!"

Crab say, "Mustn't trust shadder after dark!"

Ground Dove say, "My hears! my hears! my hears!" (won't hear what his parents tell him).

Hopping Dick go up on sharp 'tump an' White Belly go up on one tall tree an' bet one bet who can stay de longest widout eat. Hopping Dick say, "Chem chem cheery o!"

White Belly say,

> *"Coo coo coo, me hearie you!*
> *Coo coo coo, me hearie you!"*

Hopping Dick go down to de groun' pick up worm. White Belly stay up on tree all de time. White Belly fall down an' die.

Witticisms

Old-time Fools

I

THE MASTER SEND OUT ONE of them for a clock. When he get part of the way home the clock strike. An' say to the clock, "If you talk on me head again I mash you' mout'!" An' up come again the clock strike. An' he said, "Don' I tell you if you talk again I mash you mout'? An' up came the clock strike again. An' him put down the clock, say, 'If you can talk, you mus' walk!' An' as the clock couldn't walk, take a piece a 'tick an' mash it up! An' take up the clock an' put it 'pon the head. An' when he go in, Massa ask him how did the clock mash up, an' said the clock a talk 'pon the head an' him put him down to walk an' he won't walk an' he mash it up. An' the massa call the driver an' give him a good flogging."

II

MASTER SEN' THEM OUT FOR two jug o' rum, an' when they come to the river, they say they want a drink. An' one come top o' the bridge an' sen' the other down into the river an' say he t'rowing out the rum in the river, when the water taste he mus' tell him. An' he t'row out the whole jug an' he couldn't taste it. An' after he t'row out the first jug, say, "What kin' of rum is this have no 'trength?" An' him begin on the other jug an' him t'row out the whole of that again, an' him couldn't taste. An' they take the two empty jug an' go home to the master, an' they get a flogging for it.

III

DEY GWINE CUT A BIG cotton-tree. Den one of de Congo men said him don' want de cotton-tree to fall down in *him* groun', so mak one big *cotta*[1] put on head so go ketch de cotton-tree when it go fall down. Cotton-tree fall down kill him.

---

1. A ring-shaped pack made of banana leaves to protect the head when carrying burdens.

Duppy Stories

IV

ONCE A MAN WAS WALKING in the street on a night He met a duppy. His teet' was like fire; so de man went to ask for a light, did not know it was duppy. So de duppy gash his teet' at him an' he run. So de duppy went on met him again. De man did not know it was him, went up wid a complain':—"See, sir, I meet a man jus' now, ask 'im for a light an' he gash his teet' at me!" De duppy grin his teet' again an' ask, "Teet' like dese?" an' de man run again.

V

ONCE A MAN WAS TRAVELING in a dray packed with sugar. The molasses off the sugar was trailing underneath the dray. Two duppies came up and was sucking the molasses, an' say, "After the molasses so sweet, how is the sugar?" The drayman happened to hear it, wheeled his whip in the air an' give the duppy a good lick. Duppies ran off, crying, "Me dead one time, me dead one time, me can't dead two time!"

VI

ONCE THERE WAS TWO DUPPIES warming themselves over the fire. So one said to the other, "Cubba gwine to married." The other one said, "Cubba gwine to married? She don' have frock, she don' have coat. Shove fire, gi' me story!"

VII

ONCE SOME DUPPIES WERE IN a house. A man was outside; the duppies didn't see him. So they peeped all through the window to look at the moon. They said, "The moon is pretty pretty!" Another one said it was wrong, so he said, "Norra you norra me can't talk it prop-prop!"

VIII

ONE MAN WERE GOING OUT upon an errand an' night catch him on de way. An' he see a horse an' lick de horse an' de horse go after him an' he was running. An' when catch de bridge, run under de bridge mash a Rolling Calf.[2] Said, "Masha masha no hurt me, but de frighten you frighten me!" Horse said de licky licky no hurt him, but de 'brute' him call him.

Animal Jests

IX

Louse an' Dog-flea have a quarrel. Dog-flea, he said, "Brar Louse, when him ketchin' yo' a head, how you manage?" Louse said, "Brar, me gwine a knot knot." Louse said to Dog-flea, say, "Brar, when him ketchin' you, how *you* manage?" Dog-flea said, "Me gwine a seam in." Dog-flea said, "Den, Louse, when dem a comb you, whe' you go?" Louse said, "I lie down flat 'pon de meat." Louse said to Dog-flea, "Den, Brar, when dem dip a hot water how you manage?" Dog-flea say, "Come, come, sah, dat don't fe yo' business!" So de quarrel end.

X

Ground-lizard and Ground-rat were two friends. Rat said to Ground-lizard, "How black nigger sta'?" Lizard say, "Oh, dey ugly-lookin' chaps'." Rat said, "Yes? I see dem but nebber can stan' to look pon dem. Soon as dem see me dem say, 'Look Groun'-rat! look Groun'-rat!' an' take a stone to kill me, so I get out a dem sight." Ground-lizard say, "When dey buck up on me suddenly, I jump, but when I go a little way, turn round on dem an' look; dat how I know dey ugly-lookin' chap."

XI

Puss and Dog went out journeying one day and they found a thruppence. So they divided and now the trouble was they didn' know which thing to buy with a penny ha'penny. Dog said, "Brar Puss, I goin' to take fe my quattie to buy a quattie worth of 'look'." Puss say, "I won' buy 'look', I wi' buy cattle!" So the Puss buy a pair of lizard and let them go on the run, and they run to breed. That is why you see a cat always

2. "Rolling Calf" is a duppy with fiery eyes and flames issuing from its nostrils. It drags a chain about its neck, the rattle of which strikes terror to night travellers.

after lizard, and a dog is always looking, looking, looking and doing nothing.

XII

HAN' A GO MARKET. HEAR beg Han' a buy meat. When Han' come a pass, he cut piece of de meat. Den Mosquito see him, an' Mosquito come fe go tell Hear say Han' cut de meat. Den eb'ry time Mosquito go to tell Hear, Han' knock him. He come back again—"Hearie!" Han' knock him (striking his ear with his hand). Couldn't tell him yet.

XIII

MONKEY SAID TO GOAT, "I want to make a ball and I have a jacket I don't want to wear; so I sent for you to see if you will buy the jacket." And said, "Try on the jacket, see if it will fit you." So Goat try on the jacket, and Monkey said, "It kyan't fit you better!" Goat said, "Fit? fit? fit? (strutting about looking at himself) fit fe tre-ew!" So Goat buy the jacket.

XIV

ANANSI AN' TIGER WAS TRAVELING going thru' a stream of water. Anansi want to find if Tiger can tell a story. Anansi foot went right down on a sort of stone in de water. Anansi say, "I mash a fish!" Tiger holla out say, "I smell de fat!"

XV

TACOOMAH SAY, "ANANSI, YO' MA dead!"—"A' right! bit's wort' a meat fe sarve t'day."—"Anansi, yo' ma wake!"—"A' right! one somebody kyan't live a worl'."

Lies

XVI

ONCE ME AN' PA WENT to groun' fe go work. So we carry a gourd of water, go hang it up on a tree. An' when we ready to go back a yard an' we go look fe de gourd, we see dat duck come nyam off de gourd an' lef' de water hang up 'pon de tree.

XVII

ONCE I WAS CARRYING A pan of water an' I had to go' t'ru a ten bar' wire fence wid de pan on me head, an' I run t'ru an' not one drop never t'row away.

Philosophy

XVIII

ME DEAR MAN, LOOK YEAH! Jus' fancy, if life were a t'ing dat money could buy, de rich would all live an' all like me poor one here would ha' fe dead!

Riddles

Riddle me riddle
Guess me this riddle
And perhaps not!

1. My father have a thing in his yard; nobody can ride him but little Johnny. — Grass-quit riding a grass-stalk.

2. My father have a thing in his yard and never ride him till him back break. — House-roof; a man sits astride it to mend the thatch.

3. My father have a little pony in him yard and there's only one man, little Johnny, can ride it. Johnny ride with a pair of white reins and he go over a bridge.[1] — Needle is the pony, thread the reins, the crooked finger is the bridge, and the thimble is Johnny.

4. My father has a horse in his yard; it jump an' jump, an' de rein get shorter an' shorter. — Needle and thread.

5. My father have a grey horse in him yard, ride him nowhere but on him tail.[2] — Pipe.

   a) My father saddle his horse at his head an ride him at his tail.

6. My father have a horse in his yard; you can't ride him or he buck into you. — Steel-yard.

7. Me fader hab a cock in him yard; eb'ry crow him crow fire. — Gun.

   a) My father have a dog in his yard; every time it bark it bark fire.

   b) My fader hab a donkey, an' eb'ry bray him bray fire.

8. My father have a thing in his yard and he run from yard to yard. — Dog.

---

1. Cf. No. 140, p. 199.
2. Cf. No. 142, p. 199.

9. My father have a hen in his yard, you kyan' tell what the chicken be till he hatch.[3] — Wife; you can't tell whether the child will be boy or girl until it is born.

10. My father have a thing in his yard, cry for the crop once a year. — Coffee-pulper.

11. My father has a thing in his yard; the more him feed, the more him hungry. — Stove.

12. My father have a thing in his yard, have to blind it to use it. — Scissors.

13. My father have a t'ing in him yard; when it sick it look up to heaven, when it get better it look down to the devil.[4] — Bunch of Bananas.

14. My father has a cock in his yard, doesn't crow till the sun is hot. — Castor-oil bean, which cracks open in the sun.

15. My father have a thing in his yard, run off cover up the whole ground. — Pumpkin-vine.

16. My father have ten trees in his yard an' two taller than the rest. — Fingers.

17. My father got a tank in his yard, don't care how the rain come never catch water; but soon as little dirt get into it, it full. — Eye.

18. My father have a tank in his yard; when the rain fall it doesn't catch and when the dew fall it catch. — Coco leaf, because it sheds water like quick-silver.

19. My father have a thing in his yard; it button from head to foot. — Pingwing, because the leaves are stuck with pitch.

---

3. Cf. Suaheli (Velten):
    85. There is a buried thing; who can tell the sort of banana, to him will I give an amulet. — Woman with child.
4. Cf. No. 114, p. 196.

20. My father have a t'ing in him yard, cutting like a tailor cutting cloth.[5]   — Banana leaf (because when the tree begins to fruit, the leaf slits into ribbons.)

21. My father got a thing in his yard deep as well an' is not well, an' the whole sea does not fill it.
            — Sieve.

22. Me fader have a t'ing in him yard; the more you cut it the longer it get.[6]   — Grave.

    a) My father make a door an' it was too short; he cut it and it became longer.

    b) Me father have a stick an' cut it an' it become longer.

23. My father have a thing in his house, cut it every day and kyan' taste it.   — Cord.

24. We have a t'ing in the yard an' no man can tell where it end.   — Buggy wheel.

25. My father have a white house in him yard; if you go in you kyan' come out, if you come out you kyan' go in.[7]
            — Egg.

26. My father have a house without window or door.
            — Egg.

    a) There is a white house on the hill up yonder without a window, without a door; and yet somebody live in there.[8]

---

5. Cf. No. 113, p. 196.
6. Cf. No. 64, p. 190. English: Riddles (Boston):
    What thing is that which is lengthened by being cut at both ends?
            — A ditch.
7. Cf. Porto Rican (Mason and Espinosa):
    288. Una arquita muy chiquita, blanquita como la sal; todo el mundo la sabe abrir, pero nadie la sabe cerrar.
8. Cf. West Highlands (Campbell):
    A little clear (?) house and its two doors shut.
    Suaheli (Velten):
    4. My house has no door.
    Suahilli (Steere):
    1. My house is large; it has no door.
    Eastern Bantu (Seidl):
    9. There is a house without a door.

27. Me fader hab a man an' he kyan' stan' up till him belly full.   — Bag.

28. Me father have a black servant and when he feed her she bawl.[9]   — Frying-pan.

29. My father have three daughters and you can't tell me the oldest one.   — Three tumblers.

30. Me fader hab a lil bwoy sleep wid him every night; and every call him call him, de lil bwoy run.

— Dog-flea.

31. My father have twenty-five white horses in a row; if one trot all trot, if one gallop all gallop, if one stop all stop, and one cannot go on without the other.[10]

— Teeth.

32. Me fader hab a long whip and a number of cows; ebery wield him wield it, it touch ebery one.[11]

— Tongue and teeth.

Porto Rican (Mason and Espinosa):
    291. Una casa sin ventanas sin puerta ni brujería,
        que tiene un galán adentro, por dónde se metería?
Canadian: Ontario, JAFL 31:68:
        A little house full of meat,
        No door to go in and eat. — A nut.
9. Cf. Suaheli (Velten):
        24. A Grandmother sits on the stool and weeps there.
                            — Cooking-pot.
10. Cf. Nursery Rhymes of England (Halliwell):
        CXLVIII. Thirty white horses on a red hill, Now they tramp, now they
            champ, now they stand still.
11. Cf. Holme riddles:
        (125) Four and twenty white Bulls sate upon a stall, forth came the red Bull
            & licked them all.
    Yorkshire riddles (Notes & Querries, 3rd series, VIII):
        Four-&-twenty white beasts,
        And t' red one licks them all.
    Canadian: Ontario, JAFL 31:67
    Zulu:
        3. I puzzle you with a goat-ram which grazes, and white goats; it moves
            about much, but they eat in one place.
    Catalan:
        XVIII. Un convent de monjas blancas, dintre hi ha un frare vermell que 'Is
            hi repica las ancas.

33. Me fader hab a horse; eb'ry lep em lep em lef' piece a em gut. — Needle and thread.[12]

34. My father have a pony; every jump he jump he stop a gap. — Needle and thread.

35. My father have a horse and a spur; every time he spur, blood will flow. — Match-box and match.

36. My father have a horse and every walk he walk he drop silver. — Snail.

37. My father have a horse; carry him down to the river to drink and without he pull out the tongue, can't drink.
— Bottle and cork.

38. My father have a horse; hol' him a' him two ears, him bite a him tail. — Scissors.

39. My father have a rooster, got no coop can keep him but one. — Fire; only water can keep fire.

40. My father have a pig; cut him at his head he don't die, cut him at his tail he die. — Tree.

41. My father have a pen of sheep an' don feed nowhere but on the hill-side. — Lice on the head.

42. My father has a bull, can't feed but upon three ridges.
— Cooking-pot with three legs.

43. My father have a houseful of children; if you touch one, whole of them cry. — Gungo peas.

   a) My sister have a whole house o' pickney and if you touch one, everyone cry.

   b) I have a whole pen of guinea-pig an' if you touch one dey all holla.

---

12. Cf. Booke of Merry Riddles (Halliwell):
    LX. What is it goes through thicke & thin
    And draws his guts after him?
Holme riddles:
    (59) Wha that as goes throw the heye and leves his gutes after it.
Welsh-Gypsy:
    33. What goes through the hedge and leaves its guts behind?
    Canadian: Ontario, JAFL 31:69.

44. My father has a houseful of children and everyone of them has a red cap.[13]   — Woodpeckers.

   a) Me fader come out wid a whole ship-load o' Guinea people; everyone has red.

45. My father has a houseful of children; every time they come out they come out with red head.

                                   — Annata.

46. Me fader hab a houseful o' chil'ren an' eb'ryone a dem a black head.   — Ackee.

   a) Me ma ha' one Guinea ship a pickney; eb'ryone a dem head black.

   b) A woman has a whole lot of children and all come out with black heads and red dresses.

47. My father has a houseful of children and everyone of their heads turn out of doors.   — Nails in a house.

48. Me fader have a whole shipload of Bungo nager an everyone have a white head.   — Castor-oil bean.

   a) My father hab a whole house of children; everyone have a white head.

   b) Me mudder hab a whole shipload o' guinea-pig, all born at one quality head.

49. My father has a shipload of Guinea people, but all their heads is turned down.   — Bottles packed in straw.

50. Me fader hab a Guinea ship o' nager; eb'ryone o' dem a t'ree foot.   — Cooking-pots.

---

13. Cf. Suaheli (Velten):

   41. All my children have on turbans.

                          — Mushrooms.

   46. My children all wear clothes and a cap on the side of the head; who has no garment and no cap, he is not my child.

                          — Fingers. (?)

   54. I have seen twenty children in a row with bright frocks on.

                          — Crows.

Suahili (Steere):

   6. My children have turbans; he who has no turban is no child of mine.

                          — A kind of fruit.

51. My father sent for a ship-load of men and everyone come with arm akimbo.[14] — Coffee-pots.

52. My father sent for a ship-load of soldiers and everyone come with one eye. — Needles.

   a) Me fader hab a whole Guinea ship a nager; eb'ryone come wid one eye.

   b) I hab a pen o' sheep, but eb'ryone hab one eye.

53. My father have a piece of white yam that serve the whole world.[15] — Moon.

   a) One piece a afoo (white) yam nyam, serve the whole worl'.

   b) One piece of yellow yam serve the whole world.

   c) Me fader hab a half side o' bammie (cake of kasava meal) an' him share it fe de whole world.

54. Me fader hab a pepper-tree; eb'ry night all de pepper ripe, an eb'ry morning you wouldn't find one pepper an de tree.[16]
  — Stars.

   a) I go to bed and leave my pepper-tree full of peppers, and wake in the morning, there isn't one there.

   b) Me fader got a rose-tree in him yard; eb'ry night he blow, an by time de fe clean, eb'ry one gone.

   c) Me fader hab a heap a white plate pon a blue table; wash de plate in de evening an' turn him down, an' in de morning don' see one.

---

14. Cf. No. 116, p. 196.

15. Cf. Suaheli (Velten):

   77. My half cocoanut spreads over the whole town.

   — Moon.

Filipino (Starr):

   78. A single grain of rice filled the whole house.

   — Lamp.

16. Cf. Suaheli (Velten):

   72a. I laid down meal in the evening and in the morning nothing was there.

   b. I spread out my strips of matting at night; next morning I went out and found nothing there.

Eastern Bantu (Seidl):

   12. I spread my bananas on a rock; the next morning all had been stolen.

Porto Rican (Mason and Espinosa):

   225. Allá arriba hay un plato lleno de aceitunas; de día se recogen, y de noche se riegan.

55. Me fader hab a pepper-tree an i nebber ripe till night come. — Stars.

56. Me fader hab a tree full apple an' not a man can count them. — Stars.

   a) My sheet I cannot fold,
      My money I cannot count. — Cloud and stars.

57. My father has a sheet that covers the whole world. — Cloud.

58. My father has a lamp that shines over the whole world. — Moon.

59. My father have a house up on one post.[17] — Umbrella.

60. My father have two ponds; when he lie down at night, he turn up one and turn down one. — Ears.

61. My father have a well; it have neither top nor bottom, yet it hold water. — Sugar-cane.

62. My father have something without top or bottom, had it with him wherever he go. — Ring.

   a) The king of France sent to the king of Spain to get a tub without a bottom.

63. My father has a house with three doors and can walk only through one. — Three openings in a cocoanut shell; one drinks through only one.

64. My father has a gig to make; the more him pare it the bigger it get.[18] — Hole.

---

17. Cf. Suaheli (Velten):
   28. I have built me a great house; it stands upon one post.
  Hausa (Rattray) 153:
   I built a hut with only one post to prop up the roof.
18. Cf. No. 22, p. 185.
  Welsh-Gypsy: Gypsy Lore 5:241:
   29. What grows bigger the more you cut away from it?

65. My father have a thing go up chimbly chip chirrup.[19]

        — Fire.

66. My father have one thing in his hand and throw it and it support the whole of Jamaica.[20]

        — Corn-grain.

67. Me father sen' ten men fe ketch one t'ief.[21]

        — Ten fingers to catch one louse.

  a) Ten men go to Bullinton fe bring down one prisoner; only two bring him down.

  b) One prisoner stan' pon Marley hill; ten policemen go fe tek him down; two bring him to de station do, an' de sentence pass pon de finger-nail.

  c) My father tek a bwoy to court; de sentence pass pon finger-nail.

68. My fader sen' me fe go pick out a woman fe me wife; those laugh will be the bes' fe tek, but those not better left, fe they will kill me.

        — Ackee; this refers to the common warning that the fruit is safe to eat only after it has ripened and split in the sun.

69. My father plant a acre a kasava; only one white belly rat a eatey off.   — Grater for preparing kasava meal.

70. My father give me one root kasava an' a quart of fine salt; if I don clever I wouldn't taste it.

        — Egg; the salt cannot penetrate the shell.

---

19. Cf. No. 185 p. 203.
20. Cf. Suaheli (Velten):
  57. One is father of a hundred.
21. Cf. Holme riddles:
  12. In thickest woods j hunt whith eagles 10 after the chase which when (?) j doe descry j dlipossesse me of not usefull then & what j take not only that keep j.
       — A man scratching his head with both his hands.

a) I put on one coco on the fire to boil and I put in a gallon of salt, and the salt never tasted it.

b) I have a t'ing and don't care how much salt I put in it, when I go to eat it I have to put salt on it.

71. My father gave me some seed to sow; the ground is white and the seed is black.[22]   — Black ink on white paper.

72. My father was in Green Island cutting chip and the chip never fly.[23]   — Clock.

73. Mother put on a pot of food to boil; the top boil before the bottom.   — Pipe.

74. Going up to town my face turn to town; coming back from town my face turn to town. — Climbing a tree.

75. I was going up to town one morning, met a man; I tell him "Mawnin" and he wouldn't speak to me, and when I was coming back early in the evening he speak to me.
     — Trash, noiseless to the tread when cold, crackles when warmed by the sun.

76. I was going up Sand-hill and saw a man and suck his blood and throw him over the wall.[24]
     — Orange.

---

22. Cf. Irish Folk-Lore Riddles, 67:
      Riddle me, riddle me, Randy Row,
      My father gave me some seed to sow;
      The seeds were black, the ground was white,
      Riddle me that against Saturday night
    Porto Rican (Mason and Espinosa):
      151. Sábana blanca está tendida, semilla negra se va por encima, tres que la riegan y dos que la miran.
    Catalán (and see note):
      XXV. Lo camp es blanch,
          la llavó es negra,
          cinch son los bous
          que menan la rella.
23. Cf. No. 97, p. 194.
24. Cf. Nursery Rhymes of England (Halliwell):
      CLIV. When I went up sandy-hill,
          I met a sandy boy;
          I cut his throat, I sucked his blood,
          And left his skin a hanging-o.

77. When I was going up to town I met a man; his head is fire an' his mouth is bone.[25] — Rooster

   a) As I was going through Bramble hall,
      An old man gave me a call;
      His beard was flesh, his mouth was horn,
      And this old man was never born.

   b) Got to a gentleman's yard and his mouth was hard and his beard was flesh.

78. I was going over Dingledown hill and I saw a grey horse.
                            — Moon.

79. Picking juketa (?) going to town, picking juketa coming from town and can't get my hands full.
                          — Dew and sweat.

80. I gwine to town wid a hand o' ripe plantain; I hungry an' couldn't taste it. — Fingers.

81. I was going to town; I mash a plate and when I was coming back I found it new. — Ants' nest.

82. As I was going up to town I hear the bells of heaven ring; man tremble, beast tremble, cause the devil to break his chain. — Earthquake.

Welsh-Gypsy Folk-riddles:
    24. I was going over a bridge; I saw a yellow man. I lifted him up.
       I drank his blood, and I threw him down.
Lincolnshire riddles (Notes and Queries 3rd series, VIII):
       As I was going over London Brig,
       I spies a little red thing;
       I pick it up, I suck it blood,
       And leaves it skin to dry.
Canadian; Ontario:
       As I went over London bridge, I met my sister Mary; I cut off her head
       and drank her blood and left her body standing.
                        — Whiskey in a bottle.
25. Cf. Booke of Merry Riddles (Halliwell):
       IX. What is that, that hath a beard of flesh, a mouth of horn, and feet like
       a griffon?
Popular Rhymes of Scotland (Chambers):
       Page 109. Mouth o' horn, and beard o' leather;
       Ye'll no guess that though ye were hanged in a tether.
Catalan:
       Page 217. Hi ha un home que porta un vestit fet de pedassos, du
       la barba de carn y de la cara d'os.

83. Going up a lane I see a drink an' see a chaw.

 — Cocoanut.

 a) Dere's a cup an' in de cup dere's a chaw; no man to clear dis chaw.

84. A man was going to Kingston, saw two roads and took both.[26] — Trousers.

85. I heard that my father was dead in Kingston; I went there and took a piece of his bone and made increase.

 — Kasava root

86. I heave up a t'ing white an' it come down red.

 — Egg.

87. In England I am, in Jamaica I stand.

 — A man took soil from Jamaica, put it in his boots, went to England.

88. I went to town, I walk in town, I eat in town, and yet I don't know town. — A woman was breedin'. She went to town an' after she come home the baby born, grow a big man, don' know town.

89. A man going to town and he face town, and when he coming back he face down to Montego Bay.

 — Train running between Kingstown and Montego Bay.

90. A man going up to town; he walk on his head going up, he walk on his head going back.[27]

 — Horse-shoe-nail.

---

26. Tremearne, 58:

 I have two roads open, though I follow the wrong one I am not lost.

27. Cf. Booke of Merry Riddles (Halliwell):

 XXX. What is it that goes to the water on the head?

 Welsh-Gipsy, page 251:

 35. What goes to the village head downwards?

 Irish Folk-Lore Riddles:

 I go round the land and round the land

 And sleep at night on my head. — Nail in a brogue.

 Canadian; Ontario, JAFL 31:68.

91. Riding in to town, two talking to each other and none understand what the other was saying.

> —Two (?) new saddles creaking ru-u-u-u-u.

92. Four men going up to town; all were talking and not one could understand the other.

> — Four buggy wheels.

93. Four bredder walk a road and not one can touch.[28]

> — Four buggy wheels.

94. Some white ladies were walking to Kingston, and all the walk they walk they couldn't catch each other.

> — Mile-posts.

95. Three brothers in one house and never see each others' face until dead.

> — Three beans in one castor-oil pod.

96. Two sister on ribber side; no one could never wash the other.

> — Two bottles.

97. Two sawyers were sawing from morning till night and never saw a bit of dust.[29]

> — Clock.

98. Three man start fe go a heaven; one go half way an' turn back, one go right up, and one no go at all.

> — Fire: spark, smoke and ashes.,

99. A man walk around four corners of the world and make a house; rain come catch him a door, dew fall on him, sun burn him, and he have no shelter of his own.

> — Ladder.

Pennsylvania German JAFL 19:116:

> Was ist das? Fern armer Drop muss die Steg uf und ab geh uf em Kop?

28. Cf. No. 138, p. 199.

West African (Seidl), page 176:

> 6. Two things early and late together yet never touch. — Parallel roads.
> 7. Three children all alike who are constantly together yet never touch each other.

Catalan (and see notes):

> CCVII. Quatre germanas corren agualmènt qui part estan posades y agual trebal sostenan y una vol a conseguir l'altra y no s'alcansen.

29. Cf. No. 72, p. 191.

a) A man build a fine up-stairs house, and he have to sleep outside.

100. A man mek him house an' him sleep outside.
— Axe.

101. A man work for rich and work for poor and yet his head outside. — Nail-head.

102. There was an old man that live never building house till rain come.[30] — John Crow: as soon as rain come he begin to cut posts, say he will build him a house. When sun comes out, he come to dry himself; never build house any more.

103. Man mek him house, an' him bade da a do.[31]
— Ear of corn.

a) Old man in his room and the beard out in the hall.

104. Vineyard man walk through vineyard grass-piece and neither make track nor road.
— Sun.

105. I know a man talk every second.
— Sea.

a) I know a man; every talk he talk his mouth-corner foam.

106. Born from de worl' mek an' nebber a month ole yet.[32]
— Moon.

107. Baby born an' vanish. — Moon.

108. I know a baby born widout belly.
— Skelion (tin can).

109. Tallest man in Kingston don' have any belly.
— Bamboo.

a) A man stan' up widout guts.

---

30. Cf. Jones, 4; Harris, Nights, 363; Tremearne, 269–270.
31. Cf. Suaheli (Velten):
    47. There is an old man; he himself stays within but his beard is outside.
32. Cf. No. 257, p. 216.

110. Holler belly mumma, humpback pupa, pickney wid t'ree
foot.   — Cooking-pot.

111. Born in white, live in green, die in red, bury in black.[33]
— Coffee.

112. He laugh plain and talk plain but havn't any life.
— Talking-machine.

113. Going up to town me coatie torn-torn and not a seamstress
in a town could sew it.[34] — Banana leaf.

a) Mrs. Queen coat-tail tear an' never mend.

114. I think I will shoot God, and God say I mus' shoot the
earth.[35]   — Banana shoot.

115. I was tying mat ever since an' I never lay down on one.
— Pumpkin-vine.

116. If me stan' me kimbo; if me lie me kimbo.[36]
— Coffee-pot.

117. A thousand hungry men kill a thousand bullocks.
— Hunger kill men.

118. And smart as little Tommie be, one man kill the whole
world.   — Mr. Debt.

119. Woman have a chile an' fust begin larnin' larn him fe tief.[37]
— Hawk.

120. Black man dance on white man table.

— Black ink on white paper.

a) Mr. Blackman sit pon Mr. Whiteman table.

b) Black man sit down on white man chair.

---

33. Cf. Porto Rican (Mason and Espinosa):
   113b. Blanco fué mi nacimiento, amarilla mi vejez; y negro me estoy
      poniendo cuando me voy a morir.
34. Cf. No. 20, p. 185.
   Nandi (Hollis), 138:
      There lives by the river a woman who has many garments. What is she?
      — The wild banana plant.
35. Cf. No. 13, p. 184.
36. Cf. No. 51 p. 188.
37. Cf. Nandi (Hollis), page 135:
   I have a child who is known to steal.— Rat.

c) Black man dance on white man head.

d) Black man dance on white man sheet.

121. A black man sit upon a white man head.
— Ackee.

122. A white man stand upon a black man head.
— Bammie on griddle.

123. A black man sit upon a red man head.
— Pot on fire.

124. John Redman tickle John Blackman till him laugh puco-puco.[38]
— Fire under boiling pot.

a) A red man tickle a black man make him belly boil up.

b) John Redman beat John Blackman till him gallop.

125. Mr. Redman box Mr. Blackman make Mr. Whiteman laugh.
— Fire, baking-pan and bammie.

126. The white man take a red cloth tie his head.
— Tooth and gum.

127. Mr. Blackman was going to town; him drop him kerchief an' couldn't pick it up.   — Crow drops a feather.

128. Miss Nancy was going to Kingston; she drop her pocket handkerchief never turn round to pick it up.
— Bird drops a feather.

a) Miss Nancy was going up-stairs and she lose her pocket handkerchief and she would not turn round to pick it up.

b) Queen of Sheba riding out;
Her kerchief drop and couldn't pick it up.

129. Little Miss Nancy sit at the pass; everyone that come give him a kiss.   — Fly.

130. Little Miss Nancy tie up her frock and wheel round three times.   — Turn-stick in the pot

131. Little Miss Nancy like to dance and dance so rough.
— Pepper.

132. Miss D. June (?) cutting wood for a year, never get a bundle.   — Woodpecker.

---

38. Spanish Mexican, JAFL 30: 230:
   A little black one above, and red Juan below.   — Baking plate on fire

133. Little Johnny fell in the water and never drowned.
                                      — Bottle.

134. Aunty Mary cut two packey, not one bigger than the other.[39]   — Heaven and earth.

   a) Ole man Brenta sit on a stump, cut two packey not one bigger than the other. — Cloud on the earth (?).

135. Send bwoy to fetch doctor, doctor come before bwoy.[40]
                       — Boy climbing after a cocoanut; nut falls before boy comes down.

136. Dead carry the living over Napoleon's grass-piece.[41]
                       — Ship at Sea.

   a) Look through a diamond I see the dead carry the living.

137. A hen have six chickens; and hold the hen, the chickens cry.   — Guitar with six strings.

---

39. Cf. Nandi (Hollis), 141:
    I slaughtered two oxen, one red and the other white, and their hides were alike.   — Earth and sky.

40. Cf. Suaheli (Velten):
    49a. I send a man to call some one; he comes before the messenger returns.
    49b. The messenger sent is not yet returned; the one sent for arrives.
    49c. I am sent to call my friend; the friend is come, I am not returned.
  Porta Rican (Mason and Espinosa):
    174. Mandé un muchacho a un mandado; primero vino el mandado que el muchacho.

41. Cf. Irish Folk-lore Riddles:
  Irish: As I looked out of my parlour window
      I saw the dead carrying the live;
      Wasn't that a wonderful thing?
                 — Train full of people.
  Gaelic: As I was at my window,
      I looked through my gold ring;
      I saw the dead carrying the living,
      Wasn't that a wondrous thing?
                 — Ship.
  Popular Rhymes of Scotland (Chambers), 110:
    As I lookit owre my window at ten o'clock at night,
    I saw the dead carrying living.
  Welsh-gipsy: 27: The dead carries the living.

138. Two horses were galloping and neither of them could catch
one another.[42]   — Two mill-rollers.

139. One John-crow sit down on three cotton-tree.
                    — Cooking-pot set on fire-
                    stones.

140. A fleety horse get up over a broken bridge.[43]
                    — Needle and thread.

   a) A frisky horse and a frisky mare was going up to mountain
   hill.

141. John, the mule, in the stable, his tail outside.
                    — Fire in the kitchen, smoke
                    outside.

142. Stick a hog at its head and it bleed at its tail.[44]
                    — Pipe.

143. Kingston bully-dog bark, Montego bully-dog answer.
                    — Rooster; when one crows at
                    one end of the island, another
                    answers at the other end.

144. England dog bark, Jamaica dog sound.
                    — Newspaper.

145. Portland dog bark, Westmoreland dog hear.[45]
                    — Thunder.

146. Jamaica bully-dog bark, Kingston bully-dog keep silent.
                    — Great gun.

147. Rope run, horse stan' up. — Pumpkin-vine and pumpkin.

148. Old England dead an never rotten.
                    — Bottle (of ale).

149. Water grow.   — Sugar-cane.

---

42. Cf. No. 93, p. 194.
43. Cf. No. 3, p. 183.
44. Cf. No. 5, p. 183.
45. Cf. Suaheli (Velten):
    44. When the lion roars it is heard everywhere.
Nandi (Hollis), p. 145:
    A tree fell in Lumbwa and its branches reached Nandi.
                    — A great gun.

150. Water stan' up.   — Sugar-cane.

151. No ca how time hard, one coco full pot.

           — Foot in a boot.

152. One bammie shingle off Mt. Olivet church.

           — Moon.

153. One little bit o' bag hold three.

           — Castor-oil bean-pod.

154. A gully with two notch in it.

           — Purse.

155. What water wash, sun can't dry.

           — Butter.

156. Up the hill, down the hill; yet never tired.

           — Road.

    a) Up the hill, down the hill; Stand up still.

157. Chaw fine and never tired. — Saw.

158. This corner, this corner is no corner at all.

           — Ring.

159. Chip-cherry, beer, cedar.

           — White man (cedar), black-
              wife (chip-cherry), brown
              child (beer).

160. Stump to stump; dig out stump out of dogwood heart.

           — Jigger.

161. A 'tump in a pond; all the rain can't cover the 'tump-head.

           — Turn-stick in the pot.

162. There's a rope and every bump a sheet of paper.

           — Pumpkin-vine.

163. Sack a back an' not de front.

           — Finger-nail.

164. Roomful, hallful; you can't get a spoonful.[46]

           — Smoke.

---

46. Cf. Yorkshire Riddles (Notes and Queries 3rd series, 8: 325):
     A house full, a hoile (coal-hole) full,
     Ya' canna' fetch a bowl full.
   Canadian: Ontario, JAFL 31:71.

165. Knock an' stan' up.   — Mat.

166. Water a-bottom, fire a-top.

           — Lamp.

167. Hell a-top an' hell a-bottom.

           — Frying-pan.

168. Hair a-top, hair a-bottom; only a dance in the middle.

           — Eye-lashes and eye.

169. Hairy within and hairy without; lift up your foot and poke it in.[47]

           — Stockings.

170. Outside black, inside red; cock up your foot and poke it in.[48]

           — Boot.

171. White a top, black a middle and red a bottom.[49]

           — Bammie, baking-iron and fire.

172. White as snow but not snow; green as grass but not grass; red as blood but not blood.[50]

           — Coffee-blossom and berry.

173. Green as grass, not grass; stiff standing in the bed; and the best young lady is not afraid of handling it.[51]

           — Onion.

Welsh-Gipsy, 247:

    6. A roadful, a barnful; thou canst not catch a pipeful.

           — Wind.

47. Cf. Porto Rican (Mason and Espinosa) 301b, New Mexican Spanish 328:

        Pelú por fuera
        pelú por dentro;
        abre el agujero
        y ensartalo adentro.

48. Cf. Suaheli (Velten):

        97. Lift up, let it fall: *kiba kipandika, kiba kipandua.*

49. Cf. West Highlands (Campbell), II, 420:

    Red below, black in the middle, white above.

           — Fire, griddle and oatcake.

50. Cf. Irish Folk-lore Riddles: 75:

    Gaelic: As white as flour, and it is not flour; as green as grass and it is not
        grass, as red as blood and it is not blood; as black as ink and it is not ink.

           — Blackberries.

51. Cf. Booke of Merry Riddles (Halliwell):

    IV. What is that that is rough within and red without
        And bristled like a hare's snout;

174. White within, black within, red without.
— Ackee.

175. Hard as rock, not rock; white as milk, not milk.
— Cocoanut.

176. High as the world; red as blood but not blood; blue as indigo; but not indigo; high as granadillo temple.
— Rainbow.

177. When it come it does not come; when it does not come it come.[52] — Rat and corn.

178. Four sit down on four waiting till four come.
— Cat on the table waiting for a rat.

179. Six and four waiting for twenty-four.
— Six holes in four horse-shoes waiting for twenty-four nails.

180. Nine run, one come, two run.
— Nine man run for the doctor, one baby born, two nipples run.

181. Ten on to four.[53] — Ten teats on a cow (?).

182. Six is in, the seventh is out; set the virgin free.
— Hen hatching six chicks

183. Blackey cover ten. — Boots cover toes.

There is never a lady on the land
But will be content to take it in her hand.
— Eglantine.

52. Cf. Harris, Nights, 75.
53. Cf. Holme riddles:
    36. Flink flank under a bank 10 about 4.
    — Woman milking a cow.
Welsh-Gipsy, 248:
    14. In a field I saw 10 pulling 4. — Girl's fingers milking.
Canadian, Ontario: JAFL 31:67:
    Ink, ank you bank,
    Ten drawing four.

184. Two peepers, two pokers, two waddlers, and one zum-zum.[54]
    — Cow.

185. Up chip-cherry, down chip-cherry; not a man can climb chip-cherry.[55]   — Smoke.

186. Whitey whitey can't climb whitey whitey.
    — Smoke.

187. Half a 'tumpy sit down on 'tumpy; when a go, a don' see nothing but half a 'tumpy. — Broken bottle on stump.

188. Climb up Zion hill, pick Zion fruit, come down Zion hill, drink Zion water.   — Climbing a cocoanut tree, picking the nut, coming down, drinking the milk.

  a) Go up Mount Zion, drink Zion blood, eat de flesh, dash away de bone.

189. Tetchie in, tetchie out; all hands can play on it.
    — Lock and key.

  a) Tickle me in, tickle me out; all hands can play on tickle.

190. Hip hop; hip hop; jump wide.
    — Flea.

  a) Dip dup, a yard wide.

---

54. Cf. West Highlands (Campbell), 412:
        Four shaking and four running,
        Two finding the way and one roaring.
    Catalan (and see notes):
        CXLVI. Dos puntxets,
                dos ullets,
                quatre massas
                y una escombra.
    Filipino (Starr):
        a) Four posts, one whip, two fans and two bolos.
        b) Four earth-posts, two air-posts and whip.
        c) One pointing, two moving, four changing.
55. Cf. No. 65, p. 190.
    Irish Folk-lore Riddles, 68:
        Chip, chip cherry and all the men in Derry,
        Wouldn't climb the walls of chip, chip cherry.

191. Drill a hall, drill a room; lean behind the door.[56]
                    — Broom.

   a) Jig a hall, jig a room; go a corner, go stan' 'up behin' de door.

192. Little titchie above ground.
                    — Ants.

193. Every jump shiney jump, whitey hold it back.
                    — Needle and thread.

194. Miss Witty wit and wit till she wit out her last wit.
                    — Needle and thread.

195. Earie, hearie, earie, knock, pom!
                    — Brushing (the hair).

196. Papa take hairy-hairy put in blackey-blackey.
                    — Brush and blacking.

197. Unco Joey takin' long hairy-hairy somet'ing; shubbin' Aunty Mary hairy-hairy somet'ing.
                    — Making a broom.

198. Long Aunty Long-long, no one can long as Aunty Long-long.   — Road.

199. Whitey-whitey send whitey-whitey to drive whitey-whitey from eating whitey-whitey.
                    — White man sends his white boy to drive the white goat out of the cabbage-patch.

200. Sleepy-sleepy under nyammy-yammy tree; killy-killy come to sleepy-sleepy; nyammy yammy drop, kill killy-killy; walkey-walkey come nyam (eat) nyammy-yammy, leave sleepy-sleepy.[57]

---

56. Cf. Holme riddles, 225:

       (44) what is that that goes round about the house and stands behind the door.

   Irish Folk-lore Riddles:

   I go round the house upstairs and downstairs and sleep at night in a corner.

57. Cf. Porto Rican (Mason and Espinosa):

   179. Debajo de un come, come estaba un dorme, dorme; cayó el come, come, y despertó el dorme, dorme; se levantó el dorme, dorme y se comió al come, come.   — El coco y el que se lo come.

   — Man sleeping under a tree;
   snake comes to kill man;
   cocoanut falls and kills snake;
   another man comes, eats the
   cocoanut, leaves the first man.

201. Limb fell lamb; down fell lamb in the cow coram.
      — Limb falls, knocks lamb into
      the cow-dung.

202. If I had my pretty little caney, bigny-pigny could not kill
kum-painy.   — If I had my revolver, the wild
      hog could not kill my dog.

203. I was going out and I saw some pigs, and if I had my
hansom-cansom I would carry home some bigny-pigny.
      — If I had my gun, I would
      carry home some pigs.

204. I send for my man Richard to bring me tomery-flemery-
doctory to mortify unicle-cornicle-current out of my
pinkicle-pankicle-present.[58]
      — To bring my three dogs to drive
      three pigs out of the garden.

New-Mexican Spanish, 336:
  Durmilis Durmilis está durmiendo,
  Martiris Martiris está llegando
  Si no fuera por Cominis Cominis
  Durmilis Durmilis estuviera muerto.

58. Cf. Irish Folk-lore Riddles:
  As I went out a hazeum-gazeum
  I saw a shrinkum-pinkum
  Carrying away kum-painy.
     — A fox stole a goose at night.

Holme riddles, 233:
 (108) As j went through my houter touter houter perly j saw one
  Mr. higamgige com over the hill of parley but if j had my tarly berly,
  tarly berly berly j would have bine met with Mr. Higamgige come over
  the hill of parley.   — A man going ou' a hill a flee flew over
      his head.

 (237) As j went over Hottery Tottery, etc.

Popular Rhymes of Scotland (Chambers), 113:
 Ha! master above a master, etc.

Catalan:
 XXX. En Penjim Penjoy penjava, etc.

205. There is a boat an' in that boat a lady sat, an' if I should tell you the name of that lady I should be blamed, for I've told you the riddle twice.[59]

> — The lady's name was Anne.

206. I was going up to Hampton lane (a local name); I met a man, an' drew off his hat an' drew off his glove, an' he gave me his love. Take him an' call him; his name is twice mention as this riddle begun.[60]   — His name is Andrew.

a) As I was going up to St. Andrew's church, I met St. Andrew's scholar. St. Andrew's scholar drew off his hat an' drew off his gloves: tell me the name of the scholar.

b) I was going up on Oxford street, I met an Oxford boy. He took out his pen an' drew his name; what was his name?

c) Once as I was crossing the Montego Bay bridge, I met a Montegonian fellow. He took off his hat an' drew off his glove; guess me his name; I've mentioned it in this riddle.

207. I an' my dog ben up the lane catching a buck an' a doe. Whoever tell me my dog's name, there is my dog.[61]

> — The dog's name is Ben.

---

59. Cf. Booke of Merry Riddles (Halliwell):

> XV. Yonder side sea, there is a bote,
> > The king's daughter of England there she sate;
> > An if you tell her name no man it wot
> > What is the maid's name that sate in the boate.

> > — Her name is Anne; for in the fourth line it saith
> > *An* if ye tell me her name; but this riddle is not to
> > be seene on the booke, but to be put without the booke,
> > or else it will be soone understood.

60. Cf. Holme riddles, 234;

> (111) As j went by the way j met with a boy
> > j took him my friend for to bee
> > he took of his hat an drew of his gloves
> > and so saluted mee.

> Lincolnshire riddles (Notes and Queries 3rd series, VIII), 503:
> > As I was going over Westminster Brig,
> > I met a Westminster scholar, etc.

61. Cf. Dorsetshire (Notes and Queries 3rd series IX), 50:

> > A body met a body
> > In a narrow lane,

a) "Good morning, Mr. Ben; ben meke a meet. I come to borrow yo' dog go hunting. I don' know his name." "Take him an' call him; his name is twice mention as this riddle begun."

208. Megs, Pegs an' Margaret is my true lover; but it's neither Megs, Pegs nor Margaret. — Anne is my lover.

209. Trick, track and trawndy,
Which was Trawndy Grawnby?
— Witch.

210. There are 4000 people to draw in one carriage; how can they do that? — Mr. & Mrs. Thousand and their two children.

211. Mr. Lets was walking and Mr. Lets was riding and Mr. Lets was walking again. Can you tell me who the gentlemen were? — Horse, master and dog, all named "Lets".

212. My father has a long bench in his house, an' to guess me how many people sit on that bench.
— One man named "More".
(The trick is, at each guess to say More.)

213. Bees bite honey, honey run.
— A horse named Honey.

Says the body to a body,
Where hast thou a-ben?

I've ben in my wood
A-hunting me some roe.
Then lend me thy little dog
That I may do so.

Then take it unto thee.
Tell me its name;
For twice in the riddle,
I've told you the same.

Holme riddles, 237:
(137) There was a king met a king, etc.
— The men's names were King and the dogs name was Bin.

214. Twelve pear hanging high,
     Twelve men passing by;
     Each pick a pear,
     How many pear remain?[62] — Eleven; the man's name is
                                                Each.

215. A man without eyes
     Went out to view the skies;
     He saw a tree with apples on,
     He neither took apples off nor left apples on.[63]
                                 — A one-eyed man; two apples
                                   on the tree.

216. I was going up Hampton lane, I met a man have seven
     wives; the seven wives have seven sacks, the seven
     sacks have seven kits, how many were there going to
     Hampton?[64]

                           — Only one—I.

217. A duck before a duck, a duck after a duck, a duck in the
     midst of two ducks. How many ducks was going along?
                                 — Three.

---

62. Cf. Catalan (and see notes):
      CI. Dotze frares d'un convent
          dotze nespras per tots tenen,
          cada qual se'n menja una
          y encar quedan onze nespras.
   New Mexican Spanish: 152, 153.
63. Cf. Booke of Merry Riddles (Halliwell):
      XLIV. I came to a tree where were apples; I eat no apples, I gave away no
          apples, nor I left no apples behinde me; and yet I eat, gave away, and
          left behind me.
                                 — Three apples. I eat, give away, and
                                   leave one apple.
   Holme riddles, 237, (135).
   Popular Tales of the West Highlands (Campbell), II, 419:
      A man went eyeless to a tree where there were apples. He didn't leave
          apples on it, and he didn't take apples off.
                                 — There where two and he took one.
64. Cf. Nursery Rhymes of England (Halliwell), 958:
          As I was going to St. Ives, etc.
      Lancashire (Notes and Queries, 3rd series 9:86).
      Canadian, Ontario, JAFL 31:71.

MARTHA WARREN BECKWITH

218. I was travelling and six ducks flying, one before the five; and I took up my gun and I shoot one of the ducks and drop on the ground. Guess how many ducks remain?[65]
— None; the rest fly away.

219. A parson and his daughter, a doctor and his wife; and there is three apples to share among them. How will they share it?[66]
— Each takes one; the parson's daughter is the doctor's wife.

220. Run, Ricky, run; run up the Ahe river, run; run with a long trail, run up the Ahe river, run; run, Ricky, run? How many r's in that?
— No r's in 'that'.

221. Mr. Parott was sitting on a tree; some pigeons were flying by. The pigeon say, "Good morning, Mr. Parrot." The parrot say, "Good morning, Mr. Hundred." The pigeon say, "I'm not 'hundred'; want twice as much, half as much, quarter as much, and you, Mr. Parrot, to make a hundred." Tell me how many pigeons were flying.[67]
— Thirty-six.

---

65. Cf. Catalan (and see notes):
CCLIX. Un cassador surt a cassar. A dalt de un arbre hi ha quatre aucells. Etgega un tret. Ne mata dos. Quants aucells quedan dalt del arbre?
Porto Rican (Mason and Espinosa):
741. En un árbol había cien pájaros. Un cazador tiró y cayó uno muerto al suelo. Cuántos quedaron arriba?
Canadian, Ontario, JAFL 31:72.
66. Cf. Porto Rican (Mason and Espinosa):
726. El zapatero y su hija,
el sastre con su mujer,
comieron de nueve huevos
y les tocaron a tres.
— La hija del zapatero era la mnjer del sastre.
67. Porto Rican (Mason and Espinosa):
734(a). Pasaba un grupo de palomas por donde estaba un gavilán y el gavilán les dijo:
— Adios mis cien palomas. Ellas le contestaron diciéndole:
— Nosotras, la mitad de nosotras, una cuarta parte de nosotras otras tantas como nosotras y usted, señor gavilán, hecemos el ciento cabal. Cuántas palomas irían volando?
Arabian Nights Tales (Burton, Burton Club, 5:236).

222. I hire laborers for a shilling a day; I get twelve laborers. I give a man two pence, a woman ha' penny, a pickney one farthing. How many of each do I hire?

> — Five men, one woman, six pickney.

223. My father gave me a horse to go sell for ten pounds and to eat my breakfast out of the money and bring home the same ten pounds. How kould I do that?

> — Take the shoes off the horse and sell them separately.

224. In a rainy season the Cabrietta overflows a path where a poor coolie-man and his family had to cross. He then made a dray for conveying them to and from their work. Dray cannot carry more than 150 lbs. at a time. Coolie-man weighs 150 lbs., wife 150 lbs. and two sons together 150 lbs. How must they get over.

> — Two sons go over; one remains, the other returns. The mother goes over; boy returns, takes over brother returns. Father goes over; boy brings over brother.[68]

a) The same story with a fox, goose and bag of corn.

225. My fader got six sheep. He send his son to de pen. 'My son, go an' count me six sheep, but you musn' count me "one, two, t'ree, four, five, six." You musn't count "four an'

---

68. Cf. Canadian, Ontario, JAFL 31:63.
    Argyleshire, 181:
       Man, wife and sons to be ferried across.
    Ibid.
       Fox, goose and bag of corn.
    West Highlands (Campbell), 408:
       Three jealous soldiers and their wives in a boat that holds two.
    Booke of Merry Riddles (Halliwell), 72:
       Lamb, wolf and 'bottle of hay.'
    The Riddler (New Haven, 1835), 5:
       Wolf, goat and cabbages.
    Attributed to Alcuin, in Wright, Biographia Britannica Literaria, London, 1842, 1:74.

two, six". You musn't count "t'ree an' t'ree, six". You musn'
count "five an' one, six", but count me my six sheep!

> — Dis, dat, de other, De ewe, de
> ram, de wether.

226. I gwine to make a dance; I want you there. You mus'n't come
a day, you mus'n't come a night, you mus'n't ride a horse, you
mus'n't ride a mule, you mus'n't ride a jackass. An' if you come,
you mus'n't come into me house an' you mus'n't stay outside.[69]

> — You must come riding a cow,
> between day and night; and
> when you come, stand on the
> threshold, neither in nor out.

227. Under the earth I stand,
Silver and gold was my tread.
I rode a t'ing that never was born,
And a bit of the dam I hold in me han'.[70]

---

69. Cf. Grimm, 94, *The Peasant's Wise Daughter:*

"Then said the king, 'Come to me not clothed, not naked, not riding, not
walking, not in the road, not out of the road, and if thou canst do that I will
marry thee.' So she went away, put off everything she had on, and then she
was not clothed, and took a great fishing net, and seated herself in it and
wrapped it entirely round and round her, and then she was not naked, and
she hired an ass and tied the fisherman's net to its tail, so that it was forced to
drag her along, and that was neither riding nor walking. The ass had also to
drag her in the ruts, so that she only touched the ground with her great toe,
and that was neither being in the road nor out of the road."

70. Cf. "Flores" of Pseudo-Bede (III) Mod. Phil. 2:562:

Sedeo super equum non natum, cujus matrem in manu teneo.

Booke of Merry Riddles (Halliwell):

XL. On greene grass I go
    And on oaken beames I stand,
    I ride on a mule that was never folde,
    And I holde the damme in my hand.
        Solution: It is a fole ridden on, cut out of the dammes belly, and a
    bridle made of her skinne.

Porto Rican (Mason and Espinosa):

769. Ando en quien no fué nacido,
    ni esperanza de nacer;
    su madre traigo en los brazos.
    Adivina lo que puede ser.

a) On green grass I stand
   On gravel I stand,
   I ride a colt that was never in foal,
   And I beat up the mother old dum-skin in me
   hand.

b) Under de eart' I go,
   Plant trash I stan';
   I ride a t'ing that never was born
   Wid an ole be damn in me han'.

228. Little Miss Netticoat with her white petticoat,
     She has neither feet nor hands;
     The longer she grows the shorter she stands.[71]

                              — Candle.

a) Miss Nancy sits around de door;
   The longer him stan' deh, de shorter him grow.

229. Hoddie Doddie with a round black body Three legs and a
     wooden hat—What's that?[72]

                              — Cooking-pot.

230. Humpty Dumpty sat on a wall,
     Humpty Dumpty had a great fall;
     And all the king's horses and all the king's men

Irish Folk-lore Riddles, 70:

    O'er the gravel I do travel,
    On the oak I do stand,
    I ride a mare that never was foaled,
    And hold the bridle in my hand.

                   — A sailor on board ship.

  See Story No. 26, p. 33:

71. Cf. Nursery Rhymes of England (Halliwell), 93.
  Irish Folk-lore Riddles, 68.
  Holme riddles, 223:

    (27) j have a little boy in a white cote the bigger he is the lesser he goes.

72. Cf. West Highlands (Campbell), 2:419:

    Totaman, Totaman, little black man,
    Three feet under and bonnet of wood.

  Welsh-Gipsy:

    Black within and black without,
    Four legs an a iron cap.

  Lincolnshire Riddles (Notes and Queries, 3rd series, VIII), page 503, etc.

Couldn't put Humpty Dumpty together again.[73]

— Egg.

231. Round as a marble, deep as a cup;
Ten men from Jericho can't lift it up.[74]

— Sink-hole.

232. Handsome protector dressed in green,
Handsome protector sent to the queen.[75]

— Parrot.

233. Under gravel, top o' gravel;
Tell the devil I'll travel.   — Water.

234. Tires a horse, worries a man;
Tell me this riddle if you can.[76]

— Saddle.

235. Hitchity, hitchity on the king's kitchen door;
All the king's horses and all the king's men

---

73. Cf. Nursery Rhymes of England (Halliwell), page 92:
Irish Folk-lore Riddles: 68.
Hitly, Hatly etc.
74. Cf. Holme riddles, 230:232:
(82) What is that that is round as a cup yet all my lord oxen canot draw
it up.   — A well.
Canadian, Ontario, JAFL 31:67:
Round as a well, deep as a bowl, long handle, little hole.
— A frying-pan.
Yorkshire (Notes and Queries 3rd series, 8:325).
75. Cf. Nursery Rhymes of England (Halliwell), 96:
CLV. Highty, tighty, paradighty clothed in green,
The king could not read it, no more could the queen;
They sent for a wise man out of the east,
Who said it had horns but wasn't a beast.
— Holly tree.
Lancashire (Notes and Queries, 3rd series, IX), 86:
Itum Paraditum all clothed in green, etc.
— Parrot.
76. Canadian, Ontario, JAFL 31:68.
Brown I am and much admired;
Many horses have I tired;
Tire a horse and worry a man;
Tell me this riddle if you can.

Could never move Hitchity, hitchity off the king's kitchen
door.[77]   — Sunshine.

236. Flour from England, fruits from Spain,
All met together in a shower of rain;
Had on a napkin tied with a string,—
If you tell me this riddle, I'll give you a ring.
                        — Duckanoo (pudding boiled in
                        a cloth).

237. I was going through a field of wheat,
I picked up something nice to eat;
It was neither feather, flesh nor bone,
But I kept it till it walk alone.[78]
                        — Egg.

238. In a garden was laden a beautiful maiden
As ever was seen in the morn.
She was made a wife the first day of her life,
And she died before she was born.[79]
                        — Eve.

239. There was a man of Adam's race,
He had a certain dwelling-place;
He wasn't in earth, heaven or hell,—
Tell me where that man did dwell.[80]
                        — Jonah in the whale's belly,

240. Formed long ago, yet made today,
Employed while others sleep;

---

77. Lincolnshire Riddles (Notes and Queries, 3rd series, VIII), 503:
        Hickamore, 'ackamore
        Sits over th' kitchen-door,
        Nothing so long, and nothing so strong
        As Hickamore, 'ackamore,
        Sits over th' kitchen-door.
                        — A cloud.
78. Cf. Lincolnshire Riddles (Notes and Queries, 3rd series, VIII), 503.
        Canadian, Ontario, 68.
79. Cf. Popular Rhymes of Scotland (Chambers), III.
        English: New Collection, 14.
        Riddler, 18, etc.
80. Cf. Popular Rhymes of Scotland (Chambers), 108.

What few would like to give away,
Or any like to keep.[81]   — Bed.

241. Legs have I but seldom walk,
I backbite all, but never speak.
                        — Flea.

242. There was a man of Adam's race
Who had no legs, no body but waist.
                        — Ring.

243. When first I appear I seem mysterious,
But when I am explained I am nothing serious.
                        — Riddle.

244. A curtain drawn as fine as silk,
A marble stone as white as milk;
A thief appear and break them all,
Out start the golden ball.[82]

                        — Egg.

245. I came from beyond the ocean,
I drink water out of the sea,
I lighten a many a nation,
And give myself to thee. — Sun.

246. My first is a circle, my second a cross;
If you meet my whole, lock out for a toss.[83]
                        — O-X.

247. My father send me to market to carry home three-fourths
of a cross, a circle complete, a right angle with two semi-

---

81. Ascribed to Charles James Fox (1749–1806) in Modern Sphinx 17.
    Cf. Nursery Rhymes of England (Halliwell), 91.
        Canadian, Ontario, 70.
82. Cf. Canadian, Ontario, 69:
        English: Fashionable Puzzler, 58:
                In marble walls as white as milk,
                Lined with a skin as soft as silk,
                Within a fountain crystal clear,
                A golden apple doth appear.
                No doors there are to this strong hold,
                Yet thieves break in and steal the gold.
83. Cf. English: Puniana, 34, etc.

circles meet, a triangle with a cross, two semi-circles, and circle complete.[84]   — T-O-B-A-C-C-O.

248. Five letters in an invitation spell my name,
Backward and forward it answer the same;
Take away the first letter and the first of humanity race,
Take away the second and the thing that make
the water-wheel turn.
Take away the third, and the first of the alphabetical verb.
                    — Madam, Adam, dam, am.

249. Give a number that isn't even: cut off the head, you get it
even; cut off the tail, your mother's name you shall find.[85]
                    — Seven, even, Eve.

250. What word of one syllable, take away two letters and leave
two syllables?[86]

                    — Plague, ague.

251. A word of one syllable which, when two is taken off, ten
remain.   — Often, ten.

252. Give me "black water" in three letters.
                    — I-n-k.

253. Spell me a broken wall in three letters.
                    — G-a-p.

---

84. Cf. English: New Collection, 13:
    XXI. Three-fourth of a cross and a circle complete,
        Two semi-circles and a perpendicular meet,
        A triangle standing on two feet,
        Two semi-circles and circle complete.
    English: Fashionable Puzzler, 241, etc.
85. Cf. English: Puzzles Old and New, 320:
        From a number that's odd cut off its head,
        It then will even be,
        Its tail, I pray, next take away,
        Your mother then you 'll see.
    English: Puniana, 99, etc.
86. Cf. English: Riddler, 12.
    English: Puniana, 217, etc.

254. What is it that is once in a minute, twice in a moment, and not once in a thousand years?[87]

— Letter M.

255. What is it that we see every day, King George himself sees, and God never sees?[88]— Our equal.

256. What is that which if you have not you would not like to get and if you have you would not like to lose?[89]

— A bald head.

257. What is it, when Adam was four days old it was four days old, and when Adam was four-score years and four days old it remained four days old?[90]

— Moon.

---

87. Cf. English: Puniana, 217.

    Porto Rican (Mason and Espinosa):

        342. Una en un minuto, dos en un momento, y ninguna en un siglo.

88. Cf. Popular Rhymes and Nursery Tales (Halliwell), 143:

        10. What God never sees,

            What the King seldom sees,

            What we see every day,—

            Read my riddle, I pray.

    Irish Folk-lore Riddles:

        (Gaelic) I sought for it and found it, 'twas easy its finding,

            The thing that God never found and never can find.

    Welsh-Gipsy, 247:

        What is it God does not see, etc.

    Catalan, 80:

        CVI. Qu'es això?

            Lo pastò' ho veu á la montanya

            y no 'u veu lo rey de Espanya.

    Porto Rican (Mason and Espinosa); 300.

89. Cf. Booke of Merry Riddles (Halliwell):

        LXIII. What is that no man would have and yet when he hath it will not

            forgoe it?   — A broken head.

    Irish Folk-lore Riddles: 74:

        I have it and I don't think much of it; but if I had it not, there would be

            great grief on me.

90. Cf. No. 106, p. 195.

    English: New Collection, 180:

            There is a thing was three weeks old

            When Adam was no more;

            This thing it was but four weeks old

            When Adam was four-score.

    Irish and Anglo-Irish: Folk-lore Riddles, 76.

    Canadian, Ontario, 70.

258. What is that which Christ had not, Napoleon had, Kaiser has and no woman ever has?

— A wife.

259. What is it that is too much for one, enough for two, and nothing at all for three? — A secret

260. The river is bank to bank; how will you get over?

— By bridge.

261. Suppose all the tree was one tree and all the man was one man and all the axes one ax; and suppose the one ax fell the one tree and the one tree kill the one man, who would leave to tell the tale?   — Women.

262. Higher than God, lower than the devil; the dead feed on it but not the living.[91]   — Nothing.

263. There was a woman born, live an' die; never go to corruption, never see God face.   — Lot's wife.

264. There is a thing on earth that God could do but didn't, the devil had'nt got the power, and men do it.[92]

— Baptism.

265. What is the cleanest thing in a dirty woman's house?

— Egg.

266. What is the bes' furniture for a man's house?

— The daughter.

267. Why do a tailor and a plantain resemble?

— One cuts to fit, the other is fit to cut.

---

91. Cf. Porto Rican (Mason and Espinosa):

    389. Qué es lo que el muerto come, que si el vivo lo come se muere también?

92. Cf. Porto Rican (Mason and Espinosa):

    90 (Cf. 17) En el mundo no lo hubo,
    en la tierra no se halló;
    Dios, con ser Dios no lo tuyo,
    y un hombre a Dios se lo dió.

    New-Mexican Spanish, 321:

    Se que en el clelo no lo hubo,
    siendo Dios quien lo inventó;
    y si el mismo Dios lo tuvo,
    fué un hombre quien se lo dió.

268. Why do a well-dressed lady and a chair resemble?
— Because they both use pins.

269. Why does a judge and a mile-post resemble?
— One justifies the mile and the other the law.

270. What makes the devil and a shoemaker resemble?
— The devil seek after a sinner's soul and the shoemaker after a boot sole.

271. Mr. Bigger has a baby; out of Mr. Bigger and his baby which is the bigger? — Baby is a little Bigger.

272. If an elephant's four feet cover four acres of land, what will his tail cover? — The skin

273. What money in the world is the hardest money to change? — Matrimony.

274. A reason why a moth-eaten coat is like a bible?
— Both of them is holy (holey).

Notes

1. Tying Tiger

Parkes heard this story in St. Ann Parish. Milne-Home, 99–108, tells it of Anansi and "Lion," who takes the place of Tiger in earlier Jamaica story-telling. In a famous Jamaica digging-song, the words "Tiger-Lion" are coupled much as we should say "John Smith."

The story falls into three parts. (1) A bully takes for himself the food-supply of one weaker than himself, who dares not object. (2) The bully is tricked into allowing himself to be tied; when he is tormented or robbed of the food he is monopolizing. (3) He either dies, or he is rescued and (a) falls upon his rescuer, of (b) invites him to dinner, when he is again tricked by his first victim, who personates the animal who has released him and enjoys his hospitality until detected and pursued.

Compare: Callaway, 29; 358; Theal, 110; Jacottet, 20–22; Dayrell, 93–97; Barker, 55–58; Cronise and Ward, 209–213; Ellis, Ewe 274; Rattray, 2:74–82; Smith, 549–551; Lenz, 41; Christensen, 23–25; Harris, Nights, 327–329; Friends, 21–23; Ernst, VBGAEU 20:275; Koch-Grünberg, 2:141; Saurière, 95–100; Lenz, Estudios, 202, 210.

(1) The fish basket story occurs in Dayrell and in Barker (antelope in a bundle). In Milne-Home, Anansi catches the fish by pretending he is going to give them new life.

(2) The tying trick is variously treated. In Callaway, 29, and Theal, the "cannibal's" hair is plaited into the thatch, in Jacottet, the tail; in Callaway, 358, the tail is fastened into the ground. In Dayrell, the two play at tying each other (as in numbers 16 and 37) and the weaker animal refuses to untie the stronger. In Barker, the stronger animal consents to be hung in order to have his teeth beautifully filed. In Cronise & Ward and in the American versions (Harris, Christensen, Lenz, Ernst), the tying takes place under pretence of storm, but a pretence made plausible by shaking the trees as if a storm were coming. In Jacottet's story, Lion, whose tail has been thatched into the hut, prays for a storm to kill his tormentor; it comes and destroys Lion himself. In Koch-Grünberg (Taulipang), the story is mixed with the motive of the support of the stone.

Tormenting the tied victim by throwing at him the remnants of the feast occurs in Theal, Cronise & Ward, Dayrell (salt and pepper). In Callaway and Lenz, he is severely beaten.

(3) Release by "White-ants" occurs in Barker, Cronise & Ward, Smith; by "Bush-rat" in Dayrell, where the story ends, as in number 12c, by the released victim falling upon his rescuer. In Milne-Home, this motive is also suggested. In Ellis, "Bush-rat" is freed by "Snail." Compare Nassau, 46, where the swollen Leopard, freed from his predicament by Crab, turns and eats up his rescuer. The overheard invitation occurs in Barker, Smith, Milne-Home.

2. Tiger as Substitute

The two episodes do not, so far as I know, occur in African collections, and in American collections they belong to a single story.

Compare: (Mexico), Boas, JAFL 25:205; Parsons, Andros Island 82–85; Sea Islands, 40–43; Edwards, 63; JAFL 30:229); Backus, JAFL 13:22–24; JAFL 32:400–402; Harris, Nights, 12–17; 179–185; Uncle Remus 140–145; Hichiti Indians, JAFL 26:214.

In Edward's and Parsons's versions, the two episodes of tying in the garden and tying up while the water is scalding belong together; one is the conclusion of the other. In Mrs. Parsons's version, the boy says when he finds Boukee tied in place of Rabby, "O pa! de leetle man grow beeg!" Edward's version says, "Pa, dey big one here!"—"Don't care if 'e big one or little one, I goin' to scal' him!" is the answer. In Boas's Mexican Rabbit cycle, Rabbit is caught in a woman's chile-garden by means of the tar-baby, is hung in a net while water is heating, pretends he is to marry, and persuades Coyote into his place. The "dear old woman" says "Ah! How did the Rabbit turn into a coyote?"

The story is related to Grimm 8, dicussed by Bolte u. Polívka 1:68. In Boas's Mexican cycle, Rabbit escapes from Coyote by leaving him playing the guitar for a marriage couple. Anansi is represented as an accomplished fiddler in numbers 4, 10b, 14, 15, 20, 40, 43, 44, 47b, 93, 94, 131, 141. See numbers 1 and 21b and Boas's discussion, JAFL 25:248–250.

3. Tiger as Riding-Horse

The story is very common in Jamaica and presents no local variations from the form familiar in America. In Parkes's version, the "two misses" become two "post-mistresses". In a version by Knight, a school-master in the Santa Cruz mountains, Tacoomah is the horse and the story ends, "From that day the saddle fasten on Brer Tacoomah's back." Knight explained that "Brer Tacoomah is a large spider with yellow spots and a broad back shaped like a saddle," and that the story was told to explain this characteristic.

Other Jamaica versions are found in Milne-Home, 51–63; Pamela Smith, 17; and Wona, 19–23. In Wona's version, the story is made to explain "why gungo-peas are always covered with Tacoomahs," a species of spider.

Compare Parsons, Andros Island, 30 and note; Sea Islands, 53; for comparative references.

Tremearne, FL 21:205, and Tailed-Head-Hunters, 322, tells a Hausa story of a Hyena who has stolen a holy man's horse. Spider offers to bring the Hyena to him in its place, and persuades Hyena, under pretence of taking him to a dead animal, to be saddled and bridled and ridden by Spider to the holy man, who then mounts Hyena and completes his journey.

In Ellis, Yoruba 265, Tortoise rides Elephant into town to sustain an idle boast.

In Smith's Brazil version, the little animal is tied on for safety, and takes care to slip into a hole when he finally dismounts.

In Ernst, VBGAEU 20:277 (Venezuela), Rabbit rides Tiger across a river. The story is coupled here with the murder in midstream.

4. Tiger's Sheep-skin Suit

Parkes heard this story in St. Ann Parish. Wona, 62–67, tells how Anansi steals Monkey's clothes and passes the theft off on "Bone."

Compare: Tremearne, FL 21:352; Harris, Nights; 68–74; Parsons, Sea Islands, 145: JAFL 32:366.

The common theme of teaching to an unsuspecting comrade an incriminating song (as in Parsons, Sea Islands, 145) is here emphasized by a second intrigue, that of the sheep-skin suit. The idea seems related to the next number. In Wona, 30–36, Tacoomah puts on a sheep-skin and hides in the fold from which the sheep are being stolen, Anansi ties and accuses him because he wears the sheep-skin.

5. Tiger Catching the Sheep-thief

The story of the sheep-thief and the disguised watchman is popular in Jamaica, especially in St. Ann Parish, and I have given three versions in order to show the range of variation and the persistence of the essential plot. I have abbreviated White's version without other change except the insertion of the incident of the misunderstood warning, which comes from another version and commonly precedes the episode of the "refugees in the roof." Besides these three versions, Wona has the story, 30–36, and in Jekyll, 88, Tiger puts on a similar disguise at the conclusion of Annancy and Candle-fly (see number 7).

The tale falls into three parts. (1) A flock of sheep disappear one by one. (2) Tiger, or his equivalent, puts on the animal's skin in order to catch the thief. (3) The thief is caught, but escapes his captor; or he provides a substitute; or he is pursued and takes refuge in the roof.

Compare: Tremearne, 214–216; Barker, 131–132; Parsons, Andros Island, 117–119; Edwards, 67–68.

(1) The witty opening of the Jamaica versions based on a compensation motive (see numbers 22 and 63), in which the rascal takes advantage of an open-handedness common to aristocratic wealth, does not occur outside Jamaica. Compare Tremearne, FL 21:213–214. In Parsons, he pleads his wife's illness; in Edwards and Barker, he is a mere thief. In Barker, as in Jamaica, the story accepts the absurdity that all the sheep have disappeared except the last.

(2) The thief-catcher is "head-man" in Edwards as in Jamaica; in Barker he is a man who comes to town; in Wona, he is Tacoomah; in Parsons, a lion gets in with the sheep and is taken as the plumpest of them.

(3) Barker's version has a moralizing tendency; it is the friend who accompanies the thief who, at a flash of lightning, detects the trap and escapes. In Edwards, as in version (b), the rascal shifts the burden to his unsuspecting accomplice and himself escapes. Edwards and Parsons both conclude with the episode of taking refuge in the roof, as in version (c). For references see Parsons, 117 note 2.

For the incident of the misunderstood warning, compare: Tremearne, FL 21:206; Renel 2:7, 8; Theal, 165; Harris, Nights, 82; Trowbridge, JAFL 9:286.

There can be no doubt that the essential plot is a version of the Sindibad fable of the thief among the beasts, who caught the lion by mistake, told in Comparetti's translation from the Portuguese in his "Researches Concerning the Book of Sindibad", PFLS 9:144. A rich herder camps beside a village at night. A prowling lion gets among the beasts. A thief comes and, feeling the animals to see which is the plumpest, lays hands upon the lion.

6. Tiger's Breakfast

For the first breakfast trick, compare number 57a; for the second, 43. For Tiger's revenge, see number 38.

7. Eggs and Scorpions

Jekyll tells the same story in Annancy and Candle-fly, 86–89, Wona, in Anancy and Fire-fly, 24–29; Pamela Smith, in Anancy and Ginger-fly. Milne-Home, 35–39, contains the scorpion episode. Compare Tremearne FL 21:360.

The plot is in two parts. (1) Anansi goes on an egg-hunt at night with Fire-fly as guide, but is deserted because of his greed. (2) He stumbles upon Tiger's house at night, and tries to steal back the eggs which Tiger has set Scorpions to guard. The parallel of this story with number 39 is obvious. Jekyll's version takes on elements of the sheep-stealing story, number 5. A Mandeville version reads much like Milne-Home's:

> Bra Anansi an' Bra Tiger went out to go an' steal some eggs. Bra Anansi took a rubber bag an' Bra Tiger took a canvas bag. When Bra Tiger bag full, Bra Anansi jus' half. Bra Tiger would not wait any longer. He leave him an' he go away.
>
> Anansi was filling the bag, there he see a light coming, think it was Bra Tiger an' cry out, "Lor', Bra'r, Bra'r, yo' jus' coming to meet me?" But it wasn't Tiger; it was the man watchin' the eggs.
>
> An' when he went up to hol' him he said, "Do, sah! do, sah! don' carry me to massah tonight. Tie me to yo' bed-side tonight till a mawnin'!" An' when the man was sleeping, he call to Bra Rat, "Bra'r Rat, run come here let me tell you somethin'!" When Bra Rat come he said, "Jes' loose me, I hev some egg here to give you!" An' he loose him, he simply went right away,—never give Bra Rat anything.

8. Tiger's Bone-hole

The popular story of the bone-hole is better in action than on paper. A lad in Ballard's Valley gave me a similar story of John-Crow's bone-hole, ending with the dash of boiling water which has rendered John-Crow permanently bald (see number 47). After dictating the story he said, "Now I will tell it so as to make it funny", and he proceeded to retell the tale in rapid dialogue, changing his voice to imitate the speakers and representing in pantomime the action of eating and throwing the bones, of ducking to escape them, and of playing the fiddle. As in this case, the dictated stories often only approximately render the style of actual oral delivery.

Compare Cronise and Ward, 214–218. For negro ideas about the "bone-heap" see Bleek, Bushman Folk-lore, 275–283.

9. The Christening

The Jamaica version of this wide-spread tale (Grimm 3, discussed in Bolte u. Polívka, 1:9–13), has no local peculiarities. Compare Parsons, Sea Islands, 5–9 and references; also Frobenius 3:13–16.

It consists of two parts. (1) A rascal excuses himself three times for leaving his companion, on the plea of a summons to a christening, in order to rob a tub of butter which the two hold in common. (2) By smearing the innocent companion with the butter, he makes him appear the guilty one.

The first part is the distinguishing feature of the tale. A stolen food-supply is one of the commonest episodes in negro trickster stories and common tests to detect the thief occur:—(a) Taking a purge to detect stolen food as in Dennett, 92. (b) Jumping over a fire, as in Harris, Uncle Remus, 84; Nights, 253–254; JAFL 30: 193; 32:394; and numbers 21a and 36. (See Bolte u. Polívka 1:39). (c) Jumping over, or walking, a string, as in Theal, 115; Junod, 105; Boas and Simango JAFL 35:193; Compare also Monk Lewis's story of the test in crossing a river, 253–254, illustrated in number 80.

The trick to "incriminate another fellow" is, regularly, to smear the innocent victim with food while he sleeps. Compare: Bleek, 18; Callaway, 169; Theal, 93–97; Junod, 102; Dayrell, 53–54; Harris, Uncle Remus, 83; Parsons, Sea Islands, 8–14; also, Haida Indians, Swanton 113 (Bur. of Am. Ethn. Bull. 29).

The blood-smearing of the innocent victim in Leopard's Marriage Journey, Nassau, 85–95, is a particular instance of the same motive. The sheep-skin suit and the song in the mouth of the unsuspecting victim, serve as witty substitutes for this common device for the incriminating of an innocent person by the guilty.

In Arcin, 473, the common food-supply is stored in a granary of which Rabbit steals the key, eats the food, and scatters the remains in the house of the guardian Hyena.

10. Eating Tiger's Guts

The "Just so" story, number 51, is another version of the diving plot, which is popular in Jamaica. Jekyll tells it, 7–9, in form (b).

Compare: Chatelain, 205; Junod, 208; Renel, 254; JAFL 32:395; Nights, 373–377; Parsons, Sea Islands, 40.

In all these cases, the trickster proposes diving and eats a store of food while his companion is in the water. The grotesque idea of bodily dismemberment coupled with the diving episode, I do not find in any of the parallels noted. In Parsons, Andros Island, 73, Boukee and Elephant go out bird-hunting. Boukee shoots Elephant and brings him home to the family. Boukee is brought to justice because the children are overheard singing,

> *"Me an' Mamma'n Pappa*
> *Eat my belly full o' pot o' soup*
> *Bo'o' Elephin got (gut), oh!"*

For the incriminating song in version (b), see number 4.

11. Throwing away Knives

The story furnishes a good instance of local setting for an old tale, the pine-apple beeing well known in Jamaica. It takes two forms, that of leaving behind an implement necessary for the enjoyment for some food-supply, and that of throwing it away, in both cases under the impression that the adviser has done the same, as in number 13.

Compare, for both spoon and knife episodes, Theal's Hlaka-nyana cycle, 105–107; for the knife, Nassau, 85; 90; for the spoon, Chatelain, 17 (incomplete); Tremearne, 231–233. In Dayrell, 51, the abandoned implement is a drinking-horn. In the Bahama versions of the same story (Parsons, Andros Islands, 70–74; Edwards, 80–82) the episode does not appear.

12. Grace before Meat

The same story is told in Jekyll, 77. For the introduction, compare Tremearne, FL 21:502, and many Berber trick stories, e. g. Basset 1:1, 3; 2:12, 18, 76, 87. A version from Henry Spence, the Bog song leader, exactly follows the Aesopic model of Grimm 75 discussed in Bolte u. Polívka 2:119–121.

> De Fox ax de cat how much trick him got. Puss say, "I have one." De Fox say him have ten time ten. So one day Dog start de Cat an' de Fox. So after de Cat run fe de tree, never miss de tree at all, run to de top an' sit down look upon Fox now an' de dog. An' all de trick de Fox got, de Dog ketch him.

For Monkey's helping Tiger out of the hole and Tiger's ingratitude, compare Tremearne, FL 21:362.

For the escape by saying grace, compare: Bleek, 23; Jones, 109–110; Harris, Nights, 152–153 and see number 59b.

13. Seeing Trouble

The complete story is made up of three parts. (1) Some inexperienced animal wants to know "what trouble is". (2) The rascal gets him into difficulty; (3) and helps him out again.

Compare: Zeltner, 105–107; Tremearne, FL 21:499–500; Jones, 107–109; Parsons, Sea Islands, 59–61.

(1) Only Jones, Parsons and the Jamaica version (a) have the introduction, which suggests the story (Grimm 4) of the lad who did not know what fear was.

(2) One of three plots is employed to teach wisdom. In Jones (see number 30c and Gerber's Great Russian Animal Tales, 12, 16) the rascal gives his victem a bull-dog in a bag and bids him let it out in an open field. In Parsons, he sets on fire the deep grass in which his victim lies sleeping. In Zeltner, Hyena and Hare catch four lion cubs; Hare pretends to kill his two, and Hyena follows his supposed example.

In Tremearne, Hyena and Jerboa on a wedding journey are lodged in the goat-house and the fowl-house respectively. Jerboa proposes they have a feast, then counsels the host to count the fowls and the goats. None ot his fowl are missing, but Hyena has eaten a goat. In Ferrand, Madagascar, 207, it is proposed to kill mothers. One pretends to, the other thinks it real and does it. See number 136.

In Gerber's Great Russian Animal Tales, 13, the Fox, having placed some chickens under her, pretends to be tearing out and eating her own entrails. Bear tries to do the same and kills himself.

(3) The escape into a hole is very common. The usual method of rescue is to throw dust, pepper or spit into the eyes of the watcher at the hole. Compare: numbers 5c, 23, 27a, and Zeltner, 107; Nassau, 45, 46; Smith, 549; Harris, Uncle Remus, 52; Nights, 285; Fortier, 115; Jones, 108; JAFL 30:178; Parsons, Andros Island, 118 and note for references.

The "sweet" eye-water suggests such a tale as Tremearne, FL 21:364, where Goat smears honey upon Hyena's sinew, with which he is doing some mending for Lion, and by giving Lion a taste of it provokes an attack upon Hyena.

14. New Names

The trick to save a mother in time of famine from a mutual agreement of sacrifice to hunger, has a great vogue in Jamaica. I got two versions, and Pamela Smith tells it as "Parrot, Tiger and Anancy," 52–54.

Compare: Dayrell, 86–90; Dennett, 85; Harris, Nights, 233–236; 237–241; Fortier, 109; Parsons, Andros Island, 116–117; JAFL 30: 230–231.

Only in the Jamaica versions and in Parsons does the trick consist in teaching a hidden name. In P. Smith, after saving his mother by teaching her the new name, Anansi hides her in a tree and the story follows 17a. Dayrell, and Harris 237–241, tell the tree story. In Dennet, she is hidden in a cave, where she is discovered by treachery and killed. In Harris 233–236, Wolf's mother is taken first to market and sold, and Rabbit tricks Wolf out of horses, wagon and provisions by the familiar device of burying the tails; but the story is incomplete, as it does not explain how Anansi got out of the bargain. In Fortier, the two mothers are tied, one with a rope, the other with a cob-web, and one mother escapes. The tying trick precedes the tail-burying in Parson's Portuguese version, JAFL 30:230–231.

In Chatelain, 141–145, four brothers-in-law refuse food to their brother's wife because she does not know their names. A bird sings them to her as follows:

> *Listen, I will tell thee;*
> *(One is) Tumba Sekundu;*
> *(One is) Tumba Sekundu Muna;*
> *(One is) Tumba Kaulu;*
> *(One is) Tumba Kaulu Muna.*

For the hidden name theme which forms the basis of this story, see note to number 69.

15. Long Shirt

Hendrick's version of this good story is the only one I heard in Jamaica. It has a European coloring in the speaking garment, which resembles the English versions of Jack and the Bean-stalk. The setting of the dance resembles number 4, but in this story the dance plays no motivating part. For the horn as stump see Aesop, Phaedrus 2:8. The conclusion is no doubt a turn of Hendrick's own, as he was fond of explanatory endings and got one in whenever he could.

16. Shut up in the Pot

This common African story is not popular in America in this form, either because the idea is repulsive or because it is too simple to make a good story. The essential feature, that of taking turns going into the pot, is employed in number 37, and resembles the playing at tie each other of number 1. It is used in some versions of number 98. In Wona, 14–18, Anansi gets the animals into his pot by proposing a weight-testing contest.

Compare: Jacottet, 12–14; Junod, 91; Dayrell, 36–37; Elmslie, FL 3:104–105; Boas and Simango JAFL 35:168–170.

In Dayrell's version, Bat pretends to make soup by jumping into a pot which he has previously prepared with food, and persuades his companion to scald himself to death by imitating him. Yeats drew his play of the "Pot of Lentils" from an Irish version in which a stone serves as the magic means instead of the magician's person.

17. House in the Air

The story of obtaining entrance to a hidden food-supply "in the air" takes two general forms in Jamaica—first, that in which a song serves as pass-word, as in the voice-softening Rapunzel plot, number 91; second, that of the lost pass, numbers 22 and 100. The lost pass takes two directions; there is either a forgotten password or a destroyed "key."

The story is popular in Jamaica. See Jekyll, 23–25, Pamela Smith, 52–54; Backus, JAFL 11:288–289.

Compare: Dayrell, 86–90; Parsons, Andros Island, 5–7; 8–9; Sea Islands, 36; Harris, Nights, 236–241.

Version (a). Dayrell, Harris and Pamela Smith use the episode to complete the mother-eating story; the trickster hides his relative in a tree in order to evade his share of the bargain.

In Bleek, 7, 9, and Theal, 190, a trickster offers to act as carrier for the Lion's prey, conveys it to a height, then pretends to draw the Lion up with a rope but lets him fall when he is part way up.

Version (b). The version is so incomplete that its connections are difficult to trace. In Chatelain, 133, when the women from Sun and Moon who have come to draw water go back up to heaven on the cobweb that Spider has woven, Frog goes along with them to woo the daughter of Sun and Moon for his master. In Dennett, 74, the Spider climbs up to the blue vault of heaven and draws up the other animals to woo Nzambi's daughter.

Versions (c) and (d). In Parsons, Andros Island, 5–7, the trickster visits some fat pea-fields in the air belonging to "dose speerits which you call witch people" and gets a dash of hot water, as in number 1b. In version (d), the trickster himself employs the hot water in the popular John-crow peel-head episode with which the story concludes; see number 48. Backus's Jamaica version ends in the same fashion.

The idea of the liver as the "key" to the house occurs in Chatelain, 113. The trickster, after trying in vain to kill a monster by cutting off his head, gets himself swallowed and "goes to look into his hearts (i. e "liver" and "inner organs" generally, says the note) whether these are the keys."

18. Goat on the Hill-side

This well-known East Indian fable is common in Jamaica. Jekyll gives a version, 20–22.

Compare: Parsons, Andros Island, 88–89 and note for references; also Chatelain, 189–191; Junod, 123–124; Edwards, JAFL 4:52.

The ruse is one generally planned by the weak trickster for his strong but dull-witted companion, as in number 23. There is a tendency to place the incident among the monkeys, as in number 37. In Parsons's three versions the slaughter is made among them; in Jekyll's version, in a second of my own from Mandeville, and in Jacottet's form, it is the monkey or baboon who dis covers the trick. In Tremearne, FL 21:209–210, a bird gives warning; in Chatelain, a deer.

19. Dog and Dog-head

This story is told everywhere in Jamaica, but I find no African version and Mrs. Parsons says (JAFL 32:391) that, although she heard it "over and over again" in South Carolina, it was altogether unknown in North Carolina; see Sea Islands, 1–5. Such a distribution argues a fairly modern origin for the complete form of the story.

The story has two parts. (1) Two friends, who have, one a dog and the other a dog-head, go hunting, and the owner of the dog-head claims the spoils for his own. (2) His companion, who dares not dispute him, recovers the spoils by pretending that the owner is come to punish the theft.

An introduction sometimes tells how the friends come by the dog and dog-head. Each gets a present of a dog, but one is so greedy that he eats his down, beginning at the tail, until only the head is left. When his friend jeers at him, he makes a bet that his dog-head will catch the prey. The business of deciding at which end to begin to eat the dog is used as a humorous episode detached from the rest of the story, the victim sometimes escaping in the meantime.

The trick of claiming the cow as the prey of the dog-head may be related to such stories as that of Basset 2:88, in which the man lays the new-born calf beside his own bull and declares that the bull has mothered it.

For the revenge, compare Rivière, 11; Harris, Nights, 131–132.

20. Tacoomah's Corn-piece

See number 21.

21. Anansi and the Tar Baby

For the distribution of the Tar-baby story in negro folk-lore and its relation to negro practices compare: Boas, JAFL 25:247–250; Tremearne, 20–24; Parsons, Andros Island, 12–13; Sea Islands, 26–29. For Spanish see Espinosa (Cuentos populares españoles, Stanford University 1923, Vol. I, p. 80.)

Version (a). Of all the devices to catch a thief, the tar-baby story is by far the most popular in Jamaica. Despite its conformity to negro practices, the uniformity of style in which the story is treated shows that it is not here developed upon a naturalistic basis. On the other hand, the trick of the escape into the habitat does not often occur in Jamaica, perhaps because it is more amusing when coupled with the figure of Rabbit, as in 59a. For other instances of the fire-test see notes to number 9.

Version (b). Jamaica thief stories lay emphasis upon the unexpectedness of the thief's identity. In version (a) and in number 50, it is the watchman himself who is robbing the garden. In (b) it is the intimate friend. In (c) it is the father of the family. Pains are taken, moreover, to divert suspicion. In number 20, Anansi establishes an alibi by playing all night at a dance while his gang rob the field; in Junod, 102, Rabbit makes his companion put him under a mortar at night and fasten his feet, then wriggles out of the trap and returns to it again. The device in version (b) seems to be native to Jamaica.

The escape by means of a substitute is more dramatically handled than in Mrs. Parsons's Bahama versions, 15–16, but as Goat is generally a wary animal in Jamaica stories, the ending must be derived from the "Boukee and Rabby" cycle of the Bahama and Louisiana equivalents. For the substitute theme, compare numbers 2, 4, 5b, 10b, 58.

Version (c). Compare: Bleek, 80–82; Cronise and Ward, 101–111; Barker, 69–72. For the detection of the father by the son, see Cunnie-more-than-father, number 23.

22. Inside the Cow

According to Mrs. Parson's analysis in Andros Island, 2–10, the story of the lost pass takes four forms: (1) across water, (2) inside a tree, (3) to the sky, (4) inside the cow. To all these passages, a magic pass is attached, and either a violated prohibition or a forgotten pass-word traps the intruder until the master of the place appears.

In Jamaica, the story is very popular. (1) occurs in numbers 7, 39, 58, out of which, however, the pass-word has dropped; (2) is wanting; (3) is found in number 17; (4) appears in numbers 6 and 38 and in a number of current versions which contain the episode of cutting meat from inside the cow, but lack the other elements ot the story.

For the pattern of Parkes's story, which falls into five parts, compare: Tremearne, 257–260; Ellis, Yoruba, 271; Barker, 81–84; Cronise and Ward, 231–238; Nassau, 35–37; 202–207; Fortier, 31; 111; Harris, Uncle Remus, 166–168; Christensen, 108; Edwards, 77; Parsons, Andros Island, 2–10; Rattray, 2:88.

(1) The trickster discovers food in a neighbor's possession in Tremearne, Nassau, 203, Fortier, 31, Harris, Christensen, Edwards, Parsons, 3, 4, 27.

(2) His impatience leads him to create a "mock sunrise." In Tremearne, he burns the roof; in Christensen, he sets a tree on fire; in Ellis, he simulates the cock-crowing; in Barker, he makes the children rattle their spoons and sweep the floor.

In Parkes's version, Anansi wakens at the cow-boy's bell, and the reference to the "river-side" connects the story with the crossing water variant. As in Cronise and Ward, after learning the trick from his friend, he goes off alone for a supply without calling his neighbor.

In Jones, 11–14, and Harris, Friends, 6–11, the Sun promises to find food for the hungry Hawk if he can ever catch him in bed. When Rooster finally wakes Hawk in time to catch the Sun, the angry lord gives Hawk permission to catch chickens.

(3) In cutting the meat from inside the cow, in spite of warning he cuts a vital organ in Nassau, Cronise and Ward, Harris, Fortier, Parsons, 9; and numbers 17c and 17d of this collection.

In Fortier, 31 (see number 7), instead of taking one egg from each nest as bidden, he takes all. In Ellis, he forgets the password.

(4) When the owner of the dead cow comes to cut it up, the trickster hides in some organ, which the owner's daughter takes to the brook to wash. He jumps out, pretends that he was in the brook bathing, complains of the insult and gets the cow as damages. So Cronise and Ward, Nassau, Edwards. In Tremearne, he gets a whole elephant for himself.

(5) He carries the cow away into a lonely place in order to enjoy the whole, and Dry-head gets it away from him; see numbers 29, 30.

The episode does not occur in other versions. In Cronise and Ward, he gets three cows by means of the tail in the ground trick. In Harris, he is given his companion's head, who gets shut up with him and upon whom he has laid the blame of killing the cow.

23. Cunnie-more-than-Father

Parkes gave me the only version of this admirable story that I found in Jamaica and I did not find it in this form in other American collections. The essential idea is that of repeated attempts by a parent to turn over to an enemy an adroit child, who each time outwits his would-be captor. The plot is common in Africa. In Rattray, Chinyanje, 133–136; Torrend, 183–185; Junod, 158–163, a woman steals from a monster, who demands her unborn child in compensation. After his birth, the monster comes for his prey. The parent attempts to beguile the child into his hands by sending him to fetch something from the place where the monster lies concealed. Each time the child escapes. Finally the child climbs a tree and throws down fruit (Torrend and Junod) or wood (Rattray) into the open mouth of his enemy, thus choking and killing him.

For a similar sequence of attempts to entrap a weaker enemy, compare the Coyote and Rabbit cycle from Mexico, Boas, JAFL 25:205, 236, 246, and 260 referring to Preuss; and two versions of the same story by Mechling, JAFL 25:201–202.

Parkes's version includes five episodes, three of which belong to the regular cycle; the first and the last are indeterminate.

(1) The child proves too clever for the parent. Barker, 24, says, "Anansi is the Spider, and with him is generally associated his son, Kweku Tsin." Stories about the two bring out the superior wit of the son and the jealousy of the father. Compare numbers 19, 21c, 24 in this collection.

In the African stories cited above, the motive for seeking to entrap the child is one of compensation for stolen food. In the Mexican cycle, the dull-witted strong animal has been made to suffer punishment for a stolen food-supply, in place of the real thief. In Jamaica, the child's exposure of a hidden food-supply is used as the motive.

The story of the yam's hidden name is universally known and enjoyed in Jamaica. It belongs to the group of hidden-name stories discussed under number 69. See Milne-Home, 56–57, De Affassia, and compare Musgrave, 53–54.

(2), (3). The child first sticks a fire-stick into the pepper-bush behind which his enemy lies in wait, then throws bags of ants into his face as he waits under a cocoanut tree.

In the African and Mexican parallels, the trickster throws down fruit,—prickly-pears in Mexico. In every case, two fruits are thrown harmlessly, then the fatal fruit. Compare Parsons, Andros Island, 40. In Georgia, Backus, JAFL 13:22–23, pepper is the missile. In Nassau, 25–30, bags of ants and pepper are thrown to detect the pretended dead. This may be related to the bee trick in the Mexican cycle. In the Jamaica episode of the "refugees in the roof," numbers 5c and 27, after the wife and children have dropped and been devoured, Anansi puffs dust into the pursuer's eyes and escapes. Dust is thrown in Parsons, Sea Islands, 54, and in other instances in the same collection.

(4) For the episode of detecting a hidden enemy by calling upon the place where he is hidden to speak, compare Steere, 377; Rattray, 134; Renel 2:92, 93; Fortier, 110; Harris, Friends, 143–146; and Boas' Mexican cycle, JAFL 25:208 and reference, note page 248.

(5) For the trick of changing places in the coffin and the pretended pastures under sea, compare 107, 108.

24. The Duckano Tree

Tacoomah in this tale plays the part of Cunnie-more-than-father of the preceding as a spy to discover a hidden food-supply. It is a very popular Jamaica story, told by Milne-Home, 120–124; Wona, 62–66; Pamela Smith, 78.

Compare Edwards, 79; Dayrell, 26–28.

The story has three parts. (1) The son by means of a trail of ashes discovers a hidden food supply. (2) He takes all but one fruit and charms that so that his father cannot pick it. (3) Dog picks it up and swallows it, is pursued, discovered by his eyes in the ground, and the stolen fruit is squeezed out of him, thus causing the "sink places" in his two sides.

(1) For the trail of ashes compare Barker, 51–54; Arcin, 478; Dayrell, 27; Nassau, 204, 141, 155; Harris, Friends, 15–20.

(2) In Dayrell's story of The King's Magic Drum, the king gives Tortoise a tree which bears foo-foo once a year and drops foo-foo and soup once a day, but will lose the power if visited twice. The son follows and breaks the spell. The Kaffir "Iron John" story of The Bird that made

milk (Callaway, 99–104; Theal, 29–39), is the story of a food-producing animal trapped by the father and let loose by the son.

In Barker, Anansi, to punish men, gets the wisdom of the world sealed up in a jar and attempts to hide it away from everyone but himself in the top of a tall tree. His son, Kweku Tsin, follows him to the tree where he is hiding it, and, in his anger, Anansi lets the jar fall and break.

(3) In Theal, 158–168, a man whose greed in hiding a food-supply from his family has been discovered and punished, calls upon his dogs to aid him. Later his son escapes from the cannibals by slipping into a hole.

25. Food and Cudgel

The first form of this story is very common in Jamaica. It is told by Pamela Smith, Candoo, 28–30; Wona, Do-mek-I-see, 9–18. The introductory trick is generally told as an independent witticism.

Compare: Basset 11, 93–95; 102; Barker, 39–44; Dayrell, 20–28; Parsons, Andros Island, 141 and note for further references. See Grimm 36, The Wishing Table, the Gold-ass, and the Cudgell in the Sack, discussed in Bolte u. Polívka, 2:336–361.

26. The Riddle

Hendricks called this riddle test a "Nansi story," although another which he told me,—that of bringing water in a basket by daubing the basket with clay—he said was "not exactly a Nansi story."

27. Anansi and Brother Dead

The story of "Brother Dead" is one of the best known of Jamaica stories. Trowbridge, 282, says Death is looked upon as Anansi's brother. "Anansi fool 'em all; nobody can fool Anansi, only Bredder Dead," old Forbes said at the end of a trick story. Every Jamaica collection includes a version. See Jekyll, 31–34; Milne-Home, 40–41; Trowbridge, JAFL 9, 286–287; Pamela Smith, 69–70; Wona, 73–77. For other references, compare Parsons, Andros Island, 117–119 and note 2, page 117.

The story turns upon Anansi's stealing from Death's provision field, as in 17b. All the versions except Wona's version end with the episode of "refugees in the roof," as in number 5c; an episode related to the fruit-dropping or dust-blinding incident as a means of getting rid of a strong enemy who is lying in wait for a weaker; as in numbers 13c, 23.

In Wona's version, which has retained a European underworld coloring, Anansi passes fields of fat cattle and comes finally to the city of Death. He greases the hinges of the gate with the fat of the sheep he has killed out of Death's flocks, and when he flees, the gate opens for him. Nevertheless, the shadow of death jumps upon his back. He asks various friends to take it off, and finally succeeds in throwing it to earth; later he picks and eats callalu (Jamaica greens) from the spot where it fell. This latter part of the story is the "Dry-head" episode of numbers 22 and 30.

In the ordinary Jamaica version, the comedy of getting the food, bringing the wife, attempting Death's destruction, take the place of the underworld detail. Another Maroon version begins:

Anansi get a daughter he call Mat, an' he go to a place where he was hunting an' see a man sitting down all day sharpening pegs. Anansi go an' say "Morning, Brar Dead!" Not a 'peak, only keep on work all a time. He go up on his lof' have lots of dry meat, an' he tek as much an' carry it down an' bile his food. Anansi don' walk where rope is set against de water, walk a different pass.

After Anansi has left his daughter with Dead, the story runs:

Him daughter want water, say, "Brar Dead, want water." Not a answer. Him follow de pass an' go down to whe' de water deh; an' him drop in Brar Dead's rope an' he catch him. An' Dead run down an' tek him off de stick an' lick him.—"Brar Dead, I'm yo' wife! yo' wife, Brar Dead! Don' kill me! don' kill me!" Don' hear a word, not a word. Kill him an' cut him up an' carry him put him up in lof', mek fire under him, dry him.

In Trowbridge, Death is a loquacious planter and the story runs like any thieving plot. In the Maroon version the figure of "Brother Dead" corresponds with that of the "Piercer of Souls" or the "fisherman" in American Indian stories of the trickster's visit to the underworld, e. g. Relation de la Nouvelle France, 1636, p. 106; Petitot, Traditions Indiennes des Déné Dinjé, p. 33. The American Indian fisherman is spearing or angling for fish; the Jamaica figure of Death is trapping game. Both tricksters make their way in by avoiding Death's trap.

The incident of tying Death's hair in order to burn him up corresponds to the hair-plaiting in Callaway, 29, and Theal, 110, where the trickster sets fire to the hut and burns up his host.

Version (b) shows a simpler handling of similar incidents.

28. Brother Dead and the Brindle Puppy

The second story of "Brother Dead" is mixed up with obeah beliefs and it is hard to tell where the pattern ends and improvisation begins. Brother Dead, like the sorcerer, evidently sends a shadow in the shape of a brindled pup to pursue and catch Anansi. The song, meanwhile, plays a part in the conjuring. Words and tune are African. The old Maroon who gave me the trap-setting picture of "Brar Dead" quoted in the note to the last number, concluded as follows:

> "When he (Dead) ketch to a cross-path, tek him lance an' see one little maugre dog into a hole an' dig him out an' say to de puppy, 'Ai! Brar, fo' kitty a shall man bra!' If he had caught Anansi, he would kill Anansi"

I was unable to get an explanation of the sorcerer's phrase.

Compare, for the guardian dog, the story of Sarah Wintun by Lewis, 291, and see number 72. Jamaica sorcerers send a helping spirit in animal form to work their revenge.

29. The Cowitch and Mr. Foolman

The very popular Jamaica story of the "cowitch tree" is here combined with another equally popular story. (1) Anansi wins a bet to fell a tree in a cowitch property without scratching himself. (2) He loses the reward by being out-tricked by another fellow whom he has himself hoped to dupe and who pretends that the cow has sunk into the ground all but its tail.

The story occurs in Pamela Smith, 75–77; Milne-Home, 89–90; and a confused version in Jekyll, 29–30. Compare also number 52.

(1) The cowitch idea seems to be late Jamaican. In P. Smith, Anansi picks cocoa-nuts in spite of ants and wasps and gets a cow as reward.

In Milne-Home, he cuts down the tree without brushing off ants, and gets the king's daughter. In number 52, Toad succeeds in cutting down the tree the chips of which return magically to their place, and wins the king's daughter. Generally outside Jamaica, the reward is the king's daughter and the difficulty arises from stinging insects or from a useless weapon.

Compare Barker, 159–161; Tremearne FL 21:353–354; Lenz, 31–32; Harris, Nights, 216–222 and note to 222; Jones, 17; Parsons, Sea Islands, 3.

In Barker, the king promises an elephant to the man who can cut down a tree with a wooden axe. Anansi conceals a steel axe and calls the watcher's attention to various animals at a distance while he uses it.

In Harris, Wolf forbids his daughter to all wooers who slap at mosquitos. Rabbit wins her by describing where his grandfather was speckled.

In Jones, the king will give his daughter to Wolf or Rabbit, whichever will endure the sand-fly longest without slapping it. Rabbit wins by describing the colors on his father's horse.

In Tremearne, the task is to remove a heap of manure without either taking food or spitting, and Spider conceals in his quiver the means to fulfil these needs unsuspected. The story ends as in number 44.

In Lenz, the tree is to be chopped down with a single stroke by the one who wants to marry the daughter.

The test theme of the tree-chopping is familiar to European story. In Grimm, 79, the boy has to hew down a tree with a blunt axe as one of the tasks set by the Water-nix; see Bolte u. Polívka 2:140–146. In Grimm 193, the Drummer has to hew down the tree with an axe of lead and wedges and mallet of tin; see Bolte u. Polívka 3:406–417. The idea of stinging insects or plants as a test of self-control seems to be African and may be suggested by such ceremonial initiations into manhood as are described by Hollis, The Nandi, 54.

In Jamaica, the reward of self-control is not a wife but a cow. This the winner desires to eat entirely by himself. The "whole cow" theme so popular in Jamaica, occurs in 19, 22, 30, and in 6, 7, 11, 21, 23, 24, 25, 34, 39, 132 of this collection, the story turns upon a trick to secure the whole of a common food-supply.

The Foolman episode is told by Milne-Home, 109–113, of Anansi's wife and "Quanqua."

In P. Smith, the very popular "Dry-head" episode accounts for the loss of the cow, as in numbers 22 and 30.

In Barker, Anansi intends to get the cow to himself, but he loses it by the trick of stealing the tied animal. See Parsons, FL 28:411–413.

For the trick of tails in the ground, compare Harris, Nights, 234–236; 247–258; Uncle Remus, 101–103; Christensen, 89–90; JAFL 26: (Hitchiti Indians) 215–216; (General) 30:228; (Cape Verde) 230; 31: (Guatemala) 474; 32: (Virginia) 368; (Georgia) 403.

30. Dry-Head and Anansi

The "Dry-head" episode is very popular in Jamaica. From Jekyll's version, 48–49, I have corrected my version 30c as Johnson gave it and made Dry-head, not Anansi, the victim of the bag trick. Johnson was not a reliable informant. Other Jamaica versions occur in Pamela Smith, 75–76, as the conclusion to the "cowitch" story, and in Wona, 44–50.

The story falls into three parts. (1) Anansi pretends that he is about to die unless he has the whole of a fat barrow to himself. (2) He carries it away into the woods to eat and inadvertently picks up Dry-head, who devours the whole. (3) He invents an expedient to get rid of Dry-head.

Compare Surinam, JAFL 30:244–246; Madagascar, Renel 2:1–2; 57–59; Kaffir, Theal, 158–162; Upper Congo, Weeks FL 12:82–83; West African, Tremearne, FL 22: 61–63; Barker, 66; Cronise and Ward, 287–290; Rattray, 2:106–122.

(1) Rattray's Hausa version is identical with the Jamaican. The Surinam story lacks the Dry-head ending. In the Madagascar and Congo stories, the trick turns upon pretending that a spirit warns the wife against poison if she partakes of her husband's food. In Theal, Kenkebe visits his father-in-law in time of famine, is feasted on an ox and given bags of corn, which he conceals. Compare numbers 21c, 23, 24, 25, and 29.

(2) A Masai story (Hollis, 15) tells of two brothers who are given a bullock to slaughter. They carry it to "a place where there was no man or animal, or bird, or insect, or anything living," and a devil puts them to much inconvenience. The pursuit of Anansi by the shadow of Death, in the Wona version of 27, has already been referred to in the Dry-head episode. In Barker, 81–84, the stolen flour-producing stone which Anansi is carrying off, sticks to his head and grinds him to pieces, as referred to in the note to number 22.

In Theal, Kenkebe's wife and son hide themselves behind the rock which conceals his secret store, and push over a stone which pursues him as far as his own house.

In Barker, 66, the king gives to the greedy man a box so enchanted that it can never be put down.

In Sac and Fox Indian tales, JAFL 15:177, the monster-killing twins bring home a rock which sticks upon their backs until they carry it to its place again.

In the Ojibway Nanabushu cycle, Jones, Pub. Eth. Soc. 1: 117–127, Nanabushu is cooking a deer. The branches of the tree creak and he gets up to grease them and is caught and hung there. Meanwhile, the wolves come and eat up the deer. He finally escapes, discovers that the brains of the deer are still left in the deer-skull, transforms himself into a snake and crawls into the head. Turning too quickly back into human shape, he gets caught with the skull fast to his head and has to carry it about with him until he manages to break it against a rock.

(3) The regular Jamaica conclusion of the Dry-head episode seems to be the Aesopic one in which a bird carries him in air and drops him, not against a rock but, in Jekyll, "in the deepest part of the woods;" in version (c), "in a sea-ball." In another version not printed here, Anansi takes in an old man because he has some food with him; but when the food gives out, the man "become a Dry-head on him," and Anansi puts him off on Tacoomah, who leaves him by the sea so that a wave comes up and drowns him. In version (a) Anansi burns him up. Version (b) is a witticism in the same class as "Dry-head and the Barber" in this collection.

In Pamela Smith's version, Anansi shoots the bird who is doing him the favor of carrying off Dry-head. See note to number 70 and compare P. Smith, 59–64, in which Tiger, pursued by the "Nyams," begs one animal after another to hide him, but always lets his presence be known. Finally, when Goat kills the "Nyams," he eats Goat with the "Nyams."

In Dorsey, The Pawnee, 126, and Traditions of the Arikara, 146–148, Coyote, pursued by a Rolling Stone, takes refuge with the Bull-bats and is defended by them. In the Pawnee version, he later insults his rescuers.

31. The Yam-hills

The yam-hill story is very common in Jamaica. Parkes learned it in Kingston. Pamela Smith tells it, page 59 and JAFL 9:278. Sometimes a song accompanies the story. The number of Yam-hills varies.

Compare Cronise and Ward, 167–171; Parsons, Andros Island, 109.

The story depends upon the idea that it is unlucky to reveal to others a marvel one has seen oneself, or to repeat certain taboo words. A lad in the Santa Cruz mountains explained the taboo by saying that Anansi had "six" legs. Another said that Anansi's mother's name was "Six." So in Pamela Smith (JAFL 9:278), the Queen's name is "Five." Compare Rivière, 177; Krug, JAFL 25:120; Schwab, JAFL 32:437, and the next two numbers in this collection.

32. The Law against Back-biting

Parkes learned this story on board ship coming from Africa. It is common in Jamaica, and the wit by which the revenge is effected seems to be an individual invention, as it varies from story to story. In Junod's Ba-ronga version (156–158), Piti, the fool, amuses himself by the roadside instead of going to herd cattle. Everyone who reproaches him falls dead. Later he restores his victims to life by means of fire.

33. Fling-a-mile

Jekyll, 152–155, has a good version of this very popular Jamaica story.

Compare the Bulu tales, Schwab, JAFL 27:284–285; 32:434.

In JAFL 27, Turtle sets a trap and by pretending to teach other animals who come along one by one how to use it, he catches one victim after another until he is himself caught.

In JAFL 32, Pangolin offers to initiate the animals one by one and makes them climb a tree and jump upon a concealed rock, which kills them. Turtle finally circumvents the trick.

In a Jamaica version collected in Mandeville, Anansi holds a butchering at a place where there is a tree which seizes any person who leans against it and flings him upon a lance which Anansi has set up.

34. But-but and Anansi

The very popular story of Butterfly's revenge is a somewhat obscured version of an old theme—the Jataka story of The Quail's Friends, Francis and Thomas, 247–250. Compare Steel-Temple, Wide Awake Stories, 184; Gerber, Great Russian Animal Tales, Pub. Mod. Lang.

Asso. of Am. 6: No. 2:19–20; Grimm 58, The Dog and the Sparrow, discussed in Bolte u. Polívka 1:515–519.

Though common today, the story seems to be of comparatively late introduction. Old Edwards, over eighty, heard it when he was "ripe." Compare Tremearne, 231.

35. Tumble-bug and Anansi

The story of Tumble-bug's revenge is even more common than the last number. In Wona, 51–55, Tumble-bug is carrying butter and Anansi only lard. Anansi proposes that they put their loads together, sees that Tumble-bug's is at the bottom, and makes the ruling in order that he may get the butter and Tumble-bug the lard. Compare number 46 and the opening episode of the last number.

The revenge story is recent. In Wona, Tumble-bug suffers further at Anansi's hands.

In Tremearne, FL 21:213–214, Tortoise and Spider have a bull in common; Tortoise eats the liver and Spider claims in compensation the whole bull. Tortoise pretends dead and frightens Spider, who thinks it is a spirit and gives him everything.

36. Horse and Anansi

For the trick of sending after fire in order to enjoy the whole of a common store compare Koelle, 166–167; Tremearne, 255, 263; Hartt, 34; Harris, Friends, 79–80; Nights, 282–284; Christensen, 89; Georgia, JAFL 32:403.

For the trick of leaving the knife or the spoon behind, see number 11 in this collection.

For the fire-test see 21a and note to number 9.

It is clear, from the picture drawn of Horse as he starts for the Fire, that the story-teller thinks of the actors in the story as animals, even when he shows them behaving like human beings.

37. Anansi in Monkey Country

Mrs. W. E. Wilson (Wona) thinks that the second version of the story, told by Jekyll, 70–72, is not a true negro form, because of the great respect in which Jamaica negroes hold the rites of the established church.

Compare Cronise and Ward, 133–145; Fortier, 24–27.

As a device for getting victims cooked and eaten, the story is related to numbers 16 and 38 in this collection.

38. Curing the Sick

In Parkes's version, the substitution of the human for the fish victim not only spoils the wit of the story but obscures its relation to the story of Anansi's visit to fish-country as it appears in number 39. The identity of the two is proved by the structure of the story, which falls into two parts. (1) Anansi, pretending to cure a sick relative, eats her instead. (2) The mule offers to avenge her and plays dead outside Anansi's door; when he attempts to make use of her for food, she drags him into the water and drowns him, as in number 6.

For (1) compare Cronise and Ward, 226–230, where Rabbit pretends to cure Leopard's children and eats them up; Nassau, 125–126, where Tortoise pretends to bring children out of Crocodile's hundred eggs, and eats them all.

(2) In Parsons's Portuguese negro story, JAFL 30:231–235, Lob escapes from the island where the indignant birds have abandoned him, by bribing Horse-fish to carry him across. He promises to pay her well, but abandons the horse-fish as soon as he touches shore. She remains weeping on the shore. Lob thinks her dead and starts to cut her up. She drags him into the sea and drowns him. There are small touches in the story which prove its identity with the Jamaica version. When Lob's wife weeps, Lob says, "She is just playing with me, she is not going to do anything." In Parkes's story, Anansi says to the mule who is dragging him into the sea, "A little fun me mak wid you, no mean i'." In both Jamaica versions, Mule turns Anansi over to the vengeance of the fishes; in the Portuguese, he is drowned.

In Jekyll, 135–137, an old lady meddles with a jar she has been told not to touch and which, as soon as she gets her hand in, drags her to the sea and drowns her.

In Jekyll, 125, "Cousin Sea-mahmy" makes his son Tarpon carry Anansi to shore, and Anansi gets him into the pot by the trick of taking turns weighing each other, as in number 16.

In Pamela Smith, 44–46, Anansi eats the sick mother under pretence of cure, and bribes Dog to carry him across the river, but there is no vengeance; Dog himself is swallowed by Crocodile.

39. Anansi, White-belly and Fish

Jekyll, 129–131, and Milne-Home, 35–39, have excellent versions of this very popular Jamaica story, which, in its full form, is made up of four episodes. (1) The birds take Anansi across the water to their feeding-place where; because of his bad behavior, they abandon him. (2) Anansi visits Fish and claims relationship. Fish tests him with a cup of hot pop, which he cools in the sun under pretence of heating it hotter. (3) He is lodged for the night with a box of eggs, all of which he eats but one; and when called upon to count the eggs, brings Fish the same one every time, after wiping off the mark. (4) Fish sends her children to row him home. He fools them out of heeding her call when she discovers the loss of the eggs. Once on shore, he fries and eats the children.

Compare Tremearne, 265–266; Head-hunters, 324–326; Rattray, 2:88–104; Parsons, Portuguese negroes, JAFL 30:231–235; Andros Island, 2–3.

(1) The episode of the birds' feeding-place is to be compared with that of Fire-fly and the egg-hunt, number 7, and with the visit "inside the cow," number 22. In the Portuguese version, the birds take Lob to a dance and he sings insulting songs because there is no feast.

(2) The test of relationship occurs in Jekyll and in Tremearne, Head-hunters. It belongs to the same class of boasts as those of the Clever Tailor in Grimm 20 and 183.

(3) In Milne-Home, the scorpion trick is employed to guard the eggs, as in number 7, and Anansi complains of "fleas" biting him. The episode is lacking in Jekyll.

In Tremearne, Head-hunters, when Spider breaks the egg-shells, the children cry out to know what is the matter and Spider says he is hiccoughing.

The egg-counting trick generally occurs in a different connection. The trickster visits Tiger's house, eats all the cubs but one, and counts that one many times. Compare Callaway, 24–27; MacDonald 1:55–56; Theal 111; Jacottet, 40–45; Rattray, Chinyanje, 137–138; Harris, Nights, 346–348.

(4) In Jekyll, Anansi visits "Sea-mahmy," who is a mermaid, and her son, "Trapong," or tarpon, takes him home. In Milne-Home, "Alligator" is host; a "boatman" the ferryman. Lob gets "aunt" sea-horse to carry him to shore. In my Jamaica versions, the sons are the ferrymen and are generally cooked and eaten at the other end. The misinterpreted call occurs in all

Jamaica versions and in Tremearne, Head-hunters. In the Lob story, Lob mutters an insult; when asked to repeat his words, he declares that he has merely praised the sea-horse's swimming; compare Parsons, Sea Islands, 54–56. For the fate of the ferryman, see also note to number 38 and compare Anansi's treatment of Rat in the note to number 7.

40. Goat's Escape

The story of Goat's Escape is a favorite in Jamaica. See Milne-Home, 58–60; 65–66. It falls into two parts. (1) Goat and Dog are pursued and Dog escapes over a river which Goat cannot cross. (2) Goat transforms himself into a stone, which the pursuer himself throws across the river. The introduction to the flight varies but (2) remains constant.

Compare: Jacottet, note page 262; Parsons, Andros Island, 103 and note; Jones, 121–123; 133–136.

Version (a). Compare Jones, and Milne-Home, 58–60.

Version (b). In Jekyll, 46–47, Puss gives the rats a ball and only those members of the family escape who attend to little Rat's warning, for he has heard the cat's song. Compare Chatelain, 189–191, and see note to number 86, where the little brother or sister discovers by the words of a song a treacherous intention.

41. Turtle's Escape

See number 58, part (3).

42. Fire and Anansi

A less witty version of this popular Jamaica story occurs in Jekyll, 129–131.

In Dayrell, 64–65, Sun and Water are great friends. Sun visits Water, but Water never visits Sun. At length, Sun invites Water and builds a great compound to receive him and his friends. All come, take possession, and crowd Sun and his wife, Moon, out into the sky.

43. Quit-quit and Anansi

A story which turns upon teaching the wrong song to a dull-witted rival, never fails to raise a laugh in Jamaica. See numbers 4, 106 in this collection.

44. Spider Marries Monkey's Daughter

Compare Tremearne FL 21:353–354 and number 92 of this collection.

45. The Chain of Victims

Common as is the story of the "chain of victims" in Africa, Falconer gave me the only version I heard in Jamaica

Compare Koelle, 158–161; Dayrell, 6–10; Nassau, 245–247; Tremearne, 373–374; FL 21:211–212; Lenz, 39–40; Boas, JAFL 25:207–209; Rattray, 2:58–72.

46. Why Tumble-bug Rolls in the Dung

Compare Tremearne, 261; FL 21:498–499; Christensen, 96–98; and note to number 35 in this collection.[1]

47. Why John-crow has a Bald Head

The explanatory story of "John-crow peel-head" is very popular in Jamaica. See Pamela Smith, 25–26, and number 17d.

48. Why Dog is always Looking

In Milne-Home, 121, "Jack Spaniard" (a wasp-like fly) laughs at Mosquito's boast till "he broke his waist in two."

In Jones, 22, Sparrow makes the boast about his father's crop of potatoes.[2]

49. Why Rocks at the River are covered with Moss

See Milne-Home, 94–95; Jekyll, 52.

Compare Parsons, Andros Island, 119–121 and note for references; Bundy, JAFL 32:412–413, and see note to number 138.

For a discussion of Grimm 110, The Jew among Thorns, see Bolte u. Polívka 2:490–503.

---

1. See supplementary note, p. 289.
2. See supplementary note, p. 290.

50. Why Ground-dove Complains

See number 21.

51. Why Hog is always Grunting

See number 10. In Pamela Smith's "Dry-head" story, Anansi's nose turns long, and he goes about persuading other people to screw on snouts.

52. Why Toad Croaks

See note to number 29.

53. Why Woodpecker Bores Wood

In Barker, 123, three sons wish to do honor to their mother and the first declares that he will make her a "sepulchre of stone."

54. Why Crab is afraid after Dark

The story represents a very wide-spread folk motive—that of a weak being who appeals to some deity for more power, but whose request is proved to be either needless or disastrous.

In Tremearne, FL 21:360, an old woman is to teach Spider cunning. She sends him for a bottle of lion's tears, an elephant's tusk, a dog's skin. Spider secures them all, and escapes her when she tries to kill him. She says, "If I taught you more cunning, you would destroy everybody." This story is popular in Sea Islands, according to Dr. Parsons, JAFL 32:404, and Sea Islands, 14–19. Compare Bundy, JAFL 32:416–417, and note, page 416.

In Tremearne, 270–271, Snake promises Scorpion a poison that will kill a man at once. Scorpion accidentally bites Snake, and she refuses the poison lest he kill everybody.

In Fortier, 13–19, the Devil gives the little Earthworm his wish: "I want to become big big and beat everybody who will come to trouble and bother me. Give me only that and I shall be satisfied." The consequences are disastrous for the earth-worm.

In Folk-tales of the Malagasy, FLJ 1:238–239, "the little Round Boy" smokes out God's children and so wins his desire.

In Ralston, 1–20, Sukra grants all an ambitious king's wishes until he finally wishes to push Sukra himself off his seat. See Grimm, 19, The Fisherman's Wife, Bolte u. Polívka 1:138–148.

Compare the Panchatantra story quoted by Ralston, introduction to Tibetan Tales, Liii, of the weaver who asks for two pairs of arms and two heads in order to work faster, but is pelted by his terrified neighbors for his pains.

55. Why Mice are no Bigger

Compare Parsons, Sea Islands, 19–22.

56. Rat's Wedding

This story is told in Milne-Home, 63–64.[3]

57. Cockroach Stories

For version (a) compare number 6.

For version (b) compare Tremearne, 314; Parsons, Andros Island, 90–91 and note.

58. Hunter, Guinea-hen and Fish

The story as Williams tells it is made up of three parts. (1) Bird and Hunter set up the same home without either knowing of the other. (2) Bird supplies Fish with wings and brings him to the feeding-patch, then takes the wings and flies away when Hunter comes in pursuit. (3) Fish is captured as the thief, but escapes by song and dance into the sea.

(1) See Grimm 27, Bremen Town Musicians, Bolte u. Polívka, 1:237–239. Compare Barker, 141–143; Tremearne, FL 21:495; Renel 2:12–13; Parsons, Andros Island, 135; Rattray, 2:34.

(2) The episode is identical with Anansi and the Birds in number 39, but motivated differently. See numbers 2b, 5b, 21b. In Bates's Jamaica version, JAFL 9: 122–124, Mudfish is left in the Watchman's hands without the preliminary episode of the common dwelling, and the escape is effected in the same manner.

---

3. See supplementary note, p. 290.

(3) See number 41 and compare Renel 2:165; Parsons, Andros Island, 135–137 and references note 2, page 137.

59. Rabbit Stories

These three and number 17b are the only Rabbit stories I heard in Jamaica. A woman named Ellen told the stories to the lads from whom I heard them, but she refused to be interviewed. See numbers 21a, 12, 23.

60. The Animal Race

The wit of the animal race turns upon the fact that a slow animal, contrary to all expectation, wins over a swift. The story takes three forms. (1) The swift animal is so sure of winning that it delays and "slow but sure wins the race." (2) The little animal wins by hanging on behind while the other runs, and thus slipping in ahead at the end. (3) The slow animal arranges a relay by placing one of its kind along the road and taking its own position in hiding near the goal. See Dähnhardt 4:46–96.

(1) The classic Aesopic moral appears in Parsons, Andros Island, 102–103; and in JAFL 30:214.

(2) Compare Barker, 155–157; Madagascar, FLJ 2:166–168; Natchez Indians, Swanton, JAFL 26:203; Saurière, 104; Lenz, Estudios, 185, 187.

In Grimm 20 (Bolte u. Polívka 1:148–165), while the giant bears the trunk of the tree on his shoulders, the valiant tailor rides home from the forest in the branches and pretends that he has been carrying the heavier load of the two.

(3) The Jamaica stories always follow the form of the relay race, as in Jekyll, 39–43. Compare Basset 1:15; Bleek, 32; Frobenius 3:15; Rattray, Chinyanje 131; Renel 2:150–152; Schwab, JAFL 27:277; Hartt, 7–15; Smith, 543; Christensen, 5–9; Jones, 5–6; Edwards, 69; Harris, Uncle Remus, 87–91; Boas, JAFL 25:214–215; Parsons, Sea Islands, 79; JAFL 30:174; 32:394; and references to American Indian stories in Boas, JAFL 25:249; Ponape, Hambruch, Südsee-Märchen, p. 196; note, p. 347.

The story is told in Grimm 187, discussed by Bolte u. Polívka 3:339–355.

For the flying-trial for a bride, compare Parsons, Andros Island, 101.

61. The Fasting Trial

See number 149, where the bird in the tree starves and Hopping Dick on the ground picks up worms and wins the match. In this story, though incomplete, it is intimated that the bird in the tree wins.

Compare Dayrell, 153–155; Harris, Nights, 370–373; Fortier, 34–37; Parsons, Andros Island, 97 99.

In Dayrell, the birds propose to starve seven days to see which will be king. One leaves a hole out of which he creeps unobserved to feed.

In Harris, as in this Jamaica version, the winning bird takes up his station in the tree; the "fool bud" stays down by the creek.

In Parsons, one bird chooses a fruit tree, the other a "dry" tree. The song sung by the winning bird runs,—

> *"This day Monday mornin'*
> *Tama tama tam!"*

and so on for the remaining days of the week.

In Fortier, the lady-love brings food to her favorite bird. The cooing song in the Jamaica versions suggests this connection.

62. Man is Stronger

Compare Koelle 177–179; Harris, Nights, 33–38; 330–333; Radin, JAFL 28:397–398, and see Grimm 72, discussed by Bolte u. Polívka 2:96–100, and Sebillot, Le Folk-lore de France, 3:63.

63. The Pea that made a Fortune

Compare: Bleek, 90–94; Callaway, 37–40; Theal, 102–105; Renel 2:60–63; Rivière, 95–97; Tremearne, 237–242; FL 21:213–214; Barker, 177–180; Cronise and Ward, 313; Torrend, 169–172; Elmslie, FL 3:92–95; Krug, JAFL 25:113–114; Harris, Friends, 182–186, and see Grimm 83, Hans in Luck; Bolte u. Polívka 2:201–203.

64. Settling the Father's Debt

For similar "enigmatic phrase" stories compare Basset 2:147–148; Rivière, 160–162; Renel 2:82–84; 89–90; 164–165. The version, however, resembles the drolls from the Wye valley recorded in FL 16:178, 352.

65. Mr. Lenaman's Corn-field

Parkes gave me the only version I got of this good story in Jamaica; he heard it in the parish of St. Ann. Barker, 181–184, tells the same for "Farmer Mybrow," but only to the harvesting. In Cronise and Ward, 152–159, a man tries to harvest rice in Devil's Town. The Devil does all the work, but eventually the pot of rice runs back to the Devil.

66. Simon Tootoos[4]

I heard this story more than once in Jamaica.

Compare Renel 2:167–168; 283–286; Bundy, JAFL 32:420; Parsons, Andros Island, 62–65 and 62, note 1, for references.

In a manuscript story shown me by Mrs. W. E. Wilson (Wona) which she took down from her old nurse, the same song is adapted to another story of a disobedient boy. In this tale, the boy insists upon going out late at night. He is at last captured by an ogre named "Time-an'-tootoos" who carries him off to devour. Father, mother and sister refuse his cry for help, but the brother finally hears him and comes just in time to his rescue. The song runs:

> *Me muma, oh, me muma, oh,*
> *Time-an'-tootoo, oh, lennan boy!*
> *Me muma, oh, me muma, oh,*
> *Time-an'-tootoo, oh, lennan boy!*
> *Carry him go 'long, carry him go long,*
> *Hard ears baby, oh, lennan boy!*

For the story, compare Parson's Andros Island, "Disobedient Boy," 155–156, and see Jacobs's tale of Mr. Miacca, English Fairy Tales, third edition, revised, 171; Grimm, 42, The Godfather, Bolte u. Polívka 1:375–377. This is the only case in which I found the same song adapted to the dialogue of two different stories.

---

4. See supplementary note, p. 290.

67. The Tree-wife

Compare Torrend, 40–44. For the answering spittle, compare Tremearne, 210; answering tufts of hair, Theal, 131; see note to number 15 and Bolte u. Polívka 1:499; 2:526–527. For beliefs about tracing something lost by means of spittle, see JAFL 2:51, 52.

68. Sammy the Comferee

This curious story seems to be a cross between the Potiphar's wife episode with which the ballad of "Young Seidal" opens, and the African tale of the lard girl who melts if exposed to the sun.

Compare Dayrell, 1–2; Tremearne, 192; Parsons, Andros Island, 125 and note 2 for references.

69. Grandy Do-an'-do

In a Jamaica version by P. Smith, the story takes the form of the transformed mistress (numbers 84, 87). Toad betrays the witch to her suitor and teaches him the name by pronouncing which he discovers her true nature. In another Jamaica story (P. Smith, 38–40), the monster does not harm the woman who knows his name.

The story belongs to the group of fatal-name stories so popular in Jamaica. See numbers 14, 17, 23, 31, 44, 75, 88, 87, 89, 92, 93. All turn upon name customs and superstitions such as are touched upon in Tremearne, 178–182; Renel, 2:39–40; Theal 2:214; and discussed in Clodd's Magic in Names, New York, 1921; Frazer's Golden Bough (1911) 3:318–418. See also Bolte u. Polívka 1:490–498, on Grimm 55.

Compare Junod, 309–313; Tremearne, 274–278; 349–350; Dayrell, 79–80; Parsons, Andros Island, 114–115; Sea Islands, 22–23.

In this story, (1) a servant, refused food unless she tells the name of her mistress, learns the secret from a friendly animal; (2) the mistress discovers the traitor and avenges herself upon him or is herself vanquished.

(1) In some African versions, girls come to wed a desirable suitor, who kills them if they cannot tell his name. One girl is polite to an old woman, who tells her the secret.

(2) In some African versions, as in number 93, the name is fatal. In Jamaica, its possession wins a reward, and the interest is likely to

turn upon an explanatory ending. For the incident of singing the name, see Musgrave, FLR 3:1:53–54. For the bull-fight, see number 88, and compare Cronise and Ward, 55–65.

70. Jack and Harry

This fragmentary story belongs, with the Man-crow story of number 90, to a much longer African story which relates the adventures of a child-hero whose father, dying, leaves instructions that the child's will shall never be crossed. Incidents succeed one another of inhuman ingratitude and of intrepid heroism, based on the possession of magical powers, until the boy finally kills a bird-monster and performs other remarkable exploits.

Compare Tremearne, How Auta killed Dodo, 408–412; Zeltner, Histoire de Kama, 47–62.

"Harry" in this story is the counterpart of the older sister who acts as Kama's mentor in Zeltner's version, and of "Barra" in Tremearne. The four episodes are common to this and the Kama story,—the stolen breakfast, the insult to the sheltering old woman, and the two episodes of the breaking of the rescuing eagle's wing, followed immediately by the abuse of the friendly tortoise. In Zeltner, the tortoise has restored the children to life. The common-place incidents of the Jamaica version are in curious contrast with the rich and varied phantasmagoria of the Senegambian tale.

The flight which brings disaster to the kindly shelterers occurs in the story of Tiger's pursuit by the "Nyams," told by Pamela Smith, 59–65. Compare Tremearne, 344–346.

In Europe, the story of the Bear's son in folk-tale and of Robert the Devil in romance have points in common with this story. See Grimm 90; Bolte u. Polívka 2:285–297; as also Grimm's Thumbling stories, numbers 37 and 45, and note (3) to number 30.

71. Pea-fowl as Messenger

Jekyll, 84–85, connects the animal competitors with the story of making the dumb girl speak, as in numbers 95, 96. In Milne-Home, 73–77, the animals compete to sing at the king's dance. In African parallels, some peril is involved of which a bird is to bear warning. But in all my versions and in those given by Mrs. Parsons from Andros Island,

112–113, the birds summon the father of a new-born child. The song of one of my versions from Maroon-town runs,

> *Mr. Canoe-lo, Mr. Canoe-lo,*
> *I want de key of de hall door,*
> *Mistress Canoe hard labour.*

Mrs. Parsons says that the negroes of Andros Island agreed that this was the most popular story on the island.

Compare Torrend, 87–88; Junod, 140–141; Dennett, 103–104; Jacottet, 108; Theal, 63–66; Renel 1:32–34; 279–281, 282–287; Parsons, Andros Island, 112–113; Sea Islands, 106.

Peafowl's reward gives an explanatory turn to the end of the story. In Hendricks version from Mandeville, Peafowl sings,

> *Mister Conna Levrin, Mister Conna Levrin,*
> *When she's going to die, ah-h!*

The husband reaches home in haste. The lady gives Pea-fowl the promised reward, and "he took the bag of gold and the silver, and in his joy he threw it right over his head, over his entire body, never remembered his two feet. That's the reason why Pea-fowl's so handsome all over—has such beautiful feathers and such ugly feet."

72. The Barking Puppy

On the whole, the bird is a friendly spirit, the dog an unfriendly in African story. Here, as in number 28, the dog takes the place of the warning bird. The idea seems to be here that the dog, by calling his master's name, invokes his spirit.

Compare Junod, 93; Parsons, Andros Island, 165; and "The Hobyahs" in Jacobs, More English Fairy Tales, 127.

In Junod, Dove warns Hippopotamus against Rabbit; Rabbit kills Dove. The feathers give warning; Rabbit burns all the feathers but one and mixes them with dirt; then the one feather gives warning.

In Chatelain, 129, a dog warns of a murder. See note to number 73.

In Callaway, 52, a witch's flesh is ground to powder and thrown into the water in order that it may not come back to life

73. The Singing Bird

In Jekyll, 14–16, the incident of the warning bird is employed in the story of the two sisters, number 74. Version b is a poor rendering of Jekyll, 96–97.

In Theal, 217–220, the younger of two brothers secures a magic gift of cattle. The elder lets him down into a water-hole to drink and, leaving him there, goes home with the cattle. A warning bird leads rescuers to the place. See, for the same story, Jacottet, 60–62 and note; Folk-Lore Jour. of. So. Af. 1:139–147.

For the incident of the warning bird compare Torrend, 17; note 24–26; 166–167; Theal, 219; Renel 1:30–31; Dayrell, 110–114; FLJ (SA) 1:75–79. The motive is common in ballads; e. g. JAFL 20:253. In the Cinderella story, it is a bird who gives warning of the false bride; e. g. Callaway, 130–135. Not all birds, only certain species, are looked upon as "prophet birds." See Cronise and Ward, 175; Dennet, 8. That these birds may be regarded in some cases as the actual soul of the murdered person is evident from Renel's story.

In Parsons, Andros Island, 129–132, a tree sings of a murder. See Grimm 47, The Juniper Tree, and Bolte u. Polívka 1:412–423 on Grimm 28, The Singing Bones.

74. Two Sisters

Jamaica versions of this popular story appear in Milne-Home, 70–72; Jekyll, 14–16; Trowbridge, JAFL 9:283–284. Parsons Andros Island, 150–152, has equivalent versions.

The False Bride motive is very common in African story. Compare Callaway, 105–130; 303–316; Theal, 56–66; 144–147; 151–154; Jacottet, 90–99; Torrend, 66–68; Dayrell, 126.

In number 101, the true bride comes at night and sings and is detected through the words of her song. In this story, she comes at night to suckle her child; see the Child ballad version noted by Parsons, and Bolte u. Polívka 1:76–96, on Grimm 11, Brother and Sister. In Theal, 56–66, the drowned woman comes at night to suckle her child, is watched, and a net set to catch her. In Theal, 144–147, the snare and the milk are set for the false instead of for the true bride as a test of her witch nature because no witch's tail can escape the attraction of milk. This is like the old fable of the cat who became a lady, but betrayed her origin when a mouse ran across the floor.

75. Assonah

This story has some elements in common with number 90. It falls into two parts. (1) A huge beast comes daily to the house and is finally shot. (2) A boy who must discover the name of the beast learns it by chance from an old woman and wins the reward.

(1) Compare Backus, JAFL 13:27, where the animal is a bear.

(2) The connection between the first and the last part of this story, which seems to belong to the fatal name series, is lost. For the old woman as informant, compare references to number 69. For the audience, the point of the story evidently lay in the comic way in which Brown held up the imaginary monster's skin between thumb and forefinger and said, "No (is it not?) Assonah 'kin?" Assonah is generally supposed to be an elephant.

76. The Greedy Child

The idea of a water spirit who allows no one to cross a river without an offering of food, seems to be common in West Africa; e. g. Dayrell, 107–114. Jekyll, 100–101, Dry River, has a Jamaica version of this story. Compare also Tremearne, 209–210, 307–314.

77. Alimoty and Aliminty

For the exchange of colors see Bolte u. Polívka 1:124–126. For place-changing and killing of the wrong victim see the same, 499–501. Compare Parsons, Sea Islands, 128.

The incident is common in African story, e. g. Tremearne, 430; Dennett, 47; Torrend, 33; Junod, 163. The setting of the story is often similar to number 23 where a parent calls upon outside aid to get rid of a troublesome child.

78. The Fish Lover

This story is very common in Jamaica. See Milne-Home, 91–93, and compare Renel 1:203–204; 206–208 (origin of water-beings); Renel

2:268–269; Parsons, Andros Island, 61, and note for references; Sea Islands, 137.

In Smith, 573–584, a young man changes into a fish in order to escape the attentions of the ladies. He comes out when his mother calls him. He is finally lured out and caught in the meshes of his lover's hair.

In Grimm 8, Bolte u. Polívka 1:69–70, a little girl is forced by her brothers to go out and cut peat with a dull knife. Her elf-lover stretches out a sharp knife to her from the hill where he lives and tells her to call him by striking on the stone. The brothers wonder how she can cut the peat, and spy upon her. They strike the stone, take the knife and cut off the elf's hand, who thereafter disappears.

79. Juggin Straw Blue

The story is confused in the telling. It has three parts. (1) A water-being helps a girl who is abused by her aunt and sent to fetch water with too heavy a jug. (2) The water-being pursues and carries off the girl, though she is locked in an iron chest. (3) The girl's lover comes to her rescue and defeats the monster. See the next number and perhaps 99.

80. The Witch and the Grain of Peas

There are two parts to this story. (1) The witch step-mother discovers that the girl has eaten food in her house and threatens to drown her. (2) The lover comes to rescue her and fights the step-mother.

(1) Compare Jacottet, 166–175, and Lewis, 253–255.

(2) For the fight, compare numbers 69, 79, 88, 89, 90. For the fight with eggs see number 79 and compare Fortier, 11–13. Eggs are used as propitiatory offerings to a water monster, as in Dayrell, 130, and are among the most useful objects employed for conjuring. In Zeltner, 1–6, eggs are used for magical purposes in the fight with a witch, but arrows serve as the actual weapons.

81. The Witch at Bosen Corner

This nursery tale was commonly recited to me by women, and a great many versions differed only in trifling respects from the pattern employed in the oldest Jamaica version on record, Lewis, 255–259.

Here the girl breaks a jug and is sent to get a new one. Three old women appear to her one after another, the last of them headless, to test her courtesy. The cat appears, the rice is cooking. The eggs to be selected are the "silent" ones out of a number of fine large ones that cry "take me." Out of the first egg comes the jug after which she has been sent; the other two make her fortune.

P. Smith's version, 31–34, has more direct Frau Holle incidents. The good girl fulfils as she advances the requests of the grass, ping-wing and bramble, the fruit-tree and the cow. When the old woman sends her to draw water with a basket, Turtle tells her to put a plantain-leaf inside. She selects a little ugly calabash. When she is pursued by "axe-men" (as in number 82), the things she has been kind to befriend her, as in Wona's version of Brother Dead.

In a manuscript version in the collection of Mrs. W. E. Wilson (Wona), Yuckie and Jubba are the two daughters. Yuckie has a present of a string of amber beads. She puts them about her neck and says "bad dey behind you, good dey before you," but this only in dream. She loses the beads in the river and is turned out of the house. On her way, she sees and greets kindly a foot and a hand, and scratches the back of an ugly old woman, without complaining of the insects which sting her. The pot of rice, the cat, and the eggs are as above. The fine eggs say "Tek me no," the dirty ones, "No tek me." Compare FLJ (SA) 1; 111–116, where the girls pretend to throw their beads into the water and thus deceive one girl into doing so, who has then to go down to the home of the water monster to get them back.

The variants from Andros Island, Parsons, 17–26, show no such uniformity. They are sometimes confused with the pumpkin story of Parsons, 26–27, and Milne-Home, 84–88, in which the choice of pumpkins is like that of the eggs in this story.

The theme is very common in African collections. Compare MacDonald 1:298–301; Junod, 191–192; 237–242; Torrend, 75–80; Tremearne, 307–314; 401–407; Barker, 89–94; Nassau, 213; Renel 1:50–64; Bundy, JAFL 32:406; and Parsons, Andros Island, note 1, page 17 for further references. See Grimm 24, Frau Holle; Bolte u. Polívka 2:207–227.

82. The Witch and the Three Dogs

This is one of the longest stories I heard in Jamaica. The leading Maroon story-teller recited it to me in full audience, and I heard it repeated by another Maroon in much less detail. Numbers 83, 84 and 89 have points of likeness to it.

It has five parts. (1) Two brothers are out penning cattle and one, going for fire, surprises a witch in the act of feeding her family, which she carries about in her own body. (2) The witch, bent on revenge, follows them home and proposes, as a test for a husband, knocking a calabash from her head with a missile; the boy throws a frail missile and succeeds. (3) At night, the witch sharpens her razor to kill him, but each time she approaches, one of his dogs warns him. (4) The boy departs with his bride, leaving his dogs chained, but he places a pot in the middle of the floor and warns his mother when the liquid in the pot begins to boil to loosen the dogs to his rescue. (5) He climbs a tree to escape the witch. She produces axes and axe-men by tapping her body and proceeds to chop the tree, which he restores magically until his dogs rush in and tear up the witch.

Compare Barker, 123–128; Callaway, 51–54; Chatelain, 103–110; Jacottet, 58; Renel 1:86–93; Theal, 46; Tremearne, 432–441; Zeltner, 61; FLJ (SA) 1:13–17; 21–25; Lenz, 15–17; Edwards, 72; Harris, Friends, 91–100; Parsons, Andros Island, 66–70; Sea Islands, 80–88; JAFL 30:189–190; JAFL 25:259; 32:399–400.

(1) "Possessing the fire" is a sign of magic power, according to Junod, 157, note. In Edwards, "De big worrum" has fire. A father sends two sons in turn to fetch it, but as they reach after the fire the worm swallows them. The father goes with a lance that glistens, is swallowed, cuts open the worm and rescues all the people the worm has swallowed. In Renel, 88, the pursuing monster swallows people alive. Compare Tremearne, and Parsons, Andros Island, 67, 68.

In Tremearne, a hunter sees a witch knocking herself and feeding monsters all over her body. In Jacottet, an axe chops out of the body of the witch the cows which are the cause of the two brothers' quarrel.

(2) In Barker, the episode of the calabash is attached to the story of the hunter, told in number 84. The elephant whose tail he has cut off turns into a lady and goes to find her mutilator. She proposes a test similar to the test in this story. In Tremearne, the witch proposes the test, as in this story, because the hunter has seen more than he should.

(3) For this episode see note to number 83 and references. In Tremearne, the boy's father insists upon the son's taking a horse, a sword, and gourds. When the witch sharpens her teeth to eat the boy,

the horse wakens him. In Parsons, Andros Island, 68, the boy escapes the witch's razor by turning into a bucket of water.

(4) It is not clear how this episode of the life token got attached to the story. I do not find it in African versions. That it is fairly constant is shown in Parsons, 66, 67, 69. In the more common form of the story of the Two Brothers, with which this story has some elements in common, the life-token often takes the form of a knife stuck in a tree; see number 104. In Tremearne, 298, the treed husband has carried his flute, with which he warns his wife to loosen his dogs very much in the manner of Roland at Roncevalle. In Jekyll, 35, the water in a white saucer set in the sun turns to blood, but this is a Blue-beard story.

(5) Climbing a tree to escape an enemy is one of the commonest episodes in African flight stories. See number 89. Here it occurs combined with the axe-chopping contest and the rescue by dogs, who rush in at the end and tear the pursuer to pieces. In Tremearne, the woman transforms herself in various ways before the dogs succeed in killing her. They then devour every drop of her blood. In number 104, the dogs are restrained from taking part in the fight with the witch by being chained by the witch's hair. This episode is also of frequent occurrence in American Indian lore. See Parsons, Zeitschrift für Ethnologie 54:1–29 (1922).

In some cases, e. g. in Theal, Zeltner, Harris, 85–90, and in FLJ (SA), the tree-cutting episode occurs independently of the rescuing dogs.

83. Andrew and his Sisters

The story appears in Milne-Home, 114–120.

Compare Chatelain, 145–151; 103–111; Renel 1:77–81; 2:261–265; 265–267; Ferrand, 119–122; Torrend, 159–163; Tremearne, 432–441; Callaway, 53; Theal, 124–126; Cronise and Ward, 178–186; Dennett, 52; Barker, 97–101; Junod, 144–148 Edwards, 92–93; Parsons, Andros Island, 44.

See numbers 82 and 86. It is the imitative "Sharpen me razor" song which makes the story successful with an audience.

84. The Hunter

The story is popular in Jamaica and is told interchangeably of man or woman wooer.

Compare Barker, 123–128; Cronise and Ward, 261–262; Tremearne, 292–293; FL 22:457–458; Harris, Friends, 91–100; Parsons, Andros Island, 65 and reference note 3.

The point of the story is voiced in Nassau, 15; "If you find a friend, it is not well to tell him all the thoughts of your heart. If you tell him two or three, leave the rest." In Cronise and Ward, the man reveals all his resources for transformation but the last, which is "dat t'ing wey turn fas' fas' pon top de wattah." In Tremearne, FL 22, he starts to say the word for "ring" (zoba) gets as far as "zop" and is interrupted. In Barker there is a further Delilah turn to the story. He escapes twice by transformation; finally the witch gets his god, while he sleeps with his head in her lap, and burns it. Before it is quite consumed, it turns him into a hawk and he flies away.

In Harris, the version follows the story of the witch and the three dogs as in number 82.

85. Man-Snake as Bridegroom

Besides the last number, three other types of monster marriage stories are common in Jamaica, all of which, though versions overlap or vary, follow a fairly fixed pattern. They may be distinguished as the Snake husband, the Devil husband, and the Bull husband.

The Snake husband story is very common. Besides the half dozen here set down of the many versions offered me, seven Jamaica stories already collected follow the general pattern with more or less exactness. See Lewis, 291–296, Sarah Wintun; Milne Home, 54–55, The Sneake; 46–50, De Sneake an' de King's Darter; Bates, JAFL 9:121, The Yalla Snake; Jekyll, 26, The Three Sisters; 102–104, Yellow Snake; 65, Tacoma and the old Witch Girl.

The story has three parts. (1) A difficult young lady refuses all suitors, but falls in love with a Snake dressed as a handsome man. (2) He has borrowed his fine parts and on the journey home drops them one by one, becomes a Snake, and takes her to his home. (3) Her brothers hear her song of distress and rescue her just as the Snake is about to swallow her. These elements are fairly constant in modern Jamaica versions.

(1) "The pick and choose" idea occurs in Bates's, all Jekyll's and all my versions, although the idea that fine clothes do not make the man is also emphasized.

For the "pick and choose" motive, compare Zeltner, 85, where the girl refuses to marry anyone but "un homme n'avant aucune ouverture;" Nassau, 68, where she will have no man with "even a little bit of a blotch on his skin;" Tremearne, FL 22:346, where he must have "not one blemish;" and Christensen, 10, where the girl refuses to marry anyone with a scratch on his back. In none of these cases does the husband take the form of a Snake. Compare also Jacottet, 126–159, where are recorded five snake-husband stories, four of which are enchanted beast stories (two of the "Beauty and the Beast" type and two of the "Yonec" type), and the fifth is a good and bad-mannered girl story, none of which use the "pick and choose" motive.

(2) The borrowed clothes appear in both Milne-Home's versions, in Bates's, in two of Jekyll's and in two of mine. In Milne-Home, the story ends with the dropping of the clothes; in Jekyll and in two of mine, the monster carries her to his den or "stone-hole."

The clothes-borrowing idea occurs in Cronise and Ward, 178–186, where "half-man" borrows his other half; in Dayrell, 39; Fortier, 71; Hollis, Masai, 201–202; Parsons, Andros Island, 48 iv, 49 v, 50 i, 53 iv, and in Sea Islands, 46.

(3) In Jekyll, 102, and all my versions, the gir's song for help and the answering swallowing song furnish the main interest of the story; and the rescue by the brothers follows in Jekyll and in my two versions. In my third version, the Snake swallows the girl while her parents are sleeping. In Lewis's much earlier story, a jealous sorceress gives her step-daughter over to a great black dog named Tiger, who takes her away to his den. She sings until her hunter brothers hear her song, rush in and rescue her.

In Renel 1: 275–277, a girl weds a beast in disguise, because of his handsome clothes, is carried away to his hole, and finally attracts her mother's ears by her song of lamentation. In other African stories of monster marriages, the song is entrusted to a bird messenger.

For the rescue, see Jekyll's Bluebeard story, 35–37; Bleek, 61–64; Christensen, 10–14; and numbers 83 and 86.

Evidently the story has become fixed in Jamaica out of a number of different elements and does not depend upon a common source. The lesson to the over-fastidious girl, ridicule of her fear of the ordeal of marriage, and the old setting of the rescue by hunter-brothers, are drawn together into a coherent story. It is the song that makes the story popular.

86. The Girls who married the Devil

The flight from a Devil husband has also taken on a fixed form in Jamaica in contrast to the number of variants related on Andros Island and the much more complex versions known in Africa. It is possible that this is true only for the localities visited.

The story has three parts. (1) A girl marries a handsome man against her little brother's warning. (2) The man, who is usually the devil, carries her home, accompanied in secret by the brother, locks her up, and sets a cock to watch her. (3) An old woman befriends her, they feed the cock with various grains and finally escape over the river in the Devil's magic boat, pursued by the Devil.

Jekyll, 148–151, The Devil and the Princess, has a version of this story.

Compare Zeltner, 85–90; Nassau, 68–76; Fortier, 68–75; Jones, 82–88; Chatelain, 99–101; Barker, 97–101; Jacottet, 160–166; Callaway, 78–85; Christensen, 10–14; Tremearne, FL 22:346–348; Dayrell, 38–41; 98–103; Parsons, Andros Island, 49–54; Sea Islands, 45–49; JAFL 30:181–183; JAFL 12:126–130; and see references to numbers 83 and 85.

(1) In the Snake marriage, number 85, there is no rejected warning, but the hunter-brothers come to the rescue. In numbers 83 and 87, it is the despised little brother who effects the escape.

(2) In Jacottet, a girl is carried away to the land of the half-bodied people and guarded by horns that cry out. They are silenced by pouring in hot water and stuffing them with stones. In Barker, the dragon who carries away Anansi and his son sets a white cock to warn him if they try to escape. In Christensen, a fly guards the girl and Tiger comes running at its call. In Fortier and JAFL 12:128, roosters guard the girl. In Callaway, an old woman warns the Pigeons when the girls escape.

(3) The only version of the flight theme which I found developed in Jamaica is that of the evasion of the guardian cock by feeding him enough corn so that the girl can get across the river before the cock summons the husband.

In some flight stories, it is the pursuing monster himself who is silenced with the corn-throwing. In Nassau, the fleeing girl throws out three gourdfuls of seed which the Leopard stops to pick up. In Chatelain, the woman throws out calabashes of seed to the pursuing cannibal. Compare Renel 1:38–40; 2:262–263; Ferrand, 119–122.

The appearance of both the kindly maid-servant and the helpful brother in the Jamaica versions is irrelevant. The immense popularity of the theme of the despised little brother probably makes his appearance an inthrust. In Zeltner, Nassau and Jones, a friendly horse accompanies the bride. In JAFL 12:126–130, a friendly ox belonging to the husband carries the bride. So also in Parsons, Andros Island, 51–52 ii, and in JAFL 30:181, the friendly animal is taken from the husband's fields.

In Zeltner and Jones, the horse warns its mistress; in Dayrell the old mother sends her home because the girl is kind to her; in Fortier, because she is sorry for her; in JAFL 12, the old wife sends her away because she is jealous. In Dayrell, 101, a skull to which she has been kind acts the part of helper.

In Zeltner, Nassau, Fortier, Jones and Parsons, Andros Island, 52–54 iii, iv, and Sea Islands, the flight develops into an obstacle race. In Parsons, 50–51 and Tremearne, the fugitives escape by transformation. In Callaway, the sea divides; in Fortier, the Crocodile carries the girl over and drowns her pursuer. Riddling questions are to be answered in JAFL 12; Parsons, Andros Island, 52 iii; Sea Islands, 46; JAFL 30; see Jekyll, 26–28. A secret door gives a Blue-beard turn to the versions of Jones, Fortier, and Parsons, Andros Island, 44–45, and Sea Islands, 47–49; see Jekyll, 35–37.

The Jamaica version is on the whole bare of incident. Interest centers in the imitative songs of swallowing, of running, and in the boat-call, to the exclusion of any further development of the flight theme.

87. Bull as Bridegroom

The story of the beast-husband transformed by means of a song is very common in Jamaica. It occurs in Milne-Home, 42–45, and Jekyll, 73–77; 132–135.

Compare Junod, 246–253; Parsons, Andros Island, 39–43 and references in note 1.

In Parsons's Andros Island variants, the transformed beast is the wife (compare number 84) and has the form of a bird, as in Jekyll's two versions, one of which, 132–135, ends with the "Yonec" story. In all the versions I heard, and in Milne-Home, the wooer is a bull.

88. The Two Bulls

See Jekyll's version, 114–116, called "Timmolimmo," a name which is also given to the bull of number 89 in some versions. In Theal, 56–66, a mysterious and beautiful woman who goes to the river only at night is named "Tangalimlibo." Her enemies persuade her to go out by day and she is taken by the river, returns to suckle her child, and is at last ransomed by sacrificing an ox which seems to bear the same name as the woman.

In this challenge story, the bull has killed, not the mother, as in number 89, but her sons, and has unwittingly fathered his successful antagonist, who has been brought up in secret. The father's secret name is evidently learned from the mother.

For the tossing trick, see number 69.

89. Ballinder Bull

This is one of the best-known stories in Jamaica. See Milne-Home, 67–69, Garshan Bull; P. Smith, 55–58, Bull Garshananee. All follow about the same pattern, and the same may be said of other versions collected in Jamaica which are not set down here.

In a version given by Mrs. Elizabeth Hilton, the boy buys twelve buta (arrows) and a bottle of water and a bottle of rum. When he calls "Geshawnee," the bull says, "Since I have been in this place, I never heard anyone call my name." The boy stays up the tree into which he has climbed by the formula, "Bear up, me good tree, bear up! I have often seen me father fell a green tree and leave a dry one."

In a Mandeville version by John Macfarlane, the boy's name is "Simon Tootoos," the bull's "Garshanee." The woman makes him a pudding and he takes six eggs each of hen, turkey and bird. He opens three gates with song, and the giant appears in the form of a bull. He climbs a cotton-wood tree. When the bull throws arrows at him he says, "I see me father take his little finger and catch longer arrows than those!" He catches twelve, with which he pelts the bull in return.

Neither of these versions ends with the false claim.

In another Mandeville version given by a lad, Clarence Tathum, the slayer of the mother is a giant named "Tako-rimo." The son takes a yard of tobacco and a pone. With the tobacco, he bribes the watchman to give him information about the giant and an iron-crow-bar. He goes inside and sees a servant lousing the giant's head. "Massa, der is someone calling you name," says the servant. "Who would calling my name so uncommon?" answers the giant. The giant flings a sword, which the boy catches and himself flings the crowbar and kills the giant.

The story goes on to tell how the boy is imprisoned by the brother, "Giant Despair," and escapes exactly as in the tale of "Jack the Giant-Killer," while the giant falls into a trench and is killed.

In Stephen Johnson's version from Claremont, a huge animal by the name of "Grandezee" kills the mother but spares the child. To escape the beast, the boy climbs a tree and sings, "Bear up, me good tree, for I often see me father get down tall trees and ketch them up again!" He throws three pegs and pegs down Grandezee and takes out the golden tongue and teeth. The false claim follows.

In a version from Brownstown by Emanuel Johnson, "Geshawnee was a kind of witch t'ing live into de river." He has seven heads. Sammy cuts seven lances, climbs a tree and calls his name. He says, "From day I'm born, never see a big man call me name, much more a little boy!" He knocks his side and brings out axemen, rain and cattle, which attack the tree in vain. Sammy sings, "Bear up, me good tree, bear up. I oftentimes see me father cow haul down a tree an' me father say, 'Bear up, me good tree, bear up,' an' that tree bear up." Sammy kills the monster. The story of the false claim follows.

In Parsons's fragment, 145–146, the name is Kramytadanta. The boy takes a bottle of water and a loaf and sings from the tree.

Seven episodes regularly belong to the story. (1) A bull (or monster) kills a woman whose new-born son is saved and brought up by a woman-friend or relative. (2) The boys at school mock at him because he has no father, and he learns the story of his parentage. (3) He takes certain objects for slaying the monster. (4) He sings a name-song as challenge. (5) He climbs a tree which resists attack. (6) He slays the beast by hurling missiles from the tree. (7) Anansi claims the deed.

Compare Zeltner's stories of Soundita, 1–6, and Kama, 54–61; Renel 1:82–85; 117–118; Tremearne, 408–412; Lenz, 22; Fortier, 11–13; Harris, Friends, 86–89; Boas, Notes, JAFL 25:258.

(1) In the less sophisticated versions, the bull kicks the child from the "breeding" woman.

(2) See Burton's Arabian Nights Tales (Burton Club, 1885) 1:231. The mocking incident is common in Maori tales.

(3) In Zeltner's "Soundita" story, the contest with a witch turned buffalo is carried on with three magic eggs and three magic arrows. In Fortier, the boy fights the bull with flap-jacks. The arrows suggest the weapons used in the fight of Sir Percival with the Red Knight in the English romance version. See also number 79, 80, 82.

(4) By comparing this bull version with Harris, Friends, 86–89, and Fortier, 11–13, it is clear that the North American version contained the two episodes, that of exposing the bull husband by means of a song, as in number 87, and that of the challenge to conflict which completes number 89 in Jamaica. In Harris, the word used for the bull transformation is "Ballybaloo-bill," which is very close to my "Ballinder bull." The more common name in Jamaica is "Geshawnee," as in P. Smith's version and Johnson's song. But in Johnson's song, as in Harris, the boy is named Sammy and his small size emphasized. In the Harris-Fortier version, one episode is used to motivate the other. The first episode explains the rather mysterious use of the song in the Ballinder Bull story and in number 88, where the bull seems surprised that anyone knows enough to challenge him by name and where the knowledge itself seems bound up with his defeat. In Jekyll's version of number 88, when the son challenges the father by name a cow calls, "Master, master, I hear some one calling your name." The bull answers, "No, no, not a man can call my name!" At some stage in transmission a fatal name motive must have dropped out and a magic song taken its place.

This comparison with Harris and Fortier merely proves a relation with the Jamaica story. It by no means explains the original source of the American version, or its exact relation to the other bull stories collected; namely, numbers 84 and 88. Zeltner's story of Soundita, 3–5, has perhaps more elements in common with the Harris-Fortier story than any other African parallel, and further analysis may decide whether the complex Senegambian story is in the direct line or merely has gathered episodes from a common source.

(5) and (6) See note to number 82 and Bolte u. Polívka, discussing Grimm 60, Two Brothers.

(7) The episode of the mock claim appears also in the next number and in 97.

90. Bird Arinto

Jekyll, 54–57, Man-Crow, tells the same story. See also numbers 70 and 89.

The story occurs as an episode in Zeltner's Kama, 54–61 and Tremearne's How Auta Killed Dodo, 408–412.

For the golden tongue and teeth see numbers 90, 95, and Jekyll, 56; and compare Zeltner, 5.

91. Tiger softens his Voice

Parkes heard his version on Cape Coast, Africa.

Jekyll, 108–113, Leah and Tiger, tells the story. In my number 17a, it is the mother who is hidden away. In Bahama versions, Parsons, 35–39, the plot turns upon the rescue of the lost girl through song rather than, as in Jamaica, upon the voice-changing trick by which she is stolen.

Compare Jacottet, 62–69, Tremearne, 401; FL 21:492–493; Hollis, Masai, 153–155; Callaway, 142–144; Theal, 118–120; Renel 1:247–249; Frazer, FLJ 7:167–168; Harris, Nights, 251–252; 257–260; Parsons, Sea Islands, 50–52; Rattray 2:14.

See Grimm 5, Wolf and Kids; Bolte u. Polívka 1:37–42, and Grimm 12, Rapunzel; Bolte u. Polívka 1:97–99.

92. and 93. Hidden Names; Anansi and Mr. Able

These two numbers are closely related to number 69. The plot turns upon tricks to discover a hidden name. The only difference between them is that in one story it is possession of one or more girls' names, in the next, that of a person whose name the girls alone know, upon which the plot depends. All the variants play upon the idea of concealing a listener to surprise the keeper of the secret (invariably girls) into betraying each other. See Jekyll, 11–13, where the king and queen kill themselves, as in number 93, when they hear the girls' names sung.

Compare Barker, 45–49; Dayrell, 79–80; Dennet, 35–38; Parsons, Andros Island, 117.

In Dayrell, Tortoise gets the wives to call out the husband's name in fright, and he is so ashamed when he hears it that he takes to the water.

In Barker, Anansi drops down bananas sweetened with honey to the girls and they call to each other in surprise.

94. The King's Three Daughters

This story may be a fragment of the hidden name series in which the song has lost the revelation of the name, and the introduction omits the trick to discover it. If so, it has become a fixed variant. P. Smith, 35–37, tells it much as in the present version.

The story has points of resemblance to the European tale of the boy who is admitted to the princess's chamber in the form of a singing bird. See number 113 and compare Spanish-American forms, JAFL 25: 191–208; JAFL 27:135–137.

95. The Dumb Child

Parkes heard this story in Sierra Leone, Africa. In Jekyll, 84–85, Dummy, it is Pea-fowl whose song the child imitates and the story follows that of the sweet-voiced bird of number 71.

It resembles the European task-theme which turns upon making some over-serious person laugh. See Grimm 7; Bolte u. Polívka 1:59–67; and Grimm, 64; Bolte u. Polívka, 2: 39–44. See also Jataka Tales (Francis & Thomas, Cambridge, 1916), 363.

Its relation to the motive of getting a sight of the teeth is not clear. In Jones, 117–118, one of the tasks imposed by the king for the hand of his daughter is to bring him Alligator's teeth. Rabbit plays to Alligator until he shuts his eyes and opens his mouth to laugh, then knocks out his teeth. For the golden teeth see note to number 90.

In a Maori story, White 2:145–146, a chief sends women to detect an offender. They are to know him by a certain lost tooth. They identify him by singing and dancing until he laughs and exposes the cavity.

96. The Dumb Wife

I take this story to be a modern adaptation of 95, invented in the Maroon section. Another Maroon gave me a similar version under a different name. The whole point lies in the constant repetition of the burial song.

97. Leap, Timber, Leap[5]

98. The Boy fools Anansi

Jekyll, 99, uses the same motive.

Compare Callaway, 19–21; Theal, 99; Renel 1:109–110; Ferrand, 75; Rivière, 229; Chatelain, 191–195; Hollis, Nandi, 101–102; Jacottet, 260; Uncle Remus, Nights, 315–318.

---

5. See supplementary note, p. 290.

99. The Water Cray fish

In Jacottet, 166–174, Mosimoli has been killed by her stepmother for cooking and eating taboo food. When her step-sister comes to the water to fill her pitcher, Mosimoli comes out of the water, beats her and gives her muddy water to drink, singing, "My father and mother are the crocodile." Compare 79, 80, of this collection and Parsons, Andros Island, 140. The story is a mere fragment, but belongs to the very great number of tales which turn upon a broken taboo driving a supernatural visitor back to its original abode. The success of the story doubtless depends upon the song interest.

100. Ali Baba and Kissem

Versions of Ali Baba in Jamaica differ in no way from those with which we are familiar.

101. Bull-of-all-the-land

Old Forbes gave me the only version of this story I heard in Jamaica. In Trowbridge, JAFL 9:284–285, the song and the incident of the three drops of blood occur, but the king is "King Tonga" and there is no beast transformation. The husband is lost by letting a little dog kiss him, as in number 105 and in Parsons, Andros Island, 55, 59, not by his wife's burning the skin as in this version.

For the song at night as a means of recognition see number 74.

See Grimm 88, The Singing Soaring Lark; Bolte u. Polívka 2:229–273.

102. The Boiling Pot

See Grimm 3, Our Lady's Child; Bolte u. Polívka 1:13–21.

103. The Twelve One-eyed Men

See The Third Kalender's Tale in Burton's Arabian. Nights' Tales (Burton Club 1885), 1:151–160.

104. Bird and Hunter

Common as is this story in Africa, I heard only one version in Jamaica. See also numbers 82a and 103 and Grimm 60, Two Brothers, Bolte u. Polívka 1:528–556.

Compare Junod, 276–292; Jacottet, 56; Basset, 2:103–107; Rivière, 193; Dennett, 60–64; Chatelain, 89–97; Lenz, 15–17.

105. Jack and the Devil Errant

The story is told by Monk Lewis, 301–307. See also numbers 101, 111, 112, 113, 119.

Compare Ferrand, Madagascar, 102–113; Parsons, Andros Island, 54–60 and note for references. See Boas, JAFL 25:256, for the relation of the story to "John the Bear."

See Grimm 113, The King's Children, Bolte u. Polívka, 2:516–527.

106. The Magic Hat and the Staff of Life

Numbers 106–109 and 133–136 belong to the Little Peasant cycle of stories, Grimm 61, Bolte u. Polívka 2:1–18.

This number contains three episodes. (1) Three men trick another into selling a cow cheap by pretending it is a goat. He avenges himself by selling them (2) a magic hat which he claims will pay the cost of what they buy, (3) a staff of life through which they are themselves destroyed.

The first episode occurs in Heetopades of Veeshnoo-Sarma, Wilkin's translation (London, 1787), 261–262, 266. The second is episode D in Bolte u. Polívka's analysis. The third is episode G in Bolte u. Polívka; see note to 109.

107. Uncle Green and Jack

See Bolte u. Polívka 2:1–18. The story is composed of three episodes. (1) A nephew sells to his miserly uncle a means for making pots self-cooking. (2) In revenge, he is put into a bag to be thrown into the sea; exchanges places with a shepherd and gets his sheep, (3) then pretends to his uncle to have got them under-seas and persuades him to try the same means of enriching himself. The first is a modification of the self-cooking vessel, which is episode C in Bolte u. Polívka's analysis.

Compare Clouston, Popular Tales 2:243, 263, for Norse (Dasent) and Italian (Crane) parallels; Espinosa, Pedro de Ordimales cycle, JAFL 27:169, and discussion, 220–221.

The second and third are episodes H and J in Bolte u. Polívka. See numbers 23 and 108 in this collection.

108. Big Begum and Little Begum

See note to number 106. The story is a version of Hans Anderson's Big Claus and Little Claus, Grimm 61; Bolte u. Polívka 2:1–18 and contains three episodes. (1) "Little Begum" tricks "Big Begum" into killing his oxen to get gold. (2) and (3) He exchanges places in the bag, gets a drove of sheep, and tricks "Big Begum" into getting himself drowned in the same bag, as in number 107.

(1) Episode F in Bolte u. Polívka's analysis. This informant's stories were not well motivated; the version does not explain how "Little Begum" sold the pretended magic hide. In Arcin, 475–476, Zeltner, 62–72, and Parsons, Andros Island, 86, the episode is accompanied by the trick of the life-giving staff (G' and see number 106); in Edwards, 95–96, by the trick of the dead mother pretended slain (G" and see number 135).

(2) and (3) In Fortier, 88–89, as in this version, (1) is accompanied by the bag trick, episodes H and J in Bolte u. Polívka's analysis. See also number 23.

Compare the "Pedro Ordimales" cycle in Recinos, JAFL 31: 474–477.

109. The Fool and the Wise Brother

The detail of this story proves a folk rather than a literary source.

The story has three parts. (1) The foolish brother kills his mother in the bath. (2) The two brothers hide in a tree under which robbers are dividing their spoil and frighten the robbers away by dropping down a weight upon them. (3) One robber returns, and gets his tongue cut out.

Compare Zeltner, 62–72; Arcin, 477; Lenz, 51–53; Parsons, Andros Island, 92–94 and reference note; Sea Islands, 132; Espinosa, JAFL 27:119–120; Recinos, JAFL 31:473–474.

(1) See Grimm 147, Old Man Made Young Again, Bolte u.

Polívka 3:193–199, where the killing hot bath is identified with the fire bath which restores the old to youth, but which either fails when attempted by a pretender or is employed as a trick to destroy a powerful enemy; e. g. Ferrand, Madagascar, 67. In Arcin and Zeltner, the story follows this order: (1) Gold-producing animal, (2) Life-giving staff, (3) Ear cut off, the life-giving staff taking the place of the killing hot bath. In a Jamaica version from Richard Morgan, the killing hot bath is followed by the story of carting the mother about as if she were alive and extracting hush money from her pretended murderers, as in number 135 (episode G' in Bolte u. Polívka's analysis of Grimm 61).

(2) and (3) See Grimm 59, Frederick and Catherine; Bolte u. Polívka 1:520–528.

110. The Children and the Witch

See Grimm 15, Hansel and Gretel, Bolte u. Polívka 1:115–126. Numbers 83, 98, 115, 119, have some points in common with this story.

111. The Boy and the Mermaid

This fragment must belong to a story of a child promised before its birth to a water-spirit, as in Grimm 181 and Parsons, Sea Islands, 137.

112. Difficult Tasks

The fragment belongs to a story of difficult tasks, as in number 105.

113. The Grateful Beasts

See Grimm 197, The Crytal Ball, Bolte u. Polívka 3:424— 443; and compare: Chatelain, 65–81; Lenz, 25–27; Mason and Espinosa, JAFL 24:398; discussed by Espinosa, JAFL 27:212–213.

114. Jack and the Bean-stalk

See Joseph Jacobs, English Fairy Tales (Putnam, 1898), 59–68, and compare Parsons (Maryland and Pennsylvania), JAFL 30:212–213.

115. Jack and the Devil

See Jekyll, 35–37, Mr. Bluebeard, and Grimm 46, Fitcher's Bird, Bolte u. Polívka 1:398–412.

116. Jack's Riddle

See Grimm 22, The Riddle, Bolte u. Polívka 1:188–202 and compare Barker, 171–175; Fortier, 62–69; Recinos, JAFL 31: 475–476.

117. Jack as Fortune-teller

See Grimm 98, Doctor Know-all, Bolte u. Polívka 2:401–413, and compare Jones, 68–72; Fortier, 116; Harris, Friends, 32–33; Smiley, JAFL 32:370; Espinosa, JAFL 24:415–419; discussed by Boas, JAFL 25:251, and by Espinosa, JAFL 27:215–216.

118. Robin as Fortune-teller

See note to number 117.

119. Jack and the Grateful Dead

See number 113 and Boas's discussion, JAFL 25:256–257. This is the story of Thorsteinn, the King's Son in Icelandic Legends (Arnason) translated by Powell & Magnussen (London, 1866), 527–540.

120. The Boy and his Master

See Grimm 68, The Thief and his Master, Bolte u. Polívka 2:60–69; and compare Tremearne, 223–224; Mason and Espinosa, New Mexico, JAFL 24: 423–424.

121. The Language of Beasts

See Grimm 17, The White Snake, Bolte u. Polívka 1:131–134; and Aarne's study, Der Tiersprachen verstehende Mann, in FF Communications No. 15. Compare Koelle, 143–145; Basset 2:119–124; Junod, 314–317; Chatelain, 219–223; Smith, 565.

122. The Three Pieces of Advice

Compare Steere, 413; Mason & Espinosa, JAFL 24:408–411: discussed by Espinosa, JAFL 27:213–214.

123. The Brothers and the Life-tree

See Grimm 107, The Two Travellers; Bolte u. Polívka 2:468–482 and compare Dayrell, 58–60; Espinosa, JAFL 27:191–195.

124. The Skillful Brothers

See Grimm 129, Four Skillful Brothers, Bolte u. Polívka 2:165–169 and compare Cronise and Ward, 200–205; Renel 1: 215–223; Dennett, 33–34; Parsons, Sea Islands, 75.

125. The Three Sillies

See Grimm 34, Clever Elsie, Bolte u. Polívka 1:335–342, and Clouston, Book of Noodles, 7. Compare Parsons, Andros Island, 128–129; Sea Islands, 94.

126. A Misunderstanding

See Grimm 84, Hans Married, Bolte u. Polívka 2:203–204.

127. Big-head, Big-belly and Little-foot

The story is very common in Jamaica. See Grimm 18, The Straw, the Coal and the Bean, Bolte u. Polívka 1:135–137, and compare Parsons, Andros Island, 147.

128. The Goat in the Lion's Den

129. Donkey, Cat and the Lion's Head

The familiar episode of the Wolf's head which occurs early in the Reynard cycle (see Percy Society Publications 12, Introduction, pages xxxiii–xxxiv) is, in African stories, often combined with that of the

Goat in the Lion's den (or the Hyena's). Compare Rattray, Chinyanje, 149–152; Tremearne, 227–229; FL 22:63–65.

130. Clever Molly May

See Grimm 77, Clever Gretel, Bolte u. Polívka 2:129–131; and Parsons, Sea Islands, 140. From this point in the group of stories Anansi is introduced in the role of hero.

131. Dancing to Anansi's Fiddle

See Grimm 110, The Jew among Thorns, Bolte u. Polívka 2:490–503; and compare Bundy, JAFL 32:412–413.

132. Anansi Claims the Dinner

Compare Nassau, 42–44; Tremearne, FL 21:212; Krug, JAFL 25:106–107.

133. Anansi seeks his Fortune

See note to number 106, and Grimm 104, Wise Folks, Bolte u. Polívka, 2:440–451. One version from Parsons, Andros Island, 93–94, connects this episode with those of the frightened robbers and the tongue-cutting in number 109.

134. The Pannier Jar

See note to number 106. This is episode F' in Bolte u. Polívka's analysis of Grimm's Little Peasant. Compare Parsons, Sea Islands, 89; JAFL 32:372, and note for references.

135. Anansi kills his Grandmother

See note to number 106. This is episode G' in Bolte u. Polivka's analysis of Grimm's "Little Peasant." Compare Parsons, Andros Island, 87 and note for references.

136. White-belly and Anansi

See note to number 106. The trick corresponds to F' or G' in Bolte u. Polívka's analysis of The Little Peasant.

137. Monkey hunts Anansi

See Boas, JAFL 25:223–226, where the Devil is the rival sorcerer.

138. Anansi and the Pig

See Grimm 72a, Bolte u. Polívka, 2:100–106; and compare Parsons, Andros Island, 108 and note; discussion of Spanish forms by Boas, JAFL 25:252, note; by Espinosa, JAFL 27:222–227.

139. The Fifer

The story is common in Jamaica. See Jekyll, 98–99. It was told me as a "speak-acting" story, but as I could get no other of exactly the same character, I do not know how common it used to be to present a Nansi story in this way. The Nansi story is now given in the form of a dramatic monologue or rehearsed simply as a tale.

For the story of "The Fifer," six actors were required, one to represent the boy, one the father, and four others the "wild beasts." "Anansi," "Dry-head," "Tacoomah" and "Tiger" were the "beasts." Roe said that "the one who takes the son's part tells the story." The dramatization went on much like a school exercise performed by grown men, with improvised action and (probably) extemporized dialogue. It ended in a dance in which all six joined.

Compare Tremearne, 301; Harris, Nights, 370–373; Edwards, 87–88; Parsons, Andros Island, 137–138.

The story seems to be drawn from such prohibitions against whistling at night or whistling more than twice when walking at night or through a haunted forest as are quoted by Sebillot, Le Folk-lore de France 1:159, 283. He tells a Breton story of a lad who forgot the prohibition and found himself mocked and followed by the Devil, who bore him off just as he had reached home. Compare number 66, note.

141. Tacoomah makes a Dance

Medleys of this character seem to have been a popular form of entertainment and may still be common, though the examples I have were given me in every case by old men. They are composed of scraps of song or whole scenes from well-known Nansi stories, together with game-songs, imitations of animal sounds, and "rhyming," strung together much like our own musical medleys—the last line of one suggesting the first of the next. In this example, story-songs from numbers 97 and 86 are followed by a game dialogue; next by some animal imitations; last, by a specimen of Jamaica "rhyming." Other examples of this kind of improvised "rhyming" are:

> *"Mr. Might, jump up a height, after a kite,*
> *And knock his eye, upon his hog-sty, and cry out 'hi!*
> *oh, my! why should I die'."*

> *"There is a boat, and in the boat, is a goat, and has*
> *a long coat, catch him under the throat."*

142. Anansi makes a Dance

The songs of this medley at first follow the story of Goat's escape from the dance, number 40, combined with the parallel story of Rat's escape from Puss's dance. The song is taken from a popular game in which one player represents the cat, another the rat; all the others form a line with clasped hands, and Puss tries to catch Rat through the line, while all sing the song. The bull's song belongs to number 88 or 89. Anansi's fifing is possibly taken from 139.

143. Red Yam

Old Mary Roden was bed-ridden and lived in a one-roomed hut, the floor of which was falling in. The little grandchild, when prompted to "make a figure," danced quite spontaneously to the rhythm of the grandmother's quavering song. The same is true of the next two numbers. Songs sung to be danced to in this fashion have rather the monotonous rhythm of a drum-beat than any melody in our sense of the word. For the story, see number 23.

145. Fowl and Pretty Poll

Literally this means, Fowl wants to be married to Parrot in church, but Parrot has no good clothes. Parrot wants Crow to marry her in church, but he says he can't because of his peel-head (or perhaps he wants to in spite of this peelhead). Compare the witticism vi.

146. The Cumbalo

Sarah Findley was an old-time negress who lived in a little hut far out in the bush. She danced to the song with a queer jumping motion like boys playing leap-frog and with all the agility of a young girl. The dance as a wake game is performed upon two parallel bars held by four men. One informant called it dancing "Calimbe."

149. Animal Talk

Again there are, in this medley which imitates animal sounds, reminiscences of consecutive Nansi stories—Crab's words, in number 54; Ground Dove's in 50. For the fasting contest, see number 61.

Tremearne, 28, says that the imitation of animal cries is a favorite device in African story-telling. Compare Hollis, Nandi, 109–111, where a great many examples are given of this kind of entertainment.

Witticisms

I & II. These old-fashioned slave stories are from old Vassel Edwards at Retirement, in the Cock-Pit country. They belong to the "nager-trick" stories quoted by Lewis.

III. The Congo negro is said to be duller-witted than negroes from the Gold Coast. To call a man a "Congo" is hence a term of ridicule.

IV. This witticism is common. In one version, the man was said to be "walking in Kingston." Mrs. Elizabeth Hilton gave me a version she learned from Henry Roe, school-master at Retirement, which bears the marks of having been put together by some literary entertainer.

"Massa Peter was a funny sort of a buckra massa. He was 'mustafenia' (white by law). Massa Peter an' me, we go to school together. We were readin' in a 'pellin' (book) an' we were doin' jumba fraction sum.

From the day me leave school me never see Marse Peter any more till one day we buck up. A glad to see him till a couldn't glad any more. Marse Peter went a tell me somet'ing, a laugh till me belly nearly pop.

Marse Peter was the sort of boy used to go out after hours. Him ma tell him if him (she) been dead before him, she will show him token (frighten him). But Marse Peter never will believe her. One night, Marse Peter go out. When him coming back, he catch right at the cross-road where dem Taylor boy used to sit down a day-time, an' smell somet'ing funny, but he never know wha'. He been 'fraid, but afterward he no 'fraid again. An' see one man come wid litt'e fire. He say, 'I beg you a light, sah!' The man give him a light. The man has some teeth a his mouth, they long like a Jack-ass a laugh a sun-hot. Marse Peter pass the man. He meet up another man. He say, 'Look here, me frien', I meet a man jus' roun' the turning, have teeth long like a Jack-ass a laugh a sun-hot.' The man said, Teeth like these do they long?' Marse Peter run an' he run an' never stop runnin' till he meet up a mother bed. From that, Marse Peter never go af'er no girl again. Marse Peter behave a good buckra massa af'er this."

V. The witticism is used in a good many connections. In one story, a man finds a boy by the roadside and takes him home. When he asks the boy to blow the fire, the duppy says, "Me kyant blow de fire, for me dead long time an' dirt eat out all me teet'." The man beats him and he runs away crying, "Lor! me dead two time." In another version, "Rolling Calf" takes possession of a house. While he is asleep, the owner makes an iron fork red hot and catches him about the neck.

VI. See number 145.

VIII. Compare Cundall, FL 15:91, where the "Rolling Calf," afraid of the moon, tumbles over into the stream and sprains his foot. He says, "A don't mind the wet, a wet, but the 'prain a 'prain me foot'."

X. In Tremearne, FL 22:222–223, Lizard and Mouse both court a woman. Mouse tells her that Lizard is blind, can't see at night; Cock tells her that Rat is a thief, can't be seen in the market.

In Koelle, 174–177, Toad and Rat have a wager to see if one can do what the other cannot. Toad passes a crowd with a whole skin; Rat is pursued with sticks and stones.

XI. See number 48.

XII. From Alexander Archibald, near Mandeville.

XIII. From Mrs. Matilda Hall, Harmony Hall. See number 4.

XVI. This and the next two witticisms were written out by some young lads in Bethlehem, Santa Cruz Mountains.

Supplementary Notes

46. Why Tumble-bug Rolls in the Dung

In Seidel's story of the "Miracle of the Sidi" (Geschichten und Lieder der Afrikaner, 105), the devil dares the Sidi to marry a slave to a princess. The father of the princess has set to her wooers the supposedly impossible task of filling a bag with hyacinths out of hyacinth season. The Sidi fills the bag with stones and bids the slave empty it out before the king, when the stones are by miracle turned into hyacinths.

48. Why Dog is always Looking

A Jamaica negro proverb runs, "Darg say befo' him plant yam fe look like masquita' foot, him satisfy fe tun beggar." See Cundall's collection (Kingston, 1910), 211.

56. Rat's Wedding

It is not the wooden foot-bridge but any drain beside the road—the gutter—which Jamaicans call a "water table."

66. Simon Tootoos

For the music of these songs see Publications of the Modern Language Association of America, 39 (1924): 482.

97. Leap, Timber, Leap

An old man over eighty who was present at the recital of this story remembered hearing it when he was a little boy. Hauling lumber was in old days accompanied by song. The story turns upon a theme common in American Indian hero cycles, that of a trickster's claim to magical powers which he does not possess.

A Note About the Author

Martha Warren Beckwith (1871–1959) was an American folklorist and ethnographer. Born in Wellesley Heights, Massachusetts, Beckwith attended Mount Holyoke College before graduating with a Master's degree in anthropology from Columbia University in 1906. In 1920, having earned her PhD, she became the chair of Vassar College's Folklore program. Specializing in Hawaiian, Jamaican, and Native American cultures, Beckwith published numerous collections of proverbs, folk stories, myths, and ethnographies from her extensive research, often conducted with renowned ethnomusicologist Helen H. Roberts.

A Note from the Publisher

Spanning many genres, from non-fiction essays to literature classics to children's books and lyric poetry, Mint Edition books showcase the master works of our time in a modern new package. The text is freshly typeset, is clean and easy to read, and features a new note about the author in each volume. Many books also include exclusive new introductory material. Every book boasts a striking new cover, which makes it as appropriate for collecting as it is for gift giving. Mint Edition books are only printed when a reader orders them, so natural resources are not wasted. We're proud that our books are never manufactured in excess and exist only in the exact quantity they need to be read and enjoyed. To learn more and view our library, go to minteditionbooks.com

bookfinity & MINT EDITIONS

Enjoy more of your favorite classics with Bookfinity,
a new search and discovery experience for readers.
With Bookfinity, you can discover more vintage
literature for your collection, find your Reader Type,
track books you've read or want to read,
and add reviews to your favorite books.
Visit www.bookfinity.com, and click on
Take the Quiz to get started.

Don't forget to follow us
@bookfinityofficial and @mint_editions

CPSIA information can be obtained
at www.ICGtesting.com
Printed in the USA
JSHW010335160822
29340JS00001B/2